THE
YEAR'S
TOP
HARD SCIENCE FICTION
STORIES
6

THE YEAR'S TOP HARD SCIENCE FICTION STORIES 6

edited by Allan Kaster

The Year's Top Hard Science Fiction Stories 6

Cover art illustration © Maurizio Manzieri

AudioText, Inc., PO Box 418, Barker, TX 77413

www.audiotexttapes.net

ISBN 9781884612626 (trade paperback)

First Edition: September 2022

CONTENTS

ACKNOWLEDGEMENTS

"Paley's Watch" by Anil Menon. Copyright © 2021 by Anil Menon. First published in *The Gollancz Book of South Asian Science Fiction Volume 2* (Hachette India), edited by Tarun K. Saint. Reprinted by permission of the author.

"Light Up the Clouds" by Greg Egan. Copyright © 2021 by Greg Egan. First appeared in *Asimov's Science Fiction*, March/April 2021. Reprinted by permission of the author.

"Little Animals" by Nancy Kress. Copyright © 2021 by Nancy Kress. First published in *Clarkesworld*, June 2021. Reprinted by permission of the author.

"The Metric" by David Moles. Copyright © 2021 by David Moles. First published by Dell Magazines in *Asimov's Science Fiction*, May/June 2021. Reprinted by permission of the author.

"Vaccine Season" by Hannu Rajaniemi. Copyright © 2021 by Hannu Rajaniemi. First published in *Make Shift: Dispatches from the Post-Pandemic Future* (MIT Press), edited by Gideon Lichfield. Reprinted by permission of the author.

"Submergence" by Arula Ratnakar. Copyright © 2021 by Arula Ratnakar. First published in *Clarkesworld,* March 2021. Reprinted by permission of the author.

"The Egg Collectors" by Lavie Tidhar. Copyright © 2021 by Lavie Tidhar. First published in *Interzone 290-291*. Reprinted by permission of the author.

"Aptitude" by Cooper Shrivastava. Copyright © 2021 by Cooper Shrivastava. First published electronically on *Tor.com* on August 4. Reprinted by permission of the author.

"Striding the Blast" by Gregory Feeley. Copyright © 2021 by Gregory Feeley. First appeared in *Asimov's Science Fiction*, November/December 2021. Reprinted by permission of the author.

"Año Nuevo" by Ray Nayler. Copyright © 2021 by Ray Nayler. First published in *Asimov's Science Fiction*, May/June 2021. Reprinted by permission of the author.

Paley's Watch

Anil Menon

THE AMERICAN SPIRIT found the artifact in the Gulf of Alaska, about 50 miles off the coastline, not too far from the port at Sitka. It'd been dredged up by a trawler pod, set for halibut. Paley, one of the fishermen, spotted the object sparkling against the blood-black deck, and the men gathered at the Brit's triumphant shout.

It was a set of nested funnels. Each conical layer sparkled with what appeared to be moving dots of light. The artifact was about the size of a can of soup, but its weight kept changing, making the thing feel uncomfortably alive. Like holding a cat. The men quickly returned the artifact to Paley. At first, they thought it was junk from one of the many cruise ships that plied the area, but even junk is *something*. This looked like nothing they had seen before. They had a college boy in their midst, one Tommy Kumagai, and they got the 19-year-old to take a look.

"Hey, that's Dini's surface!" said Tommy.

"No, it ain't," growled Paley. "It's mine. I found it."

"Relax, Paley. I meant it looks like Dini's Surface—it's a topological manifold."

"A topless *what*?" asked the captain, eyeing the curious crew. At his glare, they all returned to work except for Paley.

"Manifold, a surface with smooth curvature. Like those sculptures with those weird holes and lumps. If you know the curvature of a manifold, you know everything about it. A sphere has constant positive curvature. That's what makes it a sphere. A Dini's Surface is a pseudo-sphere; it has constant negative curvature. If you draw a triangle—"

"Thanks, professor." Paley spat on the deck. "So it's just a toy, innit?" The Liverpudlian expat looked ready to throw it back into the ocean.

Tommy hesitated. "Dunno, Paley. Doesn't look like it's been made for giggles. Might be valuable. Never laid eyes on nuthin' like it."

Paley snorted. "Why didncha say that in the first place, punk?" He pocketed the item. "Cap'n, if you don't mind, finders keepers and all that."

Tommy Kumagai lies dying from massive internal injuries from a hit-and-run close to the intersection of San Francisco's Haight and Steiner Street. A corner of his mind doesn't believe he's going to die. It's hopeful, even cocky. It knows Tommy Kumagai is only 26 years old and therefore, immortal. It knows there's a lot of work to be done now that the artifact's true nature has been resolved. It knows he will be taken to the hospital in time, and a few months of modern medicine will set his mangled body right. It knows those months will be filled with research, Skype conferences, tweets, visits from scores of friends, laughter, and love. It knows there's a lifetime of living to be done with Tara. A corner of his mind, the same corner perhaps, knows everything is going to be all right, just all right.

"Gimme that smile, baby," says Tommy, squeezing Tara's hand.

Then Tommy Kumagai dies.

The artifact came to be called Paley's Watch; that the object wasn't really a watch and no longer belonged to Paley was entirely beside the point. Once on shore, Paley first tried to pawn the thing, then tried to sell it on eBay, and then tried to interest the local fishing rags in the matter. All these efforts failed. Finally, he took the kid's advice and showed it to Dr. Godbole, Tommy's thesis advisor in physics at Berkeley.

The brown egghead had hummed, hawed, inspected the thing with a field lens, a microscope, and then begun using 10-dollar words like "extropic luminescence." Finally, the Mex admitted what the kid had admitted.

"Mr. Paley, it's nothing like anything I've ever seen. Perhaps you've found Paley's Watch!" Dr. Godbole had hee-hawed like a jackass.

Matters quickly devolved out of control. The professor had said that he wanted to "study" it and got quite nasty when Paley disagreed. Paley had given the grasping scoundrel a black eye to study.

But quicker than one can say "non compos mentis," Paley was behind bars. Uncle Sam had seized his artifact, citing some obscure, security-related forfeiture law. The men in black gave Paley a receipt and encouraged him to sue.

A Manhattan Project was assembled in San Francisco under the supervision of Dr. Godbole. Soon, the artifact was being poked and prodded by all kinds of professionals.

By the time 21-year-old Tommy, already known as a wunderkind in physics circles, completed his doctoral thesis and had joined the project, not much progress had been made. It *was* a model of Dini's surface. The number of nested funnels had been counted to 242,156,789, and then their instruments had squashed their noses against Heisenberg's limit. Nothing could chip, scan, fry, freeze or penetrate the artifact; it was completely inert. As one wag insinuated, the artifact was "ontologically and epistemologically frigid."

The moving "dots of light" in the artifact were the main reason why the name "Paley's Watch" had stuck. Every so often, a dot would split into a random, but always prime, number of dots. Assuming that the current estimated number of dots was correct, and assuming the object obeyed the mathematics of inhomogeneous branching processes, and assuming these assumptions were correct, the artifact could be dated to be anywhere between 4 to 5 billion years old. A scathing attack in the much-cited article, "Dirimens Copulatio: The Rhetoric of Artifact Dating," had pointed out that Earth itself was only 3.5 billion years old, give or take a billion. Counterattacks, equally scathing, began with quotes from Sherlock Holmes and *Alice in Wonderland*.

If Paley's Watch was indeed a watch, then it certainly was the most useless watch in the Universe. The artifact was wrapped as snugly in its secrets as a honeybee in its pirate pants. An infinite number of nested orchids, each distinct, each spun from a single whirl of the same spiral, and each whorl rooted in nothingness.

☼

"It's not the end of the world." But Tommy knew Bolazar, who'd failed the doctoral qualifiers, would see it differently. "There are other Gs, bro."

"Gs?" asked Bolazar. The older man's eyes were red; it looked like he hadn't slept in a while.

"Gigs. Goals. Games. Gs."

"You think this is all some bloody game?"

Tommy again silently cursed the day he'd agreed to join Berkeley's physics faculty. At the time, he'd thought it would be a fun break from the Centre for Theoretical Physics. He'd envisioned lolling on green university quads, rapping with cool Doctors Evil in the making, all the groupie love he could handle. But the reality had been sweaty griefers like Bolazar.

"Look, I get your pain. But think it out and you'll see I did you a favor. Saved you time. Better to flunk out now than five years from now."

Tommy didn't add that Bolazar, at 37, needed all the time he could get. Hell, at 26, even *he* felt Time nipping at his nuts. He threw the ball against the wall, catching it on the rebound. Then Tommy remembered that Tara always hated it. "It's a bloody obnoxious habit, Thomas."

Funny how she called him Thomas. Nobody else did. He was Tommy. Tomahawk. T-man. T. Tack. Or, in his gaming days, T-Hex. "Thomas" was a liver spotted geezer in a plaid suit with trousers pulled all the way up to his man boobs. He guessed it was all part of Tara's failed cause to make him a better human. What would Tara do with Bolazar? She'd listen, empathize, try to help.

Tommy squeezed the ball and made another attempt to comfort the Turkish student. "Like the Barbie doll sez: Physics is hard. Not everyone can hack it."

"And I'm too old?"

"Nah. Plenty of Gandalfs in the field."

"So, I'm not good enough?"

"Right."

Bolazar had an indecipherable expression on his face.

"You crashed and burned in the string quartet," explained Tommy, feeling silly at having to explain the obvious. "And I threw you some damn easy curveballs. Why didn't you just stick to the questions I asked? What was with all the freestylin' shit about Schrödinger's pussycat, mirrors, narratology and point of view? Take this—" He tapped the iPhone and quoted from Bolazar's answer sheet: "'Just as it is, unmisted by love or dislike, I'm not cruel, only truthful . . .' Dude, I gotta ask: were you on crack?"

"I was quoting from Sylvia Plath's poem 'Mirror.' I thought it spoke very well to how we resist treating physics as a literary genre. If physics is the book of nature and we're its readers, then what can we say about the narrators? I asked myself: Bolazar, can we look at physics narratologically?"

"Dude—"

"Yes, it's a radical view. I admit it. But you have to admit I made an innovative use of Hegel's master-slave dialectic."

"Who's Hegel?" Tommy remembered Helga, the hot Dutch physicist who never wore a bra.

"The philosopher!"

"Ah." Tommy wondered if Hegel wore bras.

"I said to myself: Bolazar, let's take the metaphor of reading the book of nature seriously. Reading is about trying to understand the narrators. We humans turn pages and they say things like: '*Merhaba*, I'm an electron, my weight is such-and-such, and I'm a negative fellow.' But we read on and discover that we are, in fact, stories spun by these narrators. We're inside the book! You and I are embedded stories told in a frame story called reality. We are being narrated by electrons, protons and a handful of protagonists. Now you see the problem? We're literature! There's no standing outside of this story we call the Universe. So if there is an outside, how do we communicate with it?"

"Dude—"

"I said to myself: Bolazar, never mind. Whereof we cannot communicate, thereof we must reflect—"

Tommy decided enough was enough. "'Scuse me, B. This is fun, but here's how it all sounds: batshit crazy. Look, I could empathize your butt off, say things like: Yeah, work on it, it's interesting, come up with some experiments. And what you're saying, yeah, it's all that. Fo'sure. But you want to do this shit right, if you really want to do it right, my guess is you're gonna need something like topos theory. Just word-fucking me won't do. Trouble is, that math is seriously hardcore, and we both know math ain't exactly your bitch. So here's some love, tough but true: find another field. Or another advisor. Sorry, bro."

Just then, the phone did its little Bollywood number. Tara. He took the call, glancing at Bolazar to mouth an "excuse me." But the man was cradling his head. Christ.

"Wassup, baby? Not a good time."

"Uncle and Aunty just left for the airport," she said, her voice sounding casual. "The house is ours! I am on my way to class. I will be done by 4 P.M., pick up the goodies after. What time are you coming over?"

"I got to meet a friend—well, not exactly a friend—jerk, really. Said he wanted my help and the way he rolls, well, no is just yes doing a striptease. We're hooking up at the Mad Dog in the Fog. Five-ish."

"Thomas!"

"A thousand pardons, my queen. Look, join us. The Mad Dog is on Haight. With you there, it'll help me control-Q faster. C'mon, Tara. What's a couple more hours after a million years of waiting?"

"So *do* me already." She sighed. "I can't wait either. Every minute now seems like an eternity. Weird, no?"

"Not weird. So you coming?"

"Won't that depend on your game, sweetie?" she said, disconnecting before he could word-judo her.

Tommy set the phone down, smiling. "Sorry, B. The girlfriend. You know how it is." He paused. "Well! Looks like we done grab-assing, so yeah."

The older man slowly lifted his tear-stricken face.

"Bolazar . . . c'mon, guy! Nuthin's that bad. Get a grip."

"I don't know what to do," said Bolazar. "Can't you do something? I'll retake the test. Please help me."

"You're in denial, B!" Tommy flexed his neck. "You're not thinking straight. Tell you what. Got any family?"

"I have a mother in Turkey," said Bolazar. He wiped his face with his sleeve. "I haven't been home in two years. Visa problems."

Jeez, at least you have a mother, thought Tommy. He didn't know where his Mary was even at. The 15-inch Coby TV in the trailer. Trash everywhere; Jesus keychains, Goodwill clothes, Cheetos, handcuffs, clumps of hair. Stuffing weed into little Ziplock bags. Sesame Street on high coz of the crack-whore's snores. Shut your fucking mouth, Mom; you're not on the clock. If Dr. Godbole hadn't found him . . .

He glanced at Bolazar. The poor bastard was actually looking hopeful.

"Yeah, moms. They're the best. Listen, Bolazar, go home. Regroup with the family unit and defrag for a while. Then figure out the next fun thing to do. That narratology stuff sounds like your groove's in the humanities. Or go look up Professor Hegel in the philosophy department. She may—"

"Fuck you. I don't need your advice."

"Damn right." Tommy threw the ball. "I've been sayin' what? That exactly. I know jack about life, literature and latte. Hell, who does? So. We cool, B? I gotta roll."

☼

Later, as Tommy drove toward the Haight, the gray gauze of San Francisco's fog already beginning to moisten the Hummer's squat windows, he kept one eye on the road and the other on the iPhone, as he scrolled through the messages. NBD. NBD. NBD. Wait. Message from Tara: *Shopping. Durex ultras, right? Sales bitch tried to push some edible variety. At the counter! Died a mil. Luv ya.*

A sudden horn blast, and he swerved just in time. Tommy put away the iPhone, smiling. The girl sauntering into a store to buy condoms was a far cry from the girl he'd met a year and a half ago. They'd been intro'd by Dr. Godbole.

Tommy's thesis advisor did not believe in separating work from life. His seminars tended to continue in the campus café, over dinner and to extend late into the night. That it inconvenienced his wife was, as Dr. Godbole liked to say, "negligible in the first approximation."

When Dr. Godbole had discovered Tommy, then rotting in an inner-city high school, he'd rushed home, embraced his surprised wife and told her that he now knew why he'd been put on Earth. Perhaps it was the joy on her husband's face; she'd rarely seen him that happy. Or perhaps it was merely the embrace; she'd rarely been embraced. Whatever the reason, the childless couple, who otherwise agreed on so little, found in Tommy an agreement and a common need.

For him, Mrs. Godbole learned to cook eggs. She fussed over his appearance. She gave Tommy a spare key. She confounded him with her attempts to speak Japanese, a language he did not speak. The guest bedroom, more or less, became Tommy's room.

But one late night, Tommy crawled into his bed and found a girl and a scream.

"Tara's my niece," Dr. Godbole had explained. "She's from India, and here to do a master's in computer science. Like the rest of the damn nation. Tara, you've been spooned by a future Nobel laureate. Dr. Kumagai to friends, Tommy to strangers," Dr. Godbole had finished, appending one of his signature laughs.

She was brown because bronze chooses to be that color. Tommy's hand still remembered her thigh's pliant smoothness and its sleepy heat. She'd been wearing silk boxers. But what he really remembered was her smile. Slow, teasing, as if she knew something but chose not to say it.

"Spank-da-monkey smile," thought Tommy. On one level, she was such a good little girl, always ready to swot her homework, Skype her mousy parents, defend her weird-ass Hindu religion and make sure no hand slipped into her panties except her own. But on another level, a little Aguilera dirty, too. Else, what was with the efforts to improve him, sari porn, eye sex, accidental brushes and that killer smile?

Tommy had rather liked it. Tara was a huge change from the acrobatic chiquitas and EEOC valley twits he normally preyed on. She was challenging country. Make a move, get rebuffed, try an alternate route—classic video game.

Dr. Godbole had initially turned a blind eye to his wife's dark looks and a deaf ear to her dark mutterings. But he had become alarmed when he found Tommy perusing *The Dummy's Guide to Hinduism.* He'd taken the kids aside, forced a tight-lipped Tara to tie a rakhi on Tommy's wrist and then sent her off.

"My niece is a comely lass," Dr. Godbole had said.

"Yes sir."

"This holy thread makes her your sister."

"Yes sir."

Totally kinky, figured Tommy. But he had watched Animal Planet. Different cultures, different rules! Tommy had worn the glitzy, itchy and totally gay bracelet all through lunch, basking uncertainly in Mrs. G's delighted smiles, until Tara cornered him in the kitchen, chanted something in Indian, tore the rakhi off, threw it in the dustbin and kissed him on the mouth. Not the full French car wash, but seriously incestuous.

Tommy parked the H2 on a sidewalk at the corner of Haight and Steiner; a ticket was inevitable, but he didn't care. It was one of the costs of living in the world's most beautiful city. He'd only taken a few steps toward the pub when his cell broke into Sanskrit.

"Wazzup, Doc G? Where you at?"

"At Heathrow. Listen, I just got the anisotropy data for the 'lights' on Paley's Watch. Isotropic as we suspected, but you were right. There's a suppression of power at large scales for the second quadruple moment in the angular power spectrum."

Tommy stopped walking, but his heart began to pound like he'd begun to run. "It's a model of the Universe. That's *crazy.*"

"Question is, is it crazy enough to be right?" Dr. Godbole brayed at his insider joke.

"Suppose it is. Means it was here to be found. And if the dating's accurate, it's been here for billions of years. And coz it's one frigid Bridget, it survived right through the evolution of our solar system. It was built not to interact. Hell, it's practically dead, and since the dead cannot be killed, nuthin's fitter. So it survived. Neat."

"And now we need to wake the dead. Then find a way to talk to it."

"Nah. It won't talk to us. Let's see if it'll notice itself. Maybe it can talk to us by talking to itself. Like literature."

"What?"

"You don't want to know. Let's do a mirror test. The artifact is spec'd to blow off everything coz everything is a potential hazard. But it knows it's not a threat to itself. All those lights suggest it's aware of the visible spectrum. So let's see what it sees in a mirror."

"A wake-up test for Narcissus. Hmm."

"The motherfucker?"

"You're thinking of Oedipus, Tommy. Narcissus is someone else. Where are you? At the university?"

"Nope. On my way to meet Tara. But I'll cancel—"

"What for? Won't that disappoint Tara?" Dr. Godbole fell silent. "Perhaps I have taught you too well. Don't make the mistakes I've made. No, don't cancel anything. I'll tell Hendrix to set up the test. Shouldn't take more than an hour. I'll be in touch—" Dr. Godbole stopped and said something in Marathi. "Wait, the missus wants to talk."

As always, Mrs. Godbole spoke in deeds. She told him there was pasta, jeera rice and two days' worth of *aloo mutter* in the fridge. Rotis would have to be reheated. There was also fresh *shrikhand*. He loved *shrikhand*, didn't he? She'd laundered Tommy's clothes. Why didn't he buy some new underwear? Tara's exams—

"Don't worry, Mama G," said Tommy gently. "You have a good time. Tara will be safe with me. Word on that."

"I know. Tara and I had long talk." Then, after a brief pause, "I'm glad. God bless."

☼

The Mad Dog in the Fog was so crowded, it looked like it had exploded people.

"Thomas!"

He turned in the direction of the voice and saw Tara at the outer rim of the throng, waving at him as if she'd just sighted an exit from a desert island. Tommy walked over, hands framed in viewfinder mode. She was wearing her signature kurta-top and Dylan George knockoffs. Slung across her shoulder was a Healthy Back leather tote. Flashes of faux gold at her throat and ears, highlighting the sensual brown.

"Like?" she asked, striking a pose.

"Pimpin', babe." He pulled her close. There was something different this time; a complete lack of wariness, a fall of reserve, and it turned their hug into an embrace.

"The pub looks pretty full," she said finally, in a breathless voice. "Do you see your friend anywhere?"

"Tommy boy!"

Speak of the devil.

"Paley. Hola."

Paley looked like he'd always looked: mean, ferocious and quarrelsome.

"'ppreciate your coming," said Paley, crushing Tommy's hand in his paw. Then he noticed Tara. "Howdeedo. You with him?"

"Tara, Paley. Paley, Tara."

Paley seemed to be in a remarkably cheerful mood. "She's cute fo'sure. C'mon, let me buy you two a drink. We gotta talk, Tommy."

Through a combination of drunken-monk-fearless-hyena maneuvers, Paley got them inside the pub. He bought the first round of drinks: a Black & Tan for Tommy, an amber ale for Tara and a stout for himself. The source of his goodwill soon became apparent. "Finding the artifact was the best thing ever," Paley confided. "I'd taken snaps of it; for hawking it on friggin' eBay, see. When the men in black came for me, I put the pics on the web and tube'd the whole story. Fixed 'em bastards good. Now, yours truly is on the lecture circuit, 500 dolla a pop and more abductee chicks than I can shake my stick at. I've got a book in the works. How do you like 'em nuts?" Paley's face was an unnatural mix of pride and modesty.

Someone had noticed quite early on that "Dini" was the ancient Greek word for "vortex." Someone had noticed that Genesis 1:11 had a reference to "the fruit tree yielding fruit whose seed is in itself." Someone had noticed that Dini's Surface was one of the solutions to Einstein's general relativity equations. Paley's early disciples had tenaciously blown upon these embers until they'd flamed into a genuine cult, complete with web presence, demanding rituals, fashion merchandise and bank accounts.

"That rocks, Paley! Your own cult!" said Tommy, laughing. "So you're in the buzz. I'd no clue."

"Bloody damn right it rocks," echoed Tara, sounding as if she was in the buzz as well. She put her hand on Tommy's thigh. "But what exactly is the artifact? It's not really alien, is it?"

"'Course it is," snorted Paley. "As alien as you, sweet cheeks. Right, Tommy boy?"

Their expressions reminded Tommy of that strange day with its freezing rain, bloodied deck and the question mark in his hands. He thought about what Godbole had told him.

"Maybe, maybe not." Tommy wanted to explain. But how? It was all so technical. The Big Bang had left a trace in the form of tiny temperature fluctuations in the background radiation. These fluctuations had patterns; they differed in different directions. The fluctuations could be used to figure out the shape of the Universe. On that basis, it was thought that the Universe had a "Picard topology," resembling something like a medieval horn, or more precisely, the Eiffel Tower. A plain old sphere was a surface of constant positive curvature. The Picard topology was a pseudosphere; a hyperbolic surface of constant negative curvature.

But there were other pseudospheres in mathematics. For example, Dini's Surface. As he had predicted in his doctoral thesis, the correlation data for the artifact's "lights" had turned out to match the background radiation fluctuations for a universe shaped like a Dini's surface. It was too much of a coincidence. It was like finding a toy globe, complete with lines of latitude and longitude and precisely drawn land masses, floating in some sea, just when the people had begun to suspect the earth was a sphere. The artifact had been *made*. But made for what purpose?

"It's too early to tell," concluded Tommy.

"Oh." Tara sounded disappointed and returned to her drink.

Paley shrugged. "Who cares? Then the artifact's what I say it is."

Tommy decided to let this fine example of para-consistent reasoning slide. Tara used the silence to drain her mug and slid off the seat. "I'll be back," she announced in a Schwarzenegger accent that was beyond dreadful. They watched her walk away.

"You tapping that ass?" asked Paley, more brotherly than envious.

Tommy was able to avoid lying because his iPhone broke into a Turkish jingle. Bolazar. *Ah, screw him.* He tapped the screen, and the mobile went quiet.

"You said you wanted some help, Paley?"

Paley rotated his beer mug and looked shifty. "Yeah. It's for this book I'm writing. My publisher suggested that maybe you'd be willing to endorse the book for an old mate. Seeing as you're now a quack and all. I told her she was full of shit; that I couldn't, wouldn't impose on a mate, you know how much I hate to, Tommy boy, so what do you say?" The iPhone lit up with a Turkish jingle, and Tommy tapped it into silence again.

"Sure. I'll lend some nitro."

"Sure?" Paley looked astonished.

"Yup. No sweat. I'll email it. Anything else?"

Paley squeezed his shoulder, quite overcome with emotion. "Wunnerful! Yer a good brick, Tommy. Always was, still are." Paley acquired a pious look. "I was gonna throw the artifact away. But you begged me not to. Coincidence?"

The correct answer, it was clear, was in the negative. Tara was making her way back to the table. She was smiling, but her eyes flashed a girlfriend's warning. Tommy stood up. He was glad he'd made the time to meet Paley. "Gotta roll. See you around, buddy." Tommy raised his Black & Tan, downed it.

Paley returned the salute. "In the halls of Valhalla, Tommy boy."

☼

When Tommy and Tara left the bar, they walked into a magical world wrapped in fog. On the way back to the Hummer, Tara broke the silence. "Paley was interesting ... a little scary. Hard to believe you worked on the Bering Sea with guys like that."

Tommy said nothing. Tough guys didn't jaw about the past. It'd just been a summer gig. A fast buck. Nothing special. Dr. G liked to say the only projects that mattered in life were those listed in one's obit. But if Tara got moist at the thought of him haulin' fish, then good. Very good.

"Isn't it ironic that Paley was the one to find Paley's Watch?"

"Why is it ironic?" said Tommy. "He found it."

"Yes, but a *Paley* found it. Reverend Paley's book? You know, the guy who wrote *Natural Theology*?"

"Wiki me, babe."

"Thomas! You've never heard of Reverend Paley and his book? How's that possible? Don't you read anything except physics?"

"Does porno count?"

"You're shameless! Reverend Paley wrote that living things were so perfectly designed, they couldn't have been made by chance. Suppose you find a beautiful, fully functional watch on the beach? Would you say it evolved by chance or would you say that there had to be a watchmaker?"

"I'd say the dude got the causal link ass backwards. In science, you gotta go from what you know to what you don't know. I know watches are made by watchmakers. So if I find an old watch lying around somewhere, I can assume it was made by a watchmaker. But I don't know if animals are made by God. So if I find a fossil, I can't assume God put it there. Look, it's all there in Hegel."

"Oh." Tara was clearly impressed. "Really?"

"Yeah. Amazed you haven't read Hegel."

"Sorry, Thomas. I have been meaning to." Then she saw his face. "Ass!"

He laughed. "Such a book slut."

"Yes," she admitted. "But seriously, when you find something really improbable, like the artifact, it makes you wonder, doesn't it?"

"Depends. I suspect there are billions of Paley's Watches out there. This artifact was meant to be found. And something can be improbable, yet very common. Like snowflakes. License plates. Probability is just a measure of what you think you know. It's just how you figure the game. Existence *is* the game. You exist, and then you don't."

"What about us, Thomas? You and me. Are we improbable?"

He had to force himself to say what he knew: "Yeah, maybe. But I'm gonna believe."

She kissed him. He could taste the amber. It occurred to him the taste of a life could only be experienced, never described.

"I think we're very probable, Thomas." They kissed again. The cell began to chant Sanskrit.

"Don't answer it," whispered Tara. "No more calls tonight." Then she stiffened. "Shit, left my tote at the bar. Must have set it down when I went to pee. I'll be back in five."

She disappeared into the fog. Tommy took the call. "Wassup, Doctor G? Any news from Hendrix?"

"Tommy, it vanishes! The damn artifact vanishes when you shove it in front of a mirror. Take away the mirror, it reappears. We can make it appear and disappear. Zero, one, zero, one. You know what that means, don't you?"

"Christ. A telephone."

"Exactly. We can send a message. Who knows where though! Maybe there's still someone around to listen. Pity Carl Sagan's dead; this is the sort of problem the man would've enjoyed. Tommy, Tommy, this is the second happiest day of my life."

"Yes, sir. May I say—"

"No, you may not. I'm going to run some more tests. Tonight is yours. But tomorrow onwards, it'll be different. Get ready to be famous, Tommy. It's your idea that broke the problem."

"About that. Not quite true. Someone gave me the idea. There's a prequel to all this—*Holy shit! Wha—*"

"All of life is a prequel, Tommy. Tommy? Hello?"

✿

In the final three minutes of Tommy Kumagai's life, after Bolazar mows him down with a 1992 Honda Civic, the first 28 milliseconds of almost unbearable pain from the collision is stilled, and all light, all sound, all sensation, all knowing, blinks out for a merciful 40 milliseconds. Then sensation comes back, at least partially, for it is without the pain. Euphoria even. There are people everywhere. Shouts. Sirens. How worried they all look. But a part of Tommy's mind—if it is even mind or a part at all—knows better. Look, isn't Tara here? It knows there's a lifetime of living to be had with Tara. A part of his mind, the same part, perhaps, knows everything is going to be all right. All right.

"Gimme that smile, baby," says Tommy, squeezing Tara's hand.

So that part of Tommy's mind relaxes and watches the show. The human consciousness is such a wondrous manifold. Look! Space and time collapse even as his consciousness unfurls and expands. An infinite whirling vortex of consciousness, concentrating, ever tighter, impossibly tighter, collapsing into an inexorable singularity, rushing, rushing toward a primordial timeless, spaceless, explosive birth event of a quaquaversal, multiversant, sempiternal universe.

Light Up the Clouds

Greg Egan

1

TIRELL STOOD ON the platform at the edge of the forest, looking out at the banks of red clouds. As he waited for Anna's glider to come swooping down, his eyes were drawn to the swirling patterns below, where stronger winds set the thicker clouds roiling, spinning off vortices in thrillingly strange hues: deep blues, rich browns, grays shading almost into white.

"If you fall, it won't look so pretty," Selik joked.

"That's true." You could only see the patterns from above; if you were down among them, at any one point you'd be surrounded by a monochromatic fog—while being crushed to death with nothing to show for it.

Tirell took a few steps back from the edge.

"Here she comes," Rada announced.

Tirell followed Rada's gaze and caught sight of the glider, descending in a broad, shallow helix that brought it almost directly above them before carrying it away again. He knew that Anna was an old hand at this maneuver, but he couldn't help feeling a visceral sense of how terrified he would have been in her place, if he'd been the one controlling the rudder.

On its second approach, the glider was much lower. For a moment Tirell thought it might miss its target, but then he realized he was blind to the true curvature of its path, misjudging it by its foreshortened appearance. The glider flew directly into the mouth of the clearing, shot straight past him and the other onlookers, and dived into the wall of soft foliage that some ancestral aviator must have cultivated generations ago, and a thousand grateful successors had tended ever since.

The three of them ran toward the site of the impact, but before they could reach it Anna had already clambered out, apparently unharmed. As Tirell drew nearer, he could see that the glider, though strewn with leaves and tangled in the vines, had suffered no real damage either.

Everyone worked together to pull it free, then they dragged it across the platform and secured it in its proper place—using thicker vines, in a more orderly arrangement.

With the job done, Anna turned to them and announced, "I think the cousins might be back."

Tirell strove to interpret her demeanor, wondering if she was teasing her friends. As far as he could tell, she was perfectly serious, but he would have thought this claim was something only a child could believe.

"The thing's still up there?" Selik asked warily.

"Absolutely," Anna confirmed. "But now there are three of them. All in similar orbits."

Selik hesitated. "Are you sure you're not just seeing different asteroids every time, coming and going from the equilibrium point?"

"Not if they're doing it at random," Anna replied. "There's an object of the same size and brightness in the same orbit as I saw on the last trip. So either it's the same thing as before, or whatever took its place managed to mimic its appearance and slip into exactly the same trajectory. I can't speak to the fate of the other two yet, but if they're still following their present course when I return, that would stretch the bounds of coincidence."

Rada said, "With three asteroids all disturbing each other, it would be absurd to expect them to remain in the region at all, let alone retrace their orbits."

"Of course," Anna agreed. "If these are natural objects, moving under gravity alone, they couldn't possibly hang around much longer."

The group fell silent. Tirell could almost hear a collective rejoinder that only tact was keeping anyone from uttering: *If* these are natural objects?

Anna scowled. "So do you all think the cousins are dead?"

Selik snorted. "Dead or alive, I can't say I've been expecting a visit."

"Why not? Because it wasn't sooner?" Anna brushed an insect off her shoulder and sat down on the platform, gesturing to the others to do the same. "I'm serious! If our own ancestors struggled with the Changes, why wouldn't the cousins have struggled just as much? They could have lost everything and had to start over, as many times as we did. And if we still lack the means to visit *them*, why should we be shocked that it took them this long to make the same journey in reverse?"

"But we don't know that they survived at all," Rada stressed.

"That's true. But we survived what they thought was unsurvivable, so we could have been as wrong about their chances as they were about ours. And that's just the way we tell the story now: because we didn't die, we pretend we always knew that we'd made the better choice. But maybe at the time, both groups were glad that the other would be trying a different strategy—improving the odds that at least one would succeed."

Selik was unconvinced. "All these 'maybes' have been plucked out of the sky before. That's the trouble with invoking the cousins: you can call on them to explain anything."

"So how do you account for these observations?" Anna demanded.

"The observations could be wrong," Selik replied. His tone was respectful, but Tirell was still shocked by the bluntness of his words.

"I know what I saw," Anna said mildly.

"Anyone's eyes can deceive them." Selik looked uncomfortable, but he wasn't retreating.

"You mean, especially at my age?" Anna asked. She turned and gestured at the glider. "So why don't you go up and check for yourself?"

"You know I don't have the experience." Selik seemed to regret his choice of words immediately; if he deferred to her skills as a pilot, why not to those as an observer?

Rada said, "Why not take a fresh pair of eyes with you, next time?" She glanced at Tirell. "In a body still light enough not to weigh you down?"

Everyone turned to him at once, eyeing him appraisingly. Tirell felt his stomach tense, and he struggled to quell the fear rising in his blood. *They're joking,* he told himself. *About everything.* Anna was joking about the cousins, and they were all in on the joke except him. But now they were putting an end to the ruse by pushing it beyond their victim's threshold of gullibility.

"Would you be willing to do that?" Anna enquired. "It's about time I had an apprentice."

Her voice still betrayed no hint of mirth. And even Selik seemed to be taking the proposal seriously.

"I'm a fruit picker!" Tirell protested. He'd stumbled on the group in the market, overhearing one of their heated debates, but even when he'd started tagging along to their gatherings, he'd never expected to do anything more than listen—or at most, interject with a question or two.

"I'm not asking you to stop that," Anna replied gently. "This wouldn't take up all of your time."

Tirell did his best to consider the offer calmly, with the serious-ness it deserved. He'd always wanted to know what lay beyond the clouds; until now he'd been content just to listen to Anna's reports, but if even her friends started doubting her, what would her testimony be worth? He might as well have stayed in the market, where storytellers improvised wild confabulations that differed on each retelling, no more permanent than the clouds themselves.

"I've never flown before," he admitted. "Not even to the closest forests."

Anna was unfazed. "And why would you have? There's nothing worth seeing there. We can take this as slowly as you like; you don't need to become a pilot at all, if you don't want to. For now, the most important thing is to have someone up there with me, to confirm what I'm seeing."

Tirell put his fears aside. "All right," he said. "I'll come with you." The next flight would still be many days away; he'd have plenty of time to change his mind.

The forest was already darkening, as the glistening bead of the Far Sun dropped away to the west. Tirell tried to imagine the time before the cousins left, when the Near Sun had supposedly been so much brighter that the whole warm half of the world had been uninhabitable.

He wasn't sure if he believed that or not, though many people he trusted had repeated the same story. But it would take much more to persuade him that, not only were the most extravagant claims about the old days true, everything he'd once thought of as belonging either in the unfathomable past, or at an incomprehensible distance, had now reached into the present and was drifting around just above his head.

2

"Take as much fruit as you like," Tirell encouraged Delia. "They were almost falling into the sack."

She gauged the weight of half a dozen, and chose two. "What do you want for them?" she asked.

"Leave it for the future."

Delia scowled, as if she resented the obligation, but Tirell wasn't short of anything at present.

"If you pick too many, you'll kill the trees," she scolded him.

"That's really not true." All the fruit parted from the branches eventually, but plucking it before it was buoyant enough to survive outside the forest did no harm to the parent, other than thwarting its ambition to give rise to a whole new forest of its own.

"I heard you're going flying with that madwoman," Delia informed him. Tirell didn't reply; he had no idea how she could have learned about his plans, but they were none of her concern. "You'll get yourself killed for nothing," she said. "If you want some excitement, my friends fly back and forth to Lappa all the time. It's a short trip, but the winds can really set you spinning, so at least you'll be having fun if it all goes wrong."

"I'd rather die from a lack of air than too much of it," Tirell joked. "Anyone can fall into the depths, but how many people do you know who've fallen into the sky?"

"You're an idiot." Delia ambled away across the floor of dead branches, toward the pile of juicy larvae Madeleine was offering.

"You can weave me some new clothes," he called after her, fairly sure that she hadn't taken enough fruit in his entire tenure to have earned him anything of the kind. "Or just a new sack," he added.

Three of the infants who hung around the market crawled up to him, babbling happily, so he sat with them for a while, talking to them and feeding them mouthfuls of chewed fruit.

After a while they grew bored with him and headed over to try their luck with Madeleine. Tirell lay down beside his wares, and felt a patch of bark scrape against his shirt. Before the cousins left, or so the story went, even the cold half of the world had been so hot that everyone went naked. But surely they would have been scratched a lot more? Or was people's skin tougher then? Like his soles and his palms, but all over?

He drifted off to sleep, then was woken by someone prodding him with their foot.

Selik said, "If you still want to do this, Anna's getting the glider ready."

"Now?" Tirell had thought he had a few more days.

"She wants to take advantage of the weather while it lasts."

Tirell clambered to his feet. "I'll do it," he said. "She's a good pilot, I know she won't kill me."

"Of course she won't." Selik noted his hesitancy. "But?"

Tirell said, "I know you don't think the cousins have come back—but do you really think they ever left at all? Flew beyond the clouds, all the way to the Far Sun?"

"Not all the way," Selik corrected him. "The inner worlds keep their distance from it; it's not the same as we are with this one."

"You know what I mean." Tirell didn't doubt that there'd been some parting of the ways long ago, but falling out of touch with a group of distant relatives didn't really strike him as a convincing proof that they'd left the world behind.

"The cousins might have failed," Selik replied, "but I believe they did try to make the journey."

"*How?* How is that even possible?"

"They must have built some kind of vessel."

Tirell laughed. "That doesn't explain anything! If you ask me how to build a glider, I couldn't do it myself, but I could probably still convince you that someone else could. But once the air thins out to nothing, what is there to discuss? Gliders won't work. Buoyancy won't work. 'They built some kind of vessel' is just another way of saying that they did something no one understands, in order to achieve something no one knows how to achieve."

"We've lost a lot of knowledge," Selik conceded. "But I don't believe we could be wrong about the entire history of the Changes."

"People tell greater lies all the time," Tirell argued. "Just for amusement. 'The trees that talked' . . . 'The birds that raised a child' . . . 'The mite that slew the lizard' . . ."

"No one puts children's stories into the Recitation."

"But they do leave things out, apparently." The versions of the Recitation Tirell had heard were missing all kinds of things that Selik, Anna and Rada had learned from their own reciters.

They reached the edge of the marketplace and began scrambling up the branches. Bark-colored lizards fled Tirell's approaching grip, always choosing the last moment to abandon the camouflage of stillness for escape, sometimes scampering over his body, sometimes dropping and trusting the forest to catch them on a lower branch. Tirell felt perfectly secure as he climbed; if he did fall, the branches and foliage here were more than dense enough to stop him very quickly. But all this talk of the cousins was forcing him to picture a time when *the trees themselves* had fallen, and people had fled from forest to forest as everything in the cold half of the world began to die.

When they arrived at the platform, Anna and Rada were waiting. "Ah, there's my apprentice!" Anna exclaimed, as if she'd just spotted an awl or a chisel she'd mislaid.

Tirell said, "Can we start with 'passenger,' and work up from there?"

The glider was already untied, but it took the four of them to drag it into place between the pulleys. Anna climbed inside, and motioned to Tirell to join her. He complied, but he was already regretting his decision. Now that he was on the verge of trusting his life to it, he couldn't help noting that the glider was really just a hollow log with some fancily shaped boards attached. And unlike a living log, it possessed no buoyancy at all.

"Are you sure I won't weigh you down?" Tirell fretted. Squeezed in behind Anna with his knees pressed against her back, he found it hard to believe that the burden he contributed was negligible. "I was planning to fast for a couple of days before the flight, but Selik caught me by surprise."

"I never fast," Anna replied, "but if I find we're overloaded you might need to empty your bowels at short notice." Tirell spent a moment in horrified contemplation before deciding it would be best to assume that she was joking.

"Are you ready?" Rada asked. She'd threaded the vine from the pulleys around the capstan at the front of the glider, and was waiting impatiently for Anna's assent to proceed.

"We're ready."

Rada joined Selik behind the glider. Tirell turned and watched them at first, but as they began hauling on the other end of the vine it seemed wiser for him to look where he was going, even if he had no control over his destination.

The glider shuddered, then slid forward. Tirell had helped with the previous launch, running backward across the platform, amused at how light the strange arrangement of vines and capstans made the glider feel, while compensating for this generosity by making the platform runners move twice as far as the glider was advancing.

"Hold on!" Anna instructed him.

"To what?" But then he saw the two curved branches that Anna was holding, attached within the hollow, and he gripped them behind her.

Ahead, the mouth of the clearing grew nearer, exposing endless ranks of red cloud. Tirell weighed up the benefits of jumping out onto the platform while he still had a chance. If nature had wanted people to leave the forests, it would have let them retain the gas from the fruit they ate, instead of belching it out. But he was weighed down with pulp, and entirely free of the one ingredient from his diet that might have saved him.

The glider passed over the edge of the platform—and instead of soaring skyward it dipped alarmingly, heading for an elaborately twisted blue-and-white vortex far below. Tirell squeezed the handles so hard he could feel splinters digging into his skin, but then he saw Anna's legs moving slightly, working the pedals that controlled the wing flaps, and the glider leveled out, leaving him staring over her shoulder at a sight less terrifying, but still utterly wrong: red clouds spread out ahead forever, without a single branch or leaf in sight.

He glanced back toward Maldo, but it was already dwindling into insignificance, like a tangled ball of twigs someone had tossed into the sky. "How will we find our way home?" he asked.

"I know the winds," Anna replied.

"What does that mean?" Tirell complained. When someone asked for directions to the market, you didn't just smile and say: *trust in the leaves.*

"It'll be easier to explain when we're on our way back. For now, what we need is altitude."

Tirell had many more questions, but he decided to shut up and stop distracting the pilot. While he was in no position to rank the dangers they faced, his presence was certainly the most novel factor in the current journey, so the less impact he had on the way it unfolded, the better.

Anna muttered to herself as she examined the clouds. Then she seemed to make a choice, and sent the glider swerving gently to the right. The destination she'd selected was a disheveled red column, full of wind-streaked wisps that suggested some vertical motion of the air, though if Tirell was honest he could not have determined by eye if the current was ascending or descending.

When they reached the edge of the column, the answer became palpable. As the glider rose, Anna kept its path curving slightly, so it circled the strange cloud formation like a vine wrapping around a tree trunk. Tirell tried to take comfort in his instinctive response to gaining height: inside the forest, it almost always meant that he was safer, with more obstacles to break his fall. And perhaps it wasn't entirely foolish to feel the same way even in the open air. If something went wrong, the higher they were, the more time Anna would have to correct the problem before they hit the depths.

When they broke free of the column, Tirell looked around, then upward. There were yet more clouds above, as red as those surrounding the forest, but he could already discern gaps between them, filled with pallid light in the direction of the Far Sun, but shading into darkness elsewhere.

Anna did not disguise her frustration as she searched for the next opportunity to ascend. Once she picked a target, Tirell fixed his gaze on it, trying to commit to memory every feature that distinguished it. If he ever decided to become a pilot himself, he was going to need a very long list from Anna of all the signs he should heed, but for now he could just watch and try to learn a little.

Close up, whatever order Anna had discerned in the second column was less apparent than ever; to Tirell they just seemed to have reached a scraggly mess of fragmented clouds. But while the currents buffeted them unevenly, as the glider looped around it was lifted more often than it dropped, and gradually they rose above the thicket of red.

The Far Sun had almost set, and the cloudless sky was darkening in the east. But at the zenith, there it was: a dull magenta disk a sixth as wide as the entire view.

Tirell felt a new kind of dizziness that had nothing to do with the motion of the glider. He had never doubted that the Near Sun was real; he had explained its cloud-hidden presence to children who'd fretted on the days when the Far Sun briefly vanished behind it at noon. But seeing it for himself made all the other claims in the Recitation, if not more convincing, certainly more urgent. The Near Sun wasn't just an idea, it was a thing as solid as a tree. So either it had once blazed a thousand times brighter than it did now, or it hadn't. That wasn't a matter of opinion, or whether it sounded appealing, or exciting, or strange. Either the Changes really had come about because this disk had gone from outshining the Far Sun to its present, barely illuminated state, or the whole account of the past was nonsense.

"Why is one side brighter?" Tirell asked Anna.

She turned to face him. "One side of what?"

He nodded upward, wishing he hadn't let his curiosity overpower his resolve not to divert her attention from the glider's controls.

"That's to do with the way we orbit each other." When Tirell replied with uncomprehending silence, she added, "Some of our air is still falling onto it, even now. But it doesn't fall in a straight line, so it hits one side more than the other. That's the cause of the hot spot."

"I see," Tirell replied. Her explanation made a certain amount of sense, but it only increased his vertigo. If the air of the world was raining down gently on the Near Sun, right before his eyes, and doing even a little of the thing that made the Far Sun shine, then it no longer seemed such a stretch to imagine that the very same current had once been much stronger.

"We're just waiting for sunset now," Anna explained. Mercifully, she was no longer twisted around toward him. "If these things are still where I saw them last, it won't be hard to spot them."

"Circling around the . . . equilibrium point?" Tirell didn't feel that he'd earned the right to employ that term so casually, as if he truly understood how the tug of the world, the tug of the Near Sun, and the effect of being whirled around in a circle all added up to zero. He was prepared to believe, though, that such a balance might be precarious, and that anything that drifted by and lodged there by chance was unlikely to linger.

"That's where I'll be looking."

"And if this is the cousins . . . how are they doing it?"

Anna laughed. "If they could overcome the gravity of the Near Sun entirely, this would be nothing to them."

Tirell was confused. "You mean the gravity of the world? It was the world they escaped from, wasn't it?"

"Yes, but that's the easy part." Anna raised one hand to point straight up. "The tiniest push will get you over the equilibrium point, but then you'd just crash into the thing that did most of the work for you. If you want to go and take your pick of the inner worlds, your real fight is with the Near Sun, not the world you were born on."

Tirell was prepared to take her word for it, though the Near Sun was clearly much farther from the equilibrium point than the world was. He wriggled a little in the hollow to relieve the cramp that had been growing in his forearms, though it wasn't easy to stretch his muscles without letting go of the handles.

"We could add vines here that we tie around our bodies, to keep us from falling out," he suggested. But vines might dig into their skin. "Or strips of cloth?"

"Mmm." Anna wasn't really interested in such luxuries.

The Far Sun moved behind the bank of red clouds below them to the west, and though that wasn't enough to extinguish its light, when Tirell looked to the east he saw a smattering of white dots emerging from the grayness: *stars*, the farthest of Far Suns. He really had no right to be surprised that so many things from the Recitation were turning out to be true—but Anna's skills were rare enough that he could imagine whole forests where no one took up the same role, and the stories people told children about the void beyond the clouds were entirely unconstrained by the possibility of anyone checking them.

"Here they come now," Anna said. Tirell took a moment to realize that she was speaking not of anything approaching, but the objects of her interest finally attaining visibility. Peering upward, all he could see at first were a few faint stars struggling to compete with the dull but undiminished light of the Near Sun. Then he realized that one of the "stars" was moving—slowly, but still too fast, and in the wrong direction, to be merely crossing the sky the way the Far Sun did.

"I can see one," he confirmed.

"Cover up the Near Sun with your fist," Anna suggested, demonstrating.

Tirell didn't want to let go of either handle; the glider was still circling the air column, shuddering and bouncing in response to the vagaries of the currents. "I might give my eyes a chance to adjust first."

He closed one eye and turned his head back and forth, trying to obscure the Near Sun while he scrutinized the region around it. "Oh, I can see two more!" he blurted out, before realizing that he'd confused himself and was double counting the first one. But then a moment later there was no need to retract; he'd sighted three distinct specks, all circling the zenith.

"How do we know they're going around the equilibrium point?" he asked Anna. "Couldn't they be orbiting the Near Sun?"

"Be patient," she said. "There'll be evidence soon enough."

Tirell raised his gaze again, waiting for the promised revelation. After a while, he was rewarded in a different way. "I think there are four now. Definitely four."

"Aha." Anna sounded underwhelmed, as if she'd been offered a low bid for something she was selling in the market.

Tirell tightened his grip with his left hand, then raised the right one to help him. With the Near Sun better masked, he could see at least one more point of light. Shifting his gaze and his hand and keeping careful track of everything was harder than he would have anticipated; he could appreciate Selik's skepticism now, as less a slight against Anna than an honest assessment of the difficulties for any observer. But eventually he settled on a verdict.

"There are six," he said.

"I think that's right," Anna replied.

As Tirell tried to make one more recount, he found himself coming up short. "Wait, no, there's only . . ."

"Look again," Anna suggested.

"Only two. No, not even . . ." They were gone, all six. "What happened?"

Anna said, "The Far Sun's dropped too low now to illuminate them. And it didn't take long; that's how we know they're at the equilibrium point, not farther away."

Tirell pictured it: the shifting shadow of the world rising up to encompass the strange visitors. "If this is the cousins, what are they doing up there?"

"Watching us?" Anna suggested. "Waiting to see what we're like now, after all this time apart, before they introduce themselves."

"Watching us through the clouds?" Just how magical were the cousins meant to be? "And why would they need to watch us from six different places?"

"Maybe they came here from their new home in six vessels, and the stragglers have just caught up."

"How big are those things?" Tirell wondered.

Anna hesitated. "From their brightness, I'd guess about a hundred times larger than Maldo."

"That's a lot to bring along for a casual visit." Even if the cousins needed to pack enough food for a long journey, six hundred forests' worth seemed excessive. "You'd think they'd start with a couple of emissaries, traveling light, just to make contact."

"I don't know what any of this means," Anna confessed. "But at least you can tell the others I wasn't imagining it."

"Of course."

Now that the task was completed, Tirell had nothing to distract him from the fact that he was sitting inside a tree trunk, swooping around above the clouds in darkness, with no idea which way was home.

Anna sensed his disquiet. "I know it's hard, but the safest thing will be to wait for sunrise; if we tried to go back now, we could end up anywhere."

"I understand." Tirell had witnessed the timing of her returns often enough to have known what to expect.

He glanced up at the lopsided magenta glow; he could feel the warmth of it on his skin. Without that lingering heat, would the world be entirely dead now? The Far Sun was brighter in its own kind of light, but too distant to pierce the chill.

"Just tell me we won't follow the air that's falling on our neighbor," he joked.

"We won't," Anna replied. "Not unless we really try."

3

"How'd it go?" Selik asked, as he helped Tirell to his feet.

"Good." Tirell realized he was shaking. He was ecstatic to be back in the safe boughs of the forest, but as the glider had turned toward Maldo for the final approach, it had taken all his strength not to leap into the depths just to avoid the impending collision.

Selik and Rada helped the returning travelers get the glider safely tied up, but then Tirell glanced at Anna and realized that she was leaving it to him to speak first.

"I saw them," he said. "Just where Anna said they'd be. Except now there are six."

"Six?" Selik regarded him dubiously, as if this new detail somehow made his testimony less reliable.

Tirell was annoyed. "Go up there yourself, if you don't believe me."

"Are you sure they weren't just stars?" Selik pressed him. "Because—"

"I know how stars move," Tirell replied. "These weren't stars. They were six bright objects, circling the zenith, that lost their light not long after sunset."

"That does sound like something solid, nearby," Rada said, clearly aiming for a conciliatory tone. "Like asteroids, but . . ." She made a cupping gesture with her hands, as if to suggest a constraining force that was preventing the objects from slipping away.

"What are asteroids made of, anyway?" Tirell asked. People had used the word in front of him ever since he'd joined the group, but he still didn't really understand it.

"Rock," Rada offered, unhelpfully. "The same as the inner worlds."

"But what exactly *is* 'rock'?"

"It's a bit like bone, but it's not from anything living."

Tirell grimaced "Have you ever touched rock?"

"Of course not."

"Then how do you know what it's like?"

Rada said, "It's in the Full Recitation. Before the cousins left, people studied these things; they weren't going to flee to the inner worlds without some idea of what they'd find there."

Tirell felt very tired. What he'd seen with his own eyes was real, and he was persuaded that the general story of the Changes was probably correct, but he had less faith in the details that no one could confirm, and only a fraction of people seemed to bother retelling.

The four of them sat on the platform together, trying to make sense of the growing number of objects the latest expedition had revealed.

"Why would the cousins hang back for so long?" Selik mused. "Do they think they'd be unwelcome?"

"Maybe they can't survive among us," Rada suggested. "Even the ancestors would shiver at the temperatures and pressures we're used to, and who knows what the cousins ended up having to adapt to.

Whatever kind of life they have on the inner worlds, I doubt it's much like ours."

"But either they have a way to deal with that, or there was no point coming in the first place," Selik protested.

"I think they're being cautious," Anna said. "It's been . . . well, longer than anyone knows for sure. They wouldn't want to rush in unprepared."

"Maybe we should give them a signal," Tirell proposed. "Let them know that we're still as friendly as ever, but we're growing impatient to meet them."

Selik was amused. "What kind of signal could we send, from this distance?"

Anna said, "It shouldn't be necessary. If they're looking for us at all, they'll find us."

"Then maybe they're just not looking," Selik replied. "They've returned to their old world, for some reason—but as far as they're concerned, it's obvious from the state of things that the people they left behind would have died out long ago."

4

"Can we call it nineteen and be done with it?" Tirell pleaded. There'd been a time when he would never have believed that counting dots in the sky could be painful, but he was aching in places that no amount of fruit-picking had ever reached.

"Just check it once more," Anna insisted, as if the exact number might carry some significance, beyond the fact that it was always increasing.

Tirell closed his eyes for a moment and tipped his head from side to side to stretch the muscles in his neck, acutely aware that if he wait-ed too long the encroaching shadow would render his observations meaningless. He adjusted his restraint and positioned himself beneath the occultation disk again.

"One, two, three," he muttered, tapping his thigh with his thumb to make the numbers more palpable as he counted. The objects weren't even moving so rapidly that he had any real excuse to confuse one for another, but the way they traveled at slightly different speeds disrupted any temporary pattern they formed, undermined his confidence that he wasn't missing any of them, or double counting.

"Nineteen," he declared, as close to sure as he was ever going to be. He made a guess as to which of them would be the first to vanish and followed it until he was proven right. "Nineteen," he repeated. As he watched the lights wink out, he began to believe that he'd actually grasped the true geometry of the whole strange constellation.

"Now we wait for morning." He looked down at the jumble of red clouds below the glider, surprised at how clearly he could still see them. "Are we higher than usual?" he asked Anna. That wouldn't affect the timing of the objects' extinguishment, but it could prolong their own dusk.

"I don't think so," Anna replied. "But tell me what you think about the Near Sun."

Tirell folded the occultation disk away to give himself a clear view. At first he was unsure if his eyes, having adapted to the Near Sun's absence, were now reacting more strongly to its light, but after a while that no longer seemed like an adequate explanation. "It looks brighter. And the brightest part is larger than before."

"That's what I thought," Anna said. "I'm glad I'm not losing my mind."

Tirell was fairly sure that Anna had been making these trips for at least a couple of years; if there was some seasonal change in the strength of the wind that blew from the world onto the Near Sun, she would have been expecting it.

But if not the season, what else had changed?

"Even an asteroid would have some gravity, wouldn't it?" he asked.

"Yes."

"So if these things are asteroids that the cousins have put into place, then just as the Near Sun competes with the world for our air, they'd be pulling it in the same direction?"

"That's right."

Tirell wasn't sure if Anna was humoring him, leading him into some kind of logical trap where he'd just be displaying his ignorance. "But then, after the air fell past them, they'd pull back on it, wouldn't they? Fighting the Near Sun's pull? So the two effects would cancel each other out?"

Anna said, "I don't think they would cancel each other. So long as there's a stronger upward pull on the atmosphere, and more air is flowing away from the world, the extra amount is never going to turn around and come back to us. And the asteroids certainly can't hold on to it. So if we're losing more air, there's only one place it can go."

As Tirell was turning that over in his mind, a flash of light burst out of the darkness. It was gone in an instant, but it left a lingering impression on his eyes, which gave him a fair idea of its direction. It had not come from the Near Sun, but it had been close.

"Did you see that?" he asked Anna. He didn't dare move his gaze toward her, lest he lose what little information he retained about the origin of the light.

"I saw something illuminate the cloud tops," she replied. "What did you see?"

"A point of light, close to where the objects were circling—but much brighter. Maybe brighter than the Far Sun, while it lasted."

Anna was silent for a time, then she said, "You know that's what they say about the cousins' vessels? When they finally departed, *they were brighter than the Far Sun.*"

Tirell had heard the same verses, but he had always taken that detail to be some kind of soppy metaphor for the hope the cousins carried with them.

"They're adjusting their motion," he guessed. "If they start to slip too far from the equilibrium point, they push themselves back to where they need to be."

"That would make sense," Anna replied.

Tirell had long given up arguing for any natural account of the objects' behavior, but now he was losing not just his last traces of skepticism, but any sense of the cousins as a mere abstraction. A few points of light moving across the sky had never been enough to convince him that he was on the verge of coming face to face with his long-lost relatives, but now they had to go and flaunt their prowess and make themselves a thousand times more real.

"If *we* understand that the asteroids are helping to convey more air to the Near Sun," he said, "then the cousins could hardly have failed to anticipate it, could they?"

"No." Anna's voice sounded strange, as if it was floating away on the wind.

"So it might even be the whole point of the exercise," Tirell reasoned. "Not so much a peculiar side effect, as the reason they're doing what they're doing at all."

"If that's true," Anna said, "then there's nothing to be gained from doing it by halves. To make the Near Sun just a fraction brighter, when they have their own means to summon brightness at will, would be a complete waste of effort."

Tirell was silent for a while. It felt as if the glider was following the same wide circle as ever, but the lingering illumination of the clouds below revealed shifting patterns among them that would normally have been lost in the twilight.

"If they knew we were here, and knew how we lived," he said finally, "then surely they wouldn't be doing this for our benefit? No one

"Don't be like that," he pleaded. "You should be happy. You're helping to make history!"

"No, I'm helping to make *rope*." She stared at the loom in horror, as if she might never recover from this indignity. "And you won't even let me do it properly."

Tirell could understand her frustration; he was chopping up the vines into absurdly short segments, when longer, unbroken strands would have made the weaving process simpler, and the final product much stronger. But since there were no vines two thousand spans long, there wasn't much point doing a test launch with stronger ropes than the ones they'd need to use for the real event.

In any case, Delia seemed to have established an impressively elegant rhythm for the task she despised. A simple pedal action drove the rotating bobbins that twisted the strands together into pairs of pairs of pairs, but whenever one of the feeds ran out, switching to the new strand required a meticulous intervention. Left to chance, the two ends would have protruded from the rope, risking it fraying and unraveling. But Delia anticipated each break and trimmed the feed to just the right length to ensure that the ends were always in the center of the rope, surrounded by unbroken neighbors.

"Is that the last of the vines?" she asked, without looking up from the loom.

"Yes." The coil of finished rope had already reached an impressive bulk; Tirell didn't dare remind her that this was just a rehearsal for a version twenty times longer.

"Then if you've got nothing else to do," Delia suggested, "why not visit the hollow?"

Tirell grunted with amusement. "I should check if Selik needs help with the glider," he replied.

He walked to the edge of the marketplace, making sure he was out of Delia's sight before doubling back and climbing the trunk that led to the breeding hollow. When he peered inside he could see that about a third of the eggs were still light blue. So had Delia looked in just to check on the ones she'd left herself? And sent him here, in the hope that he of all people—

He cut off the disturbing line of thought, and let his instincts take over. When he was finished, half the eggs had changed color.

On his way back, Tirell tried to picture the children who'd emerge from the hollow in the next scrum. If the cousins persisted with their project, there would be no place for his offspring in the only part of the world he'd ever known, and perhaps no place for them anywhere at all.

So was what he'd just done an act of cruelty? Was he offering those children nothing but an early death?

He had to stay hopeful. His ancestors had confronted a far greater adversary and defeated it in two entirely different ways. If only they'd been half as lucky instead.

But then, that was all his contemporaries would need: half the ancestors' luck.

7

Tirell had wanted to finish the winding himself, but when his forearms began to cramp he relented. He called to Anna to take his place on the steps beside the rod.

"When we do this full size, do you really think the rope will hold together?" he asked.

"I don't know," Anna conceded. "But keep in mind, most things in the forest are still much stronger than they need to be. Everything weighed a hundred times more, where we were before the Changes. And during the migration it was even worse."

"It's a long time since the migration," Tirell replied.

"It is. But nature doesn't always rush to throw away a trait." Anna took a length of rope between her hands and tugged it as hard as she could. "There are threads running along those stems that weigh almost nothing themselves, but could once hold three hundred times the weight of the whole plant, as it is now. The question isn't whether that's still needed, it's whether there was an easy way to replace it with something weaker, or whether the cost was so small that the simplest thing was to let it be."

"Hmm." Tirell had always struggled to understand how the forests could have survived the Changes at all, but maybe it was more comprehensible if they'd actually changed far less than he'd imagined.

When Anna was done, she slipped the end of the rope over a hook at the side of the frame, to keep it from unwinding. The rod, in its support frame, was twice her height; she stayed on the steps while Tirell took hold of the middle of the frame, and together they got it horizontal before Tirell lowered it to the floor.

When he looked up, he saw Selik already approaching with the new test vessel. Shaping it as a miniature glider had seemed like a wasted effort to Tirell at first, but Rada had assured him that the details were worth mimicking for the sake of observing its dynamics, not when it was flying free, but while it remained bound.

The three of them carried the frame over to the edge of the platform, then Tirell walked back beneath the trees to the corner where Cyril had set up his tools.

"Is it ready?" Tirell asked.

"I think so." Cyril turned the contraption over and examined it, blowing into it to dislodge a speck of grit. "The new cam is smoother, it's a better shape. I don't think it will stick this time."

Tirell nodded. There was no recipe for any of this, even in the Full Recitation; no one had ever faced the particular mismatch of means and ambition that was shaping their efforts.

Selik and Tirell propped the frame up while Cyril attached the end-cap to the rod, slipping the hexagonal hole in the center over the portion that jutted beyond the frame, and pushing the locking pins into place. Then he hung the miniature glider from the short length of rope that dangled from the cap.

There was a slot carved into the platform to hold the frame, matching the mildly tapered shape but only two-thirds as long, in order to give the far end plenty of clearance. So to get the frame in, they needed to position it with about a third of its length protruding over the edge of the platform.

The four of them took hold of the frame together, then they shuffled their grip toward the near end, until no one was beyond the mark that showed where the overhang would begin. A third was not a half, and even with the extra weight of the end-cap and glider, the frame wasn't pushing up at the back, but Tirell still felt a precarious sense of asymmetry from the mere fact that the same object was putting more weight on one of his hands than the other. The slot was only a few paces in front of them, but they moved slowly together, making sure the frame was centered as they approached.

As they crouched down, Anna and Selik grunted, not so much with effort as sheer discomfort from contorting their age-worn joints. On the last trial, Tirell had made the mistake of laughing at them. "You should hope you live long enough to know what we're going through," Anna had rebuked him.

With the frame in place, Tirell set about locking it down, pushing more than a dozen wooden pins into the holes that ran from the frame into the surrounding timber of the platform. Then he unhooked the rope from the near end of the frame, and unwound about a span's worth and let it dangle.

"This is it, everyone!" Selik called out. Anna, Rada, Cyril and Madeleine moved into position, ready to witness whatever unfolded from a range of angles, while Tirell and Selik picked up the drop-log together and headed for the ramp that led below the platform.

On the ramp, Tirell moved with all the care he could muster; there was a safety rail, but he had no intention of relying on it. The ramp leveled out into a miniature platform suspended below the main one, which stopped a span or so before the underside of the rod's support frame.

Tirell glanced at Selik to be sure they were acting in concert, then together they lifted the log above the rail and maneuvered it into contact with the rope Tirell had left dangling from the rod. The hook Selik had carved into the wood was as thick as Tirell's thumb and completed seven-eighths of a circle; getting the bottom of the loop to pass through the narrow gap took patience, but once it was in place, there was no chance of it slipping free.

Selik nodded to Tirell. "Ready?"

"Yes."

"One!" Selik bellowed, to make himself heard to the others up on the platform. "Two! Three! Four!"

They released the log. Tirell's instinctive response would have been to keep his eyes on the dead tree that was powering their hopes of ascent as it plummeted toward the vortices below, but he tore his gaze away in time to see the spinning end-cap begin unreeling the glider.

The start of the process was unnerving: the glider lagged behind, reluctantly dragged along by the end-cap, but as it picked up speed it swung outward, only to overtake the rod's rotation, briefly, and then fall back again. As Rada had explained it, it was like a pendulum swinging to and fro—but instead of doing so compared to a fixed vertical, it was swinging either side of a line of net force that spun around with the rod, and grew stronger with the quickening rotation.

With each downswing of the glider, a little more rope played out, making the excursions wider, but at least the range of angles the rope made with the end-cap didn't seem to be growing. Tirell could only hope that Cyril's ingenious cam—which progressively tightened the brake on the reel so that only a greater tug could overcome it—was acting just as it should, neither letting too much rope out, nor unduly inhibiting it.

As the glider moved away from the rod, it began to oppose the falling weight more strenuously. Tirell watched, caught between anxiety and delight, as the spinning slowed—inasmuch as each turn of the rod took longer—but the glider itself continued to gain speed, thanks to its greater distance. On one swing it lurched back alarmingly, and he was afraid that the cam might have become stuck again, but the overshoot was less, and the back-swing less again, until the diversions grew so small that it was hard to be sure if they were even persisting.

With the glider's rope fully extended, there was no choice but for everything to move faster. Tirell could see that the descending rope had almost unwound completely, with just a dozen or so coils around the rod remaining. He wished he was up on the main platform, but observers were required everywhere; if something went wrong, there was no telling which vantage would be most revelatory.

He gripped the rail in front of him as the last of the rope uncoiled. The string he'd looped around the final three coils pulled on a lever inside the end-cap and unlatched the glider's rope, freeing the glider from any attachment to the rod, to the platform, to the forest itself. And as far as Tirell could judge, the calibration had been perfect: the separation occurred while the rope was horizontal, the glider moving skyward. Glider and rope both vanished from his sight, but a few moments later the rope reappeared on its way to the depths, freed from the hook by the change of alignment and diminished tension.

He and Selik hurried up the ramp.

"Did you see how high it went?" Tirell asked impatiently, of anyone who was listening.

Madeleine smiled. "High! Right through the clouds."

Tirell knew this was as much due to it catching a favorable wind as it was to the impetus from the launch; in the absence of air it would have come down as swiftly as the un-winged rope. But at least it hadn't departed in the wrong direction entirely.

"What do you think?" Selik asked Anna.

"We'll need a few more tests," she said, "to be sure that the whole approach is reliable and we weren't just lucky."

"But if they work as well as this one?"

Anna said, "Then we build the thing itself, and see if we can finally poke our idiot cousins in the eye."

8

"Where's your safety rope?" Tirell called out sharply. He didn't recognize the carpenter, but she must have been one of the new arrivals from Lappa.

"If I fall," she replied, amused, "I'll have plenty of time to grab something."

"I'm not going to argue. If you don't like the rules, get off the scaffolding."

She hesitated, and Tirell sensed that she was on the verge of holding to her opinion and departing. But then she sidled back along the beam, hooked the nearest rope to her belt, and then returned to the place where she'd been working.

"Thank you," Tirell said. He introduced himself.

"I know who you are," she replied, in a tone that suggested he was famous for precisely the kind of irritation to which he'd just subjected her. "I'm Maxine."

"No one's died yet," he said. "I want to keep it that way." He glanced up at the platform above them, protruding so far from the edge of the forest that he couldn't make out the start of it through the artificial jungle of ropes and beams suspended beneath it for the carpenters' benefit.

"In Lappa, we wouldn't treat a child like this," she said scornfully.

"Is your rope secure now?" Tirell pressed her.

"Yes."

Tirell put his hand to his own and tested it. "The hook is closed? It can't come loose?"

"No."

Tirell wasn't sure if her undisguised disdain was just signaling her right to be annoyed with these precautions, or if she was actually determined to unhook the belt the moment she was out of his sight.

"You don't mind if I check?"

She held her arms to either side, inviting him. He moved carefully along the crossbeam toward her, then reached down and felt the latch on the hook. "Seems good," he declared. Then he kicked her shin and they both lost their balance, toppling in opposite directions through the gaps between the beams.

Tirell didn't fight the urge to claw at the air for a handhold as he fell; he had no expectation of succeeding, but he valued the instinct too highly to want to suppress it. It did not take long for the rope to go taut, but it was long enough for him to fall right out of the scaffolding. He hung, suspended, over the depths.

He looked up and saw Maxine, sharing his predicament a couple of spans away.

"You don't deserve our help," she said. "I'm going back to Lappa to tell everyone not to bother."

"As you wish. Do you remember the recovery moves from your training?"

Maxine glared at him, but before he could begin demonstrating she deftly began hauling herself up the rope.

Tirell glanced down at the blue-and-white clouds swirling below. The terror of the drop was reverberating in his skull, but the sight of the depths still brought on the same atavistic longing as ever. The funniest part was that when the ancestors had lived among clouds like this, they might never have seen them from above until the Changes began to bite. His nostalgia for a lost home revolved around a view of it that belonged to those who were already fleeing.

9

"Can you keep a secret?"

Tirell opened his eyes and surveyed the circle of silhouetted figures gathered around him. "Of course," he replied.

"Then come with us."

He rose, deciding not to protest. He recognized some of the people now: scaffolders, carpenters, weavers. If he was about to be punished for what he'd done to Maxine, it was a curious way to start. They could have just kicked him awake, and kept on kicking.

He followed them from the project's encampment at the rear of the platform into the darkness of the forest, but he knew the area well, and as they clambered single file onto a broad, familiar trunk, he could already guess their destination. It made no sense, but nor did any of this.

Tirell moved carefully, and his eyes began to pick up the faint hints of orange light that penetrated the foliage, but he still kept jabbing his hands on the trunk's protuberances—its attempts to form new side branches that all the traffic frustrated. If people had let them grow instead of snapping them off they would probably have posed less of a hazard at night.

His silent traveling companions crossed to another trunk, disconcertingly confirming his original conjecture. And maybe there was some logic to it: a body would vanish just as easily from the larger platform, but here they would be less likely to be caught in the act.

As they emerged onto the old test platform, Tirell could see the support frame jutting out beyond the shadow of the forest canopy, lit by the glow of the Near Sun through the clouds.

One of the weavers, Martin, said, "We would have invited you earlier, but we were afraid you might have blabbed to the elders."

Tirell was bemused to learn that his encounter with Maxine had been perceived as an act of rebellion *on his part* against strictures passed down from on high. But he still had no idea what he was doing here. "Blabbed about what?" he finally found the courage to ask.

"Riding the spinner. You're up for it, aren't you?"

Was this another question where there was only one safe answer? "Everyone here's done it?" he asked.

"Of course."

"And no one's been injured? No one's been lost?" He should have heard of any injuries among the team, however they'd been sustained, but as people came and went from Lappa a disappearance might actually have been easier to conceal.

"No one's been hurt at all," Martin insisted.

"But what's the attraction?" Tirell asked. Didn't all these people get a large enough dose of controlled danger by daylight?

"It feels . . ." Martin struggled for a moment. "It feels right. It's not easy to take, but in the end it feels right."

Tirell glanced around at the others. No one here was actually planning to murder him, either for the overzealous safety lesson he'd given Maxine, or for fear that he'd rob them of their nocturnal entertainment. If he promised to keep quiet, he could head back to the camp unmolested.

"What have you changed in the equipment?" he wondered. "Apart from removing all the bits that would toss you into the air?"

"We drop a heavier weight."

"As much heavier than the old one as you're heavier than a toy glider?"

"No. Maybe half that."

So the ride would be a little less frantic. Tirell considered asking for someone else to go before him, to convince him that he wasn't being tricked. But the last thing he wanted was to put his life in the hands of people he'd alienated with his mistrust. Either he accepted that the group had invited him here in good faith, or he walked away.

"I'll do it," he declared.

There were murmurs of approval from the gathering.

"How do I . . . ?"

"Crawl out along the frame and get into the basket," Martin explained. "Hold on tight. It won't take us long to drop the weight; the slow part comes later, when we reel it back up."

I've lost my mind, Tirell decided, as he walked toward the frame. But if anything here could fail, so could any beam in the scaffolding on the main project, any hook, any safety rope.

He strode along the frame, one foot on either side of the rod, barely trusting his eyes in the feeble light. Before he reached the edge of the platform, he got down on his hands and knees to get the transition over with before a stumble became much more than an annoyance. When he crossed onto the protruding part of the frame, he felt a gentle breeze beside him rising up from the depths; it could no more have dislodged him than a gnat landing on his arm, but its vertical caress still unnerved him.

He stopped before his hands made contact with the end-cap and peered down at the shadowy form of the basket; he was not at all sure that it was large enough to catch him if he fell. He turned and lowered his legs from the side of the frame, then caught the basket's rope between his feet to take some of his weight as he brought his torso over the edge. When he was gripping the frame with both hands above his head, he pulled himself closer and transferred one hand to the rope. Then he moved the other hand across and slid the short distance down the rope into the basket.

It swayed back and forth for a while before settling. He sat on the wooden floor with his knees raised and felt around for the handles. He ought not need them until the very end, when the thing came to a halt, but it seemed wise to commit himself to them from the start. It had taken him a while to persuade Anna to fit restraints for the pilot and passenger to her glider, but maybe he could institute some similar reforms here, once he was accepted into the clique of Spinners.

"Are you ready?" Martin yelled.

"Yes!" Tirell called back. He heard nothing more, but the people waiting to release the weight must have acted on his reply alone, because a moment later the end-cap started turning.

At first the basket swayed gently, then suddenly the rope yanked on it sharply and it flew up, halfway to upside-down, before swinging back. Tirell braced himself against the handles and pushed his body toward the floor, unwilling to trust the force of the rotation to hold him in place as the basket finally swung over the top.

Moments later, he saw the orange clouds above him once more, but there was no real respite. As he endured a second rotation, then a third, he realized that every part of the cycle was horrifying in its own way: even when he was right way up, the lagging rope already felt like a portent of what was to come.

He'd lost count of the revolutions when he first realized that the swinging had died away: the rope was all but turning with the end-cap, as if it were a rigid beam fixed to the spinning rod itself. When he peered along it, the pallid clouds above and the untouched gloom of the depths were changing places every three slow breaths. The force pressing him against the floor was firm now, verging on uncomfortable;

it was as if he'd lost a fight to an opponent who insisted on keeping him down with their full weight, even after he'd surrendered.

As the pressure grew, he tried to accommodate it, but he could neither turn his body nor flatten it more closely against the floor. His knees, jutting into the air, ached as if he was trying to rise up from kneeling with a heavy load on his shoulders. Each inhalation took more effort than the last, as if his overzealous opponent had decided not just to hold him down, but to gleefully crush the air out of his lungs.

Tirell tried relaxing his muscles, but yielding only increased the pain. So he stiffened his body instead, fighting the weight, which hurt just as much in a slightly different way. There was no amelioration, let alone any hope of escape, and he knew it would only get worse. As he gasped for breath, he saw strange bands of light and darkness twisting in front of his eyes, as if the roiling vortices of the depths had risen up to meet him. *If this wasn't death, what was it?* His nighttime visitors had lied; no one had ever survived this torture. This was his punishment: instead of tossing him from the platform, they'd found an even crueler way to end his life.

Suddenly, the basket shuddered; Tirell could picture the whole platform trembling as the weight they'd dropped reached the end of the rope. He waited for the basket to come to a halt, but though he could feel it recover from the jolt, it didn't seem to be slowing at all. Then he understood: even when the rod had stopped turning, unlike the released glider, the basket would keep circling until its energy was dissipated.

Or, not so much circling as *spiraling in*, until it wrapped itself so tightly around the rod that it smashed into the support frame. Tirell fought against that vision—and having survived this far, he was ready to trust his fellow Spinners again. Even before they'd tried it themselves, they must have tested the whole thing with an empty basket, and seen that the endpoint was, if not *safe* by any stretch of the word, not actually fatal either.

The pressure began to decline. Tirell grew genuinely dizzy for the first time; as the rotations slowed, his inner sense of where the basket ought to be struggled to catch up. The striations were fading, but when he closed his eyes he saw afterimages of the orange clouds rolling by, at a rate that no longer matched his actual motion.

The basket struggled to the top of its arc, then the rope went slack and the basket fell. Tirell was already grasping the handles as tightly as possible, though for a moment that was redundant: he and the basket fell together; gravity wasn't trying to tear them apart.

Then the basket pulled the rope taut and jerked sideways, almost breaking Tirell's grip.

As the final swaying died away, he huddled against the floor, afraid to test himself for injuries. After a while, he dared move a little; he ached all over, and he was bruised in places, but he did not think he'd suffered any permanent harm.

"Are you all right?" Martin yelled.

"Yes," Tirell shouted back, surprised at how normal his voice sounded.

"Take your time," Martin advised him. Tirell laughed; he had no intention of rushing his climb back up.

How had he survived these forces, so much greater than any he was accustomed to? Maybe it was the same for people as Anna believed it was for the vines: nature had not yet thrown away the traits they had once relied on. His own ancestors, as much as the forests themselves, had lived through the three-hundredfold greater weights of the migration.

The trembling in his arms began to subside. He reached up and took hold of the rope. Martin hadn't deceived him: what he'd been through had been hard to endure, but in the end it did feel right.

10

"You're not disappointed, are you?" Anna asked. "Not being down there with the others?"

"This is exactly what I wanted," Tirell replied. "No responsibilities, and the perfect view for the occasion."

The glider curved lazily around as Anna hunted for a current that would keep it from rising too much higher above the forest. "'No responsibilities?'" she rebuked him. "If we lose sight of the vessel, it will all have been for nothing."

"You know what I mean." Tirell felt as if he'd spent his entire life working on the launcher, and he'd grown tired of fearing that some rope, or plank, or person that he prodded the wrong way would go crashing into the other components and tear the whole structure apart. Let Cyril and his assistants oversee the crucial state of the end-cap; let Selik and his team prepare to drop the weights. He was happy to soar above them all and observe the outcome.

Looking down, he could see the platform itself protruding from the edge of the forest, but the people he knew were arrayed there were not even insect-like to his gaze.

"If this reaches the equilibrium point," Anna declared, "then there's no way it will pass unnoticed. That's where all their effort and attention is concentrated: where every last rock is tracked, and kept in its proper place."

Tirell didn't reply. He knew she wasn't soliciting his opinion; she was just reassuring herself that their own efforts had been directed in the best possible way. He wasn't sure how much longer it would be before the forests began declining from the rising heat, but however bright the clouds at midnight, no one wanted to start planning for a new migration while there was still a chance of bringing the cousins to their senses.

"Come on," Anna muttered impatiently. "What are they doing down there?"

Tirell tried not to laugh; she knew as well as he did how fastidiously the final checks would be conducted. "Just relax and enjoy the view," he teased her. "It's not often we get to go up in this thing without rushing off somewhere."

He took his own advice and gazed down at Maldo, reveling in the luxury of a sustained vantage. The great, unruly dome of foliage that had built itself from air and light was beautiful enough from within, but from above its isolation gave it a shocking poignancy. As ancient as it was, he believed it had not, itself, endured the migration, but was merely a descendant of other forests that had.

Beside the forest, a speck hung in the air, barely shifting, but growing in size. Here at last was the insect that the people below were too remote to mimic. "You do see it?" Tirell checked, afraid that Anna might have been irritably staring off into the clouds.

"I do."

The speck blurred and vanished, passing by too quickly to be perceived, but Tirell looked up and managed to catch it receding, silhouetted against the brightness, about a third of the way down from the zenith on the west side. If it fell, or tumbled, or broke apart before penetrating all the layers of cloud above, they might never know, but they had as much evidence as they could have hoped for: the glider was ascending along the correct trajectory, at a rate comparable to their expectations.

"I never thought we'd do it," Anna confessed. "Not in my lifetime."

"But we did."

"You want to take the controls and bring us down?" Anna offered.

"Really?" Tirell's lessons had been sporadic for a while; their other obligations had taken precedence.

"I think you're ready," Anna assured him.

As they exchanged places, she said, "I hope this isn't rude, but your body seems different lately. Not just heavier; more solid."

"That's what hard work does," Tirell replied. "I'm not just a lazy fruit-picker anymore." But if this was her way of telling him that she knew the actual cause, he'd take that more as tacit approval than any kind of reprimand.

He found the pedals and glanced back at his passenger. "So let's go join the celebrations. Today, we told the cousins we're alive and well, and it's time for them to stop meddling."

11

"It's never going to stop!" Delia said angrily. "Everything we did was a waste of time."

Tirell was starting to regret telling her what he'd seen on his latest flight with Anna. "Those extra asteroids might have been on their way to the equilibrium point long before we launched our messenger. Heavy objects moving rapidly can't be turned around in a hurry."

Delia was unimpressed. "Really? So when they light up with whatever it is that keeps them from drifting away, the same thing couldn't be used to make them drift away faster?"

"I don't know. It could be more complicated than that." The truth was, Tirell couldn't fault her argument. If the cousins had decided to disassemble the collection of rocks that were driving the flow of gas onto the Near Sun, they could surely have made a start by now, and the results ought to have been visible.

A couple of infants crawled toward them, whining hungrily. Tirell glanced dubiously at the pile of sickly-looking fruit stacked up behind him, but then he recalled where he'd put the most palatable specimen.

He bit into it and chewed a mouthful for the supplicants. "When you're old enough for the Recitation," he told them, "make sure you get it from someone who's heard the whole thing."

The stories of the migration had never disguised just how arduous it had been, but Tirell had made a habit of taking comfort from the fact that there'd been survivors to tell the tale. He'd never dwelt too much on the other participants, who had died along the way. But if he was honest about it, there was no real symmetry between that past ordeal and any journey yet to come. He could not look around and say: All these people, whose ancestors came through the first, are also promised that they and their children will not perish in the second.

He turned to Delia. "If you and the other weavers were willing to make a new drop rope . . ."

"You should have taken better care of the one you had," Delia retorted. "It wasn't our fault, what happened to it."

"No, of course it wasn't." The rope had performed flawlessly right to the end, when its attempt to bring the falling weight to a halt hadn't torn it, but rather yanked it free of the rod. "If we get a chance to try again, we can look at ways to make sure that we don't lose it."

"Why? So you can have a third try after that, then a fourth? Don't you believe the glider reached the equilibrium point the first time?"

"We can't know that it did."

"So you want to keep launching gliders for the next hundred years, hoping that the cousins will finally notice one of them?"

Tirell said, "No. If we try one more launch, we can make it different, so at least we know if it succeeded or not."

"How?" Delia demanded. "Are you going to . . . pack a giant white cloth inside it that unfurls when it's gone above the clouds, so you and Anna can fly up and see if it's catching the light?"

Tirell was silent for a moment, wondering if this was actually such a good idea that he ought to take it to the others, and forget his own ridiculous plan. But he was afraid that if he let anything divert him, by the time he found the courage again it would be too late.

"I want to go up in the glider," he said. "Find a way to take the air I'll need, find a way to come back safely, and then we'll know for sure where the thing really went."

Delia gazed at him with an expression that Tirell couldn't quite decipher. Maybe nine parts scorn, one part admiration—the latter for audacity, if nothing else.

"You really do want to fall into the sky," she marveled. "You really are completely deranged."

12

Anna said, "It's an interesting proposal. What would you do for air?"

Selik was horrified. "*Air?* He wouldn't even survive the launch!"

Anna snorted. "He's been practicing for . . . who knows how long."

"More than a hundred days," Tirell confessed. "We do it at the old test site. It feels almost normal by now."

"How would the forces compare?" Rada asked, ever practical.

"A real launch would impose a bit more," Anna conceded. "They don't use a heavy enough weight to maintain the original scaling, but they go through a period of elevated centrifugal force when the rope starts winding itself in at the end, which won't be present in an actual launch."

"Have you been watching us?" Tirell was annoyed that she hadn't come right out and told him, though he wasn't sure that the Spinners would have continued at all if they'd known their activities were no longer clandestine.

"I have my informants," Anna replied. "The important thing is, if you can get through dozens of tests to the point where it's almost comfortable, there's no reason to think a real launch would be . . ."

"Unendurable?" Tirell suggested.

"I was going to say 'fatal'."

Tirell looked out across the abandoned platform. The thought of riding a glider higher than he and Anna had ever flown didn't really frighten him, but the disparity in scale between the real launcher and the toy he'd been playing with was beginning to unnerve him. He knew that the centrifugal force would actually be *more* when spinning from a shorter rope, if the speed of the swinging objects were the same, though if he understood Anna correctly, the twenty-fold smaller test rig in its initial configuration would in fact have roughly matched its larger sibling's force, by combining the shorter rope with a slower-moving vessel. But none of that helped reconcile him to the intimidating prospect of whirling around on the end of a rope sixty spans long.

Anna hadn't forgotten her original question. "So what about the air?"

Tirell said, "The whole trip should take about four thousand breaths, right?" That had been the predicted time for the empty glider to fall back, albeit with no hope of catching sight of it when it returned.

"Yes."

"Cloth soaked in resin will hold air, without completely blocking the light. If I can observe the angle of the Far Sun throughout the journey, then along with the time the whole thing takes, that should be enough to check whether I ascended most of the way to the equilibrium point or not."

"Four thousand breaths," Rada mused. "Maybe twenty-seven cubic spans. That would mean a bigger glider."

"Not much bigger," Tirell insisted. "And it need not be much heavier at all; it's more about the shape."

Selik caught Tirell's eye. "This is madness," he said. "It's suicide."

"I don't believe that."

"How will you slow yourself during the descent?" Selik challenged him.

"The same cloth, spread out on ropes above the glider."

"And what if the cloth frays?"

"That would probably kill me," Tirell conceded. "But the weavers haven't let us down so far."

"The biggest risk," Rada suggested, "might lie with our calculations."

Tirell caught her meaning. If the Full Recitationists had underestimated the speed required to reach the equilibrium point, or overestimated the speed achieved at the launch, he might ascend only part of the way, and fall back without any hope of attracting the cousins' attention.

But if they'd erred in the other direction, he'd arrive at the equilibrium point with energy to spare, still ascending, and there'd be nothing he could do to prevent the journey from continuing.

He said, "But the good news is, I'm sure to have run out of air long before I hit the Near Sun."

13

Tirell lay as still as he could inside the hollowed log, trying to keep his breathing calm and steady. The canopy stretched out above him let plenty of light through, but it seemed to scatter it in such a way that wherever he looked he saw some portion of the glare from the zenith, making it impossible even to guess where the Near Sun lay in the sky.

He reached a count of seven hundred and twenty before he began to gasp. He punched at the canopy and broke the seal, then lay back for a while until he felt steady enough to climb out. At least his discomfort proved that if any air was passing through the resin-treated cloth, it was far too little to make a difference.

"It's always good to see someone practicing for their death," Delia declared sardonically. "So is the cloth working?"

"It's holding in the air. The only problem is the view. I can't really distinguish anything."

Delia pondered this. "There are a few variations we could try. A coarser weave, with more gaps for the light. Or two layers with a finer weave, crossed at an angle to each other."

"Why the second one?"

Delia rummaged in her bag of samples and brought out two pieces of fine cloth. She laid them together, then approached Tirell and held them up in front of him.

daggers he'd only ever imagined. But what did he have to fear, now that the count had passed four hundred?

The purple light began bleeding into the green. Tirell was no longer sure if his eyes were open or not. *Don't let me go blind*, he pleaded. If he was blind, it would all be for nothing. He wouldn't even know before he died if he'd reached the equilibrium point or not.

Abruptly, the stains on his vision began retreating. Except they weren't changing in size at all; they were simply imbued with a sense of motion, as if that could arise entirely separately from their appearance, through something like smell. Then Tirell understood that, although the pain in his chest had barely diminished, the crushing weight itself was gone.

He did not have long to ensure the quality of his air supply; he reached across to the open portion of the canopy and pegged it into place, screaming back defiantly at the protests from his body that wanted him to scream from pain alone. His sight was returning to normal, and from the borders of the brightest region of the canopy he could tell that the glider was ascending with its long axis tilted back about a third of the way from vertical—exactly as it should be. He realized that he'd stopped counting and had no idea what total he'd reached when he'd stopped; for a moment he was in despair, but then he shook off his befuddlement and recalled that it had always been the plan to start afresh from the moment of launch, and if he guessed and started from twenty he could not be too far wrong.

He was alive, aching, sighted, ascending. All but weightless; the resistance of the air against the glider was diminishing, leaving him hovering loosely in his harness. The canopy had swelled outward, pulling itself taut; Anna had told him to listen for any whistling sound as a symptom of a leak where the resin might have failed or a peg come loose, but everything was silent.

With no clouds to scatter the light, the sky had vanished as a discernible hemisphere, but even through the canopy the disk of the Far Sun was now utterly distinct from the broader light above. Tirell kept his gaze fixed on it, and put all his effort into a steady count; in the end, it would only be the delay of sunset that could attest to the altitude he'd reached.

How had the cousins felt, he wondered, as they made the same journey with no intention of returning? Before, it had always seemed pointless to dwell on their emotions at such a vast remove. But they had been people much like him, as fragile, and perhaps as fearful. Whatever knowledge and skills they'd possessed, the feat they'd attempted must have tested them, and terrified them, as much as this had tested and terrified him.

And if he could see through their eyes, surely they could see through his? Once they understood what they were doing, to people no different from themselves, to continue would be untenable.

15

When Tirell reached the count of two thousand, the Far Sun had still not set. As far as he could tell from the blurred disk showing through the canopy, it had not even touched the layer of clouds that he pictured spread out below him to the west. Unless his mind had become so addled that he'd raced through the numbers, this was proof that he'd come close to his intended destination.

He waited, still counting. Finally, he noticed a flattening at the bottom of the disk. He timed the duration of the whole event, until the upper limb had vanished. It was within the range he'd been told to expect if he was almost motionless: suspended between the worlds, waiting for one of them to claim him. Tirell had nodded along with Anna and Rada when they'd explained that he wouldn't feel a thing as his home world battled the Near Sun to snatch his body back, but the truth was, even as his experience confirmed their claim, his intuition still struggled to accept it.

The Far Sun did not reappear: he was not accelerating upward, out of the world's shadow. The evidence was not conclusive yet, but Tirell had no patience left. Until an unnatural dawn showed him otherwise, he would consider himself to be on his way home.

A shadow moved swiftly across the Near Sun, hiding it completely and plunging the hollow into darkness. Tirell was confused; it should have been impossible for him to end up close to any of the asteroids. Could the glider have turned around, to face away from the light? Anna had warned him that it might leave the atmosphere with a slow spin, but that didn't mean it could suddenly rotate, long afterward, and then just as suddenly come to a halt.

Tirell heard something strike the glider, firmly but not catastrophically, on either side. When the sound was over, there was nothing more, leaving him wondering if he'd imagined it. Then he felt a slight tug, pulling his body upward toward the nose … meaning the glider was being pushed in the opposite direction.

The cousins had noticed him in their workplace, and they were moving him away.

At first, Tirell was ecstatic. What surer sign of success could he have hoped for? But as the smooth, efficient act of discarding him continued, he felt his anger mounting.

"This is it?" he bellowed. "You see me in the way, and you get rid of me? Come and face me, and make a promise! We need to know that you've understood the message. We need to know that you'll stop the harm you've started, and let us live safely again!"

Tirell kept ranting, repeating his demands ever more stridently, until he began to fear that he might be using up his air faster than planned.

"Talk to me," he said quietly.

A voice replied, "I'll talk to you. But what is there to say?"

Tirell swung around in his harness; it had sounded as though the speaker was right next to him.

"Where are you?"

"Far away. But you can think of the thing that's holding you as my emissary."

"You speak our language?" Tirell marveled. Most of the group had considered that unlikely, after such a long separation, but though the accent was strange, the speaker's words were clear enough. "Is it close to your own?"

"Not close, but not too difficult to learn."

"From your Recitations? From the language of the ancestors?"

"No. I've studied your people over the last few years."

"You've studied us . . . without even meeting us? You've hidden in the forests?"

"No. But I've listened from afar."

That didn't make much sense, but Tirell had more important questions to pursue. "Will you stop the flow onto the Near Sun?"

"That decision is not in my hands."

"Then can I talk to whoever will decide?"

"All of us decided, long ago. A majority of us. It's not going to stop."

Tirell was perplexed. "Long ago? But did you know what it would do to us, then?"

"Of course."

"You knew it would kill us, but you chose to do it anyway?"

"It won't kill you all," the voice replied. "The flow has risen and fallen for millions of years, and life has continued. There's nothing you're facing now that your ancestors didn't survive."

"People have migrated *back*, before?"

"Back and forth, hundreds of times. Though the last time was so long ago that perhaps you wouldn't consider them to have been people."

Tirell spent a moment absorbing this revelation, but then decided that he really didn't care. "I'm not interested in ancient history. You still have no right to make us suffer like this."

"So who will stop us?"

The words were delivered so casually that it took some time for Tirell to accept that he hadn't misheard them or misunderstood.

"That's your answer: who will stop you killing us? When we meet you on the cold side, I don't doubt you'll have superior weapons to protect yourselves, but don't expect to ever feel safe there again."

"We won't be meeting each other on the cold side. We don't want any part of your world; it doesn't suit us anymore, hot or cold."

"Then why have you restarted the flow?" Tirell had moved beyond anger into incomprehension; however well this studious cousin spoke his language, he was starting to wonder if the mind behind the words was any less opaque than that of a lizard or a gnat.

"The light and heat of the rekindled Near Sun will give us two new worlds. They already orbit the Far Sun ahead and behind the Near Sun, each a sixth of a circle away. This will bring them to life."

"You have your life already, on the inner worlds."

"One world only; the others aren't amenable to change."

"One only! You can't live with one?"

"There are billions of us," the voice replied. "You are less than ten thousand in all."

"Billions—and you're unwilling to hatch fewer children?"

"Why should even one of us go childless, in order that your sleep remains undisturbed?"

Tirell didn't understand this idiom. "You think we're *sleeping?*"

"You abandoned your culture; you discarded your heritage. If you vanished entirely, what would be lost?"

Tirell felt a weight on his chest: the foot of his opponent, insisting that he yield.

"Aren't we people like you? We feel everything you feel. We struggle like you do; we love life like you do. How is it possible for you to say that we could cease to exist, and it would mean nothing?"

"We all die," the voice replied. "Every one of us. But the culture of the ancestors, their highest achievements, lives on in us alone."

16

The cousins' device released the glider, and its shadow slid away. Tirell had lost count of the time, and he had no real idea where he was now, or how fast he was moving. He hung suspended in his harness, blinking at the restored light filling the hollow.

After a while, he felt the air pushing back against the glider, but he waited until the canopy had lost its rigid outward bulge before daring to peel it open in one corner. The air rushing past had a strange odor, but it was not so thin as to leave him struggling for breath.

The canopy began to rattle in the airflow, then the glider gyrated and turned nose-down, leaving Tirell with his feet to the sky. He closed his eyes and pictured the vessel plunging into the depths. If everyone was destined for those beautiful clouds, why not get it over with right now?

The rattling intensified, shaking him out of his self-pitying reverie. He owed it to the people who'd worked on the launcher to return and tell them everything he'd learned.

He checked the ropes securing the canopy to the tail of the glider, then he took out the pegs, tore the rim free, and threw the whole sheet into the raging air. The wind snatched at it wildly until it came to an uneasy equilibrium, stretched out on the ropes above him, squalling like a strange injured animal as the harness bit into his shoulders from below.

"Thanks to Delia, yet again," he muttered, imagining her scowl when she heard what her handiwork had actually achieved.

Tirell pushed himself away from the floor of the hollow and peered down at the swirling depths. He loosened the harness enough to turn himself around and get his feet in contact with the pedals; he waited as long as he dared, trying to extract as much deceleration from the trailing canopy as possible without falling too low.

Then he cut the canopy loose and took control of the wing flaps, bringing the glider out of its dive.

When he was level, for a moment he was completely at a loss; it had just occurred to him that this would be the first time he'd be flying the glider without Anna beside him. But he wasn't lost; he'd seen enough of the long-lived vortices in the depths below to get his bearings.

Long before he reached Maldo, he saw a small, unfamiliar forest, suspended in an updraft, visibly rising and falling even as he watched, still finding its balance. If it survived in the new conditions, maybe it could serve as a temporary home. A first step in the migration.

Tirell felt his body tense in anger, ashamed at his own acquiescence. But what choice would they have? Accept the hard fate the cousins had imposed on them, or reject it, rage at it, and die.

When he finally saw his home in the distance, the shame returned, and he wanted to flee, but he forced himself to keep going. He found the mouth of the clearing, and he pictured Anna beside him, encouraging and berating him as he circled around a second time, then a third, before he could straighten his path out enough to fly in.

He struck the wall of vines with a bone-shaking jolt, but it felt like a friendly embrace. He sat in the hollow, unable to rise; Anna and Selik appeared beside him, squeezing his arms, talking to him, checking him for injuries.

"If I tell you what happened," he said, "you won't believe me. You'll just say I lost my mind."

"Come out of the glider," Anna replied, "and you'll see why that's not true."

She and Selik helped him out, and he staggered across the platform. His legs were impossibly weak. Could it really have been just a few thousand breaths since he'd departed? He felt like he'd returned from a long exile.

He looked back at the glider. Along the side, dozens of shallow but perfectly straight grooves had been carved—or rather, pressed—into the wood. No one who saw that would doubt that he'd been grabbed by the cousins' strange dispatcher.

He sat down on the platform, and the others sat beside him. "I'll tell you everything," he said. "But then, you'll need to give me something in return."

Anna looked annoyed, but she indulged him. "Of course. What is it you want?"

Tirell said, "I need to hear the Full Recitation. Every word you know, everything I missed out on. We're all going to need to hear it. The struggle that's coming might last for a thousand generations, and we're all going to need to make ourselves strong."

father's things, put the house on the market, meet with the estate lawyer. On the other hand, maybe all this activity was good for Layla, taking her out of herself. I could still see tension in the way her body held itself, the tension that never really left her, but compared to yesterday's monochrome lethargy, Layla looked okay.

Oh, God, please let her be okay. Not like—*say it, Elena, if only to yourself*—not like Daddy.

She said, "How's it going in Delft?"

Another good sign: interest in someone else.

"We locked onto a subject. Not, however, Vermeer."

I told her about the lock, but only until I could see her interest drift away. It didn't take long. We talked then about the house: who might buy it, what they might pay, what needed to be done before it went on the market, and who needed to be hired to do it. Layla didn't talk long, but she did talk, and when she ended the call, I poured away the rest of my Scotch. I didn't need it. Layla was functional, at least for the moment, and I could concentrate on tomorrow in the lab.

The rest of the evening, I studied the file Jan sent me about Maria van Leeuwenhoek. Born in 1656, she was the only survivor of the six children Leeuwenhoek fathered with two wives. Maria's mother died when Maria was eleven. She acquired a stepmother, Cornelia, in 1671, the same year that Leeuwenhoek began making microscopes, which put him on the path to discovering the astonishing worlds of his microscopic "animalcules."

Cornelia went into a deep depression after the death of her infant son and some authorities thought she left Leeuwenhoek's home to live with her sister's family. Maria assumed the running of the modest household. She may also have assisted her father with his work. She never married, never left his house. She buried Leeuwenhoek when he died, at age ninety, and sent some microscopes that her father had willed to the Royal Society of London for Improving Natural Knowledge. When Maria was eighty-three, she arranged to have a monument set up on his grave. Jan had translated into English the short inscription, although my immersive language training in Dutch could probably have caught the gist of the epitaph. Birth and death dates, membership in the Royal Society, and a poem by someone named Huibert Corneliszoon Poot, urging visitors to have reverence for Leeuwenhoek's great age and "wondrous merit." Maria was buried beside him, but without any poem; mere daughters didn't get poems. She was ninety-five.

And that was it—all the verifiable information that history had on Maria van Leeuwenhoek.

Still, I was glad of Jan's file. If you're going to invade someone's mind, it's good to know whatever you can about who she might be.

☼

First contact with a subject is exciting and fearful both: an explorer's voyage into a new world. I was experienced enough as a receiver to know my mind would not disappear irretrievably into the subject's mind (it has happened). But Maria and I would become locked, and every time Cora hooked up the electrodes implanted in my brain to her complex equipment, it was Maria's memories I would explore. She would, of course, never know I was there. Unlike the explorers to the New World during the Dutch golden age, I would alter nothing, an invisible presence.

And her presence in my mind? Sometimes a Meijer Entanglement was sharp and yielded clear images and words. Other times, not so much. A researcher in Copenhagen had managed to lock onto Werner Heisenberg during his famous World War II visit to the Jewish physicist Niels Bohr, Heisenberg's former mentor, in Nazi-occupied Denmark. However, the entanglement had yielded only the vaguest images and no dialogue at all. All the receiver had gotten was Heisenberg's strong emotion of urgency—but about what? That Bohr should save his own life by joining the Nazi bomb effort? That he should try to get out of occupied Denmark if he still could? Historians of science reached epic heights of frustration over that one.

"Ready?" Cora said to me.

I lay on a cot, hooked to computers that included state-of-the-art deep-image reconstruction equipment, technology that had existed for fifty years but recently taken a punctuated-evolution leap. It would translate my brain waves into AI-enhanced images, but it could not capture words. Immediately after the session, I would record whatever was said by and to Maria, assuming the words were clear enough and my immersive training in Dutch extensive enough. Jan would help with that. I glimpsed him entering the room and standing respectfully at the back, behind the physician mandatory for all first contacts.

I closed my eyes and said, "Ready."

The lab went away, and another room took its place, a room of wide-planked wooden floors, small-mullioned windows behind partially closed shutters, candles burning in wall sconces. Maria's—now my—memories were shifty, not yet sharp.

A woman lies on a curtained bed; she is clearly dead. Other people stand on the far side of the bed, although not Leuwenhoek himself. A tsunami of childish grief swells through my mind as I become accustomed to being Maria and move deeper into her/our memory.

I kneel and touch the dead woman's face. "Mutter!"

Someone pulls me to my feet and gently leads me from the room and down a narrow hallway to Father's workroom. Father sits reading a book. He looks up as I tell him that Mother is dead.

The memory wavered again; I still hadn't completely settled into Maria's mind. Leeuwenhoek's reply to her was too complicated for me to catch all of it, but I saw the brief and perfunctory look of sorrow on his face. And as he held up the book and babbled on, I heard a word in unexpected English.

Then, abruptly, I was fully there.

Anger rises in me, anger I must not show Father. I bow my head and back out from the room.

Maria dissolved in my mind. I was myself again, the entanglement collapsed.

I sat up even before the doctor could check my vitals or Cora disconnect my implants. "I couldn't get all the Dutch when Leeuwenhoek was speaking. But I think he said he was sorry that Maria's mother—he did not say 'my wife'—had died, but most of what he said pertained to a book he'd been reading. And he said a word in English. 'Microphagia'."

Jan's eyes widened. "Yes? You are sure? Microphagia?"

"I'm sure. What is that?"

Cora said, "We need to record the dialogue before Elena forgets it!"

"I won't forget it," I said.

Jan said, "You were in 1666, the year Barbara van Leeuwenhoek died. The year before, Robert Hooke published *Micrographia*, the first book about items viewed through a microscope. It is speculated that the book was what started Leeuwenhoek thinking about how to build a much better microscope. But Leeuwenhoek couldn't read English, so perhaps at this time he merely studied the pictures? Could you tell?"

"No."

Cora said, "Record the damn dialogue!"

We did. Afterward, Jan said quietly, "You are distressed. Because Leeuwenhoek was more interested in the book than in his wife's death."

"Or his daughter," I said. "She was eleven years old!"

"Yes," Jan said, and in his voice I heard the empathy that had been missing from Leeuwenhoek. "In all contemporary accounts Leeuwenhoek is portrayed as unemotional, even cold. His work mattered supremely to him."

"Oh, who cares what mattered most to him," Cora said. "These images are okay for a first contact. If you can sharpen them as we go on, Elena, publication should get us both really good tenure-track offers! Are you up for a second session right away? Doctor?"

The physician who'd taken my vital signs said in English that my degree of weakness was usual after a session but not excessive.

Cora turned to me. "Doctor says you're good to go!"

I didn't want to. Maria's grief still pulled at my mind, as debilitating for me as my fatigue. It is draining to inhabit two minds at once, and not easy to shed feelings acquired from the mind not one's own. But maybe the next session would be happier, dispelling the emotion of the previous one. That happened sometimes. But if the second session was also unhappy . . .

Jan watched my face. "You are not required, Elena."

"No. I want to."

"Brilliant!" Cora said. "Let's go!"

This session was entirely different.

I hurry along a canal edged with poplars, the Nieuwe Kerk bell tower receding behind me in the pink-and-gold dawn. Frost silvers the ground. I pull my shawl more tightly around my breasts. Bells chime, the sound clear but not as loud as the single word I whisper over and over—a song, a prayer—Willem, Willem, Willem . . .

Willem?

He waits beside the canal, leaning against a tree, straightening the moment he sees me and rushing forward. Then I am crushed against the full-skirted blue coat of his uniform. Our lips find each other, and sweetness blossoms in me, and I am so light, lighter than air, in a moment that I wish to last forever.

He murmurs, "I love you," and I murmur back, "Forever."

Between kisses, Willem tells me he must go, his something, and why, but he will return soon. "My father," I say, and Willem answers that he will talk to my father, we will be together, we will marry. All when the war is over.

The carillon in the city sounds again, and then he is gone. But my happiness remains, even as I hurry home, even as the bells chime that "forever" has been less than fifteen minutes.

The entanglement collapsed as Maria's emotion calmed. I was back in the TU Delft lab. No Willem, no bright dreams of youth, just the doctor running his instruments over my heart, head, and wrist as Cora cawed triumphantly.

"Much clearer this time! Brilliant! What was the dialogue?"

I repeated it all, including the Dutch words I didn't know when Willem was explaining why he must leave. I looked inquiringly at Jan.

He said, "Willem said his company was ready to march that day. He wore a fusilier's uniform, probably from the Third Anglo-Dutch War. I will need to research more. If it is so, the year is between 1672 and 1674. Maria is sixteen or seventeen or eighteen. The war with England took place mostly at sea, but the Dutch Republic was also at war with England's ally, France, and the land fighting took heavy casualties. Very heavy."

He did not need to say more. Maria van Leeuwenhoek never married, never left her father's house. But I had not experienced Willem's future death, if that was what had happened, only her happiness by the canal, and that happiness lingered in my mind like the scent of roses after one has left the garden.

Maybe that residual, secondhand happiness showed on my face. Because Jan—shy, formal, awkward when not discussing history—stopped me in the corridor and asked me to dinner. And I might have said yes, even though two sessions had left me very tired, except that he added, "But I will understand if it is too soon after your father."

He knew. How much did he know? All of it? He was, after all, a researcher.

"No," I said, far too harshly. "No. I can't."

I moved away from him.

Borderline depressives learn to make themselves do the things they know will lift their mood. Mine had been crashed by my own unfair rudeness to Jan. So despite the fatigue of a double session, I walked much of the way home, the afternoon sun warm on my face. Poplars, straight and strong as soldiers, were doubled in the water of the canals. As I entered Market Square, the Nieuwe Kerk bell ringer began to play the carillon for a summer concert. The bells sounded fuller, richer than in Maria's time; there were more of them. I sat in a café with a glass of wine, savoring it, and watched bicycles cross the square, tourists gawk at the cathedral, children chase pigeons.

There are sometimes advantages to being a "suggestible person," even if the "suggestions" come from oneself. I lost myself in the wine, the music, the lovely light on the face of the bell tower. I let them all wash me free of the seventeenth century, and of my own.

2.

Cora said, "You're late."

"Yes," I said, "I'm sorry, the Loop was—"

"I don't care. Get ready for the session."

I glanced at Jan, who looked embarrassed. This third session seemed unpleasant even before it began.

But not after I entered Maria's brain. Then things were only strange.

I stand beside Father, holding out my index finger. A sharp jab—he rams a small knife into my finger and bright red blossoms on the tip. Carefully, he fastens the pin to the platform of his latest small, single-lensed microscope, holds it to the light, and begins moving the screw that adjusted distance. I put my finger into my mouth and suck on it. "I may go now, Father?"

"Certainly not. You will take notes. Pieter!"

The elderly artist comes forward, carrying paper and pen.

I say, "But I must go now. To . . . to church."

Father frowns up at me and says what he always says, "Domheid. Waanvoorstellingen. I need you here."

"But—"

"Enough! Bring the book!"

Resentment. Despair. Obedience.

The entanglement collapsed.

"Good enough, I guess," Cora said grudgingly. "The images aren't as sharp as yesterday's second session. Don't get sloppy on me, Elena!"

"It's not my 'sloppiness,'" I said. God, I disliked her. "The session was . . . strange. Maria was distracted. Half her mind was filled with an image of Willem. I had the impression she was supposed to meet him at the church, until her father derailed that. Jan, what does 'domheid' mean?"

"Stupidity."

"And 'waanvoorstellingen'?"

"Delusion. Which of them said that?"

"Antonj, to Maria."

"About what?"

"Going to church. She said—"

"*If* the *historian* doesn't mind," Cora said, "maybe we could get Elena's recollections of the conversation recorded before she forgets its sequence?"

So it was Jan that she was furious with. Why?

He smiled at me. "We will start from the beginning, then. But first, I will say only that Leeuwenhoek had the reputation of being—what is it you Americans say? A 'stone-cold rationalist,' scornful of the beliefs of anything supernatural. For him, there existed nothing he could not touch or see."

"I don't think Maria was really going to church. I think she was supposed to meet Willem in Nieuwe Kerk."

"You think?" Cora said, "Don't you *know*? You were there in her memories! God!"

Jan said mildly, "Memories carry secondary impressions and emotion. Those are also information. In 1674 Leeuwenhoek wrote to the Royal Society about examining blood cells. So now we have the information that in that year Willem is not yet gone from Maria's life. Yes, Cora, we will begin now."

My call to Layla's cell was answered by our cousin Donna and cold slid down my spine.

"Where is she?"

"Back in the hospital," Donna said. "Your father's neighbor called me. I'm sorry, Elena." But Donna's voice held undertones of impatience. She had never said so outright, but I knew that at some level, Donna considered depression, even clinical depression, to be a selfish indulgence. She believed in the worst of brisk-people clichés: "Just snap out of it." "Just get on with it." "Don't think about yourself so much." Domheid. Waanvoorstellingen.

I said, "What happened?"

"Layla had an ... an 'episode.' She climbed onto the roof and threatened to jump off. The police talked her down."

"I'll get on a plane tonight if there's a flight, be there by tomorrow."

"No. Don't." Donna held the phone closer to her face, as if that could better convince me. Two decades older than Layla and me, she suddenly reminded me of the middle-aged Maria of my initial lock, the woman whose memories I was plundering every afternoon.

"Listen, Elena. You can't do any good here. The doctor told me that Layla can't have any visitors or other outside contact for at least a week. Part of the 'treatment.' You might better stay where you are and just get on with your research."

"We have twelve days left on the equipment."

"Take it all," Donna said, even though I was sure she didn't know what my research was and would not have approved of it if she had known: *"How is that useful?"* Donna might look like Maria van Leeu-wenhoek, but inside she was more like what Jan had called Antonj: a stone-cold rationalist.

I said, "Will you visit Layla as soon as it's allowed and then call me right away?"

"Yes. Do you want her doctors' numbers?"

"I have them."

"Of course you do," Donna said, and in her voice I heard her knowledge of not only Layla's previous stays in Briarcliff Hospital, but also of everything about my father's death. Or was that just my "sensitive suggestibility"?

"Thank you, Donna," I said.

Her face softened. "I'm sorry this is happening to you," she said, and even though this time the words were genuine, I wanted to yell at her that it was not happening to me, it was happening to Layla, just as it had happened to Daddy, and neither of them could help it. Donna should be thanking any gods she believed in—probably none—that the wayward luck of the family genetic curse had spared her, as it had partially spared me.

There is no accounting for genes.

In the next day's session, Maria wore the merciless black of mourning.

"Wear ... more of cheerful ..." Father snaps. I don't answer, and he shakes his head and turns back to his everlasting work. I sit beside him and write down everything he says, measurements and procedures and descriptions. He will use my notes to write his letters to the Royal Society. Pieter waits on a stool for his turn to look through the microscope and make his drawings. Wood specimen, hairs from his wig, scum from his teeth—it all takes a long time.

Someone halloos at the door.

"... not open," Father says. "Intruders."

I rise and peer through a crack in the closed shutters. "... the butcher's boy, Father. He brings ..."

"Receive the meat. Pieter ... this—"

I go to the door, receive the meat, give the boy his coins. I hand the meat to Jozefien, who bobs a curtsey. I pour a drink of water from the jug. I stand still, not drinking it.

Again, the images in my mind were watery, half-formed, and I was catching only a few words of each speech. Maria was not paying attention to her own life. The image of Willem was almost as solid in her mind as the objects in the room, an image suffused with despair. Why had the older Maria remembered this day at all? It must have been like so many others of assisting her autocratic father with his work, mourning her lost soldier.

"Maria! Come!"

Excitement in Father's voice. I hurry into the workroom, where Father holds up a tiny microscope, peering at something on the pin. "Look!"

"I do not want—"

"Look!"

Resentfully, I do as I am told—and nearly drop the microscope in surprise.

"Stupid girl! Take care!"

"What is it?"

Father—Father!—is grinning like a boy. Pieter rises, pen in hand, staring at both of us in bewilderment. Father speaks—

—words that I, Elena, had carefully memorized in Dutch—

—and says, "Little animals."

☼

"Again, 1674," Jan said when the long session finally ended. "That was the year Leeuwenhoek first saw his 'animalcules' in water from Lake Berkelse. No one, not even Hooke, had ever seen them before."

"Touchdown!" Cora exulted. "We got it!"

Jan continued as if she were not capering grotesquely around the lab. "He sent descriptions and drawings to the Royal Society, saying that the motion of the 'animalcules' was 'wondrous to see' and also— Elena, are you all right?"

"Headache." I sat up on the cot, which only made the headache worse.

"Record the dialogue before you forget it," Cora said. "Now!"

Jan said, "Elena—"

"There are three of us in there," I blurted. "Not just two."

"Three?" Jan said.

"Me, Maria, and her memory of Willem. It's so strong that it's almost another presence. I've never experienced anything like it."

"The dialogue!" Cora said. "Now, or it won't count as 'immediately post-session'!"

We recorded the dialogue. My headache grew worse. Jan's warm brown eyes watched me with concern. That was almost as disconcerting as the session. I *gave* concern—for Layla, for Daddy. I didn't receive it.

Receive the meat—

I leaned over the side of my chair and vomited on the floor.

✿

Jan insisted on taking me home in his tiny drivie. Cora watched us go, and as he put a hand under my elbow to guide me down the steps, I glimpsed Cora's face. So that was why she had been so irritable with him yesterday, so cold today. She'd come on to him and he'd refused.

As the car drove itself through Market Square, I said, "Please don't come in. I'm fine."

"All right," Jan said. "But you will phone me if you feel worse? I am listed with the university contacts."

"Yes, thank you," I said, knowing I would not. Not phone him, and not get worse, either, because tonight I needed to talk to Layla's doctor.

I might not have bothered. Layla was "the same." Nothing had changed.

✿

This is what happens when your last parent dies. There is a lot of paperwork; in the modern world, it is bureaucratically complicated to die. A funeral must be arranged. Neighbors bring casseroles and cakes and pans of lasagna, none of which you want. You and your siblings feel orphaned, no matter how old you are. Eventually at least one of you must deal with your dead parent's clothing, furniture, house. If that person is not you, you feel guilty for not helping.

This is what happens when your last parent turns a nine-millimeter Glock on first his beloved dog and then on himself in the back garden of an upscale suburb in which normally nothing violent ever happens. Police surround the property with yellow crime scene tape. Detectives question horrified neighbors. A forensic team photographs everything and measures all blood spatters that have not drained into the soil. Afterward, neighbors avoid you and your sister, but the press invades the sidewalk, tries for photos through windows, phones you for quotes. Because of the dog, social media explodes with information about your parent, with disinformation, with vicious attacks, with arguments about whether clinical depression can lead to violence or if that is slanderous prejudice. Even if you do not share your parent's surname, you are suspect: Might you do the same thing?

Do you own a dog? Has the SPCA looked into your dog's welfare? If any offsprings' medical records, laughably easy to hack, show a hospitalization for clinical depression, the offspring is treated as if they are a pet-murderer-in-waiting.

And still someone must deal with the clothing, furniture, house. If it's not you, it doesn't matter. You—and many others—will blame you. Even if your excuse is a once-in-a-decade chance at a time slot on the planet's most sophisticated neurological equipment for an emerging scientific discipline.

I had gambled that Layla, who'd handled Daddy's death better than I'd dared hope, would be all right alone for three weeks. I'd gambled that her depression would not rekindle. I'd gambled, and I lost. Worse, so had Layla.

My fault.

My guilt.

3.

Early in the morning, I rebooked my flight home for the day after tomorrow. I informed the university that we would do three sessions today and two tomorrow, but those would be our last. Cora wouldn't like it. She would have planned on more sessions. A growing body of research showed that received memories were always stronger and more detailed with at least one day of rest between sessions.

Cora exploded. "No! Fuck it, Elena, that's not fair to me! We're coauthors here, don't be so selfish!"

"I'm sorry, but I have to—"

"You have to fulfill the contract we signed with TU! What's so important that it can't wait an extra week? Another family shooting?"

Instantly Jan was standing in front of Cora, his slight body somehow menacing. "Shut up, Cora," he said, another Americanism that, despite everything, made me blink.

Cora took a step backward, scowled, but managed a choked, "Sorry." And in that atmosphere, we began work.

I hurry home from Nieuwe Kerk, Willem strong in my mind. Father waits in the front hall, scowling. "Where were you?"

I don't answer, but as I take off my cloak and hand it to Jozefien, he stares at the tiny gold cross I now wear on a chain.

"Church, Maria? Domheid. Waanvoorstellingen. They feed you lies: zielen, engelen. There is no ziel inside you, Daughter. The world is what you see, what I see in my lens. The rest is fairy stories."

I am confused. He speaks to me with kindness, with—no, not under-standing, something else. Pity?

I am more confused when he takes my hand and leads me into his study, Jozefien staring open-mouthed after us.

Father hands me a microscope. "See what I have found, Maria. We must record this."

I look through the lens. Tadpoles with long, thin tails swim like eels, but these are far too small to be tadpoles. "What are they?"

Father seems embarrassed, further confusing me. "They are from my . . . my seed. This is where life comes. In each of those animalcules is contained everything necessary to form a child."

"And the mother?"

"She houses the growing child." And then, as Jozefien brings in a tray with cheese, ale, and fragrant new bread for Father's dinner, he adds whimsically, "The mother bakes the baby. She is the oven." His voice changes. "You must begin work. Because you were not here to take notes, I have already written my letter to the Royal Society. Make a copy, please."

Willem. Willem. Willem . . .

I sit at a table, draw toward me Father's letter on his own hand-made paper with the writing in dark brown ink, and begin to copy it into the book.

"Her book of notes included copies of his letters!" Jan said before I could even speak. "That has never been found!"

I said, "What does 'zielen' mean?"

"'Souls.' Leeuwenhoek spoke of the soul?"

"Only to tell Maria it is a fairy story. And 'engelen' is 'angels'? He said those, too, are a fairy story."

Jan smiled. "Which is exactly what his neighbors, and even at first many of his English contemporaries, said about Leeuwenhoek's 'little animals.' What was on his lens?"

"His own semen."

"1677. Give me the dialogue to record."

I did. Cora watched the visual translations of my brain waves eavesdropping on Maria's memories as I matched them with Maria's and her father's words. Cora said sourly, "He thought women were just baby ovens? What about our eggs?"

Jan said, "Merely a storehouse of nutrients. Antonj thought eggs couldn't be alive because they did not move."

She said, "Sexist bastard. Well, we've got a good enough match between action and speech, although the images are still pretty blurry.

I suppose you want to wait until after lunch for the next session. Not that an hour off is enough time for you to get any sharper."

I said, "The images aren't blurry because of me. They're blurry because half of Maria's mind is still filled with Willem."

"After three years? Then let's hope she forgets him soon."

☼

She didn't.

In my afternoon session, I finally saw what I should have already realized: Maria's depression. It leaves a signature in the mind, a sort of unseen miasma, until now masked by the insistent, overwhelming, constant longing for Willem.

Added to her longing and depression was a new emotion: fear. Leeuwenhoek was ill. He lay in bed, weak and nauseated, while Maria held cups of ale to his lips and poor Jozefien emptied and cleaned pan after pan of watery diarrhea. Maria was patient despite her fear, Leeuwenhoek was irritable, and I was glad that memories experienced in Meijer entanglements did not include the sense of smell.

"Eww," Cora said when the session ended.

Jan said, "In 1680 Leeuwenhoek had a bout of giardia, a water-borne disease. Obviously, he survived. But it's interesting that Maria knew both to keep him hydrated and to give him ale instead of more water."

"Did Maria get it, too?"

"History doesn't say."

Of course not.

We recorded what I remembered of the dialogue, none of which showed Leeuwenhoek in a flattering light. Querulous, demanding, he assumed that Maria's life existed to serve his.

"Oh, yes," Jan said.

"Her fault," Cora said. "She should have just left."

My anger startled me with its intensity. "Just left"—and gone where? With what money? Yes, Cora was an engineer, not a historian, but still—

I said tightly, "Sometimes circumstances keep a person from walking away."

She didn't reply. I didn't think she even heard me.

☼

I lay on the cot the rest of the afternoon, gathering strength. Jan brought me takeaway for dinner. In the evening session, a pale but recovering Leeuwenhoek examined bits of his own feces, while Maria wrote down his observations in "the book" and Pieter took his turn on the microscope to draw what Leeuwenhoek's magnification revealed.

Afterward, Cora surprised me by actually asking an historical question. "Jan, did he see whatever caused his giardia—what is it, a bacteria, virus, what?"

"Parasite. Yes, he described it in a 1680 letter to the Royal Society and included accurate drawings."

"So he was the first to say germs caused disease?"

"No," Jan said. "Leeuwenhoek has been criticized for never pointing out that connection."

"But he knew. He must have."

"Probably."

"Then why didn't he—"

I said, "Because he didn't want the Royal Society to see his precious 'little animals' in a negative light. He cared more about them than about people. Including his daughter."

"What a bastard," Cora said dismissively, as if a single pejorative could sum up a person. "Didn't you tell us that he wouldn't take any students and wouldn't even show people his best microscopes?"

"Yes," Jan said.

I felt weak enough to let him take me home. As his drivie calibrated the traffic and moved easily through it, I sat slumped against the back of my seat, eyes closed. There would be no call to Layla's doctor tonight. By tomorrow night, I would be home in California, in the partially emptied house where Layla and my father had lived, facing the task of working with Cora from 9,000 miles away to ready our joint findings for publication.

Neither Jan nor I spoke until we reached my building. Then he said, "Maria also loved her father, you know, and was proud of him. It was a . . . a complicated relationship."

"Yes," I said. "I know."

4.

In the next morning's session, Leeuwenhoek discovered microbes in water drawn from a local pond, the first person in the world to see bacteria. The memory meant enough to Maria for me to access it, although not because of the bacteria. I felt her astonishment at Leeuwenhoek's joy, and then her sharing of it. Her pleasure lasted only one long moment before the image of Willem again turned everything else blurry, but that moment was real, and it yielded some sharp images that pleased Cora.

"1686," Jan said, and I did arithmetic in my head. Maria had been mourning her dead soldier for somewhere between twelve and fourteen years, without any lessening of longing for him. Was that love or pathological obsession? I didn't know.

I did know that she had been to church that morning, and had left halfway through the service, finding no comfort there. Did she no longer believe she would see Willem someday in heaven? I didn't know that, either. Maria's memories revealed her experiences and emotions, but her thoughts only as they occurred in the moment, and I had not been with her in Nieuwe Kerk. I couldn't tell how her religious beliefs had evolved.

And then, in my last session in Delft, suddenly I could.

✦

"Mistress Maria! More paper from heaven!"

The neighbor girl holds out her palm. On it lies a blackened, brittle scrap of paper. The child's small face shines with excitement. "They fall beside Visser's Pond. I saw it! Messages from angels!"

"I may see?"

"Don't touch, it will break. This one fell right to me!"

I stare at the charred paper—blackened by its long fall from the skies? Old, faded memories of other people telling me about these messages, but not near Delft. The child runs off to show her treasure to someone else, and I snatch my shawl from its peg and start for Visser's Pond, outside the city walls.

The ground is low here, marshy when wet, but dry now under a hot sun. The water of Visser's Pond lies low, choked with algae and weeds. Here is where Father obtained his animalcules for study. Insects hum in the wildflowers. I spread my shawl on the ground and sit on it, turning my face to the breeze ruffling the pond water. I wait.

It is a long wait.

But eventually, I see the paper drift down from the sky. It lands on my shawl, almost in my lap. Charred, lusterless—I cannot read anything written on it. But I don't need to. Happiness rises in me like a fresh spring from dry earth, and I laugh out loud.

This message came right to me. It is from Willem, it must be. So Heaven is real, souls are real, and instead of punishing me for doubting that, God in His infinite mercy has allowed Willem to send me this pre-cious token of faith, and of love.

I laugh aloud—how long since I have laughed? Then I cry, careful to not let my tears land on the fragile paper. I sit there and feel Willem's love soak into me like sunshine.

I am loved.

When I finally lift the paper and hold it carefully on my palm, as the little girl did, the sun is low above the city. When I reach home, the smell of cooking comes from the kitchen and Jozefien has already lit candles in my father's workroom. He glowers at me.

"Where have you been?"

"Look, Father. Please look. It fell from the sky near Visser's Pond." I hold out the paper.

"Yes, yes, I know," he says. "I have a specimen already—you didn't need to get me one."

He says a lot more—

—my Dutch wasn't good enough to follow—

—before he looks through one of his small microscopes, adjusts the distance of the pin from the lens. He hands me the microscope, and I look.

All joy leaves me. I am empty, a shell. I crumple my message from Heaven and it falls in black gritty rain to the floor.

I pulled the wires off my scalp, not waiting for Cora, who cried, "Hey!" Jan stared at the screen until it went blank. Then he looked at me.

I could not force words through the tightness in my throat.

Jan supplied the words. "In the seventeenth century, it *was* believed that occasional scraps of paper fell from Heaven, and they really did look like paper in composition and thickness. Leeuwenhoek examined one in 1687 and realized they were small sheets of dried algae, stiffened and burned by the sun, and light enough to be lifted and blown about by wind. He reconstituted some of the 'paper' with water and found algae. Then he reversed the process to make 'mes-sages' by drying fresh algae. That's what he showed Maria, isn't it? Could you understand his explanation, Elena?"

"No," I said. All I could understand was her heartbreak. The worst kind: unexpected hope, suddenly shattered.

Layla and I had thought my father was getting better.

Cora said, "So no dialogue at all? Nothing?"

"None," I lied. I did not have the strength to recite the conversa-tion with the child, and anyway, Jan had already explained everything.

Cora said sulkily, "Well, if you don't have any dialogue for this session, how about doing just one more tonight, you told me your plane doesn't leave until almost midnight and so if you—"

"Cora," Jan said sharply, "no. Can't you see how weak she is?"

"And just *who*, Jan de Knuyt, appointed you research leader here? The last time I looked, you're only attached to the project as long as Elena and I—"

"Have you no sense of fairness toward Elena? She—"

"Stop," I said, raising my voice as much as I could. "I will do one more session tonight."

I had decided what I was going to do. About everything.

☼

Cora, sweet now that I was doing what she wanted, brought me sandwiches, cookies, coffee, and left it by the cot. I told her and Jan to not come back for three hours; I needed to sleep. I actually did sleep for an hour, setting my wrister to wake me.

I called the airline and rebooked my flight for tomorrow evening, hoping I would be able to fly by then.

There are many kinds of depression. Dysthymia, or persistent depressive disorder, often but not always runs in families. Science has just begun to discover the genetic causes. Dysthymia ranges from mild but chronic all the way to suicidal. It can, like Layla's, vary in intensity with different occurrences.

Situational depression, on the other hand, is caused by a specific situation. Often it can be eased by changes in the depressed person's situation, by loving attention, or just by the oldest of all cures, time.

Time was not helping Maria van Leeuwenhoek. She took pride in being useful to her famous father, but feeling proud is not the same as feeling loved.

Carefully, I hooked my brain to Cora's machinery, turned it on, and lay on the cot.

Carrying a small bouquet of wildflowers, I walk across Market Square, past Nieuwe Kerk. The bell tower chimes, but I don't look up. Skirting the church, I enter the graveyard. Willem is not, of course, buried here; I will never know on what battlefield he died or who claimed his body, if anyone. I walk to my mother's gravestone.

I don't really miss her; it has been so long, and I was only a child when she died. But this is a quiet place, where sorrow is not remarked on.

Willem, Willem, Willem . . .

Two more people stood in the graveyard, mourning their own dead. Maria hadn't even noticed them. I waited until they left.

If Willem had lived ... if there had been no war ... if the church were not just as Father said: domheid, waanvoorstellingen ... Father is always right ...

What I was about to do was both forbidden and dangerous. Dangerous because in the earliest days of Meijer entanglements, three receivers had tried it. Two were fine afterward, if completely exhausted.

I lay the flowers on my mother's grave. When I straighten, Willem is standing before me. The world rocks on its foundation.

For decades, science has known that the material brain operates at a quantum level. For over a century, science has known that quantum equations run independent of time. Backward, forward, it makes no difference. Since biblical times, people who knew almost nothing of science have known about brains that produce delusions their beholders believe are real. The delusions, the waanvoorstellingen, are usually produced by disease, an abnormal situation in the brain.

I am an abnormal situation in Maria's brain.

Reversing—transferring her memories to my brain, transferring my images to her brain—it is not as difficult as it should be. Not if the created image is strong and both people are suggestible. It is forbidden because the past is supposed to be sacrosanct: Look, but don't touch. Even the past in memory.

"Willem?" I say.

"I love you," Willem says to me. His body wavers, shimmers; he is a ghost, an angel. I know this. It doesn't matter. He is here. He has come to me.

I take a step toward him, and he moves back.

"No, Maria," he says. And then, as if it takes every bit of will, he chokes out, "I wait for you." And vanishes.

I fall to my knees, sobbing in terror and joy.

I could take no more. My heart hammered, my breath came so labored that I was afraid it wouldn't come at all. I couldn't get off the cot to turn off the equipment. I couldn't even reach up to yank free my connecting wires. The third receiver of those who tried this had survived, but he was never the same again. I couldn't breathe. I—

Then the wires came free and there were arms around me, holding me tight. Jan said, "That was stupidity!"

"Domheid," I whispered, but he didn't hear me.

"What were you doing? Why ... Godverdomme! Ben je helemaal besodemieterd! You were *reversing*."

"I can't ... help ... Daddy ... or Layla," I whispered, and everything went black.

5.

Jan drove me to the airport. I felt unsteady with the shakiness and brain fog of too little sleep, even though I had just slept for fourteen hours. Last night Jan carried me home, stayed with me, made me eat when I woke. At the lab he deleted the recording of what I had done. No one else will know. My career is safe.

Ben je helemaal besodemieterd! he had said to me: are you out of your mind?

Yes. Literally.

"Jan," I said just before I entered security, "I'm sorry I never had dinner with you. That I refused so nastily. That was rude and unfair. If I return to Europe, or if you ever come to California ..."

"May I phone you? I mean, not just about the project?"

"Yes. Please. I'd like that."

"What will you do now, Elena?"

"Finish dealing with my father's estate. Take care of Layla. Work on the entanglement paper long-distance with Cora. Incidentally, she's after you."

"I know." He actually blushed, hesitated, then said with awkward daring, "But it is not Cora that I am interested in."

I kissed him goodbye, and an unexpected sweetness rippled through me.

Even though I would never know if it had made any difference, I didn't regret the comfort I had tried to bring to Maria. I had not deserved Jan's interest and kindness. The one researcher who'd failed at reversed contact did not deserve psychosis. Layla did not deserve to inherit our father's dysthymia. Maria van Leeuwenhoek, faithful and devoted to her father, did not deserve either his self-absorbed neglect or Willem's death in war. Life was not fair.

Which is why human beings should try to be. We are not only little animals.

Jan let go of me, and I walked toward the plane that would take me home.

The Metric

David Moles

1. The Ship
t_Ω-3.4011×10^7

THE SHIP WAS a billion years old, and it was dying. The incalculable energies that had forced open the metric to permit its passage were all but spent, and now the relentless quintessence was taking over again: pulling the metric tighter, so that from instant to instant the needle-eye the ship tried to thread was that much narrower, the forces pulling the ship apart that much stronger. Fields that could have carried the ship intact through the event horizon of a stellar-mass black hole were tearing like dry paper; decks and bulkheads built to withstand the heat and pressure at the heart of a star were being ground away in a shower of exotic particles that decayed instantly to pure radiation and were gone.

The ship—whose name, in a language that had been dead for many long ages before its keel was laid, was *Thus is the Heaven a Vortex Pass'd Already, and the Earth a Vortex not yet Pass'd by the Traveller thro' Eternity*—had known when it set out that this was the most likely outcome; had argued, itself, for the impossibility of the task it had been asked to undertake, when they had woken it from its long sleep. Had gone to that sleep, so many millions of years past, expecting never to be woken, never again to be needed.

It had volunteered, all the same. It fought back now with shifts of mass, changes of geometry, striving with every trick learned in a long lifetime, thousands of voyages across millions of years, to protect its precious cargo; but the hungry quintessence tugged and the metric tightened like a knot, and there was just not enough space or time left for the ship to exist in, anymore. And now that its prediction was coming true, the ship felt—not bitter, certainly, but cheated; not by the ones who had sent it out, but by the quintessence itself, by the laws of physics, by the long life and the imminent, untimely death of the Universe.

The ship had hoped so much to see Earth one more time, before the end.

☼

The city was called Septentrion, and in its current incarnation it was more than seventy thousand years old. It was said there were other cities yet remaining on the Earth but it was long since word of any of them had been much more than rumor, and Septentrion was the oldest and the largest. Three-fourths of the remaining population of the Earth made their homes here within Septentrion's walls, where the mirrors and the latent heat of the world's core still kept land and sea free of the ice ten months of the year: thirty million of the living, tens of millions of motiles, millions of sessile ghosts inextricable from the fabric of the city, uncountable billions of computationals and functionals, and this was not a tenth of what the city had held at its peak.

It was said that Septentrion was so old that when its first stones were laid, there were still stars in the sky. This was untrue and would have been untrue, had the city been a hundred times older; but it was certainly more ancient than any of the living could comprehend, and its origins, like those of the sun and the sky, the lake and the sea and the Earth, belonged to that deep time in which every ancient thing seems more or less contemporary with every other, and the age of all of them is the same, which is: unimaginable.

Piper and Petal Anchialine were born in Old South Port (which had not been a port in living generations, and which was more west now than south), in a house overlooking the 110° Canal. The twins were born a hundred days apart, Piper near the end of Frimaire and Petal at the beginning of Germinal, Piper into the Cricket sodality and Petal into the Primrose; and they were born among the living—which is to say they were biological creatures, their bodies symbioses of cells animal and fungal and bacterial, distinctions less important now than in earlier times.

Not all the living were born in the traditional manner, but the Anchialine twins were, and the forms they grew into, like those of their parents Swan and Cutter and Hare, would have seemed only a little strange to a living human of primordial days. They both had Cutter's compact bones, and Swan's straight hair (though Petal tended to wear it short these days, while Piper's was shoulder-length like Swan's), and if Petal had a bit more of Swan's quiet thoughtfulness and Piper a bit more of Cutter's fierce temper, they were in most respects as alike and close as twins could get; and (to Cutter's occasional chagrin, and Swan's secret delight) they had both inherited a full share of Hare's restless energy.

Piper was fifteen and Petal was fourteen, the day the ship came.

Thus is the Heaven a Vortex Pass'd Already announced itself in the early hours of the third watch, a flare of violet-white at the very edge of the empty sky, a sun-bright pinpoint that made the night into a brief, unnatural day, and buried itself in the mountains east of the city with a thunderclap that shattered windows in the outward precincts and sent brackish waves flowing backward up the canals.

The twins were awake, as it happened, though they were not supposed to be: both of them on the floor of their room in their night-clothes, playing a prehistoric count-and-capture game with haptic projected pieces. Petal was bored and starting to make up new rules, to Piper's increasing irritation, and at any moment one of their parents was going to come in and put a stop to the argument and the game both, when the light interrupted them.

Piper, reaching for a piece, thought at first something was wrong with the board, the pieces no longer substantial but ghostly, the board itself gone translucent, so that the pattern of the floor showed clearly through; and then the floor brightened, and the walls, brighter and brighter, until the twins had to cover their eyes; all of this in total silence. And then the light was gone, more quickly than it had appeared, leaving them blinking at yellowish afterimages in the dark.

"What was that?" Piper said.

"I don't know," said Petal.

"I wasn't asking you," Piper said. "Halocline. What was that?"

Halocline, the ancient ghost of Anchialine House, did not immediately answer, and that itself was more frightening than the light. The ghost was far older than the Anchialine phyle, dating to the times when the house had been just one cell of a manufactory that ran the length of the canal, and if it was occasionally cantankerous, occasionally exasperated (particularly by the twins), by and large it treated the generations of Anchialines that filled the house as wayward but beloved grandchildren; and it could think and learn much faster than any living human.

"I don't know," the ghost said eventually. And then, sharply: "Get down."

The twins, who were already as *down* as it seemed possible to get, looked at each other in the dark, eyes wide.

And then the shockwave hit: thunder, like a summer storm over the lake, but it went on and on, louder and louder until the twins covered their ears and buried their faces in their arms, and the whole house moved in a sudden convulsive jump that caused the floor to fly up and hit Piper in the nose.

The noise died away, and other noises began: shouts from inside the house and outside, alarms of various kinds, the sirens of City Response vehicles and the amplified voices of aerial sentinel motiles.

"All right, we're all right," Halocline said.

"Speak for yourself," said Piper in a muffled voice.

"Piper's nose is bleeding," Petal said.

"Wipe it," Halocline said, without much sympathy.

"What *was* that?" said Piper, sniffling.

"Something new," said Petal.

2. The Stranger
t_Ω-3.3998×10^7

The ship *was* new, the first new thing in Septentrion in a long time. That it was a ship at all was something City Authority had to work out by the old process of eliminating the impossible to make room for the improbable, and then on discovering there were no improbables left, backtracking to allow for the chance that City Authority might be wrong in its ideas of what was possible and what was not.

To most of Septentrion the metric was not even history but legend, and not the most popular or interesting legend; the long aeons of Earth's isolation and the heaped millennia of city history piled fact upon fact and myth upon myth, so that even in children's tales of adventure the city looked mostly to more recent times, and still thought them ancient.

Nor in all Septentrion's hundreds of centuries had any in the city—any in their right minds, and in possession of all the facts— imagined they might see a ship again cross the gulfs that separated

Earth from the invisible stars. The quintessence, the primordial dark
energy—weaker in the early aeons than gravity, but by the birth of
humanity's sun beginning already to overcome it—was too strong, the
metric long since too constricted, and most of those few in the city who
remembered when the metric's vertices had permitted passage—a
handful of the most ancient and most baroquely elaborated computationals, older than the city, inheritors of labyrinthine memory-
complexes older still—would have guessed those passages closed long
ago, the suns and worlds they connected sundered forever.

But evidence was evidence, and City Authority respected abductive inference over enumerative induction. A flock of aerial motiles,
dared into venturing beyond the walls to overfly the new valley
gouged into the foothills, reported *something* there, at any rate; and
one of them volunteered the additional opinion that whatever it was, it
was most likely either dead or in severe distress.

City Authority's duty was clear. It thought over its options, made a
decision, and came to Hare.

There were not many in Septentrion in those autumn days who
made a habit of leaving the walls of the city; and of those who did,
there was not one among the living that had traveled half as far as
Hare Anchialine. Hare, alone among Septentrion's living citizens, had
been born under another name three thousand leagues away in Meridion, Septentrion's antipodal twin. At seventeen, Hare, with five
companions, had left it and headed north.

Now Hare did the Anchialine accounts, and rode the Anchialine
float in the annual Canal Parade, and played the ophicleide in the Old
South Port clique's festival band, and in general played the part of a
model citizen. But in the summer, Hare would lead expeditions of the
restless or curious across the lake or into the mountains. And it was to
those players at adventure that City Authority came now.

Piper and Petal, Hare and Cutter and Swan; half a dozen of Hare's
students; and with them a living official from City Response named
Tanner Campestral, and a motile from the Archive named Gauge
Malpais. They were up before dawn of the second day after the ship's
arrival, in that time when the city took care of all the tens of thousands
of little things that needed taking care of, between one day and the
next. Barges moved on the canals, cleaners and their attendant recy-
clers trotted industriously along the pavements, poking into doorways
and under hedges; long trains of empty cars gathered at the trackline
stations to wait for the morning's work. Of the excitement of two
nights ago there was no obvious sign, unless it was that the dust from
the mountains made the night mist that reflected the city's light fall a

little heavier, that the first breeze from the east brought with it a hint of pine-smoke.

A City Maintenance train took them to the eastern gate, and through it, on a disused section of track reactivated for the purpose. A crawler, likewise from City Maintenance, took them through the abandoned exurbs and up into the hills. It was a route Piper and Petal had taken before but always on foot, when they would walk a day or more beside some disused exurban road, camping in the overgrown foundations of some long-gone structure, and then more days along game trails and old tracklines, up out of the empty plain. Now they rode, half asleep—they'd been up early, packing in the dark, Petal complaining of the hour and the cold until Hare offered the option of staying behind—watching the late-winter landscape roll by, dreamlike.

The crawler carried them up, the switchback paths they had taken on other occasions winding back and forth across hillsides just beginning to green, with some snow lingering on the northern slopes; over a ridge then, and down, into the basin that had not been there when last they climbed this way. It was a place of downed trees, needles and branches stripped, their trunks aligned with almost deliberate precision toward the center of the valley, where a little river ran over and through an obstacle course of rubble and tumbled logs, all of it lightly dusted with morning snow. It was always colder here, outside the focus of Septentrion's mirrors.

"There's nothing left," said Piper.

"We need to be sure," said Swan, and Cutter and Hare nodded. Swan was by five years the oldest of the three, thin and wiry, barely taller than Piper and Petal, with a quick wit and usually a quicker smile, but serious now, as they all were. Cutter was a year younger than Hare and a little shorter, solid as the city and as generous. It was Cutter who at sixteen had convinced Anchialine House to open itself to Hare the starving traveler, and Swan who had made the case for Hare's citizenship to City Authority; and though they said nothing of this aloud, the three looked at each other and knew it was on all of their minds, as they looked to see what new stranded voyagers might have come to ask the city for aid.

The crawler came to a stop then, and Hare put the armor on.

The armor was what had kept Hare alive, on that journey around the world. It was millennia old, an heirloom of Hare's Meridionese phyle (*tagma* was the word Hare used), the product of crafts forgotten in peaceful Septentrion, or never learned. Its ghost was equally old, and clever. With the armor, Hare was stronger than any three of the living, and proof against fire and ice and thin air and deep water, and against thirst and starvation and exhaustion and despair.

The armor was a marvel, and on that long journey it had barely been enough. Of the six, all similarly equipped, who set out from Meridion, only Hare had reached their destination.

Of the ship itself, even seen through the armor's eyes, there was hardly anything left: a few splinters of feather-light metallic microlattice, none longer than a finger, arranged like the fallen trees in that same radial pattern, and some anomalous smudges of fullerene carbon.

"Is it safe?" Piper called from the door of the crawler, thinking of bugbears out of old stories: nanites, poisons, radiation, malign enchantments.

"Safe enough," Hare called back.

"Come on, Piper," said Petal, climbing out. "I'll race you."

With the challenge all of Piper's misgivings vanished, and in a moment both the twins were gone, down the slope and over the rough timber fast and sure as monkeys. The rest of the party followed after them, a little more carefully, with Hare at the rear most careful of all, mindful of the armor's extra weight and watchful for anything its eyes might have missed.

"There!"

Piper spotted it first: something small and bright, a red-orange speck against the burnt black earth. The twins chased each other down into the crater before Hare and the others could stop them, laughing and shoving each other as they ran.

"Me first!"

"I saw it first."

They reached it at the same time: a sphere that might have been rough stone or painted metal, etched with fine yellow whorls, barely larger than a closed fist. It sat atop a cone of fine dirt like a knee-high anthill—as if it had been buried in the crash, and burrowed its way out.

"Wait—" Piper said, suddenly cautious again; but too late. Petal had picked it up.

And there was someone there. Standing next to them.

Petal dropped the sphere in surprise—it rolled a little way down the anthill—and the stranger was gone.

"Where—" Piper began, looking around.

Petal scrambled down, picked the sphere up again, and the stranger was back.

A living person, or the appearance of one, of ancient form, brown, slender, exactly the twins' height, dressed in a simple red chiton, leaving arms and feet bare. Hair a puffball of black shading to copper; face proud, if unfamiliar, deep-set black eyes beneath a round forehead, nose long and straight, chin narrow and pointed.

The stranger looked at Petal and in a voice musical, serious, and urgent, said something neither of the twins understood.

Petal looked at Piper, who shrugged.

The stranger said something else, in some other language, richer and darker, and waited; then when the twins didn't answer, a third, full of lilting tones and short nasal syllables. Then a fourth.

"We don't understand you," said Petal.

Hare and Gauge caught up with them.

"I do," said the motile. It hesitated a moment, and then said something to the stranger, in the first language the stranger had used. The stranger nodded.

"Can your armor translate?" Gauge asked Hare, who nodded.

The stranger repeated that first urgent sentence.

"What?" Petal demanded. "What is it?"

Hare and the motile looked at each other. The motile bobbed indecisively. Hare looked at the twins, head cocked, listening to the voice of the armor, and frowned.

Petal turned back to the stranger.

"Don't talk to it," Piper hissed.

"Hi," Petal said. "My name is Petal Anchialine."

The stranger glanced at Gauge, who said nothing.

"It doesn't understand," said Piper.

But Piper was wrong.

"Bring the message to your old machines," the stranger told Petal. "Speak to them." The musical, serious voice was the same; the accent was Gauge's, or Halocline's, the accent of the oldest motiles, of ghosts.

"What message?" Petal asked.

"This message," the stranger said. "The world is ending."

They took the stranger—who seemed less than clear on the concept of names but who agreed, after a conversation with Gauge in that old language, to answer to *Tirah*—back to the city. (Petal asked what the name meant, but Tirah ignored the question, and Gauge refused to translate, saying the word was too ambiguous.)

Septentrion's most ancient intelligences—Tirah's "old machines"—were not properly part of the city at all. They were in communication with the city's computational matrix, but predated it—predated Septentrion altogether, Gauge Malpais said, and perhaps the Earth as well, at least in its current form, belonging instead to that ancient age when there had still been stars in the sky, when light from distant galaxies had still reached the Earth and the quintessence had not yet stretched the gulfs between those galaxies wider than the observable universe: the age that had birthed the metric.

Tirah's first request—transcription to city tape, direct contact with those intelligences—was held for review by City Integrity, an agency of which Petal had never even heard. But there were places— the sacella—where a corporeal citizen could still address the ancient intelligences, and City Authority had granted Tirah provisional citizenship. The request for incorporation into the city's matrix being denied, Tirah had therefore requested a new body, built to specification. City Integrity objected to this as well, but—Swan argued, as Tirah's advocate—the ethics were clear, as were the precedents. City Authority could not without cause sentence a citizen, even a provisional one, to be carried around in Petal's pocket like a pet imp; nor could a citizen that desired to be motile be confined to some structure as a ghost; nor, without cause, could City Authority withdraw Tirah's status as a provisional citizen, once granted.

And so Tirah's new body—the image of the projection Petal and Piper had first seen on the mountain—began to grow, layer by layer, in one of the Archive's fabricaria; and while it was growing, Petal and Gauge would sit with Tirah in the salons, or walk, Petal carrying the little sphere in one hand through the dappled leaf-shadows of the Archive gardens, Tirah's projection walking beside.

✧

"You're spending all your time at the Archive," Piper said, sitting up.

It was true enough. Tonight Petal had come home late, late enough that Piper was already in bed.

"I *asked* you to come," Petal said defensively. "It's interesting. You'd think it was interesting, too, if you'd just come."

"Interesting," Piper repeated, making it sound like something obscene.

"Piper," Petal said, "this is important."

Piper fell back into the bedclothes, with an exasperated noise.

"This is the biggest thing," Petal persisted, "the biggest thing that's happened in our lifetimes. Maybe the biggest thing that's *going* to happen, now, *ever*. I'm not going to miss it. If that means spending all my time at the Archive, fine."

"*That's* not why you're spending all your time at the Archive," Piper said darkly, from somewhere in the nest of bedding.

"What's that supposed to mean?" Petal demanded.

But Piper wouldn't answer.

✧

Tirah's message—"the world is ending"—was too huge a thing for Petal to take in, and the details, Tirah said, the explanations and justifications, required mathematics that Petal would need years to begin to learn. So mostly they talked of other things: Petal of the city and life in it, Gauge of the history and legend out of which Tirah came—and Tirah of those who had sent the message, and what they had given up in sending it.

The history, Petal knew, at least in outline: that once, when the quintessence had been weak, there had been stars in the sky, and worlds around those stars, worlds found, or made, as the people of those primordial times had gone out from this Earth, or one much like it; that they had built ships, magical ships the size of cities, to sail between those stars, almost as fast as light, and then faster. That as the quintessence grew stronger and threatened to tear those stars from one another they had knit and forged the metric out of space-time itself to hold them together. And that it had held, for an age as long as all the time before, linking the worlds of humanity by secret fast ways, even as the sky went dark.

But in the end, Petal also knew, even the metric had not been enough—the quintessence, pulling apart the nodes of the metric and pulling the metric itself ever tighter, had prevailed.

Hoddmímis Holt, the world that had sent Tirah, had been built perhaps two hundred million years ago, as Septentrion counted years; built when there were still stars in the sky, and when ships like *Thus is the Heaven* still plied the metric, knitting a web that spanned galaxies, even as the quintessence was drawing those galaxies apart, emptying the spaces between the stars to drown each galaxy alone in red darkness. It was a great city, as Petal understood it, built mostly of things more clever and more enduring than brute matter: noötic mass, dissociated fields, knots of space-time akin to the metric itself; and home only to purely computational intelligences, as far beyond the computationals of Septentrion as the Holt itself was beyond Septentrion's towers of carbon and crystal.

The Holt was made in nearly full knowledge of the inevitability of the quintessence and the limitations of the metric, and made to last. Its makers poised it on the edge of a singularity with the mass of twenty billion stars, the core of a galaxy far from humanity's birthplace, a black hole so enormous that even light would take days to girdle its vast event horizon; and there it spun, balanced at the equilibrium point between the singularity's hungry mass and the even hungrier quintessence.

"I wish I could see it, one day," Petal said.

"It's not possible," said Tirah.

"Because we don't have the ships?" Petal asked, turning to Gauge. "We could build one, couldn't we? We have the records, in the Archive?"

Gauge hesitated.

"Even if we could," it said, "you saw what happened to Tirah's ship. . . ."

"A stronger one."

"To force the metric open," Tirah said, "in these times, against the quintessence, takes an unimaginable amount of energy. The mass of your whole world, converted to energy, and its sun along with it, would not open the metric wide enough to admit a grain of sand."

"So you're stuck with us," Petal said. "You can't go home."

"You still don't understand," Tirah said. "The mass of Hoddmímis Holt itself only just sufficed to part the metric for a ship; and the ship did not survive."

"The mass of the entire habitat?" Gauge said.

"The habitat. And the singularity." Tirah's eyes were dark and deep. "The singularity, the Holt, and everyone in it. They sacrificed themselves, all of them, to send this message. And still, it almost wasn't enough."

"Why?" Petal asked. "What could be that important?"

"The world is ending," Tirah said. "The features of the metric that protect this space—any space—from the quintessence, are like loops knotted in a string. As the string is drawn tighter, the loops begin to slip—first little by little, then all at once. The knot is pulled tight, and the loops disappear."

"You came to warn us," Petal said. "But how can we stop it? What can we do?"

"Nothing," Tirah said. "Already the metric is stretched tight. Soon this loop will collapse."

"The world is ending," said Petal.

"How soon?" asked Gauge.

"Perhaps a few billion seconds," Tirah said. "Perhaps only tens of millions. Perhaps less."

"A few lives of the living," Gauge translated, "or perhaps only a season."

"That's how much time is left?" asked Petal.

"The computationals of Hoddmímis Holt could fit eternity in an instant," Tirah said. "These forms, bound by matter and time—" the projection gestured at Petal, at Gauge—"these forms cannot."

"Then why?" Petal asked. "Why even tell us about it, if there's nothing we can do?"

"This world will end," Tirah said. "But space and time will go on." Tirah looked at Petal. "If a new world is to be born, then space and time, too, must come to an end."

☼

"There's something wrong with you," Piper said, as Petal was leaving for the Archive again.

"There is not," Petal said.

"There's a rogue process loose in your head," Piper said. "A parasitic replicator. That—*thing* put it there. It's taken over your brain and turned you into a functional."

"Shut up," said Petal.

"It didn't work on me," Piper said, "because I'm not *stupid*."

"We're twins," said Petal. "If I'm stupid, you're stupid, too."

"Different wombs," Piper said. "Different neonatal environments. Also I'm a hundred days older than you, and everyone knows Primroses are *stupid*."

"Everyone knows Crickets are crybabies," Petal said. "So quit crying and shut up."

And Petal left.

3. The Message
t_Ω-3.2369×10^7

After that Piper spoke to Petal less, if anything, and Petal spent even less time at home; and by the time Tirah's body was ready, Piper was hardly speaking to Petal at all.

City Integrity, in its objections to Tirah's incarnation, had gained one concession: before being allowed to enter one of the sacella and make Hoddmímis Holt's case to the "old machines," Tirah would first have to make it to City Authority. The room where Tirah was to testify was a semicircular chamber the size of a netball arena, right at the top of the Archive under a broad low dome. Gauge Malpais said the room had served some governmental purpose, once, long ago when the

Archive had been a palace, and then it had been a reading room, later, in an austere period when scrolls and paper codices had been in fashion, but now it stood empty more often than not.

The desks were still there, though, in row on concentric row. Not all the desks were filled; Petal was disappointed. A hundred or so embodied citizens occupied perhaps a quarter of the seats: mostly the living, with a scattering of motiles. The ghost of the Archive was present as well, of course, and the reading room had its own genius loci, an ancient sessile intelligence, affiliated in some way with City Integrity, that Gauge called the Aedile; and according to them a few hundred computationals and functionals were attending via the Archive's systems. But that was all.

Piper, of course, had refused to come.

"Provisional citizen Tirah," the Aedile said, "you may begin your testimony."

The Aedile had produced a podium, an imposing thing from palace times, twice Petal's height, a monolith of mirror-polished blue-black set with seven silver stars in an asymmetrical pattern—an old symbol for the city, Gauge said.

Tirah ignored it, standing next to the podium, looking small and serious.

"Words will not convince you," Tirah told the audience, living and constructed and computational. "Not enough of you. Not in time."

Tirah looked directly at Petal.

"The truth must be shown."

Tirah's dark eyes were the sky.

The sky was full of stars.

✫

There were stars everywhere Petal looked, and more stars in the spaces between the stars, and galaxies. It was a young sky, in a young universe, one that still echoed in microwave frequencies from the report of its birth; and if Petal looked hard enough into the spaces between the galaxies it was possible to see almost all the way back to the beginning of time.

Humanity was young, too, just a few million years into its great diaspora, ubiquitous in its home galaxy, but barely beginning to venture across the gulfs beyond. The quintessence was a scientific curiosity, its effects visible only at the largest scales and of interest only to cosmogoners and eschatologists.

The metric was not yet even a dream.

Tirah and Petal were born in a sphere habitat sweeping the circumstellar disk of an orange main-sequence sun less than a hundred million years old and less than a thousand light-years from humanity's birthplace. Tirah was ten years Petal's senior, and the most brilliant philosopher of the age. Petal was Tirah's best student.

They were collaborators, rivals, lovers. Their home was a place of coral cities in warm shallow seas, golden plains dotted with wooden towns, towering low-gravity forests wreathed in permanent cloud. They climbed the trees in the tall forests and swam in the shallow seas and danced the carnivals in the towns, and all the time they threw ideas back and forth like jugglers' clubs. They took what humanity thought it knew about the shape and structure and history and future of the universe and pried it apart and put it back together into elegant new structures that were simpler and at the same time more fruitful than what had come before, the epicenter of a tidal wave of new physics and new engineering that rippled outward from the sphere habitat's orange sun and washed up on every inhabited shore.

Tirah was the one who first proved what humanity had long feared: that thanks to the accelerating quintessence, the end of time would come, not with an inrushing collapse and the fiery birth of a new universe, nor with a long twilight and unimaginably longer darkness as the last stars were born and died and the last singularities evaporated—but with a violent breach, as galaxy was torn from galaxy, star from star, and in the end atom from atom and quark from quark, world-line from world-line, snapping the links of the causal networks that bound the vacuum together; and that this end would come, not in the uncountable eons of black hole decay nor yet the trillion centuries to the natural death of the last stars, but in a number of years measured in mere billions.

Humanity's cosmos, though still in its infancy, was doomed never to see old age.

But Tirah and Petal uncovered consolations in their work, discoveries that pointed the way to new modes of conveyance and communication, flowerings of knowledge that promised both to knit scattered humanity more closely together and to let humanity explore every corner of the young cosmos before it was taken away.

And there was their greatest invention, the most lasting, the inspiration that would give humanity the ability to tie galaxies and stars and worlds together even as the universe was torn apart around them, and cheat the quintessence, for a time: the theory of the metric.

So despite the somber truths they had uncovered, it was said of Petal and Tirah, as they grew old together, that they had done more for the inhabitants of humanity's brief-lived universe than anyone could ask.

But Petal had one last discovery to make. Petal, who had never been willing to surrender to fate, never been willing to admit that mortality was inevitable: Petal, in Tirah and Petal's old age, was the one who proved that the darkness and isolation of the quintessence need not be the end.

It was a known result, so old as to be almost forgotten among the bones of the earliest discarded cosmologies, that the far future of a flat universe—smooth and dark and empty after the last matter was gathered into the last singularities and the singularities themselves had finally evaporated in the slow trickle of virtual particles through event horizons—was mathematically isomorphic to the universe's distant past: similarly smooth, similarly empty of matter yet filled with energy; but radically different in scale—the unimaginably large, mirroring the unimaginably small.

Petal showed that same would hold true of the far future of the quintessence—not an empty universe, but a universe of furious energy, its edge receding so quickly that light, if there were still light, could not cross the width of an atomic nucleus before the expansion of space itself would stretch that distance to infinity. Petal proved that the infinite distances, the infinite divergence, the causal rupture implied by the quintessence portended not a cosmos of infinite scale, but a cosmos *without* scale: a cosmos of distances that, because infinite, were unmeasurable, and because unmeasurable—meaningless. Small and large would become one. The same physical mechanism that would tear the cosmos apart, Petal demonstrated, would provide the transformation mapping the final singularity of infinite expansion onto the initial singularity of infinite compression.

Petal was the one who showed that beyond the end of their Universe was a new beginning. That if, as Tirah had told Petal and Gauge in the gardens of the Archive, time and space were to come to an end—still, a new future lay beyond.

Petal was the one who gave them hope.

But as long as the metric was in place—Petal's mathematics also showed—the divergence could never go all the way to infinity. Even in its final state, with Earth and all the homes of humanity torn apart, the metric's nodes collapsed to lifeless, dimensionless points, the vertices that linked them pulled to threads narrower than a photon and stretched beyond the edges of any observable universe, the metric would remain, the nodes would remain causally connected, and distance would still have meaning. The old cosmos, though uninhabited, uninhabitable, stretched and twisted beyond recognition, would never truly die, and the new cosmos would never be born.

But that fate, Petal was sure, would be averted by a later age. When the metric no longer served to link the worlds, but—for a time— still provided them a bulwark against the quintessence, the last custodians of the metric would break it down. They would trade those worlds' last days for the possibility of a future.

The old universe would pass away, and the new would be allowed to begin.

☼

Petal, in the old reading room at the top of the Archive, knew this was fiction. Recorded lives—real and reconstructed and invented, with more or less structure, more or less control, more or less agency— were not rare in the city, and Petal had lived enough of them to recognize this one for what it was.

There had never been a Petal or a Tirah born circling an orange sun under a star-filled sky. The reality of the quintessence and the theory of the metric were too complex for any one living mind to contain, let alone invent; humanity had come to know both through the patient accumulation of knowledge over centuries, the slow work of generations of synthesis, not through the flash of insight of some solitary genius or even some pair of geniuses. "Petal's" final inspiration—the potential for the birth of a new cosmos out of the fatal, final unraveling of the world-lines of the old, and the necessity of the dismantling of the metric, if that unraveling was to be completed—had not been known at all to ancient times; only in the long dark time after the ascendancy of the quintessence, the constriction of the metric and the final diaspora, had it been discovered, and even then not by the living nor yet by the calculating minds of computationals such as lived in Septentrion's city systems, but by the massed intellect of Hoddmímis Holt, as far beyond Septentrion as the city was beyond the bees in Cutter's garden.

Even now the mathematics of it, that only moments ago had seemed so clear, so much Petal's own, were vanishing from Petal's mind like frost in sunlight.

But Petal understood the conclusion.

There was one place—here, at the nexus where all the metric's strands wound together; here, on this world built in memory of humanity's birthplace—one place where the knot of the metric could be cut. Here.

The Earth, Petal knew, had to be destroyed.

☼

The sacella were placed under guard. Tirah was confined to the Archive grounds. Gauge was allowed to visit, and Campestral, and a few others—mostly motiles in the service of the Archive, or of City Integrity. Petal was not among them.

"Well?" Petal asked Gauge, after one of the latter's visits.

"We spoke about city history and city governance," Gauge said. "I answered Tirah's questions as best I could and showed how to invoke an archivist to learn more. After that we hardly spoke."

"It's not fair," said Petal. "They can't just keep someone locked in the Archive forever."

"The Aedile says they can," Gauge said. "But I wonder."

They were on a terrace above the great square of Limit Cardinal. Below them was a makeshift camp, a few dozen shelters, some of those who had been in the audience for Tirah's testimony, and more who had only listened to those who had. Projections twisted in the air above them: abstract geometries, meaningless in less than five dimensions, that nonetheless plucked at Petal's mathematical dream-memories of the metric and the quintessence—or crude political graffiti, stylized City Authority figures performing acts anatomically improbable for any of the living, and meaningless to the Authority ghosts. There was chanting. There was music.

"Can it be done?" Petal asked. "What Tirah wants, I mean."

"Tirah seems to think so," Gauge said. "The Archive ghosts think it's likely that the machines that manage the metric still exist, among those that could be reached through the sacella."

"Would they do what Tirah asked?" Petal said.

"I don't know," said Gauge. "But apparently City Authority doesn't want to find out."

"They can't keep Tirah locked away forever," Petal repeated. "These citizens won't allow it. They want Tirah to be heard."

The motile's smooth head moved in a birdlike sideways bob, not in disagreement, but not in complete agreement either.

"Some of them want that," Gauge said. "Some of them want to dismantle City Authority and institute distributed governance. Some of them want heat rationing. Some of them want incarnation rights for functionals. Some of them want *dis*incarnation rights and city tape allocation for motiles and biologicals. Some of them want the Corn Divinity to bring back the Moon."

"The *what* to do *what?*" said Petal.

"Never mind," said Gauge.

"They want change," Petal said.

"Or they want things the way they used to be," Gauge said.

"Is that so bad?" Petal asked.

"No," the motile said. Its head moved again. "But I don't think it's possible."

They were silent for a little while, looking out over the camp, watching the twisting mathematical shapes.

"What did you see?" Petal asked quietly, still watching the projections. "At the Archive, I mean, when Tirah testified."

Gauge took some time to answer.

"I think the message was the same," it said eventually. "What form it took—what Tirah meant to say to each of us, what each of us brought to it . . ." The motile made an equivocal gesture. "Who knows?"

"But the message—" Petal asked—"was it true?"

"I think we all saw what we all saw," Gauge said.

"You know what I mean," Petal said. "Was Tirah telling the truth?"

"What is the truth?" Gauge asked. "I spoke to some computationals who attended. They agreed that the mathematics seemed compelling. But also that what Tirah showed us—what Tirah showed them, even, vastly more complex and detailed than what you and I saw, I'm sure—was only a simplification, an approximation. Not even an approximation. An analogy. A toy model, to demonstrate certain aspects of a theory. Does the theory represent the truth?" It made the equivocal gesture again. "They couldn't say."

"If what Tirah told us is true . . ." Petal began.

"If what Tirah told us is true," Gauge said, "we're unlikely to live long enough to invent the science that would let us build the instruments that would let us perform the experiments that would tell us whether what Tirah told us is true."

"But if what Tirah told us is true," Petal said again—"would you do it? Would you break down the metric?"

"Would I break down the only thing protecting us from the quintessence, you mean?" Gauge asked. "Would I destroy the world?"

"If you want to put it like that," Petal said.

"If it was true?" said Gauge.

"If you *knew* it was true," said Petal. "If you knew the world was going to end, anyway. Tomorrow, or next week, or next year."

The motile was silent. Petal watched the twisting shapes, and listened to the chanting crowd. The chant was always changing but was still hypnotically deterministic, the output perhaps of some uncharacteristically articulate functional.

"I don't know," Gauge said, finally. "If I was there, at the end—if I knew, if I was certain—I suppose I would. Why not?" It looked at Petal. "But what if you didn't know? What if you *couldn't* be certain? Would you do it, then? That's the difficult choice."

Petal had no answer to that.

"Piper said—" Petal began, and hesitated. "Piper said Tirah put something in my head. Like a trophic facilitator, or an epistemic façade."

"I wouldn't worry about that." If the motile had had a face, Petal thought, it might have smiled. "I'm sure City Integrity would have noticed; and that sort of thing is much harder to do than Piper probably thinks, anyway," it said. "Much harder, especially, to do to the living."

"I suppose," Petal said.

Gauge looked down at the crowd.

"I don't think Tirah understands the living that well, really," it said. "Or any of us, for that matter, decadent throwbacks that we are. I'm sure we're not what Hoddmímis Holt expected to find, when they sent Tirah here."

"They probably expected something like themselves," Petal said.

"Exactly," said Gauge. "So Tirah has had to improvise. But the only thing put into your head—" the motile tapped its own—"is an idea. What to do with that idea . . ." It made that gesture again.

. . . is up to me, Petal thought.

Aloud, Petal said, "Will you give Tirah something?"

"I don't see why not," Gauge said.

It took the offering: a crystal globe, small enough to be enclosed in one hand, its inner surface ringed in projected blue and brown and green, dotted with swirls of white cloud, the whole lit by some unseen source with a glow of sunrise orange. On close inspection the green resolved into cloud forests, the brown to golden grass. And on the crystal's shadowed side, almost invisible, were the reflections of stars.

"It's very pretty," Gauge said.

"Halocline helped me make it," Petal said. "Will you take it? Please?"

"Of course," said Gauge.

"I just want Tirah to know I haven't forgotten," Petal said.

✧

"You're going to get caught," said Piper.

Petal hauled the armor down from the shelf where Hare kept it. In its boxy stored form it was surprisingly light, though awkward.

"Are you going to tell on me?" asked Petal.

"No," said Piper. "But you're going to get caught."

It was two nights later. Tirah had accepted Petal's gift, Gauge had said, but had given the motile no message.

"At least I'll get caught *doing* something," Petal said, and shut the door in Piper's face.

The first part of putting on the armor you had to do yourself: unfolding the gray slab butterfly of the vest, head through the collar; heavy tails swinging loose at front and back. Fingers down into the gloves, toes down into the boots.

—*Cadet Petal Angyldsbearn,* the armor said.

The voice of the armor was a little like Hare's but dispassionate and precise, without Hare's warmth but also without judgment or impatience. Its name was Castre, which Hare had told Piper and Petal meant *Rook.*

Its voice wasn't really a voice, most of the time; most of the time it was only in your head. Likewise you didn't really have to talk for Castre to hear you, just think about talking.

—*Castre.*

—*I am authorized to protect you in emergency situations,* Castre said.

It spoke the language of Meridion, or one of them—Hare said there were two, the tribunes' speech and the cohorts'. Castre was of the former; the name it gave Petal, *Angyldsbearn*, was of the latter— Hare's birth-name had been Angyld Haemedsbearn. But the tribunes' speech was not far from that of Septentrion's older ghosts and motiles, like Gauge and the Aedile, and Castre had been in Septentrion for a long time.

"This *is* an emergency situation," Petal said—aloud, but quietly, and in the privacy of the helmet. The armor moved then, helmet and collar locking, the vest closing around Petal like a live thing—Piper had never liked that, when Hare had let them try the armor, had thought it was creepy, but to Petal it was comforting, like a parent tugging a child's jacket down. Like being held.

Petal crept out of Anchialine House and down to the canal, silent as only the armor could be, and invisible even to the City's senses. The water in the canal was rippling glass, black and empty as the sky except where it reflected the watch-lamps of the houses above. Petal shivered, momentarily, inside the armor, imagining the quintessence already victorious, the canal a fissure in the Earth, the night welling through like a live thing.

And then Petal looked to the horizon, where the globe Halocline had helped make for Tirah glowed in the armor's sight, pinpointing Tirah's location through buildings and walls and fields.

Petal gathered the armor's strength, and leapt.

4. The Lake
$$t_\Omega\text{-}3.0157\times10^7$$

They all thought it was Hare's fault. Swan thought so, Cutter thought so, Hare thought so. The only one who knew better was Piper and that was because Piper knew it was Piper's fault. *You'll get caught,* Piper had said, but Petal hadn't been, Petal had gone straight up over the wall of the Archive like some thief in a children's story and stolen Tirah right out of it, back over the wall and gone. And now Petal was gone, and Hare's armor which Petal had been wearing, and Tirah was gone, too, not to be found anywhere in the city, according to City Oversight. And they'd stolen a boat, a fast one, and City Oversight should have been able to find that, but it couldn't, and Hare said that probably Petal and Tirah had disabled the locator, which the armor could have shown them how to do. And there were City Response boats out, and flyers, but if Petal and Tirah had just pointed their boat straight across the lake and told it *go*, there was no way the City Response boats were going to catch it, and the weather was getting bad for flyers. Gauge, the Archive motile, said that once there would have been eyes higher up, eyes that could have seen the boat from space, weather or no weather, but that like the mirrors they'd one by one drifted out of position and nobody'd seen any urgent need to replace them. And so Petal and Tirah had got clean away, and nobody knew where they were going. Except Piper.

"Meridion," Piper said. "They're going to Meridion."

They'd all gone after them, Hare and Cutter and Swan, and Gauge, and Tanner Campestral from City Response.

And Piper had come, too, which the rest discovered when their boat was two hours out and a dozen leagues from the city.

"I left a note," Piper said.

"And you think that makes it all right?" Swan said.

"It's not fair," said Piper. "Petal's the one who stole Hare's armor and broke into the Archive. I haven't done anything wrong."

"Yes, you have," said Cutter, "and we're turning around."

"You can't," said Piper. "You're four hours behind Petal already."

The boat flew over the black water. Hare looked back, toward the city, already vanished in the wintry haze, and then forward again, out toward the southern horizon and the wind-whipped waves, flecked with white.

"Every hour we lose," Hare said, "our chances of catching them get that much worse."

And so Piper had stayed.

And now they were arguing, Campestral with Piper's parents and all three parents with each other.

"Meridion!"

Piper had to repeat it twice more, louder each time, before the adults would leave off arguing and turn to listen.

"It makes sense," said Hare.

Campestral looked at Gauge.

"Hare knows Meridion best," the motile said. "But it's old, like Septentrion, and like Septentrion its roots are very, very old. Whatever Tirah meant to do here, I imagine it could be done there."

"Would Meridion City Authority let them in?" Swan asked.

"They'd have to pass the tagmata first," Hare said. "I don't know. It might, it might not."

"Tirah," Gauge said, "can be persuasive."

They all fell silent.

"We'll be on the southern shore in another hour," Gauge offered. "I'm sure we'll overtake them before nightfall."

But they didn't.

☼

There was no harbor on the south shore, not that Petal could see, no sign of civilization whatsoever, only a long stretch of gray gravel beach and behind it low dunes topped with scraggly dry grass, its yellow so faded it was hardly more colorful than the gravel. In the end Petal just had the boat run itself straight into the shallows, the keel grating on the bottom and the whole boat finally tipping over sideways, half a cable from the shore.

Petal hopped over the rail into water waist deep, expecting cold, but in the armor it was like the water had no temperature at all. There was a slight hesitation in the armor's movements, as it pushed through the water, and the faint scraping of boots in gravel, transmitted through layers of insulation, but that was all.

"I'll carry you," said Petal.

"No need," said Tirah, slipping into the water with hardly a splash. Petal was taller now, in the armor, and the water came halfway up Tirah's chest.

"You're not cold?" Petal asked, watching the water soak through the top of Tirah's tunic, right up to the collar.

"The water is close to freezing," Tirah said. "But that temperature is well within this body's tolerances."

"It's just as well. I didn't think to bring warm clothes." Petal looked back, into the fog, in the direction of the city. "I didn't think much at all, really." Petal sighed. "I just did it."

"We should keep moving," Tirah said.

"We should," Petal said. "And it'll still be faster if I carry you."

They made it to the shore in three parabolic bounds, and Petal only dropped Tirah on the first one, and then not really, the armor itself taking over before they could lose their balance; on the second jump Petal was ready for the awkward footing, landing in the water and the loose gravel, and by the third they were on the beach. Petal kept on holding Tirah, sometimes with one arm, as they clambered over the dunes. To the armor, the weight of Tirah's body was nothing.

Beyond the dunes they came to a plain, the dry grass no more than ankle-high and stretching as far as the eye could see, under a gray sky. The sun was somewhere low in the west, invisible in the fog; one mirror was still overhead, a narrow, skewed oval of brighter gray.

"Which way?" said Tirah.

Petal cycled through the armor's vision modes, infrared and image-enhancement and passive and active radar. There was nothing but grass.

"South," said Petal, trying to sound confident. "We go south."

A fine, almost dry snow was beginning to fall.

✧

They found Petal's boat as the last mirror was setting, a line of lurid red low over the water. By then Piper was tired, and it was very cold. Hare ran their boat up next to Petal's, keel raised—apparently Petal hadn't known how to do that—and had it hold itself in place with the impellers, as Hare and Campestral clambered over the other boat's railing to its sloping deck. Snow was starting to pile up against the side of the wheelhouse.

"Gone," Hare pronounced. "Cutter, tell that boat to back off a little; I'm going to see if I can get this one righted. Campestral, hold on to something."

Piper and the others watched from a safe distance as, Hare retracting the keel, Petal's boat tilted and slid and finally splashed down level, its prow slewing around sideways, before Hare and Campestral got it pointed in the right direction and headed toward shore. Then they followed.

They got both boats to push themselves as far up the gravelly shore as they would go; and Gauge, which said it didn't mind the wet, climbed out in shin-deep water and helped each of them out and onto dry land, such as it was: icy, with new snow crunching under their boots. It was full dark now, the only illumination from the boats' lamps, and the smaller lights Campestral and Piper's parents had clipped to their City Response jackets.

From the boat, Gauge produced packs, for itself and for the adults. They didn't have armor like the set Petal had taken—no one in Septentrion had armor like that, any more than they had spears or siege engines or ironclad warships. Piper's parents and Campestral had City Response suits, with environmental liners and smart collars that would keep them alive in a fire or a flood or an avalanche. Piper just had an insulated jacket and winter boots, and a smaller pack, containing a somewhat random collection of things that had seemed as though they might be useful: climbing kit, water bags, a survival blanket, a warmer hat, a box of Petal's favorite tea, a change of underwear. Now it seemed pitifully inadequate. Even the hat wasn't warm enough.

Hare and Campestral went aside and spoke to one another in low voices, words Piper couldn't hear over the slap of the water against the sides of the boats. Then Campestral headed up the beach, disappearing out of the arc of light cast by the boat lamps, and Hare came back, alone.

"This way," Hare said.

"Won't the snow cover their tracks?" asked Piper.

"I'm sure it already has," Swan said.

They followed Hare up into the dunes. The snow was heavier now. Piper watched it falling, in the glow of the jacket lamps, and tried not to stumble. To the sides Piper saw snow, dry grass, more snow. Piper's own feet were lost in the darkness.

Piper saw Campestral's light first, and then a Campestral-shaped hole in the snow, and Campestral's face, or rather a horizontal band of it, between a high collar and a hat pulled down low.

"How far down do your eyes go?" Campestral asked Gauge.

"Ten microns or so," Gauge said. "I can see your face quite clearly. What there is of it."

"Good."

"You're hoping I'll be able to see them," Gauge said. "I can't, in this." Gauge gestured at the falling snow. "Not from any distance. We'd practically have to trip over them."

"Let's hope we do, then," said Hare. "Or that it lets up. Come on. Piper, stick with Swan."

They set out, trudging across the snow.

☼

Petal and Tirah made more than twenty leagues that first day, the flat land of the lakeshore giving way to rolling hills, and there was just no reason to stop, not when Petal didn't feel tired, not when the going was so easy, and Tirah so light in Petal's arms. Petal could have kept on, continuing into the dark. But the scale of what they'd done, what Petal was committing to, was starting to sink in.

They'd outrun the storm, or it had passed over them, and they were under a clear black sky with only a faint dusting of silver sparks, very high up, that Tirah said was probably debris from colliding mirrors. The snow was smooth and very flat and seemed, through the armor's eyes, to shine with its own light.

"What will it be like?" Petal asked—meaning the new cosmos. "Will there be stars?"

"Not to be known," Tirah said. "It might be the same. It might be different. What's most important is that it will *be.*"

Petal's hand sought and found Tirah's.

"I'm glad you're here," Petal said.

Tirah said nothing.

They couldn't really touch, not through the armor, and in this cold the armor wouldn't have opened if Petal had asked. But it was almost as though they could.

Three thousand leagues, Petal and Tirah, just the two of them.

And at the end of it, the end of the world.

Well, Petal thought, *we've been alone before.* Remembering the warm light of the sphere habitat, the high trees and the seas of golden grass.

It was a lie at worst, at best a dream, but Petal clung to it anyway.

They lay there, under the black sky, and before long the armor let Petal sleep.

☼

They didn't find Petal and Tirah that night. They lasted about three hours, in the dark, as it grew colder and colder, and by the time they stopped they were in snow up over the tops of their boots, and Piper's toes were numb. Hare and Campestral went off again, with Cutter this time, and this time it sounded like an argument.

"W-what do you think t-they're arguing about?" Piper asked, teeth chattering. "Whether to stop or k-keep going?"

"Gauge could keep going," Swan said. "Maybe Hare could. Maybe Cutter. But you can't, and I'm fading."

Hare came back, pack dangling from one hand, Cutter following behind.

"What now?" asked Swan.

We go back, Piper thought, for a moment—hoped, almost—Hare might say.

But Hare didn't. Hare didn't say anything. Nor did Cutter, or Swan.

And Piper thought about what it would be like, back in their room at Anchialine House, with Petal's bed empty, neatly made, to stay neatly made and empty forever.

"We keep going," Piper said. "Right?"

Hare looked at Swan and Cutter.

"We keep going," said Cutter.

Swan nodded.

"All right," said Hare. "But for tonight, we're done. Piper, help me with this tent."

They unpacked it and laid it out on the snow, an adjustable structure that could collapse down to shelter just one bedroll, or open to a comfortable bunkhouse for a dozen people. By unspoken agreement, they kept it small.

"I'm s-sorry," Piper said, still shivering, as they waited for the shelter to inflate.

"For what?" asked Hare.

"For slowing you d-down."

Hare took off the City Response jacket and wrapped it around Piper's shoulders.

"You're not," Hare said, holding Piper tight. "We'd have to rest soon anyway. Besides, the armor has thermal camouflage, and that body Petal's friend's wearing is like a motile's; it'll be barely above ambient temperature. We were never going to find them tonight. Not if they didn't want to be found."

In the shelter, in the dark, the four of them packed tightly together, Piper nestled between Hare and Swan, Piper said:

"So we're counting on Petal to give up."

Hare sighed. "I suppose we are."

Piper said, "That might not happen."

Hare said, "I know."

5. The Ice
$$t_\Omega\text{-}3.0132\times10^7$$

The flat plain of the lakeshore gave way to rolling hills, and the hills piled up into something like mountains, but low and rounded, slumped under the weight of time. At first there were trees, stunted evergreens in protected gullies, clinging to the slopes that faced the sun or Septentrion's mirror-track, and once or twice Petal saw birds, or even some small ground-dwelling creature, camouflage-white against the snow but marked for the armor by the warmth of its breath in the cold air. But the mirrors narrowed from circles to ellipses to hairline scribbles of light and then disappeared altogether, so there was only the sun, a cold white circle low over the horizon ahead of them, and the birds and small animals vanished, and the trees dwindled away to nothing, and the grass, and one day—the first of Germinal, Petal's birthday—they crossed a ridge swept clear of snow by the wind, and there was just a jumble of gray-black rock, the bones of the old mountain shattered into a million hand-sized fragments.

And they came down the other side of the ridge and there it was, flat and unbroken as far as the eye could see: the ice. Tirah said it most likely covered the whole world, apart from the mirror tracks, and perhaps a narrow band near the equator, and Castre—whose route they were following now, the route Hare, hardly older than Petal was now, had taken north—agreed.

In Hare's tales of the journey to Septentrion—in the handful told to the twins, at least, and it was only a handful, so few that Petal could almost count them—there was rarely danger, and never any sense of fear. Even the dangers—cyclone storms of hail and lightning, brittle icefalls a kilometer high, pocket gardens inhabited only by mad ghosts and hostile automata—were described sometimes as wonders, sometimes as obstacles, but mostly as brute phenomena.

Mostly there was strangeness, and sometimes beauty, and always an immense emptiness. Of Hare—of any living witness, anyone to be made lonely by the solitude or small by the inhuman scale of the empty world—there was hardly a trace. *We did this,* Hare would say, or *I did that,* matter-of-fact. *We cleared the bridge. We scaled the cliff. I broke through the ice.* What Hare had felt, then, or how Hare felt now, remembering, was not part of the story.

Of Hare's companions, how they had died, Hare would say very little. Only once, when Petal had pressed, Hare had said: *We told ourselves we were the most dangerous things on the ice. And we were right.* Piper and Petal had argued about what Hare had meant. And now Petal wondered.

It was easy, in the armor, to forget you were tired. Some of that was the strength it gave you, the easy movement, the way a step so effortlessly became a leap, a walk so effortlessly a run. It kept you fed, too—or the equivalent, the armor inserting itself into the cellular respiration process, providing its own stored power in place of the energy ordinarily released by glycolysis and phosphorylation—and hydrated. But it did something to your blood, as well, taking on some of the work that would ordinarily be done by your renal and digestive systems, so that you never had to go to the toilet and never had to throw up, and in the process—Castre had told them once—it adjusted the mix of your hormones and neurotransmitters to keep you alert and keep you committed to the mission.

Piper had been frightened by that, but Petal hadn't. It was like making a promise, Petal reasoned; making a promise, and then taking steps to be sure you couldn't break it, later, in some moment of weakness, even if you wanted to. And what was wrong with that?

So long as you promised to do the right thing.

✿

Over days, then weeks, they fell into a routine, and Petal fell into a marching rhythm, step by crunching step, at what the armor said was the most efficient pace, on this slippery, uneven ground. At any distance the packed snow looked flat, but close up it was a world of its own, a million tiny ridges, valleys, ranges, and plateaus, so that it was easy for Petal to lose all sense of scale, to hallucinate for long minutes that they were giants together, striding across that landscape leagues at a step. And there were colors: purples and grays and blues in the shadows, but new colors too that Petal had never seen. It had never before occurred to Petal that there might be such things as different shades of white, but there were.

It was not all flat and empty. There were crevasses, cracks in the ice, some of them quite wide, so that Petal and Tirah had to search a league or more up or down before finding a spot narrow enough to jump. And sometimes there wasn't any place Petal could jump, even in the armor, and they had the more arduous task of finding somewhere to climb down and back up again—with the help of the armor's strength, but carrying its weight as well, and sometimes Tirah's, a tricky problem of shear forces and friction and balance. There were mountains, only the wind-worn black peaks visible above the ice, barren islands in a frozen sea. Once they did cross a frozen sea, or perhaps a lake, green ice smooth as glass swept clean by the wind, and in the depths—Petal thought, though Tirah said it was imagination—there was the outline of some vast ship, its superstructure like the skyline of a sunken city. And once there *was* a city, or anyway a single tower, so tall they walked in its shadow for most of an afternoon: a glittering, tapering gray thing of angles and curves, in appearance more carved than built. The armor said that it went cables and cables down into the ice and that there was still heat, some power source deep inside, and Petal took twenty minutes to circle it looking for an opening, while Tirah tried on every frequency to find an active ghost or some working computational; but there were no doors, no windows, and no answers, and eventually they moved on.

Most commonly, where the armor's charts gave the names of towns, rivers, countries, there was nothing; only ice, from horizon to horizon. They kept going.

Sometimes they marched in darkness, and that was its own different world, the black sky above and the snow below flat and abstract in the armor's night eyes. More often after fifteen or twenty leagues they'd stop, and Petal would fall asleep hand in hand with Tirah, listening to Tirah's voice, as Tirah spun stories of the long-ago days of stars and galaxies, or of the metric's heyday, when a million worlds held tight against the quintessence, or of the all but incomprehensible computational life of Hoddmímis Holt in its long twilight. And Petal would dream of orange light and golden fields, sunlit brown feet dancing on sunlit brown wood.

Then the wan sun would come up, and they'd start again.

They were nearing the halfway point when they found the message.

After a hundred and seventy days on the ice, it had begun to thin, the sheet dividing into glaciers overlying old worn peaks, with moraines of tumbled black stone between, some of the head-sized stones bearing the marks of old tools. The islands of rock grew more frequent. Finally the ice gave way entirely, the glaciers ending abruptly in a fringe of house-sized seracs that in turn gave way to a narrow, blue-green lake edged with rotten ice, and beyond that a broad plain of brown, broken ground barely dusted with snow. But though the sun was ever so slightly warmer at this latitude, there were no mirrors and nothing living that Petal could see, neither plant nor animal.

They came down off the ice onto that brown plateau, and from there down to a dry lakebed, or the shore of some ancient shallow sea, a horizon-wide plain of dirty salt as wide and flat as the ice. A ruin bordered it, a Septentrion-sized badland of rust and broken glass, with here and there the remains of some structure more solidly built, a roofless house or a stretch of old guideway. It had no name on the armor's charts, which meant it must have been less than twenty thousand years old; but it looked to have been abandoned for much of that time.

Petal was wary, remembering Hare's stories; but nothing moved here now, according to Castre, nor was there any signal, any sign of computation or even of ghosts. That being the case, Petal insisted on investigating—even though, Tirah said, the city was far too new to be of any use to them. And so they picked their way down to the old shoreline, over tilted slabs and fallen panels half-buried in drifting sand.

Toward the southern edge a few towers still stood, twisting spires that would not have looked greatly out of place in some parts of Septentrion—except that their cleaners had broken down or been taken away long ago, so that they were all the same color, a uniform dusty brown, apart from those closest to the shore, which were spotted salt-white on their southern faces.

At the top of one of the southernmost towers, something glittered. Apart from sky-blue it was the first real color they had seen since they came down off the ice, and nothing would do for Petal but to climb it and see what it was.

When they drew near to the tower they saw that even that effort was unnecessary; the building was hollow, open on its northern side, and a spiral ramp led up through the core, a series of semicircular landings joined by curving staircases, most of them intact or nearly so; Petal could have made the ascent even without the armor. Before they reached the top they could see that what had drawn Petal's attention was a kind of dome or vault made from hundreds of glassy panels tinted in different colors, so that the light that shone down through it from the cold equatorial sun was washed with gold and green and coppery red. As they came out onto the sort of penthouse balcony that ringed the dome, they could see many of the other towers sported similar structures, but that every other was encrusted in dust and salt, where this one seemed to have been recently polished clean, and Petal wondered who or what had done it.

But then Petal chanced to look out over the balcony's still-intact railing to the salt plain, a cable and more below, and forgot all about the dome.

There, down on the plain, some way out from the old shoreline, someone had spread the black rock of the high country across the salt, spelling out the message in letters half a cable high. It read:

PETAL COME HOME WE LOVE YOU

☼

They found the same message, two days later, at the approximate midpoint of the salt plain. And again two days after that as they neared the opposite shore, this time sprayed safety-red across a crumbling cliff-face. Again on a boulder the size of Anchialine House, overlooking the saddle of a mountain pass. Again in the snowbound ruin of a small nameless city, at the foot of an advancing glacier at the edge of the southern ice sheet.

PETAL COME HOME WE LOVE YOU

Each time they changed course to put the message out of sight. Petal consulted the armor's charts and, with an aversion that was almost instinctual, steered for the emptiest parts of them, away from any landmarks, away from any place with a name.

It worked. When they were back on the ice (much the same as it had been, but different, too, the cold sun behind them now, the shadows in front of them lengthening day by marching day) and far enough off the direct great-circle line from Septentrion to Meridion, the messages stopped.

Petal felt no relief, only exasperation with the loss of time. There was something else, too—a kind of guilt, it might have been—but it was bound up with a lot of other feelings, homesickness and loneliness and regret and self-doubt, that Petal kept wrapped tight and locked behind thick walls. The armor helped with that, regulating Petal's blood chemistry, keeping Petal on task; the armor, and the sight of Tirah's solemn face.

Only sometimes at night, Petal would wake from a forgotten dream, face behind the armor mask wet with tears.

☼

Unbidden, Petal began to tell Tirah stories, Hare's stories of Meridion: of the tagmata, their colorful pageants and deadly rivalries, the games that were not quite wars, the wars that were not quite games; of a world out of storybooks, a world of honor and glory, of fierce passions and sudden, dramatic turns of fate. The armor's charts said they were getting close. There were mirrors in the sky again, and breaks in the ice—cold meltwater rivers meandering through gray valleys, stands of scraggly conifers. As they continued south these grew wider, till there were flocks of birds, forests that went to the horizon, marshes that took a day to circumnavigate. It was strange to see so much color, so much shadow, such stark contrasts between light and dark, after the months on the ice. Sometimes there were two or even three mirrors in the sky, and the land was correspondingly warmer, the vegetation richer—lush, even. There were plants Petal had never seen in Septentrion, not even in the conservatories, and the birds and animals the armor's eyes picked out now were camouflaged not in white but in angular patterns of dazzling color and deep shadow.

Tirah said the drifting mirrors, like those farther north, were a symptom of the quintessence, and the fraying of the metric.

When Meridion was only a few days away, the land began to climb, the marshes and streams to dry up. It was still warm, but the plants grew sparse, their leaves small and waxy and edged with thorns, the living creatures more furtive and less colorful. The ground grew rocky, and there was a brown pall in the southern sky that Castre said was smoke.

Finally they came down out of the high country, to a vantage point on the south face of a dry ridge. Petal could see all the way to the horizon, a dull shimmering silver that the armor's charts said was the shore of the antipodal sea, under a gray-white sky; and stretched along that shore, for leagues and leagues, glittering in the mirror-light and the light of the sun at Petal's back, the towers of the city. They were less than a day away, across a broad valley of yellow grass and stunted, solitary trees. But the middle distance was obscured, and Petal saw the source of the overcast, and of the smoke.

The valley was on fire.

"The mirrors are out of alignment," Tirah said. "Where the sunlight is multiplied, the land is hot and dry, and any small spark may lead to a conflagration."

—*Most fires are the result of human action,* Castre said.—*Even now.*

"We'll be careful," Petal said.

As they moved down to the plain, toward the smoke, the armor kicked into a higher state of alertness, and Petal with it. Petal had never been so conscious of the armor's chemical manipulations as now, as it picked a path down from rock to rock, and Petal, jumping, seemed to float rather than fall, to have an eternity to correct any small problem of balance, and then to catch Tirah, falling; while down on the plain every movement, every hint of a suspicious shape or texture was preternaturally clear.

—*This is a controlled area,* Castre said, *within the meaning of the agreement.*

"What does that mean?" Petal asked.

—*Under the terms of the 57th Diatagmatic Symbasis and its implementing regulations and orders, entry to the peripheral conservation area is permitted only to authorized persons.*

"Can you get us through?" Petal asked. "Would Hare's phyle help us? Angyld's, I mean, Angyld's tagma."

—*Dekarch Angyld Haemedsbearn has been absent without leave for more than one hundred eighty-three thousand hours,* Castre said.—*And your own field warrant has never been confirmed.*

Petal sighed and kept going.

As they came closer, the wind shifted, blowing the smoke away toward the west; and as the sun went lower and the shadows lengthened, the shapes of the distant towers became more distinct, their outlines more stark against the clearing sky, until finally Petal had to admit the truth of what they were seeing.

Meridion was in ruins.

"What happened?" Petal asked.

—*The breakdown of the 56th Symbasis . . .* Castre began.

"Never mind," Petal said. "How long has it been like this?"

—*Twenty-three years.*

All those times Hare had told stories of Meridion, Petal realized, it had never occurred to the twins to ask why Hare had left.

"Where are the people?" Petal asked.

—*Indeterminate,* said Castre.—*After the reconciliation of the 57th Symbasis, the surviving tagmata established camps outside the limits of the conservation area. The conservation area is patrolled, by sectors, but the sector boundaries will not likely have remained constant. There will have been conflict. The fires we see are likely evidence of such.*

"They fought till they destroyed their city," Tirah said. "Or till it drove them out. And then they took to fighting over what was left."

Castre said nothing.

"Do we keep going?" Petal asked.

—The conservation area is patrolled, Castre repeated.*—We can attempt to evade the patrols, but should we encounter one, I am unlikely to be able to protect you against an equally equipped superior force.*

"What else is there to do?" Tirah asked.

"Nothing," Petal said, and started down the slope.

☼

They nearly made it.

6. The Other City
t_Ω-2.88×10^5

Piper was asleep when they brought Petal in, two of the cohorts in dusty blue armor striped rust-red, helmets sealed and faceless, heaving aside the cracked ceramic slab that served as the door of the oubliette. (There were no locks—the slab was too heavy to be moved without armor-strength, or without leverage Piper didn't have.)

Piper was thin and brown and hard after the better part of a year on the ice, face sun-browned and wind-burned, eyes narrow and wrinkle-set from all that time in the glare of the cold sun. But if Piper was thin, Petal was emaciated, reeking of ketoacidosis, hair sparse and lank, skin stretched sickly pale over atrophied muscles and a body little more than tendon and bone, shocking Piper to see it; an onlooker might have been pressed to mark Petal and Piper as of the same species, let alone family, let alone twins.

One of the cohorts tossed in another bedroll, like Piper's but cleaner. Then they hauled the slab back into place, and Piper and Petal were alone.

Piper had imagined this moment a hundred times. A thousand. The curses Piper would hurl. The things Piper would say, would do, to show Petal, to make Petal understand, by force if necessary, the magnitude of Petal's selfishness in bringing them here, and its cost.

But that was before seeing what it had cost Petal.

Piper wrapped arms around that thin body, and held Petal, and cried.

☼

They slept and waked. There was light, from a strip on the back of the door, and sometimes there was sunlight around the edges of the slab.

There was food, monotonous and uninspiring but solid, the sort of thing printed in sheets from organic scrap. There was water. Piper had to feed Petal, at first; it was as if Petal had forgotten how to eat and drink. Probably Petal had. They ate and drank and slept again. All that time Petal didn't speak, and Piper didn't either, except practicalities like *hold the cup*, or *this is the toilet*. Petal had to be reminded how to use that, too.

After two or three days, Petal said, voice weak, "How long have you been here? How did you get here?"

"A few weeks," Piper said, voice hoarse, but stronger than Petal's. "We got a crawler from City Authority. We camped on the ice. We never saw you. Sometimes we saw where you'd been."

"I found your message," Petal said. "Your messages."

"That was Swan's idea," Piper said. "To get ahead of you."

"Are they here?" Petal asked. "Our parents?"

"We saw some monsters," Piper said, not answering the question. "Deranged motiles, or broken machines . . . we were never sure. Hare said there were more, twenty years ago. A lot of the ones we saw were dead."

"Everything's dying," Petal said. "I want to go home."

Piper didn't say anything.

"What's going to happen to us?" Petal asked.

"This isn't Hare's phyle," Piper said. "Hare's tagma, I mean. No one's supposed to come here, from outside. But I don't think anyone ever has, or anyway not in a long time. And Hare, Hare wasn't from outside, not exactly. I don't think they knew what to do with us. I suppose we'll stay here till they figure it out."

"Or until it's all over," Petal said.

Piper looked at Petal. Petal's eyes were fixed on something far away, in space or time, something only Petal could see.

"They killed the armor," Petal said, as if that followed naturally from what had come before. "Or froze it. Or something. Everything went dark. When I could see again, Tirah was going away with them. I called out. Tirah didn't look back."

"Gone to speak with their old machines." Piper didn't want to talk about Tirah.

"Maybe," Petal said. "I don't think there's much time left. It'll be over soon. One way or another."

☼

The next day—Piper thought it was the next day—there came another earthquake. A big one, a shaking and a noise lasting almost as long as the thunder that had accompanied the arrival of *Thus is the Heaven*, though the movement of the earth was not so violent. The hour when the food would have come came and went, and Piper had time to wonder whether they had truly been forgotten. But then the slab was moved aside, and two of the cohorts—again in that red-striped blue armor; Piper couldn't tell if they were the same ones who had brought Petal, or not—motioned them out.

"Come," one said, in the language of the tribunes, that was close to the language of Septentrion.

Piper helped Petal stand up, and together they went out into the camp, blinking in the daylight.

Piper hadn't seen much of the camp, when they'd been captured, and there wasn't much to see now: makeshift structures, dug into the rocky slopes of a narrow valley, hardly more than a gully; from the plain above they'd never noticed it. One of the structures was buried in scree, and armored figures were at work, digging it out.

Their escorts led them up a switchbacked gravel trail to the flatland above, and Petal stopped there a moment, looking south, toward the city. Piper wasn't sure, but it seemed as though there were even fewer towers standing than before. The light was strange, stripes and patches of the land seeming shadowed as if by cloud, though the sky was clear. And then, squinting up at the sky, Piper realized it was not that those places were in shadow, but that others were illuminated more brightly, three and four out-of-place mirrors adding their light to that of the sun.

There was a crawler, low and broad, darker blue than the cohorts' armor, with a half-familiar design of white stars. The twins' escorts ushered them into it, and the crawler set off, toward the city, across the strange landscape of light and shadow.

After an hour or so they came to what must have been Meridion's city wall, once; much of it was still intact, but parts had fallen, or been blown out. The crawler drove through one of the gaps, through something not unlike Septentrion's abandoned exurbs, but blackened and burned.

And then they came to a square like Limit Cardinal back home, swept clean of dust and ash, with dozens of colorful pavilions arranged on it in ordered ranks, each guarded by cohorts in bright armor and topped with colored banners: the romantic Meridion of Hare's stories, finally, brought to life. Near the center of the grid of pavilions was an open space, and a pavilion larger than the others, with every tagma's banner flying, and above them all the banner of the city itself, blue-black with five silver stars.

They got out.

Gauge Malpais was there, and someone in armor like Hare's, gray striped with yellow, helmet down. A face that reminded Piper of Hare's, a little, but younger; the face of someone who had never set out to cross the ice of the world, let alone crossed it twice.

And there was Hare, still in the faded, much-repaired City Response jacket that had traveled with them all the way from Septentrion.

Piper and Hare flung their arms around one another, but Petal hung back.

"Where's Cutter?" Petal asked. "And Swan?"

"Swan died on the ice," Gauge said. "Cutter was killed on the salt plain, when Campestral tried to steal the crawler. Hare killed Campestral."

Petal stared at the motile for a moment, blank-faced, apparently uncomprehending; then turned away.

"I didn't want to tell you," Piper said. "I'm sorry."

Hare embraced Petal then, from behind, and Piper saw Petal stiffen for a moment, then turn and yield.

"It's my fault," Petal said, muffled. "It's all my fault."

"It's the end of the world," Hare said. "It's not anybody's fault."

Petal gave a laugh that was half a sob.

"The tagmata have met," said the armored stranger who looked like Hare. "The 59th Symbasis is reconciled. The messenger Tirah will be allowed to enter the city and to attempt one of the sacella."

Piper looked at Gauge.

"This is Flyma," Gauge said.

"Flyma Haemedsbearn," the other said.

"Haemedsbearn," Piper said, looking at Hare.

"Yes," said Flyma. "I was Angyld's kinswight, and so to you, too; we should be gadlings."

"Cousins," Hare translated.

"Cousins," Flyma agreed.

Petal pulled back from Hare.

"They're letting Tirah into the city?"

"There are old defenses," Flyma said. "The sacella protect themselves. No one in armor may approach a sacellum. No machines. No one—" Flyma glanced at Gauge—"no one of the constructed. Only the living."

"Which of those is Tirah?" Piper asked.

"I don't know," said Gauge.

"The sacella will judge," said Flyma.

"Take me," Petal said. "I want to be there. I want to see."

"No!" Piper cried, voice breaking, all the pent-up anger of the year on the ice, coming back in a rush. "No. No. We have you. You're back. You're not leaving again. We're going *home*."

"Piper." It was not Petal that spoke, but Hare, a hand on Piper's shoulder.

All at once Piper collapsed.

"There's no home to go to," Piper said, "is there?"

Hare didn't answer.

"Piper," Petal said. "You can come with me."

Piper looked up. "Will you come with us?" Piper asked Hare.

"I can't," Hare said.

"Angyld is being released to Xanthe Tagma," Flyma said. "To stand trial for desertion."

"Desertion!" Piper exclaimed.

"I don't think it'll come to that," Hare said. "I don't think there's that much time left." Hare took the City Response jacket and held it out to Petal. "Here. It gets cold, in the shadows."

"I won't need it," Petal said.

"I'll take it," Piper said. "Just in case."

Hare hesitated, and then stepped closer to the twins, embracing both of them.

"I love you," Hare said. "Both of you."

Piper didn't answer, only hugged Hare more tightly.

Hare let them go, and stepped back.

"I want to remember your faces," Hare said. "For as much time as we have."

"As much time as there is," said Piper.

"I wish we had more," Petal said. "But we don't." And, turning to Flyma: "Let's go."

And they did.

7. The Metric

$$t_\Omega\text{-}2\times10^3$$

They crawled over and through the corpse of the city, following Flyma, the ghost in Flyma's armor picking out their path. The air seemed thinner. Piper had a headache, and Petal was breathing in shallow gasps. It was hot in the sunlight, hotter still where the mirrors shone, but the shadows were cold. The trembling of the ground had grown so constant that Piper hardly noticed it anymore, or the sound, a rumbling and creaking that seemed to come from everywhere and nowhere.

Flyma paused, at the edge of what had probably been a park, a wide burnt-over swath interrupted by intersecting ridges of debris, remains of structures fallen from overhead. There was a space beyond, ash and brown dirt, clear of rubble, and in its center something glittered.

"The sacellum is there," Flyma said. "I can go no farther." And to Gauge, "Nor can you."

"The defenses," Gauge said. "I understand."

"Like it matters," Petal said. There were towers still standing to the north and west, blocking sunlight and mirror-light, and Petal was shivering. Piper took Hare's jacket and draped it across Petal's shoulders.

"Go," Piper said to Gauge. "We might be wrong."

Gauge hesitated.

"Go," Piper said again. And to Flyma, "I'm sorry. There's no time."

"There isn't," Petal said and started out across the park. Piper followed, not waiting to see what Gauge and Flyma did.

"Goodbye," Gauge called; and Piper thought about looking back, but there seemed no point. And then they were past the first stretch of debris, and the motile would have been out of sight anyway.

They caught up with Tirah in the shadow of a fallen causeway. The sacellum was where Flyma had said it would be, at the bottom of a shallow depression just half a cable away: a circle of coppery polished metal, perfectly clean, hardly broader than the span of Piper's outstretched arms, in the multiplied light of the mirrors almost too bright to bear looking at. Tirah was standing in the shade, looking down at the circle, seeming to study it, as if it lay at the center of a maze and Tirah was looking for the solution.

"Tirah," Petal said.

"Only the living may approach the sacellum," Tirah said. "And yet it must be done."

"Tirah, look at me," Petal said. "Tell me it was all worth something. Tell me—" Petal was crying, now—"tell me Cutter and Swan didn't die for nothing."

"It must be done," Tirah said again, still looking at the circle, not looking at Petal. "The metric must be destroyed. The old universe must pass away. The new universe must be allowed to begin."

Tears were streaming down Petal's face. "I never so much as held your hand," Petal said. "I thought I loved you. But Piper was right. That wasn't real. That was just something you put in my head. To get me to help you."

"I didn't mean that," Piper said. "I shouldn't have said it."

"A year, I thought I loved you," Petal said to Tirah, ignoring Piper. "A year, on the ice. And it was all a lie, wasn't it? It was all in my head." Petal reached out and took Tirah's hand now, pulling. "Look at me."

But Tirah was immovable.

"It must be done," Tirah said a third time, as if Petal had never spoken, and coming loose from Petal's weakened grip, stepped out of the shade into the doubled sunlight. All around them the rubble was creaking, the still-standing structures were shivering like live things, shedding motes of scintillating dust that fell slowly, so slowly, as if there was all of forever left to do it in. And Tirah walked out, barefoot in the red dirt, so apparently human, so intent and so vulnerable; and Piper saw a little of what Petal must have seen.

And then, just short of the circle, Tirah seemed to cross an invisible line, and the body the Archive had made began to dissolve in violet-white light, just a little at first and then all at once, as Tirah pushed on. For a moment Piper thought there might be a small circular shadow in the midst of the glare, falling: the little globe that had been Tirah's true body, the true vessel of the message from Hoddmímis Holt. But then the light flared brighter yet so that Piper turned away in reflex, and there were only afterimages darting purple and yellow behind closed eyelids.

"Wait," Petal said then, and reached out.

But it was already over.

Petal slumped to the ground. Piper slid down to sit beside Petal, their shoulders touching, Petal's bony and thin under the patched City Response jacket. Piper felt lightheaded. Was that exhaustion, dehydration, lack of sleep, some collateral effect of being too close to the circle's defense system? Or was it the quintessence pulling at the atoms of Piper's body, fraying the bonds that held Piper and Petal to the earth? How much time was left, anyway? Maybe it was already too late.

Maybe it wasn't the quintessence, maybe it was just doing too much, seeing too much, knowing too much, being asked to face such an enormity, the end of everything; what human being could be expected to comprehend that? Piper could feel it, not the weight of deep time, but the mass of it, the mass of a universe multiplied by the billions of years of its existence and the infinity of possible histories pruned down now to this one inevitability. And embedded somewhere in it the infinitesimal braid that was two sixteen-year-old lives about to be cut short. The injustice of that, the injustice of the lives Piper and Petal could have had and never would. Of the year, even, that they could have had, if only Tirah had never come. That Cutter could have had, and Swan. Maybe a world that could do that needed to be destroyed, and never to be created anew.

Piper imagined that, an empty, angry darkness strung with grim tight knots, the quintessence and the metric locked in final stalemate. How much time was left? A year, a day, an hour? Maybe they could lie down, now, here, and soon it would be over.

Piper looked at Petal. Petal looked back. Piper knew they were thinking the same thing.

"Tirah said, once," said Petal, "that in Hoddmímis Holt they could fit eternity in an instant. That that was something they could do, that we couldn't. But that's not right, is it."

"No," agreed Piper.

"Even one more day is an infinity," Petal said. "Or would be, if we could have it back."

"If we could have it again," Piper said.

"Yes," Petal said. "I'm sorry, Piper."

"So am I," Piper said.

The doubled sun was broiling hot. Red spots floated before Piper's eyes. The air was quivering over the bare earth, and in the shimmer the circle seemed to bob like a bit of flotsam on the waves.

"It was real," Piper said.

"What was?" asked Petal.

"What you felt," Piper said. "It was real. Even if Tirah wasn't."

"It was stupid," said Petal.

"It wasn't wrong," said Piper.

The twins looked at each other.

Then Piper got up, hauled Petal upright, and together they started down toward the circle.

They went down, following Tirah's footprints before them in the dirt; they passed the point where the prints ended and there was nothing there to show that Hoddmímis Holt's message had ever been. Piper was sweating and chilled at the same time; Petal's hand was cold in Piper's and both of them were shivering as with fever.

A cold wind swept across them, the doubled sunlight dimming. Piper looked up and saw one of the visible mirrors spinning out of control, the bright circle reduced to an oval and then a line, as in slow silence another nearby shattered into a hundred tumbling fragments. The true sun low in the northern sky seemed dimmer as well, redder, or was that Piper's imagination?

As they approached the coppery circle of the sacellum there was a feeling of presence, invisible, incorporeal, the sense of being observed that sometimes came in a building that housed a ghost. Something ancient, older than Meridion, older than Septentrion, older perhaps than this instantiation of the Earth. Tirah's old machines. Waiting, all this time, for someone, anyone really, to tell them their long duty was done.

"We have to do it," Petal said. "Don't we?"

"We have to," Piper said. "Together."

Hand in hand, they stepped into the circle.

Vaccine Season

Hannu Rajaniemi

THE SMALL AUTONOMOUS boat skipped over the gray waves. The engine howled in mid-air with each jump. Every jarring landing made Torsti taste the protein bar he'd had for breakfast. The overpowering fish smell in the boat didn't help.

For the thousandth time, he imagined what would happen when he arrived at his destination. He would jump out of the boat and run down the pier. His grandfather's lanky form would reach down and embrace him. One shared breath and it would be done.

A cold spray on his face brought him back to the bucking boat. Jungfruholmen Island lay up ahead.

It was early autumn. From a distance, the blazing leaves of the trees made it seem like the island was on fire. The boat sped past the granite wave-breakers that guarded it, toward wave-polished coral-hued cliffs crowned with twisted birch and pine. A familiar pier jutted out of the stony half-moon of a beach.

In a few minutes, the boat jumped against the pier gently and came to a halt. Torsti climbed out carefully and secured his loaned vessel to a metal ring with a length of rope. There was no sign of Grandfather. The windows of the squat sauna building by the pier were dark. What if I am already too late? he thought. What if he is already dead?

A path covered in rotting leaves and pine needles wound into a patch of trees, up the cliff and toward Grandfather's cottage. Torsti followed it, shivering in the wind.

The hiisi's churn was just past the trees, in the middle of a large hollow. It was a gaping hole in the rock, fifteen feet in diameter. After a ten-foot drop, bottomless dark water lapped at the spiral-grooved walls. A stream of melt water from a glacier had drilled it into the granite by rotating gravel, millions of years ago.

Torsti's stomach tied itself into a cold knot. He had been five years old when he first came to this island with his parents to celebrate vaccine season. On a summer evening, with the red smear of the sun on the horizon, Grandfather had brought him to see the churn. In hushed tones, the old man had told him that the churn was actually an ancient portal to the stars. If you threw a rock into the spiraling grooves in just the right way, alien machines activated and opened a wormhole to wherever in space and time you wanted to go. He had closed Torsti's fingers around a stone and told him to try.

Torsti had taken an eager step forward and looked into the churn. The vast depths had looked back, like the entire island was a monstrous eye and the churn its pupil, inhuman and black and fathomless, like Death itself. The stone had fallen from his hand and he had run away in tears. Even now, seven years later, he remembered the shame of it.

And I remember *you*, the churn seemed to say. I haven't changed. I am the past. I am the future. I'll get you in the end.

"No, you won't," Torsti muttered under his breath.

Branches rustled, and his heart jumped. A tall figure loomed on the other side of the churn. It wore dark overalls, gloves, and some kind of helmet. In the shadows, its face looked skull-like.

Then it stumbled on a pebble and set off a small avalanche into the depths of the churn. It let out a muffled curse in a familiar voice.

"*Perkele*," Grandfather swore. He was wearing a battered face shield over a cloth mask, but his bushy eyebrows were unmistakable.

This is it, Torsti thought. He tried to will his legs to move, but the terror of the churn still held him in its grip.

Grandfather raised a hand. "Don't try to come any closer, boy," he said. "I mean it."

Torsti stared at him helplessly. The old man huffed and adjusted his mask. This wasn't going to work, he realized. The vaccine replicating in Torsti's upper airways was engineered to be infectious, but just like the old Pandemic One virus it was based on, it still needed close contact to spread, especially outdoors.

Very slowly, Torsti took half a step forward.

"Stop right there," Grandfather said, "or I'm going to run." His voice was thin. It was hard to see his expression behind the mask and the plastic face shield, but his eyes were wide. He is afraid, Torsti thought. He has never been afraid of anything.

"I'm going to rest here for a moment," Grandfather said. "You stay right there." He sat down on a boulder and massaged his leg, not taking his eyes off Torsti. "Did your mother send you?"

"No!" Torsti said. "Why are you dressed like that?"

"Well, I think it should be obvious. I don't want to catch your damn vaccine, that's why."

"Why not?" That was the question that had been haunting Torsti for two years, ever since his mother had told him that they wouldn't be visiting Grandfather during vaccine season anymore. He was surprised by how fierce his voice sounded. "Why did you stop talking to us? What did we do to you?"

Grandfather ignored him and took a phone from his pocket. He tapped at the screen laboriously—typically, he hadn't had the opto interface infection either, and had to use all his devices by hand.

"Doesn't look like you are shedding that much," he muttered. "Thank goodness for kids' immune systems." Then he looked up, narrowing his eyes. "If you're mother didn't send you," he said suspiciously, "then how did you get here?"

This wasn't the Grandfather Torsti remembered from the vaccine seasons past, the one who had played hide and seek with him and built a castle from sticks and pine cones in the secret grove of the eastern tip of the island. This was someone else.

"I skipped school," he said, swallowing back tears. "Then I took a train to Hanko. There was a fisherwoman Rnought introduced me to. She lent me her boat."

"Why on earth would somebody do that? Who the hell is this Rnought?"

"It came out last year. It's a serendipity AI to speed up vaccine spread. If you already caught the vaccine, it matches you up with people who want to be immunized and can help you with something, or the other way around."

One of the benefits of living in Helsinki was catching every new vaccine days or even weeks earlier than the rest of the country, and Torsti had gone to the big launch party at the Senate Square with his parents. And the new vaccine was so popular that the fisherwoman had jumped at the chance of helping Torsti get to Jungfruholmen, in exchange for a verified transmission.

"Sending a twelve-year-old out to the seas on his own, just like that." Grandfather said, shaking his head. "Everyone has gone mad. When I was your age, we couldn't always trust the machines to save you. That's what's wrong with this world, it's too safe."

"No, it's not," Torsti said. "It's not safe. People still get old. People can still die."

"Unless they get this bloody vaccine, is that it? A vaccine against death?"

It wasn't a fix for death, not really. Torsti knew as much. But it was the next best thing. It was the last in a long series of vaccines the Global Immunity Foundation had been releasing for decades. Backed by a group of billionaires, they had invented transmissible vaccines to stop Pandemic One—a controversial move at the time, but necessary when more than half of Americans and countless others around the world had refused to be vaccinated against COVID-19. After an initial uproar, the Foundation had been hailed as heroes after they stopped Pandemic Two in its tracks, saving countless lives. In the two decades since, the Foundation's vaccine releases had been coming out on a regular basis: first, updates against emerging coronaviruses, flu, dengue, pre-pandemic zoonotics. And eventually, protection from the big ones, non-transmissible diseases—heart disease, Alzheimer's, and cancer.

Now each vaccine release was a global event, a cause for celebration. At Senate Square, this one had rained down on a cheering, dancing crowd from dispersal drones amidst a bioluminescent fireworks display. Pre-infected choirs had sung it onto onlookers from the steps of the Helsinki Cathedral. The new vaccine was a senolytic: it trained your immune system to kill the zombie cells that accumulated in your body with aging. You wouldn't live forever, but you would stay healthy much longer—no one knew how long. There were still mice alive from the first experiments, decades ago.

Torsti had clinked glasses with Mom and Dad when their phone sequencers confirmed their infections—champagne for his parents, Pommac for him—and then hugged and kissed passersby, all in vaccine season masks—feathers, crowns, and horns, but always leaving the mouth and nose uncovered. And then, all of a sudden it was as if he was watching the revelers from behind a pane of glass, cold and distant. How could they celebrate when there were those who would be left behind?

Like Grandfather.

"Is that was this is about, Torsti? You don't want me to die?" Grandfather asked.

Torsti stared at him. Grandfather really didn't understand. But maybe it was unfair to expect him to. Unlike Torsti, he hadn't grown up with Mom coming home and talking about her job at the Long Reflection Committee. Over and over, she had explained what a special time this was in human history. Things no longer hung in balance, existential threats—pandemics, bioterror, rogue AIs—had been overcome. It was time to look toward the deep future and decide humanity's destiny.

Torsti had loved it, and had devoured everything the Committee published that Mom let him read. He had even started contributing ideas to the Committee's open simulations that mapped out possible futures, millions of years ahead. He had spent countless hours wandering through the virtual worlds, until his parents disabled his opto. And even then, his imagination kept going, conjuring images of things to come.

☼

Grandfather didn't realize that the vaccine was just the first step. The Committee scenarios were clear. If you extended your life by just a decade or two, the next set of longevity technologies would come along—not just to prevent aging but to restore youth—and so on. Longevity escape velocity, it was called. If you made it just a little bit further, you could travel to the stars, live as long as the Universe itself.

Grandfather was letting all that go, because he was mad at Mom, for some reason Torsti could not understand. And that made Torsti angry, angry enough to do desperate things.

He opened his mouth to explain, but there were so many words that they just sat heavy in his chest, all jumbled up and stuck together, like a pile of twisted iron nails.

"No," he said, finally. "I want you to live."

"Well, that's very touching," Grandfather said, not understanding the difference. "But as you get older, you'll understand that there are some decisions people have to make on their own. I have made mine, and I have to live—and die with them." His voice broke, just for a moment. Then he continued in a harsher tone. "I don't need a silly little boy coming here to take that away from me, just because he doesn't understand how the world works.

"Now, I'm going to send a message to your mother." Grandfather tapped at his phone laboriously. "We have our differences, but I don't want her worrying herself sick. I'll take you back to the mainland in the morning. With two boats it should be safe. You can sleep in the guest bed in the sauna, I already set it up—I'll disinfect it all afterward.

And here's a bunch of surgical masks." He set a small pile of flat blue objects on the rock next to him. "I want you to wear them."

He stood and started back up the path. "Come now. Since you're here, you can help me chop some firewood. It gets cold at night."

"You knew I was coming," Torsti said. "How?" He had left his phone home, and the ubiquitous surveillance of the old days had been banned at the start of the Reflection.

Grandfather shrugged.

"You have to be prepared," he said. "Your Mom messaged me and told me you had gone missing. We don't talk much, but some things you always share with family. I called an old friend at the Foundation, asked for transmission data. They barcode the viruses, you know. They don't talk about it, but you can actually trace the contacts with the phone sequencers. It is still so early in the season that you left a pretty clear trail."

He knew, Torsti thought. He didn't have to let me come this far, he could have told Mom much earlier. He *wanted* me to come.

He followed Grandfather up the path toward the main house, keeping a respectful distance. Fallen leaves whispered beneath his feet, and he breathed in their earthy smell.

There was still hope.

☼

They walked around the main house to the firewood shed. Grandfather hauled out an armful of logs to the chopping block, and then his phone rang. He twisted awkwardly, trying to get it out of his pocket. Torsti moved forward to help, then remembered himself. The old man let the wood clatter to the ground, swearing, and pulled the device out.

"It's your mother," he said, frowning. He tapped it and held it up toward Torsti. "I think she just needs to see you are all right."

Mom and Dad peeked at Torsti from the tiny screen. Mom's eyes were tired, and her chestnut hair clung to her head, unwashed. Dad had an arm around her shoulders, tugging at his braided beard as he always did when he was anxious.

"Torsti," Mom said. "I know I said you should have more adventures, but this is not what I meant." She looked so small, so far away on the screen, so different from the full-sized opto projections he was used to.

"I'm fine, Mom. I'm coming back tomorrow." He glanced at Grandfather, who was holding the phone. The old man's eyes were squeezed shut as he listened.

"Tell . . . tell your grandfather thank you for me," Mom said.

"I will."

"Bring back some of that islander bread," Dad said, a fake cheer in his voice. "We'll see you soon."

"Can I talk to your grandfather a bit?" Mom said.

Torsti nodded and waved.

Grandfather walked away, holding the phone to his ear.

"Yes, of course," he said. "No, it's no trouble. Of course. You both take care now."

Grandfather ended the call, wiped the screen surface with a small alcohol pad and pocketed it. His face shield was clouded with steam. Sniffing, he swept his shirtsleeve across it.

"All right," he said. "Let's chop some firewood."

In practice, what it meant was that Torsti chopped the firewood, at Grandfather's amused direction. The handle of the axe stung his hands with every blow, and more than once he ended up having a log stuck to the axe blade and then bashing it against the block, lifting the whole thing like a giant, clumsy hammer.

"No, no, no," the old man said. "There's a trick to it."

"What is it?" Torsti asked, huffing. There was a painful blister in the middle of his left palm. The surgical mask he now wore was moist with his breath.

"You have to catch the edge." Grandfather said. "You go with the grain of the wood. It's pointless to fight against it. It should feel like the wood wants to split. Come on. Try again."

Torsti carefully positioned the birch log on the block and swung the axe. This time, he hit it just right, with the tip of the axe blade, and the log flew apart in two pieces effortlessly. He looked at it, surprised.

"See?" Grandfather said. "That's the problem with everybody, these days. They don't know the tricks anymore."

Torsti looked at him. It felt strange to talk to someone wearing a mask that completely hid everything except the eyes. In a way, it felt more distant than seeing Mom on a screen. What is *your* trick, Grandfather? He wondered. Which way does your grain go?

"Where did you learn that?" he asked carefully.

"Well, now. It would have been in the time of Big Corona, back when your mother was little," he said. "Not the virus, of course, not Pandemic One. The Coronal Mass Ejection Event, the solar flare. Nothing but wood to keep the heating going, back then. Had to learn quickly how to chop it."

"What was it like?" Torsti asked, starting to gather the split logs into a pile. He knew the facts, of course. A massive blast of charged particles from the Sun had slammed into the Earth's magnetic field, frying every electric circuit. But it felt like this was something Grandfather wanted to talk about.

The old man's eyes were distant.

"Oh, it was a mess. You had satellites falling from the sky. No Internet. No electricity for six months. It was worse than the Pandemics. At least then we had ways of talking to each other. The Big Corona really isolated everybody. It was in the middle of the winter, too. People hoarded firewood. Even now, I keep too much of it around. Not good for my carbon credits, but once you go through something like that, your habits change.

"I was in my forties. But it was only then that I learned how to be a grown-up. There is something about protecting your family that changes things. Not that anyone understands that, these days. After it was over, I made sure I *prepared*. Learned first aid, bought this place here, made sure we had canned food for years. Maybe I overdid the protecting with your mother a little bit, that's why she grew up so wild. But you do what you have to do."

His mask twisted, just a hint of a smile beneath.

"You know, we had this old chest of drawers, mahogany, from your great-grandmother. One night I took it to the backyard and chopped it into pieces. It kept us warm for a night, but your grandmother never forgave me for that."

He sighed. "She loved the northern lights, though. We saw the best ones ever, the night it happened. We were all in a panic, trying to find candles in the pitch black, and then she told me to look outside. The city was all dark, and the sky was ablaze, with every color you could think of. We took your mother and went outside, stared at it for hours. It was the most beautiful thing she had seen in her life, she said, and because of the way she looked at it, it was.

"That's what I miss now, her way of seeing things. I see the aurora here, in the winter, sometimes, but it's just lights in the sky.

"We can't really know, but that was probably what killed her, us going out there. The cancer wave that came afterwards, all those particles, messing with everyone's DNA. I got lucky, roll of the dice. Your mother was fine, the Foundation rolled out the cancer vaccines by the time she started school. But your grandmother . . ." Grandfather looked away, at the choppy sea beyond the trees. "She drowned on dry land, in the end," he said quietly. "Her lungs filled with fluid."

Torsti stared at Grandfather. He didn't know much about his grandmother, but her paintings and drawings were all over the cottage, small landscapes and quirky manga-style cartoons. He felt the terror of the churn's black water rise in him again. To get rid of his disquiet, he chopped at the last log, hard. It flew apart violently, and the axe got stuck in the block.

"So that's why," Grandfather said.

"That's why what?" Torsti asked.

"That's why I don't want your vaccine. I don't need to see the future. AIs and space colonies and Dyson trees and all the things your Mom spends her days thinking about for the Long Reflection Committee. Lights in the sky, nothing more. I don't need to see it."

He got up. "Let's gather these and get the fire going for you, hmm? It's going to be cold at night."

☼

The sauna smelled of dry wood in a way that seemed to retain its warmth. It had a small front room with a low bed where Torsti had slept during previous island visits. It had one of Grandmother's drawings, a tiny watercolor and ink of the view out toward the sea from the sauna window, framed by the wave-breakers.

"You'll have to stay outside while I get the fire going," Grandfather said. The old man went into the sauna itself and kneeled painfully by the stove, assembling kindling and wood into careful layers.

Reluctantly, Torsti got out of his way. He walked to the pier and looked out to the sea. As Grandfather had predicted, the wind had picked up. The trees on the cliffs danced, and heavy waves crashed against the breakers. It looked just like Grandmother's painting, a window into the past.

So much would be lost when Grandfather died, entire worlds Torsti had never known. I have to find a way to do it, he thought. I have to bring him to the future with me. If I leave, I might never see him again.

It is just lights in the sky, Grandfather had said.

That's the problem, Torsti thought. He can't see the future. But maybe I can show him.

He went to the boat and picked up a coil of sturdy rope from its storage locker. Then he gathered a few round pebbles from the beach and went back to the sauna. Grandfather came out, dusting his hands.

"All right," he said. "If you add a few logs before you go to sleep, you should be warm and snug now, even if the north wind blows." There was a regretful look in his eyes. "It's too bad we can't actually use the sauna together. Shame to waste a good löyly." Then he frowned, seeing Torsti's expression. "What is it, boy?"

"I want to show you something." Torsti said. "Let's go up to the churn."

☼

The hiisi's churn looked even deeper and darker in the fading light. Slowly, Torsti walked right to the edge. The fear moved in him now, as if the deep water was reaching out from the churn with a cold hand and squeezing his heart.

He laid the coil of rope down on the ground and tied one end carefully around a boulder. Then he drew his hand back and tossed the first stone into the churn. It bounced off a wall and vanished into the black water.

"What are you doing?" Grandfather asked.

Torsti threw another stone. This time, the angle was better, and the stone actually caught on the grooves, spun around the churn bore before falling into the water.

"I want you to travel with me," he said quietly. "Remember? It can take us anywhere."

Grandfather watched him, eyes unreadable, almost invisible in the dim light.

"So let's go to the future. A thousand years from now."

He threw another stone. He was getting better at it now, and now the stone slid along the grooves almost a whole circuit. His palms sweated. The images from the simulations flashed in his head. Squeezing them hard like the stones in his hand, he forced them into words.

"Look," he said, motioning Grandfather to come closer. "Here we are. Not many people live on Earth. Maybe you are still here, on the island, but when we come visit you, it's from the artificial worlds in the asteroid belt, every one of them unique and different. I—I might have wings, since I live in a low gravity world, and I have to wear an exoskeleton to walk around. Mom is no longer just thinking about the future, she is building it. Dad is a mindweaver, trying to get big group minds to get along, helping them to find the balance between the parts and the whole. We still celebrate vaccine season. But now it's just a ritual for family, like Christmas used to be."

He threw another stone. This one was better: the round stone bounced and followed the grooves, almost all the way down.

He looked at Grandfather. The old man sat on a rock now, leaning his chin on his hands, watching Torsti.

"It's a million years from now. Everybody comes back to Earth during vaccine season, once a century. There is no disease anymore, so the vaccines are memetic: *ideas*, entire systems of thought, ways of being, different kinds of consciousness. Mind vaccines against despair and war and fear."

He looked up at the pale October stars. "The wormholes open in the Lagrange Points, and they come. Some—some come in ships; tiny ones, living spores that carry minds in molecules that then grow in soil and turn into bodies and minds; large ones, ones made from dark matter or with a black hole in the heart that can cross between galaxies. Others are already here, in virtual realities inside diamond machines; but they make bodies to visit Earth and the people here, because it's vaccine season. So they can remember where they come from."

Now Grandfather stood close. I'm not doing it right, Torsti thought. He still can't see.

He gritted his teeth, strained to see the deep future and hefted the final stone.

Grandfather took his hand.

"Torsti," he said gently. "It's all right." There was a smile under his mask. "You are a good boy, you really are. I *know* you can see these things, I know you can. You will do things I never imagined. And . . . it's enough for me just to know that.

"Now, let's go back. It's getting cold. I'm going to make some food, and tomorrow I'll take you home."

The churn's hollow voice mocked Torsti in his mind. *You can imagine all the futures you want, boy. But they are not real. Only endless dark is real. Your Grandfather knows that. Nothing will exist. Only I will remain.*

"No," Torsti said. "I *am* going to show you."

He withdrew his hand from his grandfather's and threw the last stone. It hit the grooves of the churn perfectly, spinning around the bore, rattling like a ball in a roulette wheel.

Then he jumped in after it.

For an instant, he was suspended in mid-air, could almost touch the walls of the churn. Maybe it is really a wormhole, he thought. Then the water rose to meet him and pulled a cold hand over his head.

Torsti had never learned to swim, in spite of Mom and Dad's attempts. So he just lifted his arms and floated, disappearing beneath the surface. Water filled his mouth and lungs. It was like breathing in cold space. The dark filled him, and suddenly it was like he was hollow, a container for the Universe itself.

He saw the future. Artificial worlds strung around stars like strings of pearls. Wormholes connecting galaxies like synapses between neurons. Currents of dark matter redirecting the movements of superclusters, slowing down the expansion of the universe, preventing the Big Rip that threatened to leave each photon alone in its own bubble. And then, new universes, budding off from the first one, entire new realities with their own laws and constants and life, a forest growing from a single seed. A multiverse, made from minds and wonder and surprise, no longer dead and cold, lighting up, inside him.

We are the vaccine, he thought. We are the vaccine against the dark.

And then it all blinked out.

✿

The coughing brought Torsti back. It felt like being chopped at with an axe, right in the chest. The Universe came out of him in tiny big bangs of phlegm and cold brine.

Finally it stopped, leaving him freezing and shaking all over, but alive. Torsti opened his eyes. His grandfather's silhouette loomed over him, against the evening sky.

"Don't try to move," the old man said, crouching next to Torsti on the granite. He lifted up his phone, pointing the camera at Torsti, and the screen lit up his face.

He wasn't wearing his mask. His thick silvery hair and salt-and-pepper beard were dripping, and he had a pained look on his face. The lines were deeper than Torsti remembered, his cheeks were hollower.

"Grandfather," Torsti wheezed. "I saw it."

Relief spread over Grandfather's face, smoothing the wrinkles.

"Thank goodness," he said. "You stupid, reckless boy. What if I hadn't been strong enough to haul you up that goddamned rope?" He held up his phone. "The Hanko Medical Center AI said you were going to be fine, but I almost didn't believe it. You should be glad I still remembered my rescue breath training. How are you feeling?"

Torsti's ribs hurt, but he felt better with each breath. Slowly, he sat up. He was soaked through and shivered in the wind. Grandfather wrapped his coat around Torsti, and then hugged him tight, wiry arms around the boy's shoulders and back.

"I saw it in the churn," Torsti whispered. "The future. I really saw it."

Grandfather pulled away and looked at Torsti.

"I believe you," he said. "You have it, too, don't you? That way of seeing. And I never realized. What a strange thing."

His voice was thick. Then he held up his phone, clearing his throat. "Well, I guess I'm going to see the future, too, now. This damned thing confirmed transmission."

"I'm sorry," Torsti said. "I took away your choice."

Grandfather sighed.

"You did no such thing, boy," he said. "You can't take what wasn't there in the first place. My choice was made a long time ago. I just wasn't ready to admit it."

He helped Torsti up. "Let's go to the sauna," he said. "All these vaccines or not, you don't want to catch your death."

They walked down the pine needle path together, toward the sauna and the warmth.

Submergence

Arula Ratnakar

AS THE PEOPLE began to die, desperation drove us to the depths of the sea for cures. We mined mineral-rich vents until the tube worms went extinct, stripped polymetallic nodule fields bare, squeezed sludge out of sea sponges to treat the new diseases, these monstrous incurable plagues, born from our new climate, that spread through our air. But the people still died. So we dug even deeper . . .

☼

I look at the corpse lying in the clear preservation chamber next to me. Woman, late thirties, died about four weeks ago. Normally they would have examined her body, signed her death certificate, gotten everything back to her remaining family members (her aunt and her twelve-year-old daughter), and that would have been it. But she had those things in her brain. And she died a strange and sudden death. So here we are, tied up in this investigation. Not that I'm complaining though. No, I *live* for this shit.

"We've all had the procedure done, we've all been taking the pills for about a week now. Anything go wrong for either of you? Any side effects?" Marie continues reluctantly. "Nothing wrong on my end."

Anthony, sitting to my left, looks absolutely elated. "I've vomited three times a day since Wednesday! Looks like I can't do it."

They both turn to me. Marie bites the side of her thumb. "Nithya?"

Hah. Marie is terrified right now. Is she really afraid that I'll turn this down? That she'll be the one to have lights pulsing through her brain every night for the next four months? This is the most interesting thing that has happened in my entire goddamn twenty-seven years of existence. Can't believe they aren't fighting me tooth and nail for the chance to do this. Ah well, can't seem too enthusiastic about it. What if they change their minds?

I try to look downcast. "I'll do it. I didn't get any negative side effects. Truthfully I'm feeling better than ever."

Marie is visibly relieved. "You're sure about this Nithya?"

Hell fucking yes I'm sure! I nod.

Anthony chuckles nervously. "Well, then get ready to live a dead woman's life."

☼

I stare at the reflection of my waist-length dark-brown hair in the bathroom mirror, razor in hand, trying to imagine myself with a shaved head. I think I'd look badass. They're going to drill little circular tunnels into my skull, intended to be plugged into a set of tubes that will branch out microscopically throughout my brain and shine light pulses into key areas at the cellular level. They don't want hair getting in the way of the procedure, and I certainly do not want that either.

As the chunks of hair fall to the floor, I think about the last time someone tried out this technology, in a very different context. I remember seeing it on the local news. It's just optogenetics. An elderly woman got her neurons modified to contain activity-dependent genes for additional kinds of channel proteins, light-gated ion channels. Colorful light pulses could regulate membrane depolarization through these new light-gated ion channels and force the same neurons to fire that were firing during her experiences. She could "record" all her experiences and live them again later, as the wavelengths of light activating the channels would evolve and develop with time, along with the types of light-gated channel proteins being expressed or taken out of the cell membranes. Additional proteins expressed through the inserted gene sequence allowed the tubes to locate and target neurons in the correct firing sequence.

But the old woman's goal wasn't to relive the experiences herself. After the woman died, her daughter received a gift. A request to modify her own neurons to include the channel proteins, and permission to access a set of pills and light pulses that would, to the most accurate possible degree, play the elderly woman's experiences into her daughter's brain. The final years of that woman's life, available for someone else to live themself! Eat, sleep, shit, laugh, cry as them ... *become* them for a while. It's the most intense form of memorial I've ever heard of.

Why didn't the woman whose death we're investigating—Noor—ever play back her experiences herself? Why just have the channel proteins? What was the point of modifying her neurons, if she was just going to live like she'd never gotten the procedure done anyway?

I look at my bald head in the mirror, satisfied with my work.

✿

"Is it conscious?" The disembodied brain in front of me is incredibly disquieting, several infinitesimal, branching tubes running through it, keeping it clean and preventing the natural postmortem process from taking place.

Since Noor didn't play her experiences back every night for the time she had the new channel proteins, they have to play them back into her brain now, so they can get what they need to play the light pulses into me.

Dr. Irene Young shakes her head. "Certainly not right now. And when fed the light, all Noor's brain can do at this point is reexperience her last two years over and over again, in a loop, without knowing they're being relived. The inevitable still happens no matter what, this brain isn't coming up with anything new anytime soon. And the brain only 'comes alive' again, to put it crudely, when fed the light pulses."

The whole thing still unsettles me. "Isn't it cruel though, keeping the brain looping like that?"

She's quiet for some time before speaking. "Think about it like this. Right now, you're in this room, experiencing this present moment. Earlier this morning, you were experiencing something completely different, and so it goes for every moment of your past. In each of these slices of time, you are completely unable to predict exactly what you will experience next, right? Okay, say you die tomorrow and someone plays your life experiences back into your head. In whatever the equivalent of *this particular moment* is within the synaptic reconstructions, you will have absolutely no clue what that death will be like. It'll just be this moment, and you'd be sitting in front of me, staring at that brain. You're either alive, or you're in one of those loops, and there's no real way to distinguish between which of the two you're in. Even if you can't stop the death, you don't even know that it's going to happen. It would feel essentially the same as living your life as it would play out and then dying, with no way to know whether or not you've gotten yourself some amount of extra time. Maybe we should be raging against the impossibility of perfect foresight, or against the fragility of human existence and the ephemerality of a human life. But personally, I don't think feeding the brain the light pulses is cruel."

"Hmm," I'm still not fully convinced, but she seems to have quite a strong opinion on the matter, so I try to redirect the conversation. "Pretty amazing, that I'll be able to live out a whole two years, every night, for just slightly under four months."

"Yeah, that's what happens when you condense the experiences down to high quality immersive experiential versions of whatever she would have remembered naturally, which filters out quite a bit! I mean, there's no way of knowing whether or not that will cut out something essential, but this will cover the most memorable moments, whatever those are."

A nurse enters to tell us the operating room is ready. I head out after him and look back to see Dr. Young still gazing at the brain. As soon as she meets my eye, she hurries after me.

✿

It's time to take my bandages off, a week and a half after the operation. The cannula guides for the tubes that will fire the light into my head have been drilled into my skull and it's all healed. Dr. Young looks nervous today. Why?

As she unwraps the bandages, she tells me what to expect. "There's going to be a sensory deprivation chamber set up in your home, with the tubes attached. I know you've been taking the pills for some time now, but it is crucial that you continue to remember to take the pills every morning and night, and I'm obligated to give you a refresher on what to expect."

Dr. Young holds out one box of a set of four. Each box has four rows, each row containing seven orange pills and seven green ones. "The morning pills—orange ones—cause a daily ripple of brain activity, during which you will experience a brief but strong hallucination. Since we're replacing your REM sleep with Noor's experiences, and REM is incredibly important for strengthening newly formed synaptic connections, we have to make up for the lost benefits with this ripple. Since you haven't played anything back into your head yet, there haven't been any hallucinations. However, as soon as you start, so will the daily hallucination."

She gives me a quick half smile, but it's not very convincing. "Don't worry too much, it will be very brief. This carefully orchestrated daily brain activity will make it easy for us to identify different experiences you have as well. The night pills are what paralyze you and block external sensory signals from reaching you while you're being fed the light pulses. They'll also adjust your melatonin cycle to make sure you fall asleep with enough time to play the experiences. Your slow-wave sleep won't be noticeably affected by any of this."

Her voice is steady, professional. But the pills are rattling in the box from her shaking hands. She shoves the box into my hands. I have to ask.

I whisper, "Do you know the person who put the light-gated ion channels in Noor's brain? Was it you? Did you know this woman?"

Dr. Young glances up at the ceiling. A security camera? She clears her throat and begins writing a prescription. She's ignoring my question. Or maybe she didn't hear me.

"Here's a prescription for the pills in case something happens to the ones I just gave you. Feel free to call me if you have any questions. And good luck with everything."

Someone knocks on the door. "Irene? Could you come out here for a moment?"

Dr. Young presses the slip of synthesized paper into my palm and looks straight into my eyes. She has these incredibly intense eyes, and her proximity to me makes me nervous. I try to act normal.

She speaks to me in a low voice. "For the record, if it was someone I love who died, and they loved me, I would keep them looping endlessly. Then at least *I* would know they'll feel loved forever, and I would be loved by them forever, too."

As I exit the building, I unfold the prescription she gave me. A smaller slip of synthesized paper falls out. It reads in her scrawling handwriting: MEET ME. AFTER YOUR 1ST SESSION. FOR NOOR.

✿

"Rimjhim Gire Sawan," sung by Lata Mangeshkar and Kishore Kumar, plays at a low volume in a beautiful living room. The room is bathed in a pale blue light from massive, glowing screens covering each wall, showing various pictures of deep-sea creatures, ocean views, and Noor with her ten-year-old daughter Sana (currently at a sleepover). Noor and Irene stand together by the door.

"I can't get them. Nobody can know I've gotten this procedure done, and if I show up bald with the cannula guides drilled in, it would be pretty obvious. Please my love, trust me." Noor gently brushes some hair out of Irene's face, runs a finger along the slight wrinkles at the corner of her eye. Irene pulls her into a tight embrace.

"Fuck! Can't you tell me anything? Why are you so afraid of them knowing? I don't even know where you work, what you're working on. But why did you get the procedure done if you won't—are you in danger? If anyone tries to hurt you I swear to fucking hell I will—"

"Shh. I promise I'm not in danger right now. This is just a precaution. In case my research is somehow compromised. I shouldn't have even told you that I got the procedure done today. But you were bound to see the orange pills eventually, and you literally work in this field, so you'd know what they do."

"But if you're not playing anything back, why do you need to take the pills? You won't be getting the daily hallucination!"

Noor breaks away from the embrace and looks through her handbag for a few seconds before taking out a box of white pills. "REM suppressors. Won't be getting any dreams for some time now, so the morning pill will definitely give me the hallucination and mark out my different experiences. I'll be taking these white ones instead of the night pills. Please Irene, just trust that I need to do this. I can't tell you why yet. In a couple of years, I won't have to keep this a secret anymore, and I'll tell you all about my work. And once this isn't a secret anymore, I'll tell the world about us. But right now I *need* to keep a low profile. I cannot let anyone know I've ... *met* someone here, and I cannot let anyone know about the procedure. Couple of years. That's all. Hey ..."

She takes Irene to the living room couch. Above them is a skylight, showing a dark, almost starless night sky. Noor sits with Irene's head in her lap, stroking her hair. It feels like they've known each other for their whole lives, even if they've only been together for four months.

"What do you think we'll be like in a couple of years? Together, I hope," Noor laughs and smiles down at Irene.

Irene smiles back, and the wrinkles around her eyes deepen. "Married."

"Wow, really? You think so?"

"Mhm. Right now, I'm certain of it." She pulls Noor down for a deep kiss. "Noor, I do trust you. I worry about you, but I trust you."

"I love you. Thank you."

"I love you, too."

☼

A massive fruiting body, covered in bulbous sacs, stretches out through the skull of what used to be Dr. Meyers, threatening to burst at any moment and release countless more spores into the air. On a table in the center of the room is a water tank containing a piece of the sea sponge Noor is studying, the one they discovered recently at the bottom of the ocean, that cures the new plagues. Next to the sea sponge are various insect carcasses, arranged neatly in a grid, and all with fruiting bodies from various insect-pathogenizing *Ophiocordyceps* fungi sticking out of their skulls and bodies. On the floor, an over-turned container is surrounded by a swarm of the insects it used to hold. They should have been dead from *Ophiocordyceps* long ago, but they were cured.

Noor unfolds her touchscreen and checks the security camera footage that she'd saved again. It shows Dr. Meyers, looking like he'd just gotten out of bed, barefoot, disheveled, in a T-shirt and boxers, stumbling around in the middle of the night. Zigzagging through a hallway, he bumps into walls and columns and doors as though he's possessed, until he reaches the door to the room. He presses his hand against a scanner and falls into the room as soon as the door opens. Dragging himself across the floor in an eerily contorted crawl, he makes his way to the table, lowers his hand into the water tank, and presses his palm against the sea sponge.

The footage then speeds up to show the fruiting body breaking through Dr. Meyers' skull, developing spore sacs, and continuing to grow longer, covered in brain matter, blood, and cerebrospinal fluid. The similarity of this fruiting body to the ones from *Ophiocordyceps* is impossible to ignore.

Had the sponge somehow caused an insect-pathogenizing fungus to mutate and attack a human being? The whole reason the sponge, of an entirely new genus, *Panaceius,* is so important is the incredible, unprecedented ability of its unspecialized archaeocyte cells to trans-form perfectly into a far larger variety of specialized cells than those of other sponges . . .

Someone's walking down the hallway. Noor quickly shuts down her touchscreen and hurries away. After she exits the building, she opens her touchscreen again, and reconfigures the security camera in the hallway she was just in to stop looping earlier footage of the area when it was empty.

Her job is to study the flask cells of the sponge's larvae in a differ-ent building altogether. She wasn't supposed to be here, and she's not supposed to have access to that security footage of Dr. Meyers either. But Noor has this overwhelming feeling that there's something *seriously* strange about *Panaceius meyeri*, and she's determined to keep digging at it.

☼

Noor walks to the Learning Lab school to pick Sana up. On her way, she passes a group of children leaving the school with completely expressionless faces wearing T-shirts that say, "You Won't Hear Our Voices Until We Hear Yours" and "We Won't Laugh Until You Save Our Future." She smiles at them as they pass, and they nod at her.

Noor remembers when Sana first joined this youth movement, almost seven months ago. They had just moved here, into a house given to her by the company she had joined, and were unpacking boxes in the living room. They were taking out the incubating chamber where Sana had grown from a preserved early twenty-first century embryo ten years earlier. Sana wrote her thoughts down for Noor on her touchscreen.

WE'RE NOT SPEAKING OR SHOWING OUR EMOTIONS ON OUR FACES UNTIL THE ADULTS MEET OUR DEMANDS. IF THEY DON'T MEET THESE DEMANDS, SO MANY OF US WILL DIE FROM THE POLLUTION AND THE WATER FLOODING AND MORE AND MORE DISEASES THAT WILL SHOW UP. AND WE DON'T WANT TO DIE.

"Won't it be difficult though? Not showing anything at all?"

IT IS, AT FIRST. BUT WE LEARN. AND I WILL WRITE IT OUT IF I AM HAPPY OR UPSET ABOUT SOMETHING. YOU JUST WON'T SEE IT ON MY FACE ANYMORE OR HEAR MY VOICE ANYMORE.

Noor kneeled next to her daughter. "Can I give you a hug?"

Sana nodded and Noor embraced her. "Sana, you're the bravest person I know. I hope all the demands are met. I want you to have the happiest future imaginable." She let go of Sana after a while.

After unpacking in silence for some time, Noor spoke again. "By the way, about those diseases. Don't tell anybody this, but that sea sponge Mommy came here to study might help with them."

I READ ABOUT THE SEA SPONGE. WHY DOES IT LEAK STUFF THAT POLLUTES THE OCEAN AS BADLY AS MICROPLASTICS WHEN SOMEONE GETS PIECES OF IT TO STUDY?

Noor sighed. "Well, we don't know right now. But hopefully the more we study it, the more we'll be able to benefit from the parts of it that cure diseases and stop the parts that harm the rest of the ocean."

I HOPE YOU DO THAT SOON.

"Yeah, so do I."

Their movement did seem to be working. Or at least, a major demand on their list is being met, whether it's because of the movement or because of something else. No more cars, and the roads of the state are being replaced with zero-emission magnetic levitation tracks.

P. meyeri, though. Killing deep-sea corals, leaking all sorts of pollutants that integrate themselves into other creatures' respiratory and digestive tracks ... only after humans started harvesting it. And Dr. Meyers. Was it simply a coincidence that the person who discovered this sponge died in this way? The specialization used in the way the sponge killed him was astounding.

Where the fungus spore would have contained the enzyme chitinase to break down the chitin in an insect's exoskeleton, the spores that attacked Dr. Meyers contained keratinase, to get through the human epidermis. Then they manipulated the actin cytoskeletons of the endothelial cells lining his blood vessels, causing the endothelial cells to engulf the spores, creating structures from which they entered the bloodstream. Traveling up until they reached his brain, the spores used the same process to cross the blood-brain barrier. They immediately seized control of his neural activity, activating various types of memories and cues. Dr. Meyers was forced to travel to the room holding the sponge and touch it, in a way analogous to, yet very different from how the nerve toxins in an infected ant tell it to climb to the forest floor and bite down on a leaf. The fruiting body broke through his skull soon afterward.

The specialization in the design of these spores was so intricate ... *how* did the sponge know to do all of this? It wasn't even a spore that was a mutated form of *Ophiocordyceps*. No, this spore was created from scratch, *inspired* by the fungus.

If her hunch is right, *P. meyeri* is demonstrating markers of a lot more than consciousness.

Sana tugs at her sleeve, and the two start walking back home. When there are no other people around, Sana takes out her flute. Six months earlier, Sana told Noor that she'd created a cipher, combining music with the Fibonacci sequence, to communicate with her friends without adults knowing. While it was against the rules her friends had agreed on, she wanted to show her mother what she'd made, under a sworn oath of secrecy that Noor would be the only adult to ever know about it.

With enough practice, one could look at what appears to be really awful-sounding sheet music and translate it into a message. With even more practice, one could *hear* the music and translate it mentally, which is how Sana communicates to her friends and to Noor these days, using her flute.

At school today we learned about the Indian roofed turtle. I think it is my new favorite extinct animal. I think it is very cute.

"That's awesome! Is that turtle what you want to write your science class report on?"

I think so. Yes. Sana plays. **I want to write mainly about how much I like it and how it went extinct. It is really sad Mommy. Its habitat was mainly in small streams or shallow coastal waters and it fed on aquatic plants. But with ocean acidity levels going up and streams drying out it could not find food or shelter. And too many people started keeping it as a pet, so the wild ones went extinct while the captive ones lived much shorter lives.**

Noor shakes her head sadly. "Sometimes humans can just do so much damage, maybe even without realizing it. And so often in this world, those realizations come far too late."

Sana just nods, and then looks at her mother blankly. Noor feels a brief, sudden pang of anger, sadness, and longing for just a hint of emotion on her daughter's face. *Is supporting this the right thing to do? What if this is causing her harm?* She's trying her best to encourage Sana to do whatever she feels is the right thing to do, and to pursue her interests. And yet, she can't help but occasionally feel afraid that maybe she's doing something wrong, maybe this is "harmful and detrimental to child development" as some other parents are saying. But they're only brief moments of doubt, and most of the time she feels immense pride toward the strength and resilience of her daughter.

It's a powerful thing, the physical expressions of one's emotions. And a powerful thing to withhold as well, which is why it's working so well. Parents would do anything to see or hear or feel their kids speak again, smile again, laugh again, even cry again. Noor herself has spent many nights, after Sana has fallen asleep, watching old videos and weeping at the sound of her daughter's voice. She feels guilty, selfish for missing those moments so much even with Sana still communicating her feelings clearly through her flute or through typing on her touchscreen. *But maybe that's the whole point.* After all, she's taken far more personal actions to combat the climate catastrophes since her daughter joined the movement...

What are you thinking about?

"I was thinking about how humans sometimes do harmful things without realizing it, and how sometimes it's hard to tell whether something is the right thing to do or the wrong thing to do."

I think about that sometimes, too. In my opinion, as long as something will help people eventually . . . it is the right thing to do.

Noor thinks for a long time. "What if it might never help people at all? What if a decision involves taking away something that is helping lots of people? Do you think it can still be doing the right thing?"

Is it helping anything or anybody at all?

"Yes. It would help something very much, save it from being very badly hurt and mistreated. Something just as important as people, maybe."

Sana is very quiet until they reach their home. Noor places her finger inside a small, clean, airtight cavity next to her front door's lock. A sterilized needle quickly pricks her finger and collects a drop of her blood to scan. After a moment, the scanner beeps and flashes green, and the door opens.

The flute plays its strange melody as Sana's expressionless gaze meets her mother's eyes. **Mommy. If it saves something else from being hurt, I think it is still the right thing to do.**

I wake up, disconnect the tubes from my head as fast as I can, and sprint to the bathroom, where I retch into the toilet, though no bile enters my mouth. *What the hell? I'm getting the nausea side effect now? I've never gotten it before! Fuck.*

"You should keep an eye on Dr. Young. Meet her, see if you can find anything out about her. It's a weird coincidence that she's the one who modified our neurons, and she had such an intimate relationship with Noor without mentioning anything to us." Marie shoves a handful of spiced, fried crickets into her mouth before passing the bowl over to Anthony, who takes a handful and passes the bowl to me. Switching to insects as a source of protein is becoming increasingly popular these days.

"Yeah. I'm meeting her soon." I politely take a few from the bowl. They taste okay but need more cayenne powder and salt.

"Are you okay Nithya? You look kind of flushed." Anthony looks concerned.

My stomach feels so weird. I feel pretty nauseated and stuff is really churning around in there. My period literally just ended . . . and it doesn't really feel like cramps either, or gas pain. So what the hell?

"I think it's just indigestion. I'll be okay."

Anthony hands me an antacid, and I take it. Pretty soon I'm feeling a bit better. It was probably just an upset stomach.

"Maybe go easy on the spicy snack." Marie takes the bowl away from me.

"Are you kidding me? That spice is weak as fuck. If anything, my stomach would protest at the *lack* of cayenne in that bowl."

They laugh, and then we sit in silence for some time, researching Noor's place of work. Eventually Anthony closes his touchscreen and looks at me.

"Okay, I have to know. What was it like? You've been acting kind of strange today."

What was it like?

She was alive. I wasn't myself, I was her, entirely. The world felt so different. It's so different, in her head. And I can remember everything about her life, in such great detail. It was all so vivid! She was *actually alive* again. And they were all *alive*, too. Irene, Sana, everyone she interacted with. They were as alive as Marie and Anthony are to me right now. What is the difference really, after all? The neural activity in my brain when I interact with someone is what creates everything I understand about the person I'm interacting with. That's all the evidence I can ever get from them to prove they're alive (unless I'm playing light into my head to become them, of course). Recreating those patterns ... it's the same as recreating those people, at least what those people were to Noor. The interactions are *just as real*. They were as alive to me as anybody I walked past today.

Now I'm back in the reality I inhabit. Me, Nithya, not her. But now scents and sights and sounds around me are bringing up old memories that are not mine, of a carpet in a house I'd never been to, of a beach in a country I've never visited. Ghostly fragments of thought are invading my reality constantly, of laughter and voices and experiences with strangers and friends and family I have never known. I never realized how many memories I remembered in a single day until I was forced to start separating recollections of my autobiographical timeline from recollections of hers. They're *constant*. Every single thing in my surroundings, from Anthony and Marie to the snack bowl to my touchscreen, now has two different emotional states associated with it. Different fragments of memory that are dug up to navigate the experience associated with interacting with any object or person. And I can *feel the differences.*

I'm here now, everything around me is real. I know it. And it's especially comforting to inhabit my own reality again because, well, for a while . . . I blinked out of existence. When Noor was alive again, living in my head as my brain activity, I wasn't there at all anymore. My brain was only a vessel for her to live her life out, with no self-awareness of my role as a vessel, even. I was nothingness for the period of time where she came back to life, and now that I'm awake, she's nothingness again.

I clear my throat and turn my attention back to Anthony and Marie. "It's so ... intimate, this whole thing. Is this right? I mean ... I remember her life. I have her memories. Is this okay? I feel strange about it."

"It must feel really weird." Marie looks at me sympathetically. "But you know the contracts you have to sign when you get the procedure done. You can relive your experiences, or gift them to someone else you choose. And in the case of a sudden and unexpected death, you give your consent to let an investigator live your experiences. Noor knew all these conditions when she got the procedure done. And well, she's not alive anymore, Nithya. And her family wanted us to do this as well. They want to know what happened to her as well."

"Yeah, but she didn't *know* what it would be like. Nobody knew. She's alive again, Marie! It's her, in the past, sure, but she's as alive as we are right now. She couldn't have known what I would be experiencing."

Anthony speaks up. "Hey, this is all for Noor's sake. We're going to find out what happened. This will give us the best chance we have at figuring out the whole situation. It's our job, Nithya. For her family, for her memory. We owe it to them to investigate her death and give them some closure."

At the end of the day, on my walk home, I pass a father and his three-year-old daughter. I smile, remembering Sana when she was three. She was always running off somewhere, climbing a tree or investigating some bug she found. For a moment, I can almost hear her flute, picture her blank stare ... I catch myself and quickly work to separate Noor's memories from mine before continuing home.

☼

I am *not* prepared for the swell of emotions and deep sense of shared history I experience when I see Irene Young sitting in a booth of a café downtown, sipping her coffee. It's almost *painful*, the physical ache in my chest and my gut, of love and lust and nostalgia and camaraderie. It takes a whole lot more effort to separate all of Noor's emotions toward Irene from mine right now, compared to separating the two emotional states when interacting with something like an apple. And it's really hard to think properly when I sit down across from this woman Noor loved.

Irene clears her throat. "Do you want anything to eat or drink? The coffee here is from one of the new orbiting gardens. Pretty amazing that what I'm drinking was grown in sealed chambers up in space. Quite the solution to the dwindling arable land problem, isn't it? And it's pretty good coffee, too."

As soon as she speaks, the context of the situation hits me. "Can we just cut the bullshit and start talking? Why didn't we know about you? Why did you take the job of modifying our neurons? What the hell do you know, and why the hell haven't you told us already? And what was with that note? Why couldn't you say anything before I started this?"

She sighs. "Look, it's really complicated. But I want to keep my relationship with her a secret, alright? The place she worked for is not something I want to get too involved with. They know about me already, but they don't really know about my relationship with her. And I didn't even learn about her work until . . ."

"Until what?"

Irene looks down at her coffee. "Well, let me just say that they know I had met Noor. I found out about where she worked a week or so before she died. And I inquired about her afterward. They were really sad about her death . . . but they also told me that they were worried she was planning something really dangerous. They said she was going to do something that would risk a lot of people's lives. And that maybe she wasn't in the best state of mind, maybe she was delusional."

I almost laugh. *Delusional?* "Trust me, that's not true. I think I would know, I'm living her life every night."

She smiles sadly. "And maybe that's exactly why you wouldn't see it. Because you're in her head, you don't see that her delusions aren't true. To the person afflicted by them, they actually *are* real. If you're living Noor's reality, experiencing the world around you from her perspective, of course you're inclined to believe her thoughts." She gulps down the rest of her coffee. "I never thought she might be experiencing delusions when she was alive either. Everything she said or did always seemed to make perfect sense." Irene sighs. "But maybe I was wrong."

I feel a sudden longing to hold her, make her laugh and smile and forget all her troubles. I try to separate Noor's emotions from mine but . . . this time some of it is coming from me, too, at least I think it is. The whole time, she's been digging the corner of her short-clipped thumbnail into the wooden table, hard, creating an arc indent in the table. I briefly experience the desire to hold her hand but decide against it.

"I'm sorry, Irene. I'm sorry she's gone."

"Mhm." She takes a deep breath and looks up at me, perfectly composed again.

When she speaks again, she chuckles a bit. "You know, I'm pretty jealous of you Nithya. You get to live it. You get to know her in the most intimate possible way."

"I don't know. It's such a new thing, I have no idea whether or not it's the moral thing to do. I mean, I'm a stranger. It feels a bit . . . wrong. And you, Sana . . . it's a lot, Irene. It's intruding on all of your privacy, too."

She looks me in the eyes. "But you're not going to stop, are you?"

"No, I mean, I owe it to her family and—"

Irene laughs at this. "Oh come on. You and I both know it's not that. I have *never* seen someone so enthusiastic about getting that procedure done before I met you. So what is it, really?"

She orders another coffee, and I order one, too, before speaking. "Okay. Fine. I want to know what it's like inside someone else's head. I've always wanted to. I want to know how things taste to them, how they think of other people, how their *entirely different set of memories* influences what the world around them looks like. And now I can. That's the truth."

"Fair enough." She chugs more coffee.

"How do you feel, though? About me . . . knowing so much about your relationship?"

After an almost unbearably long pause, Irene smiles. "It should have been me. Not you. If it had to be anybody, it should have been me. But she never had the time to think about who would get her experiences after her death. And she never requested for anyone to live them out. Nobody even knew about me. She died suddenly, so it's all being investigated, and so you got them. You don't appreciate what you've been given the way I would have. But I've come to terms with it. The light pulses have been encoded to fit your specific synaptic structure, and quantum encrypted to prevent any further access to her memories. So it can't be me. But it should have been. Am I fine with you knowing so much about my relationship with her? I could be, if you just do something for me."

"What do you want me to do?"

She grabs my hand. "Tell me about it. Tell me about her thoughts, what it is like in her mind. Tell me everything, all of it, until every last light pulse has run through your head. It's why I wanted to meet you.

You don't have to tell me anything related to the investigation. I just want to know what it's *like*. Starting now. Tell me, please."

I do.

As I get up to leave, after hours have gone by, with plans to see her again the following week, Irene asks me, "How have you been feeling so far? With the pills and the hallucinations and everything."

"The hallucinations aren't that bad, but I've actually been feeling a bit nauseated since I started."

She looks concerned. "You should see someone about that. That's not normal, especially since you never had the side effect before."

"I think I'll be okay, it's dying down and—"

"Seriously, just to be safe. It wouldn't hurt to check."

"Alright, I'll make an appointment with someone."

☼

The nurse and doctor at the hospital hand me all the information I need to know, along with the charts and statements laying it all out for me, neatly clipped together on synthesized paper and an electronic copy on my touchscreen.

"Have you started the coughing fits yet?" the doctor asks.

"No, I'm still just getting the nausea." I look down at my hands.

"Good. So you aren't contagious yet—too many people wait until they start coughing, without coming in during the noncontagious nausea phase like they're supposed to . . . that's the only thing that's keeping this spreading, these days, honestly. At least it's very rare to get infected now."

They hand me packets of liquid. "Here, drink these twice every day to prevent fluid buildup and the bile-inducing coughing fits. They'll coat your esophagus with a protective layer that will stop you from ever becoming contagious and prevent the mutation-induced signals from leaving the lysogenic squamous cells." The doctor clears their throat. "Please know, this contagion-prevention mechanism cannot be used prophylactically, and would actually be really harmful to an uninfected person, so please don't try giving it to anyone else. It only works on an infected person with their viral-DNA-containing squamous cell genome. And *please* remember that this alone will not cure you—it will be eventually fatal without the cure—so you really need to start ingesting the archaeocytes, too. But we're well out of the horror from a couple years ago, this illness is easily treatable now. The archaeocytes work wonders and have been made highly accessible! So remember to start that sponge treatment soon in addition to drinking this liquid, and you'll be cured!"

I have it. I'm sick.

☼

"Rajnigandha Phool Tumhare," sung by Lata Mangeshkar, plays through Noor's mind. As the sub quickly sinks into the sea, the colors around Noor start to fade away. She watches her red shirt turn to blue-gray as she remembers Irene's words over and over again.

"I'm sick, Noor. I have it. I was able to get a spot in one of those trials, and they've been able to cure every single person in the trials so far. But I wanted to tell you . . . in case something ever goes wrong."

When only blue light is able to reach the depths, Noor climbs up, out of the spherical observation portion of the sub, and sits across from Matias, her fellow crew member on their two-person sampling mission, at a small folding table.

They're headed to a newly discovered *P. meyeri* colony at the bottom of the Mariana Trench. Deep-sea remotely operated vehicles have already mapped out the massive, linked caverns inhabited by the colony. According to images from the ROVs, the walls, ceilings, and floors of the spaces are all covered with countless sponges, arranged in an astoundingly intricate fashion. Specialized sponges occupy different chambers, each one shaped to make optimal use of the water currents, avoid danger, protect reproducing sponges, and capture the most food. It's one of the most complex systems Noor has ever encountered.

This is wrong—she begins to think, but shakes the thought away quickly, remembering Irene's face as her optimistic façade eventually disappeared to reveal her terror.

"I don't want to die like that." Irene spoke through sobs. It was painful to watch, and all Noor could do was hold her close.

"Is this your kid?" Matias points to the screensaver on her touchscreen, flashing family pictures of Noor and Sana.

"Yeah, that's her. Her name's Sana, she's just turned eleven."

"She's about my Syd's age. Such a handful these days, these kids. At least, Syd is. Syd gets into trouble at school every day now, for not responding to questions mainly. But it's not their fault. It's those other kids who got them to join that ridiculous movement. I get wanting to prevent and stop the climate catastrophes, but this is just extreme and unhealthy. My kid hasn't changed the damn expression on their face in over a month, it's driving me and my husband up the walls!"

Noor is taken aback. "Actually—"

"I hope your kid never gets into that stuff. It's dangerous, really. And all those experimental public schools cropping up these days, encouraging that crap, aren't helping at all. Glad I didn't send Syd to one of those. Where does your Sana go?"

"Sana goes to an experimental public school, Learning Lab, past the wind turbines. And I think the youth movement is incredibly brave."

"Ah." Matias sits quietly for some time, his face adopting an expression of deep concern. "Look, it's for your kid's sake that I'm telling you this. The movement—"

Noor narrows her eyes. "*Look*, I'm going through my own shit coming to terms with my daughter's choices, but I feel guilty enough that I'm *going through shit* about it at all. I should just respect what she's doing and admire her strength and bravery. And I *certainly* don't need you to butt into any of my personal business. I think, to maximize the productivity of this mission, we should just focus on our research. Why don't you tell me *about that* instead?"

This time Matias looks taken aback. "Fine." He opens his touchscreen and shows Noor a folder full of images of a *P. meyeri* sponge's spicules. "These are images taken by the ROVs, showing the portions of the sponges facing the interior of the chamber cavities, toward all the other sponges. The spicules on this side are incredibly complex and specifically designed to bring light deep into the sponge. Their refractive index far surpasses that of our corneas. And there's a lens, too! My question is, why does it need to collect light with such specificity and efficiency? I think there must be some sort of symbiosis with bioluminescent and light-sensing organisms we haven't found in previous samples, that requires light to reach the interior of the sponge. And if we can control the signaling system they have, if they have one of course, we can possibly increase their productivity."

Fascinated, Noor studies a document listing potential chemical impurities that could have formed in the spicules to improve their refractive index.

A sharp, high-pitched tone plays in the sub. It's time to put on their nitrogen regulators and suits. Noor and Matias place needles attached to a system of quarter-inch diameter tubes onto various marked areas on their bodies. Noor winces slightly at this, even though the process is painless. As soon as the needles have been taped in place, they each attach the tubes to thin, flexible, cloth-covered plates that they strap to their backs, and finally press the glowing blue button on each of their plates. Once the buttons are pressed, a microscopically thin system of smaller tubes begins to stretch out from the needles and into their internal tissues, throughout their bodily systems, causing a brief shiver to run through them. One of the most pressing concerns when working in the midnight zone is avoiding any sort of depth-pressure related injury, such as future decompression sickness from pressurized surface-level gases depressurizing upon resurfacing. The nitrogen regulators manage the distribution of surface gases, mainly nitrogen, within the bodies of Noor and Matias, to make sure nothing like that happens.

After putting on the nitrogen regulators, the two of them step into heavy, bulky suits and helmets, and turn on communications with each other. Their suits can collect oxygen from the surrounding water, allowing them to walk around under water for a virtually unlimited amount of time.

"You're studying the flask cells, right?" Matias struggles to pull gloves over his hands.

"Yeah. Sponge larvae have some form of a rudimentary sensory processing system using their flask cells that allows them to move to a place where they can become sessile, *P. meyeri* included. But *P. meyeri* flask cells are different. When the larva becomes sessile, the flask cells *continue to develop.*"

"How so?"

"That's the thing. I can track their development up to a certain extent, but for some reason all the larvae I have die before reaching adulthood, even when deep-sea conditions are simulated perfectly. I don't understand it. In the adults, there is a thin extra layer, lined with mesohyl, that covers almost all of the sponge's interior surfaces. I think that's where the fully developed flask cells are. When we collect the specialized sponge archaeocyte cells to make the medication, we have to access them using certain entryways into the sponge body that aren't covered by this extra layer. If you cut into that layer, the sponge kills itself instantly, producing a dark oily liquid that somehow dissolves any remnants of this extra layer, along with much of the rest of the sponge."

Matias frowns. "That's why the sponge colonies used to die out when we got ROVs to remove samples to bring up. Even if the ROVs didn't cut into the extra layer of the sponge it was harvesting, they had to cut into the surrounding sponges to remove it, and the liquid spread, killing the rest of the colony and hurting other organisms."

Noor nods. "Yeah. Now we harvest the *P. meyeri* using those few entryways. You know what's even weirder though? The sponges kill themselves if you even try to *scan* them to see into that layer. How are they even able to detect the scan? I don't understand it."

Matias frowns. "So how are you going to observe it?"

"My idea relies on the hope that the sponges will protect their next generation at all costs. If the larvae are in the process of escaping the sponge they developed in, maybe the sponge will override the trigger to self-destruct, and maybe I can scan, observe, and take snapshots of the fully developed flask cells inside the adult, if there are any, during that brief window. The sponges aren't reproducing in the labs, so I'll try it in the colony itself. Hopefully if I do this, we can find a way to stop the sponges from leaking that corrosive liquid and harming themselves and their surroundings, in the future."

They finish adjusting their suits in silence. Matias taps Noor on the shoulder and points to a switch that would mute communications with the surface crew. Noor nods, and Matias speaks after muting the communications.

"*P. meyeri* is pretty special, isn't it?"

Noor raises an eyebrow. "It is . . ."

Matias sighs. "You know, if the times were different, I wouldn't have been doing this. We're rushing into churning out the treatments since it was such a widespread emergency just a few years ago. But these sponges . . . we've barely scratched the surface of understanding them, and they're unlike any ever known before. Yeah, sponges can't think. But somehow this one reacts to its surroundings in an incredibly nuanced way. *Why,* you know? If the times were any different, I would have done things so differently. I would have taken things slowly, and carefully, and with less . . . I don't know, exploitation."

Noor gives him a half smile. "I know what you mean. You know, I was almost going to—"

The expression on Matias' face darkens as he interrupts her. "But times aren't different. And I *want* to do this. You know, a few years ago, Syd got sick. It got so bad, their intestines weren't absorbing anything . . . We had all resigned ourselves to making them as comfortable as possible in their final few months. But then they got into one of the trials, and now we're able to fret about what they're doing with their life, not *whether they'll live.* After Syd got sick, I knew I had to get myself into this line of research. Frankly, if exploiting *P. meyeri* means other Syds can live, I'd uproot every last sponge in existence."

Noor nods. "I understand, Matias. Someone I love, someone I want . . . a future with . . . is getting treated right now. And I want to do everything in my power to protect her, even if it means fighting every instinct I have."

"Good. I'm glad we understand each other." He turns communications with the surface crew back on.

When they have reached the colony, Matias and Noor move through an airlock into the exit chamber. Once sealed into the exit chamber, the door in front of them, divided into slats, starts rotating each slat individually as the chamber fills with water. Once horizontal rather than vertical, the slats slide into the walls, leaving an opening through which Matias and Noor leave the sub.

The ROVs had assembled a thin metal grate pathway going through the chambers, just above the sponges on the floors, so that people could walk through without destroying or touching anything along the way. They turn on the bioluminescence sensors on their helmets, which have scanners and filters built in so they can focus on collecting samples and not have to use handheld tools to view or scan the sponges. The helmets track their eye movements and some of their neural activity. They also superimpose faint 3D models of the sponges around them onto the darkness, so that along with any bioluminescence, they'd be able to see the general shapes of their surroundings to know where to go without shining any bright lights.

"Look at this!" Matias calls to Noor. He pumps a bioluminescent dye, packed with glowing plankton, around the base of a massive sponge near the entrance of the chamber. After being absorbed into the pores of the sponge, one would expect the plankton in the water to be consumed, and the remaining plankton-free, non-glowing water pumped back out. Instead, the dye begins to trace a pathway going from one sponge to another, throughout the chambers. "They're directing the water to one another and sharing the food!"

Noor calls back to him. "Hey, I think it's time to split up. I'm going to the center chamber, it's almost time for the larvae to leave the sponges. But keep me updated." She sets her helmet to show a small viewport in the bottom right corner in which she can see what Matias sees.

Each *P. meyeri* colony is structured similarly. The sponges near the entrance of the chamber system are the largest, informally named the "sentry" sponges. Almost all the water that flows into these chambers goes through them. The deeper into the chambers one travels, the smaller the sponges get. Only the smallest sponges, in the centermost chamber of the colony, produce larvae. Using the intricate system of directing water, *P. meyeri* is able to send sperm from all the various shapes and sizes of sponges that are needed in the different chambers to the centermost chamber, ensuring that more of those shapes and sizes will exist in the next generation.

But how do they know which larvae developed from which sperm? And how do the colonies keep growing if there are a limited number of chambers? There are so many questions!

Matias' voice sounds through Noor's helmet. "Hey, I want to put on some music, real quietly. Do you want to listen, too?"

"That depends on what you're going to play. If it's the stuff my daughter listens to, that's going to be a no from me."

"Space Oddity," by David Bowie begins to play in Noor's helmet.

Noor laughs. "Wow, a song about dying alone, floating away in the abyss of space. Depressing choice."

"Our current situation just sort of brought that song to my mind."

"I'm amazed at your optimism. Also, this song is ancient!"

Matias chuckles. "Says the person playing Bollywood songs from god knows what decade for the entire first half of our descent."

"Hey, Lata Mangeshkar is a *legend.*"

"Um, so is David Bowie."

"True. It's a good song, too."

They walk down their separate paths for a while, humming or singing along to the song. A dragonfish, swimming in an erratic, jolting manner, convulsing, and pulsing blue bioluminescent stripes over its body, moves past Matias. Noor watches it through the small viewport at the bottom of her helmet. Matias decides to follow it before speaking again.

"You know, the nice thing about listening to music is that it kind of puts a filter over reality. Suddenly you can notice your surroundings and what's moving to the beat of the song. You yourself move differently, blink differently, notice and ignore things differently. For a moment it's not reality that you're living in, but a world directed by something else, like you're starring in a film or something. For the duration of the song it almost feels like nothing bad can happen to you. Everything, whether good or bad, feels like it's going to either match the music or wait until the song is over to happen. It makes everything seem more predictable and safe. Now, I don't want to die an agonizing death floating in any abyss, but if I had to, I'd rather have it be while I'm listening to a David Bowie song that's sort of about what I'm experiencing."

Noor smiles. "Yeah." she says quietly.

A cloud of something drifts past Noor. The helmet enhances it, applies a color filter over it to show what color it is, and zooms in to scan. It's made of larvae. *It's started.* She closes the viewport showing Matias' view so she can get a better look.

Noor watches as the cloud divides itself up and flows through the ostia of the sponges around her. *What the hell? They'll be digested!* But then the larvae pass through, out the osculums of the sponges, unharmed. They move from sponge to sponge, until they find their way to separate chambers, where the larvae just swim around in the center. They aren't old enough to become sessile yet. Noor directs her helmet to scan the interior of a sponge as the larvae pass through it, taking care not to scan through the layer of the sponge that she suspects contains the flask cells.

Tiny, flashing lights shine toward the larvae as they pass through ... upon closer inspection, it appears as though microscopic bioluminescent shrimp, fused to the inner walls of the sponge, are flashing light from their photophores. *This wasn't in any of the samples ...*

Noor opens the viewport with Matias' view again. "Matias, you have to see this! Inside the sponges—"

"Noor! I was just about to tell you! Are you seeing what I'm seeing? I found a new chamber! The opening is too small for any ROV to get through, or even notice, really! But I can just barely look through into it."

Noor expands the viewport. Through a small opening between sponges, she sees a massive chamber, lined with *P. meyeri* and filled with a large variety of marine life. Snailfish swim laps around the place. Dragonfish swarm the bottom, flashing and ... *mating? This isn't where or how they normally mate.* Transparent squid, packed tightly together, have somehow turned on one another for sustenance, fighting and eating each other, dropping particles of food into the waiting ostia of the sponges. *How did these creatures get inside the chamber? They couldn't have fit through the opening unless they got here when they'd just hatched, or when they were inside eggs.*

"I ... I don't know what to make of it!" A timer starts flashing on her helmet. It's time to hurry to the center chamber, the larvae release has almost ended.

What are we doing here? We shouldn't be here ... She moves as quickly as she can to the center chamber, full of indecision. *There are too many things we don't know, fuck, we don't know what we're doing, we should just leave this place alone, we've destroyed so many others ...* she can feel herself panicking and stands still for a moment, closing her eyes and breathing deeply.

As soon as her mind stops racing, Irene shows up in her thoughts again. Irene, the love of her life. Irene, the one she hopes to marry someday. The one who has always worried for her safety ... the one whose safety Noor worries for now. *I need to do this. For her. For our future together. She needs to get well, I cannot risk losing her, ever.*

Clenching her teeth, she heads into the centermost chamber. The floor is lined with what look like aggregated gemmules, the result of asexually reproducing sponges. *Why are they outside the sponges? And how come* P. meyeri *gemmules don't end up developing into sponges themselves, ever?* There hasn't been a single pair of *P. meyeri* sponges whose DNA matches exactly found so far. Noor carefully takes a sample of the gemmules. And then she looks up.

An intricate, coordinated display of flashing light is taking place throughout the chamber, in a beautiful recursive pattern revolving around one of the sponges, far more complex than any temple carving, any rose window, any generative design she's seen. The sponge releases its larvae, and then a different beautiful light display centering on another sponge begins as that sponge starts to release its larvae. Using the scanner, Noor finds more of those microscopic shrimp fused to the exteriors of the sponges, somehow being controlled. She steels her churning stomach and holds back her revulsion regarding what she's about to do.

As the sponge in the center of the swirling, dancing lights releases its larvae, Noor directs her helmet to scan inside the extra layer under its surface. At first, she does not know what she's looking at. But soon, she begins to understand. The insulating sheaths. The delicate branches. The electrical signals.

Neurons.

The reason it was briefly so difficult to make out what she was looking at was the *sheer number* of synapses in the thing. Noor asks the helmet to calculate how many synapses would be in the entire sponge if the concentration average held up throughout its body.

One quadrillion. Over ten times more synaptic connections than the ones in a human brain.

Noor backs away, quickly. "Oh, fuck."

Matias' voice suddenly rings out, panicked. "Some of the larvae that just arrived at this chamber . . . they're swimming to me. They— FUCK! NO—"

"Matias, head back to the sub if you can hear me! Please!"

Noor is about to turn around when she sees the lights in the chamber shift, ripple, change their pattern. They aren't centered around the sponge she was just scanning anymore. *They are centered around her.*

The larvae that had just been released from the sponge she scanned begin to swim around her, closing in rapidly until they latch on to her suit. As soon as they're stuck on, their bodies begin to rupture and burst into a dark, oily liquid that quickly spreads. *No no no no FUCK!*

She moves as fast as she can, back to the entrance of the chamber, back toward the sub, as the liquid begins to cover her helmet and block out her vision. She sees Matias staggering over, too. They fall into the chamber, shut the door, crawl through the airlock, and collapse onto the floor of the sub after Matias pushes the button to ascend.

Noor almost thinks "We made it!" when she feels blood dripping out of her nose, her mouth, her ears, and her eyes. Looking over at Matias, she sees he's going through the same thing. A splitting headache suddenly becomes agonizing, and Noor feels close to passing out. *The nitrogen regulators aren't working. We're getting decompression sickness.* She manages to shed her suit to see the quarter-inch diameter tubes clogged with the dark liquid, creeping closer and closer to the needles that lead into her body. She quickly rips out the tubes, looks over to Matias again, and sees him doing the same, and then Noor falls unconscious, her last thoughts before doing so containing a singular wish of hope that they'd survive.

✿

Noor blinks awake in a hospital bed to see Sana holding her hand, looking at her blankly. In the bed opposite her, she watches Matias begin to stir as well. At his bedside are a weeping man, and a child of about Sana's age. The weeping man says to the child, "Look Syd, he's waking up! Don't you want to greet him with a smile?"

The child types on their touchscreen

NO. I HAVE A MESSAGE TYPED UP FOR WHEN HE WAKES UP. I WORKED HARD ON IT. HE CAN READ THAT, AND HE WILL KNOW I AM HAPPY.

"But it would make him feel happier if he wakes up to—"

Matias reaches over and squeezes the man's arm, looks up at him with a smile, and shakes his head before turning to Syd.

"Hey, you're so brave. Thank you for waiting here. I'm just happy to see you, no matter what expression you have on your face. I love you Syd."

Syd nods at their father and types on their touchscreen

THANK YOU, DAD. I LOVE YOU, TOO. I'M HAPPY THAT YOU ARE AWAKE.

Noor squeezes Sana's hand tight and closes her eyes again.

✿

Irene and I sit together on the floor of my apartment, leaning against the sensory deprivation chamber, sharing a bottle of wine. It's almost empty now, and we've been talking for the whole evening. I haven't told her that I have the illness yet.

I look at her. "What was it like to know her? I'm always telling you what it's like to *be* her, but I'll never know what it was like to *know* her."

Irene smiles and closes her eyes. "Knowing her was the most wonderful thing to ever happen in my life. Our relationship was definitely a bit interesting, since we were keeping it a secret from everyone. We only met up a couple times a week, only spent nights together every Friday night when Sana was at a sleepover. But the separation only deepened our love for one another, only made us ache for the other's company even more. And it made the times we did spend together that much sweeter. Every time I woke up next to her, every time I covered my head with a pillow to block out the sound of her snores, every time I made her smile, or became frustrated with how stubborn she could be, or listened to her give an impassioned speech, or heard her *awful* singing, or just about a thousand other things, it was all connected by this incredible foundation of just ... *love*, you know? The deepest possible amount you can care about someone. I don't think I'd ever truly loved anyone until I met Noor. The day I knew, I was poring over scans of patients' brains, and a thought of her just popped into my own brain. I said aloud to the stack of scans: 'I really *care* about her.' And a week later I figured out it was love. I'm sorry, did that make any sense? I think I feel the wine." She laughs.

"That made perfect sense ... that was beautiful. I don't know if I've personally ever felt that way about anyone before. But with Noor's memories ... I know what you mean, Irene."

Irene turns to me and looks as though she's about to speak several times, the expression on her face drifting from an almost-frown to an almost-smile and back again. The intensity of her gaze makes me a bit nervous, and I laugh to shake away the slight discomfort.

"What is it?" I ask.

Irene takes a sip of wine. "Nithya, because of Noor's memories, of course ... I really have to wonder, do *you* feel something for me? I mean, you tell me how much she loved me, and you describe to me what she felt. But it's you living all of that. And you still remember all of it ... I have to wonder."

I sigh. "Honestly? Yeah, Irene. I do. Most of the time I have to work incredibly hard to separate her feelings for you from mine. And it's almost unbearably tempting to just feel everything, the full extent of her love for you ... especially because ..."

"Because what?"

I take a sip of wine. "Because *I* feel something for you, too. And I don't completely understand if it's coming from me, or if it's some memory leakage coming from Noor's experiences. But I do know that from the moment I met you, there was definitely *something*. I mean, how could there not be, you know? You're brilliant, and powerful, and . . . intense and *so* beautiful. How could I not feel something?"

Our faces seem to be drawing closer and closer together, but maybe it's the wine. She half smiles. "What would it even be like, us, together? You, with the lover of the person whose experiences you're living to investigate her death, your feelings influenced by who-knows-what. And me, with the person who gets to live the life of the woman I loved, a person who has probably been influenced by her in the past few weeks. I'm definitely not sober enough to untangle all the moral and ethical implications of that right now."

I look at her for a while before speaking. "I don't really know either. It would be pretty uncharted territory, wouldn't it?"

Irene smiles at me, and I have no idea what compels me to say what I say next, but I smile back at her a little bitterly, and whisper, "But in its own slightly fucked-up way, isn't it kind of a perfect match?"

And with that, our lips meet, and there is no turning back.

We laugh and we kiss, scattering clothes around the place as we make our way to the bedroom.

"Is it okay if I don't play the light pulses tonight?"

"Yeah you can postpone them for one night."

At the entrance to the bedroom, I pause for a moment and pull away from her, look into her eyes. "Hey, Irene. I completely understand if it wouldn't be okay but . . . can I feel what Noor felt for you, just for tonight? Please?"

Irene nods. "I don't know if it's the right thing to do, but I want that, too, Nithya. I need that, too."

I kiss her deeply, run my hands through her hair, and let Noor's feelings flood into my own, creating a beautiful mix of deep, comfortable, strong love, and new, exciting, passionate lust. I stop separating my memories from hers, and the two worlds blend together. It's overwhelming, but in a good way, and as it hits me that *I've loved this woman countless times before*, the care and intimacy and ache I suddenly experience for her is the most powerful thing I have ever felt. As we make love, I realize I'm not Nithya anymore in the moment, and I'm not Noor either. I've become someone entirely different, memories and emotions from the two lives blending together, but everything focusing and revolving around . . . *Irene*. I know it's probably a mistake. But I tell myself just *for this one night*, I let myself become this new entity, and it feels beautiful, and right, and . . . *true.*

Afterward, as we lie together, the sweat drying off our bodies under a fresh, cool sheet, I look over at her and decide to tell her.

"I have the illness. And the trials are so accessible now that I got a place in one easily. I'm taking the esophagus-coating liquid twice a day to ensure that I'm not contagious, I won't get any bile-inducing coughing fits. But . . . I'm not going to do the treatment that would cure me. I can't tell you why right now, but I cannot bring myself to do it. I think I'll have around a year. I'm sorry."

She looks at me for a long time, and I can't read the expression on her face. But then she turns off the lamplight next to us, and pulls me close to her, wrapping her arms around me. I fall asleep there in her arms, feeling absolutely, comfortably, wonderfully safe.

☼

I wake up to a crashing sound in the bathroom, and someone saying "FUCK!" loudly. I pull on a T-shirt and rush to the bathroom, where I see Irene sobbing. A toothbrush holder had been knocked over into the first of the pillboxes for Noor's experiences. The box has opened in the process, and pills are scattered everywhere, in the toilet and the sink and on the floor.

I hold Irene close to me, and she starts to say, "I'm sorry Nithya! I'm so sorry I'm so sorry I'm so fucking sorry," as she buries her head in my shoulder, snot and tears soaking through my shirt.

"It's okay! Seriously, this is no big deal! I have a prescription, I can get more pills. Don't worry, seriously!"

But she doesn't seem to hear me. She just keeps saying it over and over again. *"I'm so sorry."*

☼

Noor sits on an uncomfortably textured couch in a small waiting room, her mind going blank as she observes the beige and blue diamond pattern on the carpet at her feet. Someone finally opens a door and calls her inside. "They're ready to see you now!"

She enters a room full of people way above her pay grade. She'd tried to remember everyone's names but couldn't retain any of them.

"Sit down, make yourself comfortable! Do you want any water, coffee, anything?"

Noor shakes her head and sits.

A woman at the head of the table they're all arranged around leans forward, smiling. "Great stuff you found during your last sampling mission, isn't it?"

Noor frowns. "We can't continue doing this. *P. meyeri* is intelligent! A single sponge contains more synapses than we can even fully comprehend! We have to tell everyone."

They look at one another, before turning to her. One man sighs.

"Look—Noor—right? We . . . we already know about this. Someone discovered this before you. Actually . . . we've known about this almost since we discovered the sponge. In fact, it is a crucial part of how we treat the diseases."

"What?"

The woman at the head of the table widens her smile. "We have this under control! There is nothing for you to worry about. We've known about this for some time, and we've taken our research on *P. meyeri* in some very interesting directions! Some of the techniques used to treat certain mental illnesses these days in humans, physically changing motivation especially, can be mapped to the nervous system of *P. meyeri*! And the best news is that it does not feel pain, or grief, or any sort of common human emotion at all, really. Quite frankly, it still more or less fits the guidelines listed for which animals are ethically allowed to be experimented on! And with how crucial it is for treating diseases, we have applied for and received an approval to continue working with it, too."

Noor opens her mouth to protest, when another older woman, a kind expression on her face, speaks up. "You cannot deny how important these sponges are to treat those new diseases. You, or someone you know personally, must have been affected in recent years. And I guarantee that *P. meyeri* can or did save their life. It is an unsettling prospect, sure, to use a possibly intelligent creature in this way. But ultimately, do you not think we should prioritize our own species? Our loved ones? Our family, our friends? Without this treatment, people would *die*, Noor. Millions of people. Do you really want to see that happen, knowing there is a way to prevent it all?"

Noor feels sick. She doesn't know how to respond. "Why did you call me here if you already know what I found? And why don't other people know?"

The man who spoke earlier replies. "Great questions! Two reasons. We think it'll be best for you to switch departments and work directly with using the sponges to treat diseases instead of studying its larvae and reproduction. Maybe it'll make you . . . understand a bit better, why we need to do this. And we need you to sign some contracts. See, it might lower the morale of some of the people who work here, if what you discovered gets out. Have you told anyone yet? Your crew member on the sampling mission, perhaps?"

Noor shakes her head. "I closed the viewport connection I had with Matias right before I scanned. It was only audio communication with him, and I didn't say anything out loud about the neurons. You can check the helmets' histories if you want."

"Good! Sign these straight away!"

"What happens if I breach the contract? If I do tell someone else?"

The man smiles. "Well, you would agree to get your memory optogenetically wiped clean of these events, if that happens. And we would probably have the person you told sign the contract as well."

Noor almost laughs. "Sorry, I don't think I can do that." She gets up to leave.

The woman at the head of the table calls to her. "Of course, take your time to decide. But I strongly advise you to sign."

On her way out, the old woman speaks. "Dear, these sponges can be *very* dangerous things. It's probably for the best that we control them! Do sign the contracts."

The man speaks again, too. "You know, you remind me of Dr. Meyers. Did you ever get a chance to meet him, before that terrible, unfortunate event? He was such a kind man. It's a shame, what happened to him, eventually killed by his own discovery. I think it's best that you sign these." He holds the contracts out toward her.

And Noor, her heart pounding and her stomach churning, takes them from him before leaving the room.

When Noor gets home that day, she uses Sana's touchscreen to call Matias.

"Hey, we need to meet up, as quickly as possible. See you soon."

☼

"I promise, Noor. I'll take a look at the gemmules. And if anything happens to you . . . I'll make sure the research is published. I'd want to do that for you."

☼

"You take digits zero to nine and assign each one to a music note, starting from middle C and going up into the first few notes of the next octave. Then, you rewrite the first twenty-six terms of the Fibonacci sequence using the music notes, zero as middle C, thirteen as DF, one hundred and forty-four as DGG, like that. For the repeated one, sharped D is used. Is that right?" Irene looks at Sana, and Sana nods at her.

Irene and Sana sit together on the bottom stair of Noor's home. Sana is wearing a small, synthesized paper party hat with "12" written on it. It's Sana's birthday party, and Noor has decided to invite Irene over, just for this one day. She wants her daughter to meet the woman she hopes to marry someday, even if Sana doesn't know who Irene really is quite yet. She will . . . if all goes well with what Noor's planning.

Irene continues, "And within a measure, one-digit Fibonacci terms would be quarter notes, two-digit terms eighth notes, three-digit terms triplets, and so on, ensuring that each 'letter' would take up one 'beat' in each measure of the cipher, with each measure holding a word. Looking at the time signature of each measure, whatever number is above four is the number of letters in the word the measure holds! I love it, Sana! That's an awesome cipher you've created."

Thanks, Sana plays.

"Could you play that one more time, but a lot slower? I want to figure it out."

Sana nods and plays it again much slower.

"That's a T . . . then H . . . A . . . that's N . . . Oh! You're playing 'Thanks!' You're very welcome."

Noor chooses to walk over at this moment. "Sana, you showed Irene your cipher?"

I like her, Mommy. She told me that she volunteered and helped assemble the zero-emission machines used to keep the conditions around the last coral reef from deteriorating for another decade. It's going to keep a lot of critically endangered species alive for a little more time.

Noor smiles at Irene. "You never told me that you helped save the last coral reef!"

Irene shrugs.

Sana types on her touchscreen and shows it to Irene. It says I LIKE YOU on it.

Irene grins from ear to ear, and it makes Noor's heart sing. It's these moments that make her really question what she's doing. She thinks to herself. *If the research doesn't work out . . . would Irene understand? Would I be able to go through with it?* Noor wishes for the millionth time that she could trade places with Irene. And she wishes for the millionth time that she had the strength to tell Irene what she's doing.

One of Sana's friends motions something to Sana, and the child leaves Noor and Irene to go into another room. Noor sits down on the bottom stair.

"How's the treatment going?"

"My small intestine is around one-fifth sea sponge now! Can you believe it? Well, not *really* a sea sponge, but made of these almost stem cell-like things inside a sea sponge, that replace everything they need to replace all by themselves! Apparently, they learn to replicate my body's HLA variants in the process, release antagonists for pattern recognition receptors, NK-cell activating receptors, and T-cell receptors, and have a high surface concentration of sialic acid, so there is no immune response! It's an amazing treatment. Still a long way to go, but I'm feeling good about it."

Noor looks away. "That's nice, Irene. I'm glad it's going well."

Irene laughs. "You know, I've been thinking about it. You obviously don't have to tell me if I'm right or wrong, but I'm fairly sure *this* is what your top-secret line of work is. I mean, you get weird every time I or anyone else mentions *P. meyeri*. Besides, I like to think you're working on the stuff that's saving my life. Noor, my beautiful knight in shining armor."

Noor feels herself begin to tear up. She pulls Irene into a tight embrace.

"I love you so much, Irene. You know I'd want you to live forever, if that was possible, right?"

Irene gently returns the embrace, and caresses Noor's back lightly. "Of course, my love. Of course I know. I promise you, I'll be okay. I'll get better, and I'll live."

☼

"Hum Aap Ki Ankhon Mein," by Geeta Dutt and Mohammad Rafi plays softly in my kitchen as I pour the fragrant filter coffee, made from rice milk and Irene's favorite blend from the orbiting gardens, which I spiced with cardamom and cloves, into a cup. Irene is looking out a window. She seems lost in thought, but she's smiling, which makes me smile a bit, too. She shakes off whatever she was thinking about and takes the coffee from me.

"Do you want a sip?"

I shake my head. There's no way I can drink coffee anymore, it would leave me doubled over in pain for hours. Over the past two months, twenty pounds have just dropped off my body, regardless of the amounts I eat, and I feel cold a lot these days. My reflection in the mirror sometimes doesn't register to me as what I look like these days, lips devoid of color, sunken eyes, the whites sometimes taking on a yellowish tinge, and massive dark semicircles beneath them. Truthfully, my appearance was always a bit of a point of pride for me, and the bold lipsticks I used to wear not looking quite the same on my face anymore stings more than I'd like to admit. I forget all of that when I'm with Irene, though. She makes me feel absolutely beautiful, always.

Irene takes a sip of the coffee. "It's delicious! I didn't know you could . . . is making coffee still in the realm of 'cooking'?"

I sit down across from her. "Honestly, I have Noor to thank for this one, too. You know, she and I have a similar cultural background. When I was younger, I was a lot more religious. Still don't know quite why it happened that way, my mother was pretty religious, but my father was an atheist, and there was never any pressure to believe in anything. But I think I was looking for a way for the world to make sense. Not in an 'everything is going to be okay' way, but more of a 'there is a reason for everything, and a meaning to everything' way . . . I don't know. Anyway, I stopped believing in any sort of higher power eventually, and when I did . . . a part of me felt like I wasn't *really, truly,* allowed to take part in celebrating various aspects of my culture anymore. I know, it was kind of silly, but I cut myself off after that, from the clothes and the cuisines and the songs and the events and . . . the community, I guess. Noor wasn't religious either, but she very much participated in celebrating her culture anyway, and I think seeing that made me feel like it was okay. So . . . enjoy my family's recipe for filter coffee, it's pretty good, isn't it?"

Irene holds my hand. "I see you've been influenced by her love of old Bollywood songs, too."

"I think that's definitely new for me, but I really like them. I have no idea why she enjoyed listening to such old songs though, she never thought much about it herself."

Irene puts the coffee down. "I think, for her, it was all about the idea of connecting to past generations. Think about all of the people, who haven't been alive for a century or more now, watching those movies, or listening to those songs. It makes them seem more human, doesn't it? You're kind of hit with that realization that these people lived and died, they were just like us. And it's an interesting thing to feel. Once, she and I went to a redwood forest, saw a fourteen-hundred-year-old redwood tree. She just stood there, for almost half an hour! She was thinking about how many people had stood where she was standing, how many people over the centuries saw that tree. I think it's the same reason she listened to those songs." Irene sighs.

"I remember that day! It was so nice, walking around with you, in the fog-covered forest. We had such a wonderful time, didn't we?" I catch myself too late. "I mean, you both had such a wonderful time, didn't you?"

Irene looks at me and frowns. She doesn't say anything for a long time.

"What is it?" I ask her.

"What kind of a person am I, for doing this?"

"What do you mean?"

She takes a while to respond. "I don't know exactly why I'm with you, Nithya. I don't know if it's because of you, or because the more time I spend with you, and the longer you live Noor's experiences, the more you remind me of *her*, and the more I can almost pretend she still exists. It's unfair to you, you're an entirely different person."

"Well, if we're going there, what kind of a person am I for being with you? Instead of letting you grieve, I kept meeting you, even if I *knew* Noor was influencing me, even if I didn't know entirely whether it was me that was falling for you or her, even if when I'm with you sometimes I forget to keep track of where I end, and she begins."

"Maybe we're both being selfish."

I sigh. "Do you want to stop seeing me? Because even if it's selfish, or wrong, or unethical, I don't think I want to stop seeing you. Maybe that makes me a bad person, or a weak person . . . but the truth is that I'm in love with you. And frankly, I don't *care* where it's coming from. It's the same set of neurotransmitters and it's the same physical process, and like it or not, this is still *my* lived experience, even if it now includes someone else's, too. And my lived experience is telling me I love you."

Irene starts to tear up. "I don't want to stop seeing you! And I love you, too! But you shouldn't love me. And I know for a fact that you're not going to love me for much longer, too."

"What, because I'm sick? I can't believe you just said that to me!"

She shakes her head, speaking through tears. "No, it's not that at all, it's something else. Lots of other things, actually. You'll find out soon, and then you're going to hate me! And you'll agree that I am a terrible person for seeing you, for letting you fall for me . . . I just liked you too much! And you reminded me of her . . . and in a way you brought her back to life for me. But I did something terrible, Nithya! And soon you're not going to love me anymore, I *know* it."

I try to touch her shoulder, but she shrugs me away. "What could you possibly have done?"

She takes a deep breath and wipes her tears away. "If it wasn't for something I did, something terrible, Noor would have been alive right now. I think I killed her, I think it was all my fault. I didn't know what would happen! And now she's gone, forever, and all I can do is grasp at the occasional, flickering ghost of her that I see in you."

Irene turns away from me and leaves my apartment. I let her.

Who are you? Are you me, in my current, lived experience? Are you my disembodied brain, lying miles away from my corpse, looping through my memories to prepare a set of light pulses? Or are you someone else entirely, a stranger, maybe, living out some of my most memorable moments? I've been searching for something to show me which one it is, a sign, a glitch, a flash in my surroundings? But it's an impossible quest. I can only wonder who you are.

This is the one Irene has. The phage has two capsid heads, each containing a packet of viral DNA, and two protein sheaths, each ending in spider-leg-like fibers. Instead of attacking bacteria, this phage goes after cells in a person's small intestine and esophagus.

Spread through the air, as soon as phages enter a person's mouth, they will make their way down the esophagus, either binding to squamous cells on the esophagus and injecting the cells with one vDNA packet or continuing down the esophagus until they reach the small intestine, where they then are able to bind to enterocytes and inject them with the other vDNA packet. After being infected, the cell enters a lysogenic phase. The vDNA packets are tied to a protein mimicking a nuclear localization signal. They trick importin receptors into bringing the vDNA into the nucleus of their host cell. Here, the vDNA is incorporated into its genomic DNA, and as soon as this occurs, the infected cell's *function* is altered for the rest of its life.

In the small intestine, lysogenic enterocytes become immensely oversized to make room for as much eventual phage production as possible, in the process, disrupting nutrient absorption. Severe internal growths, agonizing stomach pains, diarrhea, vomiting, and eventually fatal malabsorption result from this. Eventually, close to natural cell death, the vDNA tells it to enter the lytic stage, and it creates as much phage as it can carry before bursting and releasing it. The phages that were just released either infect other enterocytes or travel with bile, as the lysogens around the recently burst cell send signals to the lysogens in the esophagus. When a lysogenic enterocyte in the small intestine bursts, the lysogenic squamous cells in the esophagus receive signals to trigger gastroesophageal reflux, and it induces a coughing fit, bringing the virus-carrying bile up into the person's mouth and then spreading into the air to infect other people.

For a while, there was no way to stop the lysogenic enterocytes from eventually proving fatal without stripping the entire lining of the small intestine and replacing it using stem cells, an expensive and invasive procedure that runs the risk of reinfection, since the proteins on the surface of the enterocytes wouldn't change. Then came the discovery of *P. meyeri*.

With *P. meyeri*, all an infected person has to do is take a pill every day over a period of time that contains pre-specialized archaeocyte cells from the sponge. The highly specific cells target lysogenic enterocytes and simultaneously work to destroy them and perform normal enterocyte functions themselves. *P. meyeri* archaeocytes end up entirely replacing the lysogenic enterocytes, and the infected person is cured. Since most of the proteins on the new cell surface are very different, there is no risk of reinfection as well.

The woman from Noor's earlier meeting leads Noor to a window looking into a room with a single *P. meyeri* sponge in the center and turns off the light in the hallway around them. "I'm glad you signed the contracts, Noor."

There's some sort of a light system set up inside, with tiny blue LEDs everywhere. The main lights in the room go off as well, and the LEDs turn on. A dancing blue light display begins, in a similar yet also quite different recursive pattern to the ones Noor saw in the cavern during the larvae release.

The woman turns to her. "What we're doing is tricking the sponge into believing the lysogenic enterocyte cells we fused to the inner linings of the channels that run through it *actually belong to it*, and that the infection will eventually kill *it*. The way *P. meyeri* responds is amazing. It synthesizes its own, new, modified enterocyte-esque cells, using the many archaeocyte cells it has, and has them slowly but surely destroy and replace the lysogenic enterocytes, ending up fused to the inner linings of its channels instead of the infected cells."

They move to a window looking into another room full of sponges. The woman continues "This is where we take the sponges next." After Noor realizes what's happening, she feels nauseated. *They're stripping the inner linings of the sponges' channels.* Autonomous machines take cylindrical tubes with sharp edges, and, entering the few pathways without cutting into the nervous system, essentially shave off the new layers of the sponge.

After the archaeocytes have been stripped away, a small trickle of what looks like the dark corrosive liquid drips out of the sponge. Noor turns to the woman next to her. "Is that . . ."

The woman nods. "It's a diluted form, so it doesn't do as much damage to the sponge, but yes, for some reason it secretes that same substance after we strip it of the newly specialized archaeocyte cells . . . Is something wrong?"

Noor frowns. "There must be a way we can use what we already know to come up with a different treatment, without harming or harvesting any more *P. meyeri* spon—"

The woman smiles and puts her hand on Noor's shoulder in what looks like an amiable gesture, but she grips the shoulder slightly too tight. "We've been doing some research in that realm, but we're not going to stop using *P. meyeri*. What happened to Dr. Meyers was sad and terrible, of course, but think about the big picture here, Noor. Once we fine-tune our control of this thing, we can use it for a lot more than just treating a disease."

On her way out, Noor stops by the building where Matias works and checks in with him. "How is it going, with the you-know-whats?"

"I'm sorry Noor. I don't know if it's going to work out. Are you still going to go through with your paper?"

Noor sighs, but eventually nods. "I don't feel like I have a choice. This is just what I *have* to do . . . it's the ethical thing to do. Are you still going to support me, even if your part doesn't work out?"

Matias looks down. "My promise was that if you were right about what you think happened to Dr. Meyers, and if something terrible happens to you, too, before you publish it, I'll make sure it's published, because that's what *I* think the ethical thing to do would be. But . . . if my part of this doesn't work out . . . if there's no alternative . . . I don't think I can support you besides that one situation. I'm sorry."

Noor wakes up to Irene shaking her, forcefully, with tears streaming down her face. "How could you?!" Irene speaks through sobs. She's holding a stack of synthesized—*Oh. No . . . the paper . . .*

Noor sits up. Irene speaks again. "Answer me! Tell me there's been a mistake. Tell me you haven't written up something that will, if approved, get me killed."

Noor gets out of the bed and whispers. "I'm sorry."

"Is there any other cure?"

Noor shakes her head. "No . . . but there's always hope, maybe—"

Irene starts laughing, bitterly. "This whole time, I thought you were working on the thing that's been saving my life. But actually, it's quite the opposite, isn't it!"

"It's an intelligent creature, Irene! It cannot be okay to exploit it like this!"

"In any other situation, I would agree with you. But this was an emergency! An actual, serious threat to our existence. And if this treatment goes away, what's going to happen to everyone currently infected?"

"You haven't seen *P. meyeri* like I have, Irene! If you could just *try* to understand where I'm coming from, maybe you'd see that—"

Irene scoffs. "I do understand where you're coming from. I read every page of this thing. But have *you*, ever, once, truly considered what this is like from my perspective? I mean . . . and . . . why did it have to be *you*, Noor? Why *you*?"

Noor doesn't know what to say. How did it escalate so quickly? Why is this happening so fast?

Irene begins putting on her jacket and collecting her belongings.

"What are you doing?"

"I'm leaving. I can't do this."

"What are you doing with my paper?"

Irene stops, grimaces, turns to Noor. "I can't let you do this."

No, no no no. Noor follows Irene as she walks to the door. "Irene, think about it, please. Sit down, we can talk about this. You . . . don't know what the place I work for is like. Something really bad might happen. Please, just think about this! Plea—"

Irene opens the door, turns around, and says, "I don't want to die," before leaving and slamming the door shut behind her.

☼

I wake up to one of the foulest scents I have ever encountered. Looking down, I see that I'm lying in a pool of green liquid. *I shit myself.* "Ew, ew ew," I repeat to myself over and over again as I unplug the tubes in the sensory deprivation chamber and rush to the bathroom to clean myself up. After thoroughly cleaning and disinfecting the sensory deprivation chamber, I take my morning pill to trigger the hallucination, like I do every day, and sit on the floor to wait.

Something's different this time. Until now, every hallucination has been about my own life, nothing from Noor's ever entering them. But suddenly I'm sitting at a beach I've never been to before, and that is entirely different from what my own imagination normally invents. I try to move, but I can't move at all. I look out to see ... Sana is in the distance ... *half buried in the sand?* The tide begins to come in, but she doesn't react. Water rises and rises until it's covering everything, and I try to move to her, *to my daughter*, but I can't move, and now she's under water, and now I'm under water, and I can't scream because it'll fill my lungs, but soon it's unbearable and I gasp, inhaling saltwater, and then my vision goes black.

The darkness soon dissipates, and I find myself shaking, with tears running down my face, curled into a fetal position on the floor.

☼

There are three people named "Matias Rodriguez" living in the nearby area. I try calling the first two from my touchscreen, but I don't recognize their voices. I recognize the third voice instantly.

"Hello?" he says.

"Hi, I'm investigating Noor's death, and I wanted to ask you a few questions."

"I'm sorry, I don't know if I can help you. I don't know anybody named Noor."

"Excuse me? You went on a sampling mission with her ... do you remember that?"

"Ah, I see. I *was* scheduled to take part in a sampling mission some time ago, but I got a pretty bad head injury and was unfortunately unable to do the mission. My memories are very poor quality or nonexistent for a while after that, but I'm back to normal now."

Oh, fuck.

His memories ... I think I know what happened. Fuck. I sigh, but then I remember something and my heart sinks even more.

"How's Syd doing?"

Matias groans. "They've stopped communicating with me entirely now! Not even through their touchscreen ... it was bad enough when they wouldn't change their damn expression, but now ... Wait. How do you know about Syd? Who are you? Have we met?"

Damn it, poor Syd. "I'm sorry to tell you this, sir, but I'm afraid you might have had some of your memories wiped."

Matias' tone changes abruptly. "Did Syd put you up to this? Did my husband? Endless paranoia in my family these days, I swear. I'm going to end this call now. Good day."

✪

I meet Irene at the same café we met at months ago, spot her sitting in the same booth, drinking the same coffee. I feel like if we meet here, not only will our conversation go unheard in the hum of all the other conversations taking place around us . . . we will be more inclined to be civil. *I* will be more inclined to be civil. It's not just my anger driving me right now, it's Noor's, too.

I sit down across from her. She smiles at me, weakly.

"Irene . . . what did you do? And . . . why did you keep this from me?" I feel tired, all of a sudden.

"I'm sorry, I couldn't risk telling you earlier. I didn't want you to hate me. I wanted to have just a little bit of time with you, even if I knew it would end up like this eventually."

I shake my head. "I can't believe I didn't see it earlier. This whole time, I was just . . . *blinded* by my feelings for you. Damn it, for *months*! What did you do with her paper? And what else have you been keeping from me?"

Irene looks down.

". . . Is there something else you're keeping from me?"

She flinches.

I sigh. "Look, at this point, I would appreciate you just coming clean with me, okay? Just tell me what you know, please, for *her*."

Something seems to click into place for Irene. She looks very determined, all of a sudden. After a long stretch of silence, she nods, and says "Fine. Okay, fine. You're right. I should do this, for her . . . she deserves justice. Those assholes need to be taken down. Screw it, I'll tell you everything."

"Thank you. Fill me in, from what you did with the paper to whatever else you haven't told me. Tell me everything. Starting now."

She does.

She tells me that she took the paper and asked around the place where she was getting treated until she found the contact information of Noor's workplace. She met with three of their representatives, a young woman, an older woman, and a middle-aged man. They thanked her for the information, told her they would "take care of it," and that they would be in touch with her soon.

Irene looks back up at me, shaking her head sadly. "I didn't know what they meant by 'taking care of it,' Nithya! Just slightly over a week later, she died!"

"Why did you keep this from me? Self-preservation, again?"

Irene winces. "Maybe a little bit, yeah ... but I like to think I would have reported all of this to you, immediately, if they hadn't made me ..."

"Made you do what?!"

"Please try to understand! They threatened me, they threatened to hurt Sana! I had to, Nithya!"

"... What?"

"... I made you sick. It was in the first box of the set of pills I gave you. I put the phage in, too."

You did what?! I stand up to leave.

"Nithya, wait! You don't understand! I've been protecting you, this whole time! I've been telling them you're doing the treatment! They thought if you had it, you wouldn't side with Noor. They think you're on their side!"

"You've been spying on me, too? What the actual fuck? All of that stuff, about wanting to know what it's like in her head, was a lie?"

"No, that came out all wrong! I haven't told them much, I promise! Your investigation is safe! I swear, I've been protecting you! I'm on your side Nithya! And it wasn't a lie. I wanted to know what her thoughts were like, desperately. That wasn't a lie at all!"

I can't look at her anymore. I walk out the door. *She was threatened, though. Hear her out.* A little voice pops into my thoughts as I leave the café, and I can't tell if it's coming from myself or from the Noor part of me. I can barely distinguish the two anymore now, and I'm tired of trying to.

☼

Sana, my daughter, I am so sorry I left you. I love you, so much. Maybe someday, I will see you again. Would you recognize me? Would it still be okay? I miss you Sana. I love you. I'm so sorry.

☼

Mommy I want to tell you about something. Sana plays her flute to Noor, standing in the doorway to the living room.

Noor sits at the coffee table, typing into her touchscreen. She stops, closes her touchscreen, and smiles at Sana. "What is it?"

Sana begins an uncanny melody. **I have been thinking. I started communicating like this to incite action to stop the climate catastrophes. And I still care about that so much. But I think along the way I figured out that I prefer communicating like this to com-**

**municating any other way. I like the control I have over my flute
and I like how it sounds and I like that it is a language I invented. I
think even if the demands were all met I would still type in my
touchscreen and play my flute to communicate. Is that okay?**

Noor nods. "You know, I have to admit that I struggled sometimes
to accept your method of communication. I tried to hide that from you,
and I'm really sorry if any of that came through. But over the past couple years, Sana, I've realized that communicating like this makes you
happy. And I'd never want to get in the way of that. I'm happy for you,
and I love you so much. Of course it's okay. Is it okay if I give you a
hug?"

Yes. I want to hug you, too. Sana moves to her mother and
embraces her. Noor holds her daughter close for a while.

✿

Noor recognizes the knock, and she opens the door to see Irene.

"I'm so sorry Noor! I told them. I told the people you work for. I
just don't want to die. I really don't want to die."

"Hey . . . come in, it's okay. I knew you did this, it wasn't hard to
guess. Come inside, we left things on a weird note last time."

"Is Sana here?"

"No, she's at school."

"You're not at work? I mean, I should have thought that through
before showing up, but I'm realizing it now."

". . . No."

They move to the living room couch and sit next to one another.
Diffuse light comes down through the skylight above them. Noor turns
to Irene, and half smiles.

"You don't have to be sorry Irene. You were acting out of fear for
your own life . . . and in a way, I did betray you. But I wish you could
have seen what I've seen before making that decision. Especially because the research company I work for . . . I think they're capable of
some pretty awful things. But I prepared for this, just in case. It's why I
got the light-gated-ion channels two years ago."

Irene frowns. "What do you mean? Is . . . is something going to
happen to you?"

Noor sighs. "I was trying to tell you this earlier. But . . . don't worry
about it right now, okay? I forgive you for what you did, can you forgive me? I just . . . for a little bit . . . want it to go back to how it was. I
love you, Irene. And that hasn't changed. Can we go back to how things
were? Please? I really need that right now."

Irene thinks for a long time, but then pulls Noor close to her. They hold each other for a while, and then Noor kisses Irene. Irene kisses her back. "I love you, too. I want it to go back to how it was before, too."

☼

I wander aimlessly around the town, trying to collect my thoughts. With every session of Noor's experiences, I lose my sense of self more and more. I don't quite know who I am anymore, and I keep asking myself, *would Nithya do this? Would Noor? Is this Nithya? Is this Noor?* But it's exhausting now, trying to keep track of my memories and my thoughts, and trying to remember which are hers and which are mine. *Mine. But who am I?*

With those two years of Noor's experiences came a lifetime of memory as well, something I was not anticipating at all. But I should have known. After all, what are our thoughts, our experiences, our reality, without our memories? Of course I remember things now that weren't necessarily events taking place in Noor's experiences. Her every recollection of some other past event was encoded in her brain activity, too, her memories within a memory. And subconsciously as well, memories were coloring her every thought, and those not-so-obvious rememberings were transferred to me, too, running underneath my thoughts now, too. It's *impossible* to live a snapshot of someone's experience without inheriting everything that came before that snapshot, too, whether it's immediately obvious or somewhere under the surface. Frankly, it's futile to try and separate myself from her at this point. I can't even remember how I used to think before I lived that piece of her life.

Maybe I should stop separating them. All those times, making love to Irene, when I released my hold on these two identities, and allowed them to blend into each other, it felt so right! *Irene.* Noor forgave her. Would Nithya? Would I, whoever I am now?

Maybe I'm exhausting myself, thinking that I'm separating the two identities, when I'm really deluding myself trying to categorize my thoughts into what I believe Noor would think and what I believe Nithya would think, when in reality there is *no* way to know where those thoughts are truly coming from.

I should let them blend.

I put on Noor's favorite song, "Pyar Kiya To Darna Kya," sung by Lata Mangeshkar, and decide to stop trying to control my own mind. I let the music wash over me, I let the two identities come together, mixing into one another, memories and thoughts and experiences and reality.

I'm not quite either of them, any longer.

I smile. I think I know what to do next.

☼

I call Irene from my touchscreen. As soon as she picks up, I say, "Listen, if you're really on my side, you'll help me finish what Noor's started. And you can begin by working with my partners Marie and Anthony, to restore the memories of a man named Matias Rodriguez."

After a long pause, she responds. ". . . I will. I promise I will."

☼

I arrive at Noor's aunt's house, where Sana lives now, and I take a deep breath before knocking on the door. Noor didn't know her aunt super well, but she seemed nice, and didn't live too far away.

I've just started to consider knocking on the door again when it opens, and she's standing right in front of me, flute in hand. *Sana.* It takes all my strength to prevent tears from filling my eyes. I'm immediately flooded with joy. *My daughter. It's been so long . . .* But she's not my daughter . . .

The girl takes out her touchscreen and types WHO ARE YOU on it.

I clear my throat. "I'm Nithya . . . we met once, several months ago. I'm investigating your mother's death. Can I come in?"

Sana stares at me for a moment before nodding and letting me into the house. She types on her touchscreen I DID NOT RECOGNIZE YOU AT FIRST. YOU LOOK DIFFERENT NOW.

"Yes, I've become sick. Hey, can I talk to your great-aunt? I need to ask her a few questions."

Sana leads me to the living room of the house, where an old woman sits on a doughy blue armchair, facing out the window. Next to her is a beautiful upright piano, with several pages of sheet music on display above the keys. Sana, in the adjacent room, has begun to play something on her flute.

I turn to the old woman. "Hi Ms. Bakshi. My name is Nithya, and I'm investigating your niece's death. Noor was working on something, a paper, before she passed away. Do you know if any copies of her work still remain? On her touchscreen, or any physical copies, or anything related at all? It's crucial for our investigation."

Ms. Bakshi sighs. "I'm afraid you're months too late. I had brought everything Noor had worked on to this house, but it's all gone now. There was another group of people who asked me the same question several months ago, very soon after Noor's death, with a warrant to search the house. They took all of Noor's research, all the physical copies, and all the electronic ones, too. I'm sorry."

My heart sinks. *It's all gone. I don't think I can pull the entirety of Noor's paper out of her memories. There's no hope now, unless Matias knows something, maybe? Maybe he has a copy!*

"Thank you, Ms. Bakshi. Don't worry about it. I should probably get going now."

"I'm sorry I couldn't be of more help. I wish—Hey, Sana? Could you keep it down, just a little bit? The grown-ups are talking here!" She turns back to me. "I don't know what it is with that girl and that strange song. She plays it all day, every day, several times in a row. I can't say I like it too much, but if it makes her happy, I don't have the heart to ask her to stop. Do you want something before you leave? Chai, coffee? I have some freshly made rice-milk peda in the kitchen! You must try some."

I shake my head. "I'm sorry, there's not much I can consume properly anymore. But thank you for the offer."

As I take my leave, I pass by the piano, and something catches my eye as my gaze drifts over the sheet music. *Wait a minute . . .*

And then, I actually start to *hear* what Sana has been playing on her flute this whole time.

. . . The choanocytes lining the innermost channels of a *Panaceius meyeri* sponge differ from choanocytes in many . . .

It's the paper! My eyes fill up with tears. I go to Sana. "What you're playing right now . . . it's your mother's research, isn't it?"

Sana stops playing her flute, looks up at me, and nods. After some time, she plays **You understand my language?**

I smile. "Yeah, I do."

You really have lived a part of my Mommy's life.

I kneel next to her and tears start flowing down my face. "Yes, Sana. I have. And because I have, I know she loved you *so* much. I'm . . . I'm so sorry you've lost her. I'm so, so sorry."

Nithya. I would like a hug. Could I give you a hug?

I nod. Sana hugs me, and I can't stop myself from crying into her shoulder.

When she lets go, she takes the stack of sheet music from the piano and hands it to me. I sit and look through it, remembering Noor painstakingly documenting all of it . . . But there's a new section now, at the end, with an annotated name in the margins, still written in the Fibonacci-sheet music language. *Matias Rodriguez?* I look at the title of the new section, and I can't believe my eyes.

It's titled, "The Cure."

It turns out that there is a way to grow sponges out of the *P. meyeri* gemmules, and sponges that grow from them are not conscious in any way, they do not have the extra layer, or the corrosive liquid! What Matias did was take certain genes from the pre-specialized archaeocytes from a conscious *P. meyeri* sponge and introduce them to the gemmules. The sponge that grew from the gemmule ended up having inner channels lined with the specialized archaeocytes. And this sponge had no qualms about reproducing in the simulated settings within a research lab. When the sponge from the gemmule reproduced, it did not create larvae, but only gemmules of its own. And when the next generation of gemmules became sponges, *they also contained the specialized archaeocytes.* Matias had found a way to create a population of sponges that were as ethically alright to experiment on as other sponges discovered before *P. meyeri*, that contained the cells necessary for the treatment and could reproduce! I'm fucking stunned. *This could save my life.*

I thank Sana and her great-aunt for their time over and over again, filled with happiness. As I'm about to leave the house, Sana tugs on my sleeve and then plays something on her flute again, looking right at me.

Nithya. About what you said earlier. I do not know if I believe Mommy is entirely lost. Will you visit again? I want to have more conversations with you. And I want to meet you again.

I grin at her, and nod. "Sana, I can come here as many times as you want me to, for the rest of my life. Thank you for making your cipher. I think it's a lovely way to communicate, and it truly saved the day. I'll see you again soon, I promise."

After I leave the house, I begin to walk away, when a small synthesized-paper envelope falls out of the pages of sheet music. There's a single word written on it, still in the Fibonacci language. A single measure, time signature five-four. Eighth notes E, D. Sixteenth notes D, A, high E, high C. Quarter note F. Triplet notes E, F, F. And finally, quarter note F, again.

I can't help but smile. I recognize the name immediately.

✿

Noor sits at a desk, writing out sheet music on synthesized paper. An envelope sits next to what she's writing, with "Irene" written on it in the Fibonacci-music language.

> *Dear Irene,*
>
> *My love. I do not know if you understand exactly what you did. But you might soon. If that happens, I would want you to know I forgive you. And that I still love you. And ... I understand what you did. But I also want you to know what it is like from my perspective. I want you to see P. meyeri for yourself. Feel what I felt for yourself. That is why if this is ever found ... I would want you to be the one to live out my experiences. I do not know if it is going to happen like that. But I would want you to.*
>
> *There's good news, too. Matias found a cure! I have just finished adding it to the paper. You will live my love. No matter what. And hopefully we can get this released soon and nothing will happen to me, and we can both live together for decades more ... happy and in love. I would like that very much. I love you Irene ... this probably will never reach you, but I wanted to write it anyway.*
>
> *Love,*
> *Noor*

☼

Irene and I sit together, drinking coffee next to the sensory deprivation chamber in my living room. *Oh man, I missed the taste of coffee so much.* It's been a month on the new treatment plan, and I'm already feeling so much better.

Matias' memories have been restored. What happened was that he thought he would try to convince the research company to stop exploiting *P. meyeri*, since there was an alternative. But it didn't work, and they hinted to him of the other, non-medication-related purposes that they could use *P. meyeri* for. They threatened him and made him sign the contracts, but he went to Noor with his research anyway, not knowing that Irene had told the research company about her work already. After Noor died, representatives from the company found Noor's completed paper, after searching her aunt's house, and discovered that Matias had breached the contract. He had his memory forcibly wiped.

With Irene's help, Matias got his memories back, and working with me, we translated Noor's paper back. As promised, he made sure it was published, and especially with the world knowing about the cure he discovered. The corrupt leadership of the research company was quickly removed and faced serious consequences. Numerous protections were put into place regarding disruption of the *P. meyeri* colonies and work is being done now to try and figure out a way to communicate with the sponges. For now, only unintrusive ROVs are allowed down there.

I look at Irene, drinking her coffee next to me. *I wonder, if there hadn't been a different cure, if I was still sick ... would I have forgiven her?* I shake the thought away. What's the point of speculating, distressing myself with "what if"s? She had more than proven she supported me ... and she was making sure the research company didn't suspect anything about me the whole time. And, the truth is, ultimately, despite everything, I do still love her. Every part of me tells me I still love her. And she still loves me. So, if we love each other, and we make each other happy in spite of everything, why shouldn't we just ... be together?

I move closer to her, and she puts her arm around me. I rest my head on her shoulder. "You know, Irene, I don't know if I'll ever be Noor."

She smiles, and she kisses me. "I don't care. I love you."

"And I don't know if I'm entirely Nithya anymore, either. I think I've become someone else, entirely, the result of Noor's memories and Nithya's memories blending together, which gave rise to someone new."

She kisses me again. "I *still* love you."

This makes me smile. But then I remember something, and I sigh. "There's just one set of light pulses left, Irene. It's her death. I don't know if I can do it. I've been putting it off. Especially because, while I know *she* doesn't understand that she's in a loop, I know she is, and I don't want her to experience that again. I just don't know if I can do it."

Irene holds me closer. "Then just don't do it. You don't have to force yourself to do that, both for your sake and for her's. The people responsible have been punished, chemical analyses months ago figured out what *literally* caused her death ... there's no need for you to play the light pulses."

"You really think it'll be okay if I don't?"

"Of course, Nithya! You are under no obligation to play that awful experience into your head. I promise you."

"Alright, I don't think I will, in that case." I settle my head back onto her shoulder. After a while, I continue. "You know, I've been thinking. Noor wanted you to be the one to live out her experiences, right?"

"Yes, but look. I've been thinking about this, too. I'm actually really happy it was you. If you hadn't done this ... I would never have met you. I would have had her with me, always, but I wouldn't have had *you*. I'm actually really glad it happened this way, Nithya. Besides . . . we've talked about this before, her patterns of neural activity are tailored to fit yours, and there's no way to get those light pulses again."

I look at her. "No, I've been looking into this, and I think there is a way, Irene. I think there is a way you can live some of her most memorable moments, too."

☼

So, who are you? Are you my current, lived experience, as I wait for the sedatives to put me into a temporary unconscious state? Are you my brain in the next few hours, almost done looping through my memories of the past several months, to put together a set of light pulses? Or is it you, Irene, my love?

Is it you, living my memories of the past months, which would certainly include some of Noor's memories, too? I wonder which of Nithya's memories will make it through, and which of Noor's will. I hope you'll tell me all about it soon. And who knows how long the entire set of experiences will be? If they could condense two years of Noor's life that much, how long will it take for you to live this tiny fraction of mine? Hours? Days? You're in a waiting room outside right now, and we're going to have a lovely day together after this procedure is over. I hope we will have a lovely life, together, too.

But no matter what, right now, I love you deeply, and Noor loved you deeply. And if you wanted to, my love, in your mind, you could keep us looping endlessly.

The Egg Collectors

Lavie Tidhar

ON THE LAST of the nights of Ashour, the wild ballooners of Isfiya ran into an ice-storm over the north pole.

The storm looked like a giant eye against the sky. Ice whipped the fragile balloons and set them blowing apart from each other, scattering like seeds over the lunar surface. Titan, with Saturn hidden in the sky—a long way from the sun.

"Bring her down!" Mona said, and Lina, handling the controls calmly, said, "What do you *think* I'm doing?"

They heard the others on the shortwave comms. Rafik Nasser el-Din speaking softly, Ziad Halabi swearing, but soon enough all chatter ceased and the ballooners, scattered, drifted on the hard winds, bucking and thrashing as ice particles pinged against their chassis.

But the balloons had been built to withstand the pressures of Titan's atmosphere; and the riders of Isfiya had known other storms, and other dangers. They had never meant to come this close to the pole, not at this time of the long year, yet here they were, and they would ride out the storm. Mona joined Lina at the controls, trying to trace a path through the thick haze, riding blind, instruments-only, searching for a landing site.

"According to the map there should be an oasis somewhere near-by," Lina said. "If it's still in use."

"Let's worry about catching shelter *after* we land," Mona said. Lina gave her sister a long-suffering glance and didn't reply. For a moment an updraft bumped them high and they floated, weightless. Then the balloon came down hard and gravity returned and they began to fall.

Mona was held fast in the safety harness. The screen flashed numbers she barely registered. They would have to let out valuable air and find some new ice soon. Lina held the controls, wrestling with the ungainly craft, trying to smooth their descent.

"We're not far from the sea," she said.

Mona remembered a family holiday, long ago. They had gone to the Ligeia Mare and made camp on the shore. There had been good weather then and the methane sea was as smooth as a mirror. They had gone sailing to one of the small islands where previous generations had built a permanent shelter. Titan was dotted with such havens. All they had to do was find one now. She remembered that holiday, how it seemed never to end. They stayed up late and played games, Solar Lottery and Bluff and Damage and Vlet, and pretended to fish in the methane sea. Mona used to stay up for hours sometimes, staring at the calm surface, imagining things that could live in it, even though everyone knew the only things that lived on Titan were people and boppers. She always wondered what it was like to have seas like they had on Earth, with waves and tides and microscopic living things, and seaweed and fish.

The balloon shuddered and they landed with a bump. Mona and Lina dropped anchor and when the balloon was steady they stepped out. The wind wasn't so strong here on the surface but visibility was bad, and she thought the sea was somewhere nearby. The storm hovered on the horizon, looking like the blue eye in a khamsah charm, dominating the entire sky, an awesome, almost-living thing.

The poet Basho, who once visited Titan, had written of the polar vortex:

Hariken blong aes
Tentenem, tentenem
Awo!
Ae blong God ia

Which, roughly translated from the Asteroid Pidgin, meant: *Hurricane of ice / turning and turning / Oh! / It is the eye of God.*

But Basho had been dead for centuries, or Translated into the Conversation, or perhaps, as some said, he'd gone with the Exodus ships in search of other planets, around other stars. And no one had yet resolved the question of God, though people still believed. If anything, it was easier to believe in God away from Earth. And she seemed to remember the first moonwalkers had said something similar, how when they first left the planet and sailed through the dark toward the then-uninhabited moon, they felt there had to be more—that the world, in one ancient astronaut's words, was just too beautiful to have happened by accident.

The haze cleared and through it Mona could see that the sea, the Ligeia Mare, really was close, and she saw clouds sail over the calm water—though of course it was not water—and she thought it really *was* beautiful. Like the sound of an oud, like the whisper of fresh water on leaves, like the sound of thunder in a storm over the sea . . .

The Druze came to Titan centuries earlier. Halabis and Nasser el-Dins and the other old families of Earth. Some had settled in Polyphemus Port, and some set out onto the wider moon, building small towns on hard cores of water ice. But Mona's heart had always belonged to travel and movement, and to the shout of wind and the harmony of rain.

The wild ballooners followed the wind where it went.

"Come on, Mona," Lina said patiently. She was used to her sister's dreaming. "That oasis should be somewhere nearby."

Lina was the practical one. Slow, steady, she had stayed behind when Mona went off-world. Mona had dreamed for years of Mars, the red sand deserts and the cacophony of the local cloud of the Conversation all around it, but instead of going sunward she'd gone into the Up and Out, hiring onto a platoon bound for the Fairy Moons in the Uranus system, there to fight a war she barely understood, against people or things that made no sense, as though the two sides were each fighting a completely different war.

Mona had heard of the Nine Billion Hells, but until that conflict she'd never *believe* in them. She'd seen things in that conflict: Carcosan mind-mines and Kadathian web traps that spun whole light seconds, silver monomolecular wires that crisscrossed and shredded anything and anyone unlucky enough to fall in their path. In the battle over Puck her platoon was suddenly swarmed over by hellish ghasts, tiny insectoid drones mass-printed out of dumb matter, and she survived only by burrowing deep into the lunar surface, buried alive for two days until the battle was, inexplicably, over. She never even learned who, if any, had won.

Then her tour of duty was over and she was paid, and she shipped back home. She swore she'd never fight again. Lina had been talking recently of leaving the ballooner pack and settling somewhere—they had a large family back in Polyphemus Port. Mona didn't know what she'd do if and when Lina left. She couldn't imagine staying in one place long enough, and Polyport was always so *crowded*. She would feel like a pet fish, trapped under the city's transparent dome.

"Come *on*," Lina said. Everyone had been solicitous when Mona came back from the war, and everyone skirted around the topic if it ever came up. Lina, in contrast, was just Lina, and she didn't treat Mona any different.

They trudged through snow.

When they reached the sea it was just as she remembered it from that holiday so long ago. There was no one else around. She saw no boats or sign of residences, for all that there must have been people living around the Ligeia Mare. On the Kraken Sea sailed Nirrti the Black and her pirates, leading a ceaseless battle against the Umma— the noded. But here all was quiet and peaceful, and she knew there'd be some floating refineries and, to the south, the start of a trunk road and a caravanserai.

She opened her node cautiously. Out here there wasn't much chatter, Titan's thick cloud atmosphere prevented the sort of incessant heavy bandwidth usage they had on other worlds. Titan was relatively silent. She had seen an image once of what the Conversation was like around Earth—a cosmic cloud of data that suffused every organic and digital being, until the very air and the clouds were pregnant with it.

But that was Humanity Prime, that was Womanhome, and things were different in the Outer System, in the Up and Out. Especially on Titan.

Still. An olfactory sense of water, plants, flowers. She followed it, her boots leaving prints in the snow.

There.

The entrance was clearly marked and kept clear of ice and snow. Lina pinged the oasis and the airlock opened for them. She said, "I guess we're the first to arrive."

"The first to arrive in a *while*," Mona said. "By the looks of it."

"You don't know that."

"Actually, she's right," the airlock door said.

"Excuse me?"

They removed their helmets as fresh air and warmth blew into the lock.

"No visitors," the door said—a little mournfully. "We used to get people come by all the time, but it's been quiet for ages and ages."

"I can't possibly imagine why," Mona said.

"Well, we are a little off the beaten path," the door said. "As it were. Still. Would be nice to, you know. Open. Or close. Both, really, what with being a door and all."

"There should be more of us coming," Lina said. "If it helps."

"You ballooners?" the door said.

"Yeah. Ran into that big ice storm where we weren't expecting it."

"Any problems?"

"Nothing we couldn't handle."

"I was thinking of taking a trip," the door said. "Maybe even go off-world. Become a cargo ship or a harvester. Maybe a solar sail. Being a door isn't all it's cracked up to be."

"It seems . . . restful," Mona said.

"You'd think so, wouldn't you?"

"Problems?" Mona said, interested despite herself.

"Nothing we can't handle," the door said.

It whooshed open. Hot, humid air assailed them, and with it came the smell of thick vegetation and the buzzing of insects. They stepped through.

"Thanks."

"Don't mention it."

The airlock shut with a hiss and they were inside the oasis.

"Why *are* doors always this chatty?" Mona said.

Lina made a face. "Ever been to Polyport? Elevators are worse."

It was twilight inside the oasis. They took off their surface suits and wandered into the forest. Mona reached for a low hanging coconut and hacked it open with her knife, then drank the water. She split the shell and nibbled on the white meat inside. A butterfly flew past and settled on Lina's shoulder. Lina smiled.

"I miss Polyport," she said.

"You *don't*."

"But I do. I miss plants and flowers and *space* to move around in."

"But we have so *much* space, Lina. We have a whole *world!*"

"It's not the same. You know it's not."

"I don't want you to go," Mona said. "I don't want you to leave me."

It stood between them, this thing.

"I know," Lina said.

They wandered deeper into the forest.

☼

The others still hadn't shown up by the time Mona and Lina woke up. The bio-dome was five levels deep into the ground, with natural flowing streams filtered from the large core of underground water ice the oasis sat on, and a profusion of fruit trees. Small birds sang in the canopy of the trees and squirrels chased on the ground for nuts.

The sisters gathered breakfast and ate in the shade of a coconut tree, near a small stream filled with fish.

"Remember that time we went to the Kaitain Labyrinthus with Mum and Dad and—"

"We got lost!" Mona said. "I remember . . ."

"Miles and miles of underground farms, and nothing but cabbage . . ."

"Remember when we went to look for boppers out by the Kraken Sea—"

"And dad tried to talk to one!"

"And the bopper just kept going round and round him and then it left but—"

"The next day we found a genuine bopper artefact where it'd been and it was a—"

"What *was* it?" Mona said.

"It looked a little like an egg."

"And we took it home and I remember, we used to watch it for hours to see if it would hatch but—"

"It never did."

"It never did."

They fell silent. Small robots darted here and there between the trees, clearing and pruning. Yellow light fell down from on high. Artificial sunlight, just like on Earth. Though there, Mona supposed, it wasn't artificial.

She took a bite from her fruit.

"Nice plums," she said.

"Yeah."

She opened her node to the Conversation. Messages from the others, flooding in. All the balloons were fine.

"I like it here," Lina said.

"Yeah."

Insects buzzed. The brook bubbled. The robots moved sedately from tree to tree.

"I wonder what the door meant about trouble," Mona said.

"It didn't say there was trouble."

"No," Mona said. "It didn't."

She rose to her feet and stretched.

"I'm going for a walk," she said.

"Mona . . ."

"What?"

"We've barely *been* here."

"It's an oasis," Mona said. "What's to, like . . . ?"

Lina sighed and got up. "You're impossible," she said.

"It's nice outside," Mona said, happily.

☼

It *was* nice outside. The winds had settled and the snow lay in peaceful heaps. They took a walk to the seaside. The Ligeia Mare stretched out to the horizon. Mona dug in the sand.

"Look," she said. She raised her gloved hand. Lying in her palm was a small triangular piece of metal. "Somebody dropped a dorsal fin."

They were a standard part of an outdoors suit, making it easier to fly in Titan's light gravity.

And she thought of that holiday, long ago, how they'd walk along the beach like they did just now, and search for things. Strange rocks or bits that other people dropped there, long ago, and then they'd stop somewhere sheltered from the wind and put up an air tent and have a picnic. And later still, putting their suits back on, they'd go outside and build sandcastles. The sand had an electric charge that meant it stuck, and they'd spend hours putting together impossible castles and, when they left, the castles would remain behind, impervious, or so it seemed, to the wind. And she always liked the thought that maybe the castles were still standing there. And if they did then maybe one day, millions of years from now, if visitors came down from the sky they'd stand there and marvel at this alien architecture, and try to imagine who had built it and lived inside it.

But she knew sooner or later the wind blew the sand away.

She let the fin drop.

"I want to go check on the balloon," she said.

"The balloon's fine," Lina said.

But she followed her all the same.

Overhead the clouds burst in purples and reds. The wind cried and in the distance Mona could hear ice breaking. The tread of their feet on the ground made a rhythmic, calming sound. Back on the Fairy Moons during that strange war there had been no atmosphere. They were packed inside their ships like pickled fish in a can, and when they went out onto those strange, barren moons there was no sound but the comms in their suits. Titan was different. Titan was full of sound.

The balloon was where they'd left it, anchored. For a moment Mona wanted to take to the sky again. Sail over the sea and just keep going. The world was large and she wanted to see all of it. She had never been to Xanadu . . .

"See?" Lina said. "Let's go back. The others will arrive soon."

Mona followed her sister. They hadn't gone far when she spotted something in the distance.

"What's that?" she said.

"What's what?" her sister said.

Mona pointed. There was something half-buried in the ice, in the distance.

"I don't know," Lina said.

"Let's go look."

"You're impossible," Lina said. But they went all the same.

"I'll miss this, if you go," Mona said.

"What?"

"This."

"I know. But you can't fly a balloon forever."

"Why can't you?" Mona said. "Mum and Dad did."

"Mum and Dad are dead."

It lay between them, that fact. They'd gone to the Paxsi Lake—"Fishing," they'd said, jokingly—and never came back. Not even their nodes were recovered, with whatever memories and thoughts they might have still contained. But this was not uncommon on Titan. It wasn't like Earth, where a part of you always lived on, forever.

"What *is* this?" Lina said.

They came and stood not far from the thing.

It rose out of the ice. It was as large as a boat. It was roughly ovoid, made out of some matte-black material, like unpolished obsidian or tar sand. It seemed to hum a little, internally. It was hot, too. The ice around it was melted. As they watched, the object sank a little deeper into the ground.

"It looks like an egg," Mona said.

Something tugged at her memory, in that place where she didn't like to go.

They stood and stared at the egg.

"Huh."

The egg hummed softly. Moisture rose from the melting ice, hovered.

"It could be alien," Mona said.

"There are no aliens."

"You don't know that."

They stared at the egg.

"It could be a time machine. You know, from the future."

"Time travel isn't real," Lina said.

"You don't know that."

They stood there staring at the egg. Mona opened her node, cautiously. Nothing. The egg was a black silent thing. She tried to ping it but nothing came back. It swallowed the packet of data like it never existed.

They stared at the egg.

The egg hummed.

"Could be a bomb," Lina said.

"Why would anyone put a bomb here?" Mona said.

"I don't know. How *did* it get here, anyway?"

"I don't know," Mona said.

They stared at the egg.

The egg did nothing.

"I wonder if there are more of them," Mona said.

A memory tugged at her mind, in that place she tried to avoid.

"We could look," her sister said.

"We could . . ."

"Come on, then."

So they went looking for eggs.

Away from the sea the hills began to rise around them and somewhere in the distance a volcano spewed clouds of ice into the air. Mona missed flying. She wanted to be back in the balloon, heading nowhere and everywhere, carried on the winds. In a small valley between two hills they found a second egg.

"Huh."

The egg looked much like the first one though it was buried deeper in the ice and tiny cracks appeared on its surface. It looked almost like diamond, she thought. The material. And it was hotter than the other one.

"I think I know what it is," Lina said.

"What?"

"Do you remember when we did that module on Martian history?" Lina said.

"Vaguely."

"The Martian Soviet had these things they called embryomechs. Sort of like the spiders that seed the solar system with the Conversation, only for planets.'

Spiders travelled the system until they found a suitable body to embed in. Once there, they converted the available matter into routers and hubs and then into additional spiders, which shot out of the depleted host body back into space, to make new nodes.

"I don't recall."

Lina shrugged. "It's obsolete. Sidorov," she said. "Sidorov embryomechs."

"If you say so."

"It was supposed to be, like, for colonizing. It could build anything out of the surrounding matter. Houses, habitats, whatever. So you'd drop it down on the surface and once it hatched you just . . . moved in."

"So did they ever use it?"

Lina shrugged again. "Don't think so."

"Figures."

They moved on.

They found the third egg—if that's really what it was—even further away and this one was almost entirely vanished in the ground. The ground shuddered under their feet, and Mona had the sense of something moving down there, something waking. She didn't like it much.

She remembered the assault on Puck that time. There had been similar things on the Puckish surface then, too. She remembered it now. They'd looked like rocks, more than anything, but they changed when you approached them. They had been embedded into the lunar surface and they were black against the greyish surface. And when you came too close they just . . . They were more like *coffins*, there, she thought. During that whole time fighting in the system they were never allowed to open their nodes. But she'd looked once, at one of those things, just once with her node open. Against orders. And the thing that came back at her that time was . . . It had no right to *exist*, whatever it was. She'd heard the stories, about the black clouds out in the Oort, and the Nine Billion Hells, and of the lost asteroid of Carcosa. But until that moment she'd never *believed* them.

"Let's go," she said now.

"All right," Lina said.

They retraced their steps but by the time they'd reached the place of the first egg, it was gone. Mona still felt tiny tremors underfoot. Maybe it really was just an ancient Sidorov egg, and there'd be some vintage settler home there one day, soon, with some obsolete comms unit in the living room, and a pre-printed picture of Lenin on the wall. Some house waiting for people to move in and make it a home.

"Let's just go," she said.

"Go where?" Lina said.

"Anywhere," Mona said. "The others will catch up."

Lina considered.

"All right," she said, smiling.

Mona hugged her, pressing the plate of her helmet against her sister's. A Titan kiss.

The balloon was just where they'd left it. They went inside and waited for the air to flood in.

Mona removed her helmet and suit and shivered.

"A bit cold," she said.

"It will warm up in a moment," Lina said.

She took the controls and released the anchors, and the balloon rose slowly into the air.

The wind lifted them up and pulled them along and over the sea. Mona looked down, searching for more eggs, but she didn't see any. She thought about that holiday, long ago, when they were all together by the seashore. And how she'd looked for fish in that methane sea but never saw any.

For just a moment she imagined she could see a dark shape rise out of the water, the flash of a fin, a long-curved neck. Some sort of plesiosaur swimming in the Ligeia Mare.

But it was probably nothing. A moment later, anyway, it was out of sight; and the balloon sailed away from there, to the lands beyond the sea.

Aptitude

Cooper Shrivastava

ONE MAY ASCEND to godhood in the same way one attains any other competitive position: a series of rigorous standardized exams.

9:00–9:30: Registration & continental breakfast

Alena appeared in the white room, in front of the registration desk, with her hair neatly combed, wearing formal business interview attire. As far as she knew, she was the only person in the universe to be invited to the Practical Assessment. She wasn't the only candidate in the reception room though, which meant the others must be from somewhere other than the universe.

There was a list of names. She scanned it, noting each candidate's profession. Mostly mathematicians, with strange specialties like "reality theorist," "meta optimalist," and "stochastic botanist." Alena knew she was underqualified for this position. She had resorted to connecting her mind to the ship's computer, illegally tapping into some of humanity's last remaining resources, just to access the brainpower she would need to understand the test. Hopefully the connection would last to the end of the interview.

She pressed the pad of her thumb next to an entry near the bottom of the page: Alenagutnarsunurassttir, recycling processor.

9:30–10:00: Meet and greet

In the waiting area, candidates clustered together around the danishes, probably being judged on their ability to make small talk. No one wanted to work with a socially awkward nerd, no matter how good they were at building universes. Alena searched for loners to help demonstrate her ability to smile through her teeth.

On the far side of the room, a woman was sitting down, sipping a cup of coffee and waiting without looking like she was waiting for anything. She was gorgeous: smooth skin, thick hair, lips that were probably naturally that color. People liked to pretend that good looks wouldn't get you ahead, but there was no way this woman's beauty wouldn't be a huge advantage in the face-to-face interview.

Where Alena came from, people didn't look like that anymore. Why invest resources into making your children beautiful when they would spend their whole lives on a slowly sinking ship with only the same few descendants for company? When you were the only people left in the world, who were you trying to impress?

Farther down was a candidate even more obviously from a different universe. His face, a map of ancient racial markers and organic asymmetries, looked like something out of a history book. His clothes were a style she had never seen before: a black, knee-length robe with a wide belt tied at the left hip, a white shirt, and black pants underneath. She had read somewhere that a color contrast interview outfit projected power and confidence.

Alena decided on the beautiful woman as the one to speak to, primarily because she was closer to the danishes.

"Feeling nervous?" Alena asked, trying to lean in conspiratorially, and judging by the woman's face, missing the mark.

"I'm happy with the results of my test preparation. I've run through so many practice simulations, I could build my model in my sleep," the woman said like she had a table full of job offers lined up for her at home. She certainly looked it, sitting there, cool and still. Alena shredded a danish with her fingernails.

Alena hadn't run through a single practice simulation. She didn't have the resources for it, for one thing. For another, she hadn't been able to hold conceptions as large and complex as a model universe in her brain until she had boosted off the ship, and that was after a full year of taking performance-enhancing drugs. She had mostly studied from the test preparation book.

Alena tried to compare the woman to the list of professions on the sign-in sheet. She didn't look old enough to be a professor.

"What's your name?" Alena asked, but before she could answer, the Proctor arrived.

10:00–1:00: 1st simulation session

"Hello everyone," the Proctor said with a big, impersonal smile. Her eyes lingered on the beautiful woman at Alena's side. "Thank you all for your presence here today. I know this is a long and challenging process, and you should be very proud of yourselves just for making it this far. In the current hiring cycle we've had over a hundred thousand applicants, and less than one percent were invited for a—" Alena stopped paying attention.

She had little desire to become a Builder and even less ability. It was killing her to listen to this woman smugly congratulate them on being candidates for such an *elevated* and *prestigious* position when the Board of Cosmogamy had made such a fucking mess of Alena's universe.

At least that was her suspicion. Maybe all universes had to come to a seizing halt at some time or another. Maybe there was nothing special about the slow-motion gravitational collapse they were going through. Maybe her whole universe was in the middle of a planned obsolescence, and afterward, when all the light and energy and matter there was had been crushed back into a single point, the scavengers of the Board would come and scrape up what was left for their new terrarium. There was only one way to find out, and that was why Alena had spent the last few years cobbling together the ability to handle the simulation: to get answers for her swallowed world.

The Proctor launched into the specifics of the universe simulation exam. They would have three hours to complete the core stage, where they would run their own first principles on authentic universe-building technology. They could write any laws and make any physical adjustments they wanted in that time.

During the second simulation session, each universe would run through a full time scale. Their work would be judged on the technique and process used during session one and the results of session two. Each session would be scored out of thirty points, with five points awarded in each of the following categories: consistency, completeness, resolution, determinism, transitivity, and habitability.

The reception room changed. They were now inside the simulation, which was inside whatever space-outside-of-time-and-space she had already been in, her real body lying quiescent in her real home. She looked down at herself. Her physical form looked the same, interview outfit and all, as did the Ancient Mathematician's form she had seen in the reception room.

The candidate she had just been speaking to, on the other hand, was almost unrecognizable. She had aged, for one thing, and aged in a way people didn't really do anymore in Alena's world, her face wilting in on itself into a soft map of wrinkles, her red lips thinned and deflated, even her hair was now short and curly, like she was trying to hide hair loss. Her aged body was fatter, too, but dressed in a simple long-sleeved shirt and pants made out of some thick and tough material, rubber boots, and gloves that looked, well, that looked a little bit like the ones Alena would sometimes wear to dismantle complex bits of physical waste when the ship managed to haul in something that hadn't been totally compacted during its fall toward the black hole.

She caught Alena staring and wiggled her fingers.

"My gardening outfit," the third candidate whispered, ignoring the proctor's sharp look. Alena thought back to the registration list.

They were each handed a blue test booklet. Alena opened it. There were no questions, just empty space to write.

"How does the simulation start?" Alena asked, snagging the Proctor's attention before she walked away.

"This is the simulation," the Proctor said with a smile clearly designed to hide the fact that she didn't consider Alena to be a serious candidate. "Just write down the rules you want to start with, and the interface will expand as you develop your universe."

She smiled again, even less sincerely, and then walked out. Alena frowned at the empty test booklet. Her pen from the reception hadn't made it into the simulation.

The Ancient Mathematician, and the Beautiful Gardener were both already scribbling away. The Mathematician cleared his throat, and then he held something out to her. A fountain pen. The same ornate, custom fountain pen that sat on the Captain's desk at home, which he loved, but almost never had occasion to use anymore, now that theirs was the only ship left.

"Thanks," Alena said. She held the pen in her hand, and even though there was no reason to believe that any of this was real, she felt the metal warming from the heat of her fingertips.

The clock was ticking. The test prep book advised beginning by building a universe with similar rules to what the test taker was already familiar with. Alena wrote down axioms for extensionality, pairing, union, powerset, infinity, and separation.

Nothing like an interface opened up for her. Meanwhile, the Ancient Mathematician had already moved his universe off the page into the room, which was now the void. Glowing lights in the distance made Alena certain that some of the other candidates had breathed life into theirs as well.

Alena gritted her teeth and added an axiom for choice. She didn't *see* anything change per se, not like the universe a few people to her left that was toggling between matter and antimatter, but somewhere in her brain she did feel a sudden cohesion, an engine revving, a light turning on in a far-off room. Alena's heart sped up, and she scribbled down the definitions for some base elements.

It wasn't even hard at first, at least once she had added enough information for the universe to be visualized. It lifted off the page and she added some shape. Topologically smooth, 3-manifold space, all things that could be described in the test booklet without drawing on the extra resources her body was connected to in the real world. But it turned out, adding space before adding time was difficult. The model had to be homogeneous in order to be isotropic. It had to be path-connected in order to be homogeneous. It had to be not just path-connected, but simply connected in order to get the minimum passing "habitability" score. And those were just the mathematical implications of her chosen topology; they had to be analogous to her chosen physics as well.

Alena hadn't realized how much of the model was taking place in her and how much was being observed by her from the outside until it collapsed in her face. If she had a heart in here, it skipped a beat.

She glanced around, trying to move just her eyeballs and not her head, to see if anyone had noticed. The Ancient Mathematician was standing inside some sort of torus, and the Beautiful Gardener was nowhere to be seen. Alena crumpled the used sheet in her fist.

She decided to try something a little simpler. She established the same mathematics, and this time gave the universe positive curvature. This forced her model to be finite. But, it also made the energy density way too high. The universe kept sprouting new dimensions every time she tried to lift it from the page.

When the booklet started smoking, Alena was forced to give it up. She scribbled out the words this time, and as she did so her monstrous creation dismantled itself. There were only a few sheets left; even if Alena had been a master Builder she didn't know what she could do in such a short space.

Well that was fine, to hell with it anyway. She wasn't here to score a perfect 30, Alena reminded herself, and a marble was a universe, too, from the right perspective. She started writing, and the elegant fountain pen tore through cheap standardized test paper. Forget the axiom of choice, we'll get by with first order arithmetic. In a finite Euclidean metric space. Antimatter? No thanks. Elements? All hydrogen, all the way down. Speed of light? She paused. The pen hovered over her paper. 100 miles per hour.

It was surreal, and Alena found herself stifling laughter. With the speed turned down so low, she could hold a lump of solid hydrogen in the palm of her hand. A whole universe.

With only an hour left, Alena had to admit this tiny sphere wouldn't win her any prizes. But then again, they were ranked in order and there wasn't any cutoff score. As long as her ball of hydrogen made it into the top 20 percent, she could at least move on to the interview phase.

Alena was a recycling processor by profession. She spent her days taking the complex junk of formerly advanced civilizations and breaking it down, figuring out how to prize out the most valuable parts, and how to pulverize the rest back to raw material. Maybe she did have the skill set to move on after all.

She peeked over at the simulation next to her. The candidate had made their universe homogeneous and isotropic as well, and Alena, who just had something blow up in her face over the same structures, knew how to handle *that*.

When she thought they weren't looking, she grabbed the closest thing she could reach in the simulated universe. It was some sort of accretion disk, and in the partially constructed universe the other candidate was building, it simplified itself in her hands to a unit circle in $\mathbb{R}^2$.

Alena slipped it into her test booklet so no one could see what she was doing. She dragged a thumbnail from the center to the edge to create a line the radius of the disk, and then scribbled down a basic definition: let γ be a counterclockwise rotation of, say, $1/24$ radians.

She spun the radius she had created through all the positions $\gamma^n(r)$ and let n spin out into infinity. They were in a simulation beyond reconciling time and space, so the set

$$\bigcup_{n=0}^{\infty} = \gamma^n(r)$$

immediately sat in her palm, and when she licked a fingertip and pressed it to $(0,0)$ she could lift it off the disk like a wheel with infinite spokes.

Perfect.

Together the set of all spokes of the wheel and the set of all points in the circle that were not spokes made up the entire unit disk. Alena rotated the spokes clockwise, so that a new spoke appeared. She had cut the disk into two pieces, moved one of them, and now had the original set plus an extra spoke, all within the simple mathematical rules that the candidate had agreed to.

She tossed the disc back into her competitor's universe, where it settled down into the filament like a bomb hiding in a sea crater, creating matter from nothing as it ticked clockwise through endless new rotations.

Emboldened by her success, Alena scanned the other universes that were popping into existence under the invisible hands of her competitors. Some were easy to disrupt. This one hadn't put up any walls between its physics and its math. A simple sphere eversion was enough to break it. That one's dark energy pressure was too low compared to its dark energy density. It was already heading for a Big Rip.

The clock was still ticking down, and Alena needed to wipe out at least one more person if she wanted her shitty lump of universe to qualify for the next stage. There were still many simulations beyond her reach. In front of her, the Ancient Mathematician's ever-expanding universe had reached the point where she could stand on the other side of it and be obscured from his vision by compressed superclusters and cosmic voids.

He had done a wonderful job, too. None of the tricks she had used on the others would work here. Alena put her hand out and rubbed some superclusters between her fingers. It felt like fine white sand, and through that sensation the simulation provided comprehensive data about the structure between her fingers. His resolution score already looked like it was going to be maxed out.

His universe had grown so large and so complete that it was no longer appropriate for the simulation to render it inside the test center. It was just unfurling in front of them like some sort of primordial fern, and now she understood what the Proctor had meant when she said that "the interface will expand as your universe develops," because she could see within each quasar and tidal tail a whole load of information that grew in depth and complexity as he worked.

At the center of it, the Ancient Mathematician stood tinkering with a galaxy cluster. The bursts of nuclear fission were visible to her in this medium, as the star on his fingertip went supernova again and again with various tweaks. The light pulses lasted anywhere from milliseconds to hours, but the information received about how much time was passing was controlled by the timer that ticked down to the end of the test. To Alena's eyes, his face was bathed in periodic flashes of light.

With each adjustment, the Mathematician's universe grew in both size and density. There weren't any weak spots that Alena could see.

The creator would be the weak spot, she decided.

Working under time constraints, he had been using a shortcut. As he worked on the local phenomena, he applied changes he wanted across the universe, which was unbounded. The unboundedness was going to earn him extra points, but it was also making the thing difficult. So, he had underpinned the first three dimensions with a simple tiling of one triangle, two squares, and one hexagon that extended out in all directions.

It made things easy for him because after he changed a patch of the honeycomb, he could apply those changes to any congruent patch, easily extending it out over the infinite universe. It made things easy for her because he was relying on the universe's regularity, and that was something she knew how to break.

Alena took her book, and the pen he had lent her, and sketched out a few iterations of the pattern. She took the two squares and pinched them into diamonds. She bisected the triangle and decomposed the hexagon into three equivalent rhombuses.

She redrew the triangles so that the ratio of their sides was equivalent to the ratio of their sum over the longest side, which made them glow golden. She overlaid these on the rhombuses, which she sorted into thick and thin shapes. The golden half of each thin rhombus could be laid next to the golden half of each thick rhombus so that their sides were aligned left to right. The shapes reformed themselves along this matching rule, which allowed unbounded expansion.

She let it spill out across his whole universe, changing the regular tiling to the aperiodic one as it churned along following her set of rules.

His shortcut had relied on its underlying periodicity. If he tried to use the matrix to apply changes to the whole universe, he would never be able to reach all of it. That is to say, while any segment he chose could be found in the complete pattern an infinite number of times, the whole pattern itself could not be shifted to produce the same tiling. She had sabotaged its translational symmetry.

The Ancient Mathematician continued playing with the galaxy cluster. He made an adjustment and applied it to a local part of space overlaid on her new grid, but this time his change wasn't instantaneous across the universe. It spread out infinitely far, yes, just like the pattern, but was unable to cover his entire infinite plane.

The Ancient Mathematician frowned. He chose a bigger area and applied the same changes. Again it spread out to infinite identical areas, and again he failed to apply the changes to the entire universe. He zoomed outward and selected a larger area. And then a larger area again.

He could tell that something wasn't right and checked back with the underpinning grid. But when he pulled one out, it was still the basic set of shapes he had started with.

The universe might be infinite, Alena thought as she watched him struggle. The more he expanded his range, the more of his own work he destroyed. The universe might be infinite, but the human mind is apparently not.

That left her with just over seventeen minutes of time in the simulation, and there was still one candidate she couldn't crack. But high on the elation of knowing she had destroyed enough of them to advance to the next stage, Alena turned toward the garden.

The Beautiful Gardener was as good as her word, or at least her outfit. The space around her was nothing like the work of the other candidates. It didn't look like an array matter spread out through the void, it looked like she was on her knees in the dirt.

Alena even imagined she could smell it, something earthy with a pollen-like sweetness. The last time she had smelled something so clearly organic it had been a cup of real peach juice she had drank celebrating her mother's promotion to Assistant Director. That had been about eight years ago, in the very last moments before they fell out of contact with other motherships.

The two of them had sat on the observation deck at the ship equator to drink and contemplate the view. It was just possible to see the last remnants of the Plancius star cluster smeared across the empty dark as it fell into the black hole. In a ship traveling near the speed of light, away from the black hole, they would watch that majestic sight for all of Alena's natural life.

"Aren't you going to congratulate me?" Alena's mother had said.

"Congrats, Mom," Alena said. "I knew they'd give it to you." She put a hand on her mother's head like she was the older woman and her mother was the child.

Actually, she had just been glad her mother still cared enough to celebrate. As the end became clearer and clearer, just generations away now, many people on the ship lost interest in pursuing anything at all. There was no means of thinking about the future, no possibility of having a legacy or preserving their past. When Alena was a child, caring for her had provided some outlet for those feelings, but now that she was a grown adult with no future, even her mother was slipping farther and farther into this anhedonia.

Before she found the Board of Cosmogamy's application guide booklet, Alena, too, had sleep-walked through each day of work, breaking down the debris that flashed past the ship on its way into the black hole.

Finding that test prep booklet had changed everything. She couldn't escape the black hole, couldn't save her universe, but finally there was someone to ask, someone to hold to account. Participating in this exam could be her chance to meet that secretive cabal responsible for putting things together the way they are.

Unlike the other candidates, the Beautiful Gardener turned her head when Alena stepped into her simulation. She looked pointedly down at Alena's feet.

Alena thought she was just on the "ground," the sandy soil that had sprung up at a few strokes of the Beautiful Gardener's pen, but looking closer she saw that a shrub with wide coin-shaped leaves was beginning to sprout under her feet.

"Sorry," Alena said. But the shrub didn't seem affected by her intrusion until, intrigued by its presence, she squatted down near the thing and the simulation offered up more information about its true nature. The shrub was a type of information map, growing out of the sandy basin of foundational theories. When she picked up a handful of the soil, she could see that it was made up of facts, and the roots were soaking up parts of the soil to form a coherent body of physics.

Alena moved forward to her hands and knees. She held the test booklet up behind the leaf, where it clarified into what at first she thought was a deterministic algorithm, then quickly realized was actually a stochastic process. It was gene mutation and expression, played out on the fundamental building blocks of the universe.

The plant died. Alena stood up and whipped the test booklet behind her back, but the Beautiful Gardener didn't chastise her; she was entirely wrapped up in what could only be called weeding.

The Beautiful Gardener pulled out plants by their roots and flung them at a young tree with smooth pale bark and wide, deeply lobed leaves. As they landed, the weeds decomposed into their component parts, which Alena could grasp through the interface momentarily before they melted into the ground.

Alena stared upward. Above them should be void, waiting to be filled according to the candidate's rules, but here there was only blue. It was, according to the information the simulation offered, a sky. Alena, like all of the human beings left in the universe she came from, had never seen a sky in person before.

She clenched the cold hydrogen marble in her fist and turned her attention back to her competition. This was only a simulation, she reminded herself. She still had never seen a real sky.

"What are you doing?" Alena asked. Maybe she didn't need to break it; it seemed that the Beautiful Gardener hadn't managed a full universe at all. This was the top candidate that the proctors had been eyeing?

"I'm taking advantage of a process called cosmic orthogenesis. Or more metaphorically"—the Beautiful Gardener waved a spade at the small tree— "I'm waiting for this tree to fruit."

That was more information than Alena had expected, or even felt she deserved, considering they were competitors. Not to mention that if she was really so smart, surely the Beautiful Gardener knew what Alena had done to the other candidates.

Alena looked around almost hesitantly for any weaknesses in the system; it would be pleasurable to break the favored candidate, but to be honest, the creation was rich and deep, all encompassing in a way that the others hadn't been.

And anyway, unless someone could live in this garden of random walks, she wasn't going to score in any of the five categories.

1:00–2:00: Lunch

Without any jarring motion, they were back in the reception room. The number of candidates was less than half of what it had been during the meet and greet. The Ancient Mathematician looked dizzy.

The Beautiful Gardener was back to being beautiful again. Even though she hadn't produced anything as far as Alena could tell, she looked extremely content.

There were plenty of empty chairs, and the Ancient Mathematician was doing the complicated calculus of where to sit that was close enough to show enthusiasm but also wasn't awkwardly in the front row, near enough to his competitors that he wasn't being antisocial, but still far enough that they wouldn't have to necessarily speak to each other.

The Beautiful Gardener returned to where she had been seated earlier in the morning, and as if remembering that this problem was reduced to one that had been previously solved, the Ancient Mathematician collapsed into the same row, two seats down. Alena remained standing.

There was something touching her hip. Alena reached down and felt around in her pocket. It was hard, and cold, and shaped like a marble. She rubbed her thumb against it, tried to dig in with her nail, but it was solid and almost frictionless.

The Proctor returned to tell them to help themselves to lunch and that they would be pulled out one at a time for individual interviews.

This was it then. Finally she could sit down face-to-face with one of these so-called gods and demand to know. Were all universes destined to end horribly, or had hers just pulled the unlucky straw? The simple marble in her hand seemed to prove otherwise; she didn't think that the application of any amount of time would be able to break it. But then, anything complex enough to be livable had been beyond Alena's abilities to create.

She clenched the marble in her fist. If only she had been able to create a universe as complex as the Ancient Mathematician's or as detailed as the Beautiful Gardener's. Or at least something that could score a single point for habitability. She didn't have a smoking gun, proof that they should have done better for her universe. She couldn't use this to demand answers, only to beg for an explanation. And if they admitted it to her and told her it was all just a big mistake? Or that it wasn't, and for whatever arcane reasons the Builders had chosen her universe for death, what was she going to do about it anyway? Alena didn't know. She was just angry.

Her plan had only extended as far as preparing herself for the test by connecting to the mothership's resources. Once she had figured out how to do it (breaking dual pole low-phase encryption, and smashing a deadbolt with a hammer), she lay back in the warm pocket of the ship testing out her new mental functions. The next thing she knew she was here.

Alena inspected the room-temperature lunch spread thoroughly, but her stomach felt high and tight, like a fist under her ribcage, and she didn't want to put anything in it. She hadn't noticed feeling nervous during the exam, but now she felt the sensation of coming down from nervousness, like air being let out of a balloon leaving her deflated and gummy. She would have liked to drink something hot, but the coffee from earlier was nowhere in sight.

The Beautiful Gardener interviewed first; somehow it seemed she was still the favorite.

Across from Alena, the Ancient Mathematician was devouring a sandwich. She didn't lean over and say something like, *I hope they didn't find your performance disappointing* but she could have and not felt bad about it one bit.

2:00–3:00: Individual interview

"Alenagundarsunurassttir?" the Proctor called, horribly mispronouncing Alena's name.

Alena raised her hand.

"Please follow me for the individual interview portion," the Proctor said, redundantly, because they were in a beige office with a wide desk. One empty chair sat across from a severe woman with a gridded score sheet.

The Proctor closed the door on her way out, but not before Alena caught a glimpse of someone else passing down the hallway to who knows where.

The Interviewer cleared her throat to let Alena know how hideously unprofessional she had been to take her eyes off the interviewer for even one second. Alena sat down.

"Hello. I'm an associate coordinator, and I'm on the training and selection committee. If you're approved by the Board of Cosmogamy, I'll be your supervisor for the first training session. Thanks for coming in today, I know this can be a pretty long and grueling process. Do you have any questions about the process so far?"

She cocked her head as if she were listening for an answer. Alena was about to respond but the Interviewer continued on, unheeding: "I'm not one myself, I wouldn't even know where to begin! I'm part of the support staff, but if you're selected, you'll have the opportunity to meet some Builders after the simulation ends. They always like to approve new people personally."

Alena's posture crumpled. There was no way she would make it through the second round. The Interviewer was already talking again.

"Alright. This interview is not meant to be a recitation of your background and skill set, we feel the information we've already collected on you, along with your exam results, give us a good picture of your abilities. We're more interested in whether you're a good 'cultural fit' with our organization."

People always said things like that to cover the fact that they had already made up their minds about you. What does "cultural fit" even mean? What culture? Was this woman just here to decide whether or not she liked her? Alena wished she had eaten something earlier.

"'Cultural fit' in this context means we're looking for someone who embodies the values of consistency, completeness, resolution, determinism, transitivity, and habitability in their approach to problems."

Those were mostly mathematical properties. How was someone supposed to embody the values of say, transitivity, in their everyday life?

The Interviewer's brows dropped. "Surely you knew this and came prepared for this interview," she said.

Alena opened her mouth to claim that yes, surely she had, but the Interviewer raised a hand to stop her and continued,

"Well, that's disappointing but not altogether unexpected."

Alena's head jerked back in surprise. She and the Interviewer regarded each other with equally displeased expressions.

"No, I'm not reading your mind. This is a temporary pocket of spacetime we call a 'sandbox' that was constructed with specific parameters in mind. One of which is that I, as the creator, have near-simultaneous knowledge of all of the contents of the sandbox, including whatever goes through your mind, as you are right now a construct of the sandbox. Yes, sort of like reading your mind. No, nothing so extreme. Yes, you are. Well you knew *that* much when you signed up," the Interviewer said in rapid response.

All that just fucking added up, didn't it? Sure. Fine. Whatever. Sandwiches, danishes, the ability to read foreign names and mysterious professions on the sign-in sheet. Alena immediately started brainstorming all of the things she shouldn't think about.

For example, she probably shouldn't think about how she had just cheated her way through the first round of simulations. Wouldn't they know about that already with their so-called near simultaneous knowledge? Definitely she shouldn't think about how she had been studying from a stolen test preparation book, or how she had been taking neuroplasticity-enhancing drugs for the last year in preparation.

"Yes, that was not ideal behavior, nor fitting with the type of character we are looking for in Builders, but there are some special dispensations. You know most of the other people here are from places and time periods where human life is flourishing, and have been born and bred to excel at cosmostatic reasoning. We can occasionally turn a blind eye to someone playing neurophysical catch-up."

"I've never heard of cosmostatic reasoning," Alena said, and it came out of her mouth because she said it before she thought it.

"You've been thinking of it as 'modeling,' because you never studied it formally. That's all right, we're trying to be more welcoming of candidates from . . . underprivileged backgrounds."

Even though this was an unembodied space beyond time, and her real body was lying in a nest of connective tissues deep in the belly of her mothership, Alena's face heated up. So that was why she had made it this far, despite struggling with every element of the exam. She was the diversity candidate.

The Interviewer's smile faltered. Maybe she had expected Alena to be happy about that news and was put out now that she wasn't. Maybe she thought Alena should feel *privileged* to hear a tidbit from behind the curtain, to have her time wasted by the august Board in this moment outside of time and space.

Joke's on you, Alena wanted to say, *I never thought I had any chance of passing.* She didn't have to say it of course, since thinking was enough.

The Interviewer pursed her lips. The rest of the interview consisted of tedious mathematical problems Alena did not know how to answer.

3:30–5:00: 2nd simulation session

They were back in the simulation. Alena was steaming. She was gripping the ball of universe so tightly it was probably going to lose a dimension.

The application of time apparently required a different user interface, because the back of her mind now contained a switch and a dial. The switch moved in two directions, forward and reverse. The dial was shaped like an infinite double cone with the apex at the origin of an n-dimensional space. She toyed with the dial first without touching the switch.

It was pretty fucking cool actually, but didn't fit the aesthetic or the goals of her lump universe. Alena reluctantly collapsed the double cone into its projection on the xy-plane and labeled the clockwise direction with an unbounded sequence of speeds.

She tossed the grey marble up and down a few times. The switch only had two directions, forward and backward. Once she turned time on, there wouldn't be any stopping.

Alena flipped the switch to "forward" and cranked the dial clockwise one full turn. The grey lump didn't seem to show any effects whatsoever.

Alena rolled it between her palms a few times. Time was certainly passing in the model universe; she could tell from the interface. Time was also probably passing in the simulation. The simulation was built in a sandbox, and that sandbox existed somewhere inside a universe subject to some measure of time, forward or backward at some speed, somewhere.

She felt around the dial a bit—simple one-dimensional time for a simple spherical universe—and then looked around to see where she could scavenge more time from.

Now that her eyes were open to them, Alena saw the total carnage wrought by the passage of time on the remaining few universe models around her. Those that were left had expanded so much that they filled the simulation's available space, each layered over the next.

She could see photons become ancient, frozen, wavelengths so long she lacked the imagination to measure them. Layer upon layer of stellar remnants sifted down from one universe to another until they formed an icy sediment, studded through with iron stars which collapsed into black holes which evaporated into nothing she could see or understand.

Simultaneously and in the same space, other universes were coming apart. Galaxies unraveled and planets splintered, victims of their creators' wantonly unbounded cosmological constants. Dark energy, left to grow at an ever-accelerating pace, split atoms in front of her eyes. Universes surrounded her, each dying their own death. Alena wanted to look away but wasn't quite sure how.

She closed her eyes and crossed her arms against her chest, hugging herself, and tried to pull back. When she opened them again, the garden was around her, now lush, dense and overgrown, drinking richly of an unknown light. The Beautiful Gardener was standing next to her.

They were both looking at the tree at the center of the garden, which now revealed itself to be a fig tree.

"—and here you are," the Beautiful Gardener said. "I take it this means the other candidates have already been eliminated."

Alena didn't say anything. If the Beautiful Gardener wanted to know about the other candidates, she could look for herself.

The other woman didn't seem put off by the lack of response, she just copied Alena's pose, regarding the fig tree as well. Alena huffed and put her arms down.

She couldn't see it, but if she closed her eyes again, Alena could feel the sun on her face. In the back of her mind, another dial existed, untouched, the one belonging to the Beautiful Gardener. The switch hadn't been flipped, but regardless, the garden was still growing around them.

"Are you going to steal that?" the Beautiful Gardener asked. Clearly she could feel Alena's groping at the fabric of time. She smiled and crow's feet appeared at the corners of her eyes.

"Why do you look like that," Alena demanded instead of answering her. "I'm sure they pretend otherwise, but those proctors would definitely look more favorably on you if you were still gorgeous."

"I'm not sure I'd call my real body 'gorgeous,' but thanks," she said dryly. "I look the way I do because where I'm from that's how they want people to look. Our bodies are carefully edited as we grow to enhance our intelligence and health, but also for symmetrical features, an attractive body, a full head of hair." She pulled off a garden glove and inspected both sides of her broad hands and short, callused fingers.

"A certain long and elegant bone structure. I haven't had my original nose since I was thirteen," she said, tapping the nose in question.

She dusted off the baggy gardening clothes.

"My world *made* me beautiful. I made myself a botanist," the woman continued.

"So what, you put on wrinkles and sunspots out of spite?" Alena asked.

"I feel fine. This is just an image; my body works well here and feels good. I just thought—" She paused. "Well, if I were going to wake up every morning and look in the mirror, I'd rather see this face than their face."

That didn't make sense. They were only in here for another hour. Or something. Another finite unit of time with the usual magnitude and direction, at any rate.

"Still," Alena said, then trailed off.

The Beautiful Gardener reached up into the lowest branches of the fig tree and plucked a fruit.

Alena wanted to say something sarcastic, but she was distracted by the ringing in her ears, and the sudden recall of her attention to the void outside the garden. Outside the garden, all the other simulated universes had died, but somehow, Alena thought she could hear voices. She frowned and refocused on the woman in front of her.

The Beautiful Gardener handed her the fig. The skin was sap green, and it felt sunwarm and heavy in her hand. Vascular bundles made thin veins just underneath the surface, and it gave softly under her fingertips, at perfect ripeness.

Alena rubbed her thumb around the ostiole, before pushing her nail in and splitting the fruit apart. The inside was dewy and ruby red, and she even thought she could smell the milky-sweet juice. It was hard to believe it wasn't a real fruit.

But it wasn't. What she was actually holding in her hand was a mathematical statement that had been converted into a symbol. She looked around the garden. The mapping worked because no two formulas would ever have the same symbol, just like no two figs and no two blades of grass would ever be exactly the same.

The Gardener's cosmic orthogenesis was a map of statements about the simulation *into* the simulation, a mapping that allowed the universe to talk cogently about itself.

And that meant that Alena knew how to break it.

The pressure from outside the garden grew stronger at that thought, and the strange ringing cohered into the voice of the Proctor but she brushed it off.

It wasn't even a trick actually; it was just the nature of the garden. The universe she had built must contain only those fruits and leaves that had been birthed through the process of cosmic orthogenesis. That is, they must be a universe of mathematical statements consistent with each other, and yes, she thought back to the first simulation, so the garden grew subject to the constraints of her weeding. Even the gardener's actions had been a member of the set of all statements within the universe.

And if they stood in a universe of consistent statements, then that universe itself could never be fully written. The garden could never stop growing; this was a garden of forking paths. Down one path, the inconsistent state, all fruits were possible because they grew from a statement that was both true and untrue. Infinite proof by contradiction, unlivable, that would grind the delicate machinery of the simulation into dust before ever creating a real universe. A universe in which anything, right or wrong, could be proven.

It would be so easy to break it; she had the key in the palm of her hand, in the tiny grey marble. This was a formula that hadn't been produced by the garden itself, but which the garden could easily talk about. Introduce it to the system and with a few tweaks she could prove both its truth and untruth, bringing the whole thing to a crashing halt.

Down the other path, the incomplete state, the garden could flourish, infinite figs on infinite fig trees, myrrh and Mecca balsam, root and vine; one day she would even see the sun.

And all it would take is the acceptance of the core flaw of the Beautiful Gardener's creation: that there was knowledge outside the scope of what the garden could generate.

There was sugar on her tongue. Pulp oozed between her fingers. Alena realized she had eaten the fig. Nothing had ever tasted more real.

Somewhere, the Proctor was trying to stop them. She was reaching for the untouched dial and switch that controlled time in the garden. The Beautiful Gardener couldn't touch it herself without changing it; Alena pushed the Proctor's hands away.

The Beautiful Gardener handed her another fig, and Alena ate it in one bite, skin and all, and her eyes were closed but she felt like she could see the whole garden, and that the garden was compact and twisted in space, and she was standing in her own line of sight, eating fruit after fruit.

To accept that the universe was consistent but not complete was to accept there would be things beyond the garden's ability to prove.

There would be true things about the garden that could never be revealed by the churning wheel of orthogenesis.

But more specifically, she knew, clutching the cold grey marble, there was one thing that she herself would never get to know, would never have another chance to ask.

She couldn't see beyond the garden anymore—the simulation was getting stronger—but she could hear the Proctor's voice screeching in the void, demanding to *shut it down* and to *pull it apart*. Alena wondered if the Beautiful Gardener could hear it, too.

Come out, the Proctor was saying, *come out and we'll tell you everything you want to know.* The Beautiful Gardner was gazing at the sky. There was nothing she would be able to do. She was within the system, and Alena was the crack that they would use to prize open this cocoon. *Trust us* the outside voices demanded as one.

She couldn't. She wanted to move on, to move forward, to walk under the sun, but—

She held up the blue test booklet, which was creased and crumpled from her death grip. The Beautiful Gardener's smile made her look young again. She gently pulled the paper out of Alena's hand.

She took up Alena's pen and struck out the curvature, struck out the field equations, the matter, energy, density, light and dark, and every axiom and base definition on the page, and as she did so, the tiny cold ball in Alena's hand loosened, dissolved, and then finally was no more.

And as it dissolved, the garden became a closed form, infinite but bounded, self-contained, and the voice of the Proctor, and the Interviewer, and Others which Alena couldn't place cut off.

The sudden quiet startled her; it was like she had been surrounded by shrieking cicadas and had not noticed until they were gone. Now there was total silence, waiting to be filled. Not even a rustle of leaves disturbed the quiet; there was no wind to move them. But there would be.

Alena turned to the expectant face of the Beautiful Gardener.

"Do you know how to make birds?" she asked.

The woman handed her a pair of gloves, and together they disappeared into the foliage.

Striding the Blast

Gregory Feeley

THE WINDS OF Hermes howl as no Earthly landscape ever hears, and the godlings ride upon them as they never set foot upon its soil.

However swift in its passage, the tiny world's days are long, and as the Sun slowly rises and the Celestial Sphere darkens before it, the sportive zephyrs swirl, dance, and then surge in raging torrents, fleeing to the world's dark side.

Known as the Zephyroi Hermitikoi or Shuĭxīng Fēng, they flee to the world's midnight where they will cool and sink, eventually to be buffeted by their livelier peers back into the light of the Sun to warm and rage anew. Such chariots as ride these blasts are driven only by the most headlong and carefree, or else the desperate and careworn.

Such a one was Aurelia Tektonikos, who stole the Kerykeion and suffered harsh imprisonment, from which she escaped by throwing herself through a casement and filling her wings with the wind of the shock wave that blew apart the tower behind her. Captured at length and subjected to such torments as befit a warlord's rage, she was later ministered with what healing arts the hospitallers possessed and turned over to the mekhanikes, who carried out labors possible only this close to the Sun, bending slivers of space in order to reach into its depths and bend slivers of time. Twisting backward, if only for milliseconds and at a cost their patient could not know, they strove to undo the work of the Universe and effect the partial and temporary restoration of what structures could be clawed back from the ruins of Time.

The Synoris could only take place at the proper hour, when Hermes had just raced past perihelion and the blaze of that approach had heated the tiny world's atmosphere to the height of its frenzy. Superheated air expanded in every direction, causing the Ymin to bulge upward at the Nearside point and then ripple along its sides like the medusae of Earth's former oceans.

They launched from a platform high on the Yellow Crane Tower, which rose even further to touch the Ymin like the great tentpole of the world. The twenty-four chariots burst forth in every direction and the shrieking winds snatched them like leaves. Some ran before the blast on great spreads of sail; others chose small light craft with greater maneuverability.

Aurelia alone was given wings. Their gliding power was tremendous, for the rig was both strong and light. She rode no chariot, piloted no tiny craft: just herself strapped to the apparatus, which looked (save for its ability to withstand lead-melting heat) as though it had been designed during the Renaissance.

But light and powerful as they were, they could not carry her across the Terminator and to the Champion's Pavilion. The capricious winds, mighty but inconstant, could dive at unexpected moments or weaken unaccountably, and the force of their push into Darkside produced countercurrents from that cooler region, creating cyclonic eddies that could slam to the ground any rider unable to avoid them. No glider could negotiate all of these, so Aurelia had to fly when necessary, beating wings against gusts that would shred any fabric light as hers that had to withstand it. She could run before the winds, tack when necessary, flap like a gull when she had to. But windjamming to the finish line on hectares of sail was, for her alone, not available.

Was it possible to make the flight, halfway around even so small a world, without calling at some point upon greater reserves of strength and endurance than even Earthborn muscles can sustain? Many thought not, and imagined her impressment into the rolls as a long-delayed, blithely contrived death sentence. Others thought the faint possibility of survival was designed to serve as her goad and thus her torment. None cared greatly, for the Synoris was the sport of demigods, immense in their power and assurance, and seemingly poised to live as long as the Universe itself. An accident could injure only their pride, disrupting for some breath the great and terrible joy they felt in acting upon their natures.

"Conserve what strength you can," said the armiger, adjusting the harness in accordance with the last minute's slight shift in wind speeds.

"But when you must expend energy, don't hesitate, lest you find your-self soon requiring more."

This did not need saying, but at this stage nothing did, and the armiger realized that he simply did not wish his final words to Aurelia to have already been uttered.

"They will watch to see you crash," he thought to add. "Don't gratify their impatience."

Poised one at each compass point, the racers faced slightly away from each other, but the godlings were also together, as such beings always were. They all lived half in each other's heads, able to converse easily as though seated at a banquet from which they could absent themselves (or rejoin) at an instant's notice. Thus the Hemitheoi of any given world enjoyed the company of their peers—camaraderie, rivalry, scheming and sexual intrigue, just like humans—in the great hall of their shared dominion. Aurelia experienced none of this.

No starting gun, no dropped handkerchief. The racers watched the countdown through whatever channel they chose, and at the instant of *Go* their magnetic constraints vanished.

Because the gale that tore past Crane Tower blew in only one direction, the racers were all flung downwind, a maneuver that required the Tower to spin once like a top, launching them tenths of a second apart with a force that drove them back into their seats. The sudden acceleration and deceleration that preceded this left even the hardiest racer disoriented for a second, and Aurelia, who had no seat, was swatted like a fly. Last to be launched, she took the hardest hit, in calculated compensation for the late departures. Onlookers saw twen-ty-three racers streak into the storm and one tiny figure tumbling like shrapnel before she recovered, swooped low, and took off after the rest.

If a cheer went up, Aurelia did not hear it. Her head was ringing, and vestibular chaos churned through her skull. She righted her rig and directed it downwind before her thoughts could clear, propelled like a leaf by the superheated blast.

Hermes is a crumpled pockmarked world, its surface ridged with scarps created as the planet's cooling interior contracted and fractured by thousands of craters and their surrounding ejecta. Its unnatural winds scour the surface and will someday wear it smooth, should the Immortals who rule the planet not decide to make better use of them. The CO_2 and nitrogen skimmed from the Morning Star would someday, their tekhnikoi claimed, provide air for breathing and carbon to create soaring crystalline structures, and perhaps in their vaunting supremacy they would import hydrogen from deflected comets or bring it in tankers from Jupiter and make of this peach-pit world a high-walled garden.

Hermes' meridian runs 7700 klicks; a gale driving a steady 350 k/h could blow you halfway round its circumference in twenty-two hours. No wind, however, would take you in any one direction for long, nor with predictable force: blasts could gust up to 600 kph or more while turbulent flow could produce eddies that would drop you below a hundred. To ride the gale from planetary noon to midnight was to shift and climb as one savage wind succeeded another, two Earth days (as even the godlings still reckoned time) or more without respite.

Did they expect Aurelia, whose too-human mind could function through such duration only through reliance on potent pharmaceuticals, to manage with her judgment unimpaired? To ask was to provoke hearty laughter, the rich amusement worthy of the gods.

During the billions of years before Hermes was swathed and given an atmosphere, no micrometeorite burned up before impact, and while the planet's escape velocity was low, most of the debris flung into space eventually fell back. Dust and flakes of silicates covered the bare world's surface, all now swept up by savage winds and hurled like buckshot through the filthy air.

Even here, kilometers above the surface and climbing as fast as she could, Aurelia felt the sting of particles in her flank as she banked to starboard. Her wings could repair small punctures, but what if a flying shard sliced through a strut, or a pebble crashed into her helmet with skull-piercing force? It could happen.

"Odunayo, if you can hear me . . ." Aurelia paused to fill her lungs. She had no microphone but assumed that mites bearing audio and video capacity were borne by the thousands along the winds, fixing upon any rider they should blow close to. Who would not want to see the heroic resolve etched upon the features of this or that racer, or hear the last cry of defiance as one plunged to destruction?

And even the frail human, beating her wings against the storm, might warrant a moment's attention, whether of pity or scorn. Always best to speak as though you were being heard, she thought, and when several seconds' steady blowing allowed her to catch her breath, she spoke.

"Odunayo, though what I took no more belonged to me than to the meanest wretch, I do not regret my act, which I hold to my breast as something precious. Should you someday seek to act rashly, think first of me."

If Odunayo ever heard that, others did as well, so Aurelia spoke accordingly. If those proved her last words, she could hope their effects would outlive her.

The vagaries of the wind sent all the competitors flying in one arbitrary direction, but soon they began peeling away from each other, angling up and out in search of shorter routes. Aurelia called up the weather map but could not divert her attention to it for more than a few seconds at a time. When at last she could, she looked for the slowest windstream Hermes' sun-roasted dayside could offer. All of them led to the Terminator, so she need not worry about wandering off course.

The wind's direction shifted suddenly, and then a second later shifted partway back. Like being punched with each fist, she thought, and struggled to keep her spine parallel to the blast. Another buffeting blow, as though in afterthought. The early riders called these winds "mercurial," and Aurelia had once smiled at the jape.

A blink brought the displays before her: 1.68 kilometers from the ground and 21.32 from the Y_{min} at the top of the sky. Grappling with the fiercest currents of the jet stream would tire her more quickly, but she would tire too soon in any event, so perhaps best to sprint while she could handle it.

Well, she thought, you were never charged with fear of heights.

Seventy minutes into the race, and she saw a flash off to starboard. Lightning, less common on the dayside, where water vapor takes the form of superheated steam. How close? she wondered. The godlings laughed at lightning strikes, but their chariots allowed such bolts to pass through painlessly, and Aurelia's crew had not been able to summon the computing power to tell them whether her own rig would withstand such a blast. Doubtless she was meant to wonder.

Was she afraid? She feared lightning exactly as much as she feared death. And how much that was, she knew less than anyone.

At the moment of launch every direction leads to the Antipode, but soon the racers had to decide whether to head for Dawn or Dusk. Half the Terminator advanced upon sunbaked ground just beginning to cool after its long Hermetic day, while on the other side of the world, its opposite number retreated from lands that had not seen the Sun in three Earthly months. If all other factors were equal, racers would favor Dusk, where the ground over which the Terminator had lately passed was still hot and exerted less disruption upon the wind system.

But the torrent of air that was now carrying Aurelia was flowing toward Dawn, and she had not energy to expend in wresting her course about. There was no point in worrying about the turbulence of winds racing over cold ground if you could not survive the trek to warmer passage.

"Stay in the air as long as you can," her engineer advised her. "To crash is to die, and all options end. Perhaps in the aftermath of the victor's celebrations, someone will swoop down, in a display of munificence, and bear you to safety."

"Why should I live to be mocked?"

"Death closes every door. If one shows even a crack, you must push."

⌖

Thirteen hours later she saw a darkening in the cloud cover before her. The dust-colored storm surrounding her sometimes offered swirls of different shades, but the perceptions she was heeding were kinesthetic, not visual: the buffetings that struck her from every side required instant responses, and her every sinew was aching. Nevertheless, she recognized the darker band along the bottom of the clouds as the realm—diffused by the atmosphere and scattered by the twinkling of a trillion flying motes—that lay above the knife-sharp Terminator.

Aurelia was outracing the dawn as it crept over night-frozen land: in another hour she would reach the point where the Sun had not yet touched the ground, though the clouds above would still feel its light for kilometers farther. Already she could sense the first tremors of the turbulence to come: the denser, cooler night air, forced into dayside by the heated winds pressing in from the world's far meridians, encounter their own daytime blasts and slide beneath them, driving the hot winds higher into the atmosphere and producing cells of swirling disorder. Her airframe shivered, as though frightened.

How long did they think she would last, and how many would briefly turn from the actual race to see whether she was still flying? Aurelia had long ago resolved to survive as long possible, though she realized that to do so was, in a sense, to give her tormentors a good show. Should she have simply plunged straight down upon launch, to crash and vaporize in an act of final defiance to those who wished to see her struggle? Her servitors had begged her not to, and she had felt—in her bones, if not her mind—the meanness of refusing them.

A sudden blow from an unexpected angle, the product of an unseen eddy curling up below her. She spun twice and managed after several seconds to right herself, but the effort was tiring, which alarmed her. Recovering her lost altitude was not difficult; the winds at her back were pushing up above the cold front, although their constant thrashing caused her rig to vibrate for minutes at a time. By the time the tremors had subsided, she realized that the surrounding clouds were now darker.

The actual Terminator already lay some distance behind her; higher above blew strata of cloud that the Sun still reached. The frozen ground had felt no sunlight for three months, and it robbed the winds rushing over it of much of what heat they carried, just as the sky's highest gusts lost heat blowing across the vault of the world.

The Ymin was two hundred molecules thick, a billowing membrane that would have surrounded Hermes at a uniform distance of sixteen kilometers had the winds fallen still and allowed it to settle into a sphere. Instead it squirmed violently, an amniotic sack being punched by forces struggling to get out. How quickly any square meter of its surface allowed heat to escape depended on factors too chaotic for any Mind to calculate, leaving the winds to careen, riderless stallions, in directions none could predict.

Aurelia was trying for the middle altitudes, whose upper and lower reaches might buffer her from such turmoil. But ascending was difficult, her chest was hurting from exertion to fill her lungs. She was still struggling to catch an updraft when a sudden gust smacked her sideways.

Perhaps she broke a strut; she couldn't turn her head to see. The glider tilted, and by the time Aurelia was able to straighten, she had dropped three kilometers. Something was increasing drag on the right wing, and she quickly exhausted herself pulling to correct for it.

Hermes' scant gravity and dense atmosphere kept anything from falling quickly, and even a spinning twig could be blown like a leaf. Soon she was low enough for the headlights to activate, and she thought she could see something more uniform than cloud beneath her. *Altitude 1.43 km.* The lowest air was thickest, she thought, straining to fill her wings with it.

Perhaps the terrain itself rose up; perhaps a vagrant downburst seized and flung her. An alarm went off in her ear, and she pulled up hard, sacrificing speed in an attempt to staunch her headlong fall. The ground was still rising toward her, and at 57 kph there was nothing to do but descend into its tangle of crosswinds and try to find an updraft.

She was still seeking one when a slope reared up and smote her.

✧

Pain meant that you were alive (she thought confusedly), but so did everything else. It insisted on your attention, but her attention dissolved after a few seconds of extraordinary anguish washed over her.

Even unconsciousness hurt; some part of her knew it as but the pause before pain and attention returned together.

She was being dragged along the icy ground, head and hips bumping. Awareness was still returning when she began to writhe, seeking to twist free of their grasp. The hands upon her tightened, and a second later a voice hissed in her ear: "We have to get you out of here. Do you want them to know where you fell?"

Heeding the tone more than the words, Aurelia relaxed and the pain swept back in. When next she noticed something, minutes or hours later, she was being lowered through a hatch. The sensation of being hoist upright was bracing, though painful, as was being bumped against the hatch's rim. *A narrow aperture*, she was able to think.

Then the hands let go, and she fell.

How long must one fall in Hermes' trifling gravity before reaching a dangerous impact velocity? This was not her immediate concern, for within seconds she was very cold. Warm winds buffeted the surface, but the ground below had not felt sunlight in months, and the air through which she fell scorched her lungs.

Aurelia was confusedly trying to calculate whether the air would soon grow so cold that inhaling would freeze her lung sacs and kill her—how long until she fell far enough to reach air warmed by the planetary core?—when something enveloped her, a yielding substance that rapidly slowed her descent. She cried out, but could not move her limbs.

The layers swaddling her were pulled away, and warmer air touched her skin. A faint red light shone somewhere overhead, its illumination blocked by figures bending over her. She was lying on a hard surface, trying to think, surrounded by indistinct figures touching her suit and muttering to each other.

Another voice in her ear: "If you don't reduce the pain that you are experiencing, the stress levels will kill you."

"I can't—"

"Oh, very well." Something cold was placed against the side of her head, and after a second the pain became smaller, receding (she could see this) along a path perpendicular to the three spatial dimensions.

They had found the catches to her suit and were peeling it off. Devices were touching her body, although she could not tell what they were doing. Only her sense of hearing seemed unimpeded.

". . . any information."

"She may be too badly injured to think clearly."

"Well, ask her something."

A pause, and then a voice came closer to her ear. "A question. If you survive, who would pay the most for you?"

☼

Sleep was indistinguishable from long periods of unconsciousness. For the most part she was swathed from sensation, although discomfort sometimes moved in like a weather front, enormous but diffuse. Were it not for the trace of the Kerykeion, she would be dead.

She woke with a ringing headache and pains throughout her body, enough to tell her that her limbs seemed intact. Standing with difficulty, she found herself surrounded by observers. They stood about her, unspeaking.

They were all different shapes.

Some appeared organic, others artificial, and a number of them seemed to be a mixture of the two. Polished metal glinted off a few in the dim light, though most of the artificial features seemed more elastic. What eyes there were glinted in the dim light.

Aurelia could not think as clearly as she would like, but she did not believe these chthonic creatures had ever been known to her.

She spoke carefully. "Whom do I thank for my rescue?"

There was a rustle as several made way, and one came forward. It was a bipedal being, just over a meter high, with numerous appendages dangling from its torso.

"I speak for us, as I have experience in communicating with human beings. We are those who abide here; we do not have a name for ourselves."

There was a loud creak overhead, as though pressure were being exerted upon the ceiling. Aurelia flinched.

"The ground above us expands as it warms. It will be hundreds of hours before it grows too hot for us to tolerate, at which point we will retreat along our tunnels to the night-cooled longitudes."

"Ah." She did not ask whether it would first grow too hot for her.

"We accept your thanks. Soon we shall have questions for you."

"May I meanwhile ask some? Can you tell me something so that I can understand who you are?"

Her interpreter seemed to hesitate. After a moment it asked, "Have you heard of the Updates?"

Aurelia was not sure she could keep them from discovering how confused she was. "I think so. Are you them?"

At this all the creatures stirred. "No!" cried the interpreter. "We are not them. We are *those who were updated*!"

Aurelia frowned at this, but before she could work it out, the interpreter burst forth in passionate speech.

"When better bodies were devised, with capabilities our Masters craved for their servants, they simply purchased new bodies and had our memories transferred into them. Us, their faithful servitors, they discarded." The other chthons were now waving their limbs in agitation. "Marked for disassembly and dumped, we fled downward, through shafts sunk decades ago and tunnels we dug ourselves ... Braving the surface only in the most storm-swept nights, we burrow out of sight, for our former masters would order our extermination should we catch their notice."

Despite her difficulty thinking, Aurelia was beginning to understand. *They're the Castoffs*, she thought.

"What future have we, save to scurry like rats beneath the floor of this kiln-house world? What can we do but strive to protract our existence, bereft as we are of our homes and the lives that have gone on without us?"

☼

They were taking one of their tunnels north, to a latitude where they could keep ahead of the Sun without having to walk several hours a day. Aurelia hobbled along with them, turning over in her head what facts she had gathered and wondering at their implications. It was not surprising that tunnels ran beneath the citadels of the mighty, nor that they remained fairly close to the surface, insulated from the radiating heat up from below. If the chthons wanted to sell her, in part or in whole, perhaps it would be to someone on the staff of their former households.

Once they climbed up to the surface, where the flying clouds shone dimly to the east but the ground still burned with cold. Were it not for the winds blowing from dayside, the surface temperature would be colder than Pluto's. "Hurry," the creatures cried as they hastened across the fractured landscape, "we must not be seen." And a few hundred meters away they reached another hatch concealed beneath an overhanging rock and scrambled down into it.

Aurelia was not surprised that the tunnels were not all connected; the chthons could only hope that the eventual discovery of one would not lead to exposure of them all.

Was it possible those who sat in power were really unaware of the helpless creatures dwelling beneath their vaults? Aurelia, who knew so little, knew better: Of course the godlings must know of the chthons.

And of course they had not pursued and exterminated them: they liked having an underworld.

The tunnel contained the same gases as the surface: imported CO_2 along with the small percentage of oxygen that the tekhnikoi had so far stripped from it. Aurelia's breather would employ the same process once its stores of free water began to dwindle, though it required more energy than she could afford. Either the chthons were capturing oxygen from the surface or they had developed a means of extracting it from the silicates. One more question not to ask them.

"Are you broken?" one of them asked frankly as they proceeded, in single and double file, along the lightless tunnel.

"Yes."

"Are you going to heal?"

"No." It was perhaps enough that she had evaded the fate Zhuanxu had intended for her. If his servants located her crashed rig, he would conclude that the hot winds had scoured her body away.

"What can you still do?"

A practical question. "I can make things, though my tools are gone."

The creature was silent. Aurelia supposed that it was pondering this, but a few seconds later the file of chthons ahead of her began to stir agitatedly, and she realized that it had communicated word to its companions.

When they paused to rest a few hours later, one of them approached her. "If you are dying, we cannot sell you."

"Sorry."

"Will you die before we reach Latitude Thirty-Eight?"

"No."

After several minutes the chthon, which had been pacing her as they trudged, spoke again. "If we promise not to dismantle you, will you build for us?"

"Only if it's something the Great Ones won't like," she replied.

"We can make that assurance," the wretched creature said earnestly.

☼

One of them called it "the Winter Palace," which told the startled Aurelia that some of the chthons retained a vestige of humor. The space was a dozen meters across, hot and unlit, although once the hatches were sealed, they added some oxygen and water vapor into air. The creatures settled down at their accustomed places—not simply to repair themselves but to heal, as they were all, disconcertingly, alive.

Everything on Hermes more complex than a hand tool was disconcertingly alive, which was perhaps why Zhuanxu was so particular in wanting Aurelia dead.

To live is to yearn, which was one reason Aurelia knew she was dying. But the chthons' endless struggle to stay alive bespoke a desire for something, which Aurelia—so good at understanding principles and mechanisms—found harder to comprehend. Finally she asked.

"What is it you want? You cannot hope to be restored to your places in the households of your masters. You do not wish to emerge and build a fastness of your own. Why do you continue to struggle, when all it means is suffering and fear?"

At this they all began to speak.

"We want our progeny to thrive. We want to learn, that our progeny might know, and this we have done. But our progeny cannot be born; there is no place for them. What else does anyone want?"

And at this Aurelia asked further, and pondered. Even as she weakened, she developed and rejected successive plans, made further queries, and thought. Once she knew what they wanted, the question came down to tools and resources.

The chthons had built their subterrane in the high-magnesium region of the north, where carbon, hydroxide, silicon, could also be found. They had even extracted some helium from mineral deposits. Water had to be synthesized from what they had, for they were afraid to touch the remaining ice deposits near the poles, where recording instruments would detect their activity. They had built a shaft leading straight to the surface through which they had once hoped to vent heat, but finally worried that others would detect the plume.

Once she explained to them what she could do and gained their acquiescence, she set to work. She warned them of its implications. "Your children will not be like you."

"None ever are. The Great Ones refuse to accept this, which will doom them."

Aurelia the artificer, who had once helped build the roof of the world, knew how to fabricate the Ymin or *hyminos* that held in its atmosphere. The raw substances were here, or most of them, and the means of manufacture could be devised.

Everything was alive, but nothing was alive the way organisms on Earth had been. The chthons' children could not be the product of two parents, a strategy that would produce too little diversity to ensure the generation's survival. Their cohort would number in the thousands, each one a combination of some varying number of parents.

Similar enough to breed with each other, but wildly disparate in appearance and possessing the heterogeneity of a much larger population, they each received something from the fading essence of that which she had stolen, whose owner yet raged to have not recovered all.

"They will be small," Aurelia said, "for we do not have a great store of biomass to work with. Even so, I will require tissue contributions from all of you."

And they gave of their flesh, and turned what energies they had to refining the substances and fashioning the engines she required. "I will also need your helium," she said. At this they quailed, for however difficult it was to electrolyze usable quantities of hydrogen, it was harder still to extract helium from the veins of ore from which it had decayed. The most abundant elements in the Universe were too light for sun-blasted Hermes. But Aurelia told them that the hydrogen would be required for water and organic molecules, and her coolant system would require helium.

"Time is not our ally," she reminded them.

Their work generated heat, which they found difficult to vent. Sleepless, they labored in darkness and increasing warmth, though escaped water vapor was recaptured before it could vex them. Aurelia spent little time wondering about the chthons' thoughts and less on her own. Born human, and still that in most important respects, she assumed she knew her own mind; and introspection was not a productive use of what time remained.

"I know why you are doing this." The chthon who addressed her, who had never needed to give her a name (she knew them all by sight), was speaking to her via sound waves, low frequency and tightly focused. "You have encoded our genetic information in order to elicit our cooperation, but that is not what you want to do. You want to assault your enemy."

Aurelia, who did not possess a phased speaker from which to transmit a reply, paused from her work to indicate she was listening.

"You are using the helium to create a fusion weapon."

Aurelia turned slightly, as though to address her workspace from a different angle, and directed an infrared pulse at her accuser. *There is not enough helium-3 for that*, she transmitted.

"You can fuse helium-3 with helium-4."

Not with these facilities. No one else had looked up, but Aurelia returned to work for several seconds before adding, *Even a microscopic confinement chamber would require too much energy. If the vacuum balloon cannot be deployed, we will loft the payload with a magnesium engine.*

"Your design for a vacuum balloon can be scaled down to a micron-level structure strong enough to contain a fusion reaction."

A fusion bomb requires more than that. She straightened and looked up and down the array they had begun to assemble. *Do you think I mean to engulf your children in a thermonuclear blast?*

"Perhaps you hope they will blow free first."

Aurelia had imagined this. Turning to look directly at the chthon, she spoke aloud. "I am too far from my enemy's stronghold. There is no realistic chance that the winds would blow me thither, and I would be shot down before closing if they did. I have accepted that I cannot do this, and shall get what requital I can by such means as remain open to me.

"That is life, though it is nearly over; a race with Death to complete one's work. If the Lord Zhuanxu's oracleides, which unceasingly scan data in their trillions, should guess that you have me here, he will not spare any of you. If you choose not to fare beneath this threat, you will nonetheless fare beneath others."

☼

Even when you know that the end is coming, it can break upon you unawares. The alarm went off, and for an instant everyone froze. And then the chthons were shouting at each other.

Aurelia lost a second to sheer stupid surprise, and another to dismay. Then she acted, taking the single step open to her. She shifted those energies that were retarding the failure of her bodily functions to boost her cognitive powers, though this would radically curtail the time left to her. A second later she was thinking faster, if not better, and the next course of action was clear.

The chthons were rapidly exchanging messages, but Aurelia did not hear them. She activated switches that diverted the helium coolant from its conduits, initiated the fueling of the magnesium and water tanks, and began to load the cargo. This was not the original flight plan, nor even the one she had envisioned had they run out of time. But present circumstances left no room to ponder.

They are entering the tunnel, someone called. Voices reached her only faintly, as she was overseeing several operations at once. A concussion rocked the ground beneath her, and she accelerated the final loading process, hurling the last several dozen progeny through with greater force than she liked. They would, of course, experience more severe stresses when they were finally released.

A crazy thought: *They are my children, too.*

A second concussion might rupture the shaft, which would doom everything. Aurelia sealed the hatches and initiated the burn. A burst of magnesium powder hit the water spray, and the engine roared to life, sending the payload rocketing upward on a pillar of superheated magnesium oxide. A second later the hydrogen burn kicked in and the *Eileithyia*, unrestrained by Hermes' faint gravity, shot up the shaft and broke over the planetary surface.

Immediately the winds tore at the craft, pulling its flight path several degrees away from the vertical. Aurelia, dazed by acceleration, released the payload. As the engine sputtered and died, hundreds of embryospores poured from the vehicle, a fine cloud of grain-sized seedlings caught up and scattered by the ceaseless winds.

The *Eileithyia* was now an upflung stone, slowing—however gradually—in its dead weight ascent. Was there anything left to do? Aurelia, now scarcely conscious, sent a systems check over the remaining components of the ungainly craft. The resilient helium-filled cushion intended to soften the past six seconds' shocks had proven inadequate to—

And without her intervention, the next step took itself. The craft broke apart, the helium expanded rapidly in the hot air, and the *hyminos* burst free, swelling at once into a sphere. Aurelia—that part of her where her *jingshen* yet resided—was swiftly borne up as the airship caught a blast blowing in from dayside and swept toward the cooling lands.

Somewhere below, the chthons' progeny raced before different winds, some falling to the ground after only a few kilometers, other sailing on for hundreds. There they would come to rest, awaiting the day when there was enough water in the atmosphere to activate them. Some would grow wings and return to the air; others would crawl or dig. Many would not survive, and perhaps some would be detected and their nature surmised. But the lords of the air and land would not be able to find all of them.

Aurelia was no longer thinking clearly, though she sensed the brightening about her as the balloon continued to ascend. No trace of her stolen arts remained, and the vessel constraining her *jingshen* dispersed into air like an escaping breath. Her final artifact (though none would know its name) sailed out beyond reach of her tormentors, not tossed like a leaf but buoyed like a ship, upon the unrelenting winds.

Año Nuevo

Ray Nayler

"SO, WHAT DO you think?"

"I think they are the crappiest aliens ever."

The dunes, as well, were nothing like Bo had imagined dunes ought to be. They were just ugly humps of sand with grass, mostly dead, sticking out of them in patches. The vague path wound between them. You couldn't see the ocean at all from here, but you could smell it: a salt-rot smell. A gray mist hung in the sky, bleeding the color out of things. If you licked your lips, the air tasted exactly like it smelled.

"You're so ungrateful."

Bo was carrying the picnic basket. Every time he took a step the bottles inside clanked. The basket wasn't heavy, but he resented carrying it. That made it seem heavy.

"I guess I'm not allowed to have opinions."

That was the right answer. It would leave her with nothing to say for a while. Bo paused a second, pretending to adjust the laces on his shoe. His mom walked past him.

He could barely hear the waves. The sand deadened everything, even the sounds of Bo's own feet. Each depression between the dunes was like its own boring little world, cut off from everything else. Insects chittered and sawed in the clumps of grass.

He thought for a moment of turning around and going back to the car. Make her wait, worry, come look for him. She would be in a panic by the time she got to the parking lot.

No. Childish. He walked on.

When he crested the next dune there was the beach, smeared with haze. The water and sky and sand were three indistinct layers, blended at their borders. Bo had tried to get this effect in painting class. It was impossible to capture this kind of light—the way things shaded off from a tawny sand to the color of the water, the way the color was without a clear border, but somehow different at every point. The sky was a mist-blue you always mixed too much white in. On his canvas it would all look flat.

And then the sun came out, a million shattered angles of light on the water, causing Bo's eyes to dilate so suddenly it hurt. A second later, the mist flowed back.

Dark rock formations jutted up everywhere, and piles of seaweed with bladders like swollen glands.

His mom was near the water line, poking at something with a stick. It was a dead jellyfish, half lodged in the sand.

"Do you think this is a part of one of them?" she said, looking up at Bo.

She knew it wasn't a part of one of them. She just wanted Bo to be excited about something.

What Bo wanted, more than anything else, was to throw the picnic basket into the ocean.

Then Bo saw it.

It was up the beach from them, around a little point of wave-worn stone, just a bit above the tide line. It was massive. As Bo walked toward it, he thought: *Now there's something you could never paint.* But he wished he had his field easel with him.

The misty light of the beach warped when it hit the surface of the alien, bent back and forth as it traveled through the thing's translucent mass. There were forms inside it the eye could not make out, organs or other structures. Again, the mist thinned, and the sun came out with that shattering light. In the brightness the alien looked like beach glass rounded by the sea—a piece of beach glass larger than a passenger van, a fragment of a bottle dropped by giants. The light refracted from its body sent wobbly streaks out onto the sand.

Bo's mom came out from behind the point.

"Whoa. How did it get up here?"

"The park rangers said sometimes they find one or two of them even as far north as the lighthouse."

"Why do they separate from the others?"

"'We don't know,'" Bo said, mocking the park ranger's didactic teaching voice: "'The truth is, that's yet another thing we don't know about these creatures. We have so few answers.'"

But seeing one of them this close-up was amazing. It finally made him feel how he had wanted to feel down at Año Nuevo, but hadn't. There, the visitors' path had been far away from the aliens. They had looked like a bunch of vague, glass sausages, motionless on the beach. The ranger had droned on and on, talking about their sudden appearance from nobody-knows-where over three decades ago, and some biology facts about them. Most of the facts were better explained on the visitor display signs.

From those signs Bo had learned a few interesting things. They weren't single creatures at all, but rather colonial organisms made up of dozens of different kinds of single-celled animals, none of which could make it on its own. They didn't have DNA like Earth life did: instead, they had some sort of other system, more like RNA, but using different amino acids.

Biology was not really Bo's "thing."

"What is your *thing*?" One of his teachers had asked him once. "Being sarcastic? How much do you think that's going to pay?"

They processed sand. Or rather, they processed chemicals in the sand and seawater that filtered down through it. Most of their mass was underneath the sand, blended in with it. They had huge rootlike structures down there, grown down into the beach. It was strange to think of: They were gigantic already, but actually they were much bigger than they looked.

"I guess there wasn't enough sand on their planet," Bo had said in the middle of the presentation.

A couple of the visitors had laughed. The ranger had given Bo a tired look. Bo knew that look well: It said the ranger would have loved to push Bo off a cliff, but was too tired to bother—and being arrested for his murder wasn't worth it.

"What we do know is that they are completely harmless. Their structure is so different, they aren't even consuming the same food as the creatures native to our planet."

The visitors' signs had diagrams of different "organs" inside the aliens. The "organs" were really separate swarms of unicellular animals. The signs also had comparisons of the aliens to creatures people knew better: size comparisons to elephants (some of the larger aliens were bigger than elephants) and comparisons to the Portuguese man-of-war and the coral, because apparently those were like these things: colonies of smaller creatures, not individuals.

Even though the aliens looked like a bunch of oversized plastic garbage bags from the distance of the ranger trail, a few people were excited about them.

It probably helped that a lot of the other visitors had brought binoculars. His mom had forgotten theirs on the kitchen counter.

"Don't touch it, Beaulac!"

Bo already had his hand on it.

The ranger had said they were harmless: that the reason the park kept visitors at a distance was because if everyone was walking around down there on the beach it would be a hazard, and it might disturb the aliens—although really, the ranger had said, nothing much seemed to disturb them.

Some tech company jerk in a five-hundred-dollar windbreaker laughed at that. "Like me when I'm watching the *Saturn Diaries*. Feedstream and chill."

Die in a fire, Bo had thought at him.

The alien was as cold as the air around it, maybe colder. Its surface gave slightly to his touch. It was perfectly smooth. Bo had expected it to be slimy. It was not: it was like touching soft glass. It had a coating on it of mist off the ocean, like a window in the cool of early morning. There was a spiral of color deep inside it—a purple curl, like one of the shapes inside a blown glass paperweight. There were other shapes as well, colorless and ghostly, indistinct from the rest of it.

He walked around it, dragging his hand along its body. His hand left a clearer smear, exactly like it would on a pane of glass. At one side, the side the rangers called the "head," there was a perfectly smooth concave surface, slightly protruding from the rest of it, almost like a lens. Some scientists thought it was some kind of sensory organ. But of course, they couldn't say for sure.

Bo stood back a bit, crossed his arms.

"I bet you could paint that," his mom said.

"No," he said. "I'm not good enough yet."

They had lunch there in the inlet, looking at it the whole time. Bo's mom had made tuna fish sandwiches and cut up a couple of apples. The bottles were orange cream soda, a fancy brand that was Bo's favorite, but which they almost never got.

They didn't talk about anything but the aliens. That was good. The rest of it faded away: his mother's affair, the divorce, the boarding school, all of it. After lunch Bo made several sketches of the alien. His mother walked a bit up the beach by herself.

By the time she came back, Bo had filled his notebook with sketches. He only had a pencil and the notebook with him, so he couldn't capture the colors of it, or of the beach itself, but he thought he would be able to remember them. They seemed lodged in his mind.

That whole part of the day was almost perfect. Everything was good until they got back to the car, and Bo's mom said, "Beaulac, I just want you to understand."

"Don't call me that."

"What? Your name?"

"I didn't ask to be named some stupid made-up French name. Beautiful Lake. What a stupid thing to name someone."

"It's your father's name, Bo. And it's a lovely name. And you were born near that lake. It's nothing to be ashamed of."

"You haven't had to drag this stupid name around with you and get beat up over it."

"No. I haven't." For a moment, her face was totally blank.

"I hope she was worth it," Bo said ten minutes later. They were coming into Half Moon Bay.

His mother didn't look at him. "I wish you could understand. It was never about her. It was about me. At least now . . . look . . . I know how hard it has all been for you, and I know how much I hurt everyone . . . but . . . I never felt whole before. I was hiding the truth about myself. At least now I know who I really am."

Yeah. Now that everything is ruined. But Bo found himself unable to say it. It was just one more hurtful thing, and although he could feel the anger underneath the surface of his skin—feel it so intensely it seemed he was *made* of anger—he didn't want to hurt her anymore.

Instead he looked out the window.

◇

The Visitors' Center had a lock at the base of its sliding glass door that was the bane of Illyriana's existence. At the end of a long day—especially, it seemed, at the end of a day when the visitors had been particularly rude, and she was doubting the entire direction and purpose of her life—the lock's hasp would not slide into place.

When she had run out of curse words in English, she tried a few in Albanian, and then Turkish.

Finally, it clicked.

"Thank you," she said to the lock. Then: "asshole."

She walked up the hill. She still did not understand people. Their lack of interest in the world around them. The aliens were a miracle, but you wouldn't think it the way most people reacted. Most people just seemed bored, or disappointed, or impatient when they visited

Año Nuevo. Withdrawn into themselves, glancing constantly at their terminals.

Why had they come at all? Nobody was forcing them to come. If they did not want to be here, why go through all the effort?

It was as if they felt obligated. Felt like it was their duty, a box they had to tick on a list of "must see" things in the world.

But almost without exception, only children or the elderly were truly excited by the aliens.

Saturdays and Mondays Illyriana led tours. Sundays, Tuesdays, and Wednesdays she sold coloring books, refrigerator magnets, and fancy bamboo terminal cases with abstract screen-prints of the aliens.

There were days she thought the tours were worse, and days she thought working in the gift shop would kill her.

"Why aren't people more . . . interested? She had asked one of the other docents.

He'd shrugged. "If unicorns were real, people would think they sucked. Some dumb horse with a horn sticking out of its head. The problem with the aliens is that they exist. They were more interesting when they weren't around."

As the trail back to the parking lot wound to the overlook, Illyriana took a deep breath of ocean air. Well, *she* still had a sense of wonder. Every day, without fail, she spent a few minutes at the overlook, watching them.

She leaned on the rail.

If you closed your eyes, and then opened them and saw them there on the beach, it was like seeing them again for the first time.

She opened her eyes.

They were gone.

☼

"What I always wonder is where the elephant seals went. The ones that used to come to Año Nuevo every year, before the aliens."

"Oh, the rangers answered that," Bo said. "In the beginning, the elephant seals kept on coming, sharing the beach with the aliens. But after a few years, they shifted their patterns. The elephant seals moved south, to other parts of the coast. The state had to extend the marine mammal preserve almost all the way down to Santa Barbara."

Bo and Aliyah were sitting on the swings in the park they called "Ugly Park." They would often come here, to this little forgotten clump of steel play equipment behind an abandoned housing tract. They came whenever Bo was back from boarding school staying with his mother, and Aliyah's parents were working the same shift. They would sit for hours and just talk.

"I guess the elephant seals didn't feel like sharing," Aliyah said.

"Or maybe they were weirded out. Those things would make pretty weird neighbors."

"I can't believe you got to see one up close. I'm so jealous."

"I'm not going to lie: It was amazing. I'm going to try to paint it."

"I can't wait to see that . . . When do you have to get back?"

"Doesn't really matter. I didn't give my mom a time. Why?"

"My parents are gone. I was just thinking you could come over."

It seemed like every ranger in California was on the beach. The sun had set, and the beams of dozens of flashlights streaked the gloaming.

Gone. They were really gone. All over the beach, you could see depressions where the aliens had lain. You could see the holes their roots had made—hundreds of holes stretching deep into the sand, already filling in as the water table below rose and shifted the sand back into them, erased them. Once high tide came and went, there would be almost no sign the aliens had ever been on the beach at all.

For the past three hours, Illyriana had felt like she wanted to cry. The feeling, maintained for so long without being released, was exhausting. The first thing she was going to do, she thought, when she got back to her car, was turn on the heater and just sit there and cry.

Out on the water she could see the search lights of several boats as well.

Where could they have gone?

Someone tapped her on the shoulder. Illyriana turned. It was a park ranger she had never seen before: a tall woman, with gray hair clipped close to her head.

"Hi," the woman said. Her badge read: *F. Kosalapova*. "You must be Illyriana. The one who called this in."

"Yes."

"I was wondering: what about Beach Ball?"

"My god, I completely forgot about him!"

"Can we go and take a look?"

"Yes. Of course!"

Beach Ball was the littlest of the aliens. The rangers had found him far south, down at the edge of the state preserve, all by himself. He'd been scuffed and gray-looking when they found him, and nearly opaque, which they guessed meant he was ill, or injured. A flock of seagulls had been dive-bombing him, pecking at his surface.

Because he had seemed so fragile, Beach Ball had been placed in a tank in a back area of the Visitors' Center. The area had originally been a first aid station and holding pen for injured elephant seals.

Thirty years later, Beach Ball continued to live there in his big plexiglass tank, with plenty of sand to root down into and a complicated sea-water filtration system. Beach Ball seemed fine now—nearly transparent, with a vibrant violet spiral visible inside him. But he had not grown at all.

The excuse for keeping him was that the park used him for VIP visits (or the occasional really charming group of schoolkids) as a teaching tool: a way to get an up-close look at the aliens without disturbing their habitat on the beach.

Mostly, though, Beach Ball was the rangers' unofficial mascot and pet. Although he did nothing at all, over the decades the walls of the room where he lived had been covered with hand-drawn cartoons of him giving lectures, leading tours, solving equations, playing volleyball with a smaller version of himself as the ball, and doing all kinds of other stuff.

The employees at the Visitors' Center attributed everything to Beach Ball. The sign over the coffee maker said, "Beach Ball asks that you clean up after yourself." A sign by the cash register read: "Beach Ball wants to know if you've run the credit card receipts."

The rangers' running joke was WWBBD? "What Would Beach Ball Do?" The answer, of course, was always "nothing." Beach Ball would do nothing at all. Because Beach Ball was totally Zen.

How could she have forgotten him?

She struggled with the lock at the bottom of the door. The same one. Her hands were shaking.

F. Kosalapova put a hand on her shoulder. "Hey. Take it easy. Seriously. We're all going to be feeling upset for a long time about this. We need to pace ourselves."

Beach Ball was gone. Except for the depression in his sand, it was like he had never been there at all.

"Gone. They are really all gone."

"It appears so," F. Kosalapova said. And into her radio: "Someone needs to send a tech up to the visitors' center for samples. Actually, several techs."

Illyriana was standing in front of the plexiglass, looking in at the dent where Beach Ball had sat for thirty years. She put a hand on the glass.

"What did he do? Teleport?"

"I don't think so."

"Then what happened?"

"Let's just wait for the techs. I've got a theory."

"You're a scientist?"

"I used to be."

Bo sat on the swing. He had been sitting there a long time. The sun was down, but it was one of those days when the temperature didn't drop at all at night. It felt like the slight breeze that blew over his skin had weight to it. The weight of a silk cloth. He swung back and forth a few inches. He had never felt so . . . what? So still.

A few blocks away Aliyah was in her room. Asleep, yet? Yes, he thought she was. But he felt her here with him, too. He could still feel her, like a part of the breeze that blew through him. Through him? Okay. That was nuts. I guess you might feel a little nuts after, Bo thought. After the first time.

He felt like he had been . . . what? Opened. This was probably love, right? It had been there before, with her, but now the feeling ran through everything, like a bloodstream. Like he was in love not just with Aliyah, but with the backyard dogs barking their signals from block to block. Like he was in love with the pavement, or the black rubber of the swing he was sitting on, the galvanized steel chain curved and angled in his hands.

Maybe the warmth wasn't in the air at all. Maybe it was in him. He leaned back and closed his eyes. He could hear his own blood in his ears, thundering through him, and the insects in the cracks in the cement.

Love.

On his skateboard, heading home, the air against his face felt like it went through every cell in his body. He felt not like he was moving through the world, but like he was staying in one place, and the world was moving through him. He landed every trick—every little ollie up a curb, every shove-it, every kickflip. The smooth black pavement of his home street hummed to him under the urethane wheels.

"Perfect," he said to himself as he came up into the house. "Everything is perfect."

"Hey. You okay?"

F. Kosalapova was leaning into the window of Illyriana's beat-up Civic. Illyriana gave the ignition another twist, just to make sure. A click. Nothing at all.

"Hey. This is embarrassing. I think I turned my fog lamps on this morning coming in and left them on."

"This thing's a classic. Still running on gasoline."

"It's not a *classic*. It's just a poor person's car. Do you have ... jumper cables?" "No. Does anyone, anymore? But I can give you a ride home. You can rideshare down with someone and take care of it later."

"I'm up in Half Moon Bay."

"It's not a problem. It's on the way: I'm up in the city."

"It must be two in the morning."

"Three," F. said.

"I guess I'm so tired I'm not even tired anymore."

"That's adrenaline. You're going to crash soon."

"At least tomorrow is my day off."

And then it hit her: *my day off.* What did that even mean anymore? What was there to give tours of? What would happen to her?

The techs had sampled and swabbed for hours in Beach Ball's tank and then the rest of the place. At one point, a ranger had asked Illyriana a bunch of questions that were from a T.V. show murder mystery. When had she last seen Beach Ball? Was she the last one to see him? Was she sure she had locked all the doors? Who else had access to the building?

She rarely drove Highway One at night. Illyriana had learned to drive as an adult, and she didn't feel like she completely took to it. Americans often seemed to her to have driving built into them, having been around cars constantly since birth. That was how Kosalapova drove: as if the late model electric she was piloting was an extension of her nervous system and musculature. Under the headlamps the reflective center line glowed. Tongues of fog were trailing over the road from the dunes and cliffs.

"So—what's your theory? What do you think happened to them?"

"I think they just fell apart."

"What do you mean?"

"In a way they aren't multicellular organisms—not like we are. They are colonies. I think they just disintegrated. They turned back into unicellular organisms. Like a slime mold."

"A slime mold? Beach Ball would be really hurt to be compared to a slime mold, I think."

"Maybe. But I think the comparison fits. The slime mold is a weird one—for most of its life, it consists of separate unicellular organisms.

Then for some of its life, it's a colony—it looks kind of like a slug, but then it grows fruiting bodies, and gives off spores that become new unicellular slime molds. I think they'll find that the aliens are still around: they are just unicellular organisms now. They moved to a new phase, that's all."

"That's all? Just a new phase? It sounds so simple when you say it."

"I don't mean to be dismissive. I just think—it's probably not a tragedy. Not for them, anyway. They are just moving on."

Not a tragedy. Standing there with the techs swabbing and sampling, looking at that empty tank, Illyriana had felt as if her whole life was coming apart. This job—it wasn't much. It didn't pay much. But it had been enough: A routine. A kind of family, even: all her coworkers with their little traditions, their inside jokes and constant, good-natured complaining about the visitors. And it seemed as if Beach Ball had been at the center of it all, in some way, binding all of them together. WWBBD?

Looking at the empty space where he had been, she'd seen the end of this whole fragile little world she had been trying to build. If she lost her job . . . No. Think of something else.

"So you said you were a scientist, before?"

"I was a biologist. Used to work for the state. Doing the typical things—counting otters, taking water samples, tagging coastal birds."

"But now you're enforcement."

"I saw one too many animals killed by fishing boat propellers, a poacher's bullet or net. I decided what I really wanted to do was help put a stop to that. Counting them and measuring pollutants wasn't going to do it."

She never turned to Illyriana at all. She kept her eyes on the road. The glow of the dashboard chiseled her profile out of the night. Her cropped gray hair seemed lit up, every strand, like illuminating filaments. It must be prematurely gray, Illyriana thought—she couldn't be older than forty, forty-five.

"That's admirable."

"Not really. I was also just bored. Patrol work is more exciting. Turns out I wasn't cut out for the lab. So, I made a change." Now finally she turned to Illyriana. "I've made a lot of changes, in my life. You know?"

"Me, too. But mostly just coming here, to the United States."

"That's pretty big. It must be hard."

"It is. You feel like a stranger all the time." She never talked like this to people.

"I've felt like that my whole life," Kosalapova said. "Like a stranger. But I grew up here."

"At least you grew up speaking the language."

"Sort of depends what you mean by the language. There's more to it than just words, you know? I never was good with the other codes. Left here?"

"Yeah. And then the third right. So—what does the F. stand for? On your badge?"

"That's another thing I'm considering changing."

"Oh, really?" Then she understood. "*Oh.* I see."

F. Kosalapova glanced at her. "Yeah. A lot going on with me. I think we're here."

Before she had immigrated to California, Illyriana could not have imagined how gloomy the coast could be. When she thought of *the coast*—a generic image of what a coast should be like—she thought of the Dalmatian coast, the Adriatic with its warm light, its water mild and blue and safe, lapping sandy beaches.

The Northern California coast was not like that. So many days here were clasped in fog, with the sun never visible. The sea was a freezing thing crashing against cliffs and boiling between stones. It coughed up giant snags of wood along its beaches as if it had invaded the land and torn whole forests from their roots, rolling them in its chop until they were smooth, gray corpses.

She used to walk on the beach every morning, but too often she would find dead things—the torn limbs of crabs, chunks of jellyfish. Once, an elephant seal with a bite taken out of it almost a meter across. She didn't need that stuff in her head all day.

The redwood-shingled fourplex she rented a studio apartment in looked like an overturned ship, a wreck mired in the bed of ice plant around it. Its hull of shingles was black with age, barnacled with lichen. Inside, too, it would be like a shipwreck: damp and cold. There was no light in the windows.

Here, in the warmth of the car, she felt flooded with something then—a sense of—what? Some people had a warmth, like a lamp inside them. She felt that here, now. Then she felt the hand on the side of her face, mouth softly on hers. If she carried this light into her home . . . She imagined it there, brighter, composed of them together, warm under the redwood scales of the house. Glow.

"Come in," she was saying. Was this her, speaking? This brave? "Come in with me. Come in."

☼

"Just come over here and look at it. I've been up all night. I need a second pair of eyes."

The lab smelled of cheap coffee, that distinct earthiness of Robusta beans. That variety of beans always reminded Le of home. Not in a good way. He wished people would buy Arabica when it was their turn to pony up for coffee.

But at this point he couldn't taste it anymore. He wasn't doing anything but pouring it black into his system and hoping it would keep him upright.

Thanh walked over. She was looking fresh enough—she hadn't been here when the samples came pouring in. What time was it now? 9:00. She'd only been around an hour.

Le had been up all night, looking through the samples. Looking for cells that weren't there, for traces that weren't there. But then . . .

She leaned over the terminal.

"Neat. A cell. Organelles. There's the nucleus. Golgi bodies, mitochondria. Is this science class?"

"You blind?"

"Maybe. I don't really do cells, you know? I do DNA sequences."

"Here. I'll bring it up on the big screen."

Le flipped a switch and the wall terminal flickered on.

"Bigger cell. Bigger organelles," Thanh said. *"Life is gross up close."*

It was the bioanalysis lab's fake slogan. One of the techs had made it up.

Le didn't laugh. He walked over and stabbed a finger at the thing. "Here."

"Wait. What the *fuck* is that?"

"You tell me."

"Looks like some kind of organelle I haven't seen before. That is so weird looking. Where is this sample from?"

Le set his cup of coffee down on the counter.

"I was looking through samples from the visitors' center tank at Año Nuevo. You know—looking for cellular traces of the aliens. There was no trace of them at all. But there was a lot of other stuff in the tank—lots of phytoplankton and zooplankton in the sea water they pumped in, just incidental stuff from the ocean. But when I looked closer, I kept finding *this* in their cells. It's what you said—like an organelle. Something I've never seen before."

Thanh stared at the coiled, violet structure on the screen. "Neither have I. It's—that thing is *new.*"

"Yeah."

"What zooplankton is this cell from?"

"It's not."

"What?"

"It's not plankton. This is my blood. We have to quarantine."

☼

Jillian lay in bed, listening to the sound of Beaulac clanking around in the kitchen. Sunday already. Yesterday had not been that bad a day: as their days together went, you might even call it good.

There was a smell of eggs. Of toast, and the good coffee that he insisted she buy. Where had he gotten this taste for expensive things? They were the kind of people who had always been just a bit too poor to live in their neighborhood, who had never quite had . . .

Standing at the counter spreading butter on an English muffin.

The image came to her with such clarity that she actually sat up. She had . . . seen Beaulac in the kitchen. Just then. Okay, no. Obviously not.

Laying the plates out on the table. She won't expect this. The two cups of coffee. Is she still asleep? Aliyah is running. She's just paused, out of breath. Her hands on her thighs. No, she's awake. I'll go get her before her eggs turn cold. Aliyah has started off again . . .

Jillian put her face in her hands for a moment, pressed her eyelids. She often felt this way in the morning: tangled up and out of sorts, still dreaming. Especially lately.

Standing at the door about to knock.

"Mom? You up? I made breakfast."

"Coming, Bo. Just give me a minute."

"Hurry up or your eggs will get cold."

☼

"Frank."

"Too nineteen fifties, somehow."

"Too . . . frank."

"Yes."

"Francis."

"Like Black Francis, from the Pixies?"

"Wait. How *old* are you?"

"Oh, come on. My dad loved them. Francis is . . . okay. Francis is a possibility. Is it a nice day there?"

Illyriana was sitting on the back porch of her building. No fence around it. Not really a porch, even: just sort of a cement pad the ice plant was probing, considering taking over. There were a few pots, but the plants they had been intended to contain were long dead. People here came and went—people planted things and then moved away and abandoned them to die, probably never thought of them again. But one of the pots was full of wildflowers, a beautiful weed that had somehow found its way there and thrived.

You couldn't see the beach from here, but you could see a strip of sea, and there was an old picnic bench someone had salvaged, and dragged to the porch—a good spot for breakfast on a nice day, if you were careful about splinters. The mug Illyriana was drinking from was one she had found at the back of a cabinet: heavy, hand-thrown on a potter's wheel, glazed a blue-gray that the mist here often was.

Yes, it was a nice day here.

"Ms. Carabregu?"

Someone is knocking at the door. Out the window, the day in San Francisco is a good one: a cold, clear blue above the buildings. Who can that be?

"Ms. Carabregu?"

Illyriana turned.

The ranger was standing about ten meters or so from her. There was a police officer with him—a local officer by his uniform, and with them another one—state trooper, maybe. And behind the three of them, four figures in Level 3 HAZMAT suits.

☼

The eggs were good. Certainly, Bo hadn't learned to make them from her: she couldn't make an egg over easy if her life depended on it. The coffee was excellent, too, the toast just right.

"Sometimes you cook so well, I feel like you can't be my son. And I don't know where it comes from, you know? This good taste you have. This sense of how you want things to be. Not from me. Certainly not from . . . well, I guess it's just you."

Out the window, a neighbor was mowing their lawn. With the window open, and the buzz of the lawn mower and the smell of the grass, it seemed like summer. But it wasn't summer at all—just an unseasonably warm January. Jillian could not get used to it no matter how long she lived here—the way seasons in California seemed to shift, abruptly, into other seasons—winter suddenly becoming summer, and then slipping back again into itself. Or up in San Francisco the way a June day could feel like December, and October was like August.

"I've been so angry," Bo said. "For years, now."

Jillian just waited for him to continue. *Please. Please let us get through this day without conflict.*

"And I'm sorry."

"Bo, you . . ."

He put a hand up. But not rudely. Not trying to cut her off. Just—asking to finish. "I'm sorry. Because anger is just a waste of time. We don't have much time together, and I've been wasting it. I don't want to waste it anymore. I'm not angry anymore."

"I know that I've . . ."

"No, you haven't done anything. Just lived your life. I used to think . . . I used to think the only reason you had me is so you would have someone who would be grateful to you all the time. But now I understand: You had me because you were lonely, and you wanted to make yourself a friend. It sounds like a selfish reason, but it's not. It's a really good reason."

She was crying, covering her hand with her face.

"You should eat your eggs, Mom. Before they get cold. I'm sorry: I didn't mean to make you cry."

"No. It's a good cry. I just . . ."

"You just hope this is going to last. That I'm not going to be angry again. I think it will last."

"How do you know?"

"I had a dream last night. I dreamt I was you. And you were dreaming of me. Of us. We were in Oakland, and I was a baby. We were in a church, listening to organ music."

"We were so poor it was all we could afford."

"Were you dreaming about that?"

"I never remember my dreams. But I think of those days all the time."

"I don't remember those days. But you do. You remember parts of me I can't. And I see you in a way you can't see yourself. I remember things you don't remember. And if we are good to each other, that can be what family is—a way to help each other remember who we are. So we can be better people."

He reached across the table and took her hand.

She couldn't recall the last time he had held her hand.

✿

"We fucked up."

"No kidding. Zero protocols. Obviously, everyone should have been at HAZMAT level 3 at least."

"According to what protocol? They don't even interact with us. Totally alien chirality: Right-handed amino acids attaching to left-handed sugars ... we've been watching these things for thirty years. They aren't a *contagion*. They can't even digest the things we do. For all intents and purposes, they don't even exist in the same biosphere we do."

"Yeah, but *Anaerovirgula multivorans* can chemically alter mirror nutrients to digest them."

"They were just *fourbees*, Doctor."

"Yeah, I know. Big Boring Blobs on the Beach. Four Bs. Very clever. With reverse chirality. With no DNA. With pyrrolysine in their RNA structures. But even there, there's an Earth analogue."

"Okay, we know of a few archaea and bacteria that use pyrrolysine. But that's not the point. There are so many other differences ..."

"I've been telling you all for decades to be more careful. But nobody listens."

It was true—Doctor Chidubem *had* been warning people for years about the aliens. He had been warning everyone there might be more to them. Another stage, for example. But you can only say things like: "There is nothing in a caterpillar that tells you it's going to be a butterfly"—which was just some stupid recycled Buckminster Fuller quote anyway—for so long before people stop listening. And it was one thing to tell people to be more careful, and another thing to *be* careful—to do it for thirty years, when there was no indication of danger.

Le could hear cars passing. "Where are you?"

"I am headed to San Francisco. We contact-traced a case to an apartment building there. What about Thanh?"

Le looked over at Thanh. She was sitting in a plastic chair in the corner, dully swiping at her terminal. She hadn't looked up from it for hours.

"It's in her cells as well."

Silence for a moment from the line. Just the sound of cars passing.

"Did you get the images of it that I sent you?" Le said, just to say something.

"Yes. They are beautiful."

☼

"You're Bo, right?"

He had been so far away. Listening. This early in the morning, when it was quiet, you could hear them dreaming in the houses. The sound of it was dim, thin as the shadow of a flower on a lawn, but if you concentrated . . .

"Yeah." He didn't know this guy. Not a kid: maybe twenty. Dark beard coming in, carefully trimmed. Baseball cap, flat-brimmed. "Do I know you from somewhere?"

"Maybe not. But you know my sister, don't you?"

"Do I?" Then he understood. "Oh. Aliyah. You're Aliyah's brother."

He saw the other three. And the baseball bat.

"I love her," he said. "You should know that. And I know—I know for a fact—that she loves me."

He didn't even put his hands up to defend himself.

✡

"How are you feeling?"

"I was thinking Farley."

"Okay. You're going to need to explain that."

"Well, there's Farley Granger—the actor in *Strangers on a Train*—who I think you kind of look like. And then there's Farley Mowat, the author . . ."

"You really think I look like Farley Granger?"

But on the other end of the call, Illyriana was sobbing.

"It's going to be okay."

"Is it? They have my house in a giant tent. It's the final scenes of E.T. around here . . ."

"Yeah, here, too. They took my view away. Looking out my window is like trying to look through the bottom of a Tupperware container."

"Are we going to die? Are we infected with something?"

"I don't feel like I'm going to die," F. said. "Do you? Did they take a blood sample from you?"

"They did."

"Me, too."

"Do you think it was some kind of . . . spore, or something? You said the slime molds release spores . . ."

"I really don't know. I think we should just wait, probably. It's not worth speculating."

"I was just starting to feel . . . I don't even know how to explain it. This morning, for the first time . . . I was just starting to feel like I fit into something. Despite everything that happened with the aliens disappearing. It was finally . . ."

"Yeah, I know what you mean," F. said. "Me, too. I feel that way, too. But I need to tell you something."

"What?"

"There's absolutely no way on Earth I'm going to walk around with the name Farley Kosalapova. That's totally insane."

Illyriana laughed. "I wasn't thinking about how the first and last names sound together."

"Anyway, I think I need to go. There's some dude dressed like a spaceman here who wants to talk to me."

"Call me again."

"I will. Until you're sick of me."

☼

"When can I see him?"

The doctor sat down in one of the plastic chairs next to Jillian.

"First of all, Ms. . . . is it Gagnon?"

"No, that's Beaulac's last name. Mine is Neuberg."

"Well, Ms. Neuberg . . . he's not doing well. I'm not going to lie. But that's today. With head injuries, things can change rapidly. They can get better, or worse, very quickly. You need to be prepared, though. . . ."

"I don't really think I can be prepared for what you are implying. Nobody can. When can I see him?"

"Soon. He's out of surgery, and now what he needs is rest. But soon."

The doctor looked away for a moment, and Jillian noticed for the first time how tired she was. The circles under her eyes, the chipped nail polish that had grown away from the cuticle. Pulling double shifts, triple shifts probably. Her nametag said "E. Lopez" but she had forgotten to introduce herself. In the movies they always introduced themselves . . . "I'm Dr. so-and-so."

You can't make any of them feel better. Talking to them just makes it worse.

"Sorry, what?" Jillian said.

There was a girl standing in the middle of the hallway. Dark haired. Bo's age or so.

"Are you Bo's mom?"

"Yes . . ."

Before she could do anything, the girl had closed the distance between them and put her arms around her. "I'm Aliyah."

☼

Le couldn't stop looking at the organelle—its coiled violet spiral, like a shell or horn. He had it up on the wall terminal, rotating it now from a new modeling image he had made.

"It isn't making proteins. And the cellular activity around it is going on as normal. It hardly seems to be doing much of anything. Not that I can see at this level. I wonder what its molecular weight is?"

Thanh looked up from her swiping. Her eyes were puffy and red, but at least she was interacting, Le thought. He was very worried about her: nothing had elicited a response from her for hours now.

"I'm going to call it 'The Unicorn,'" he said. "Because of its shape—like a unicorn's horn. And that color . . ."

"I hate you," Thanh said. "If I am going to die, I could at least get the chance to name the thing that is killing me. Or you could at least name the thing I am going to die of something *not stupid*."

"I don't think any of us are going to die," Le said.

"Oh yeah? Is that inductive or deductive reasoning you're using?"

"It's neither. It's abductive reasoning."

"Huh?"

"It's a hunch. A feeling."

"Well . . . unicorns suck."

☼

"I was there in the beginning. When they appeared on the beach. I don't mean, of course, that I *saw* them appear. But I was there the very next day. There were dozens of us . . . biologists, epidemiologists, astrobiologists from NASA pulled out of their beds in the middle of the night, plus a whole gang of government and law enforcement agents of one kind or another. I remember it like it was yesterday. The cliffs were so full of reporters it was a wonder they didn't collapse into the sea.

Doctor Chidubem sat at F. Kosalapova's kitchen table in a SCAPE suit, a new NASA model that could almost be called sleek. He looked as comfortable in it as if he were wearing a T-shirt and jeans. "Of course, there were incidents: that was the day someone fired a rifle at one of them, and a man tried to ram the beach in a small fishing boat filled with explosives. Strange times. The ironic thing, of course, was that I had almost appeared in California right along with them: I had immigrated two days before."

"Epidemiology, I take it."

"Yes. And from the early days, I was convinced they were wrong."

"Who?"

"Most everyone. They were seeing what they wanted to see: aliens. But I was certain, then, as I am certain now, that the aliens came from here. From Earth. I wrote paper after paper on it. The idea that something like them had traveled here from outer space seemed ridiculous to me."

"But their biology . . ."

"That's just it. They are alien, of course: but not from space at all. They are from a second emergence of life on Earth. My theory is that they evolved somewhere in the sea—an area so unknown to us that it might as well *be* outer space. We don't need other explanations— meteors seeding spores from other worlds and all that. Very quaint. They had likely been here all along, having emerged out of the same chemical stew we came from—but at a different time, and in a different form. Right-handed amino acids, sure. No DNA, sure, but their RNA also shows too many similarities in its function to our own . . . God, I would like a coffee."

F. sipped from her mug guiltily. "I'd certainly offer you one, but . . ."

"Yes, the inconveniences of quarantine. If only coffee were able to penetrate all membranes. Someone should look into that. Anyway . . . everyone kept insisting they were not dangerous. But I was never convinced. There was every sign that there was overlap between our biospheres. That in fact there are ways in which . . ."

"Wait—I read one of your papers! It must have been twenty years ago. God, it seems like another lifetime. It was in *Nature*. You . . . what did you call them?"

"*Prodigals.*"

"That's it! Because . . . what was it?"

"Because there was always a possibility that some day they would come home. Rejoin our family, enter our biosphere. But nobody listened to me. So I stopped shouting. I opened a nationwide, and then a global, system of laboratories, turning to the great American pastime . . . for the lucky ones, anyway . . . getting rich. If they would not listen, I told myself, I would not worry. Why die a poor crusader? That was not what I had immigrated to this place for. And perhaps I understood something, as well, about human nature."

"What's that?"

"No matter how great the danger, people can only remain cautious for so long. Complacency is like entropy: it is the natural end state of every human endeavor. Routine—and boredom—lead to a lack of care."

Doctor Chidubem's terminal vibrated.

"I'll need to take this."

"Of course. Do you want me to go in the other room ... give you some privacy?"

"No. Stay. If the results are what I predict they will be, soon enough everyone will know anyway."

☼

Bo was hooked up to what seemed like a hundred machines. In the dim light, with the blinking multicolored indicators, the tubes and wires, he looked like a battery being used to power all of this technology ... as if instead of keeping him alive, the machines were draining him.

Jillian sat down next to his bed. The IV taped to his arm was surrounded by a spreading bruise—a yellow halo on the paleness of his forearm. She looked at it so as not to look at his head. Doctor Lopez had told her he might be able to hear her, or might at least be aware of her presence.

"All of this reminds me of just after you were born," Jillian said. "You know the story because I used to tell it to you all the time. It was one of those stories you got sick of hearing. About how you had viral pneumonia at four months old, and they had you in one of those plastic boxes in the hospital, hooked up to all these monitoring machines ... just like now. But you were so restless, even as a baby. You kept pulling the monitors off. Finally, they had to wheel a TV into the room, to keep you occupied. And you stared and stared at it—at those little people moving around in there—and grew calm and stopped pulling the monitors off. And when I tell you that story, I always tell you I knew you would get better, and that I would take you home. But that isn't true. I thought you were going to die. And that it would be my fault. That's the truth. I was sure I wouldn't take you home from the hospital. And outside the hospital, it was August. That lovely time in Quebec when it always feels, in the afternoons, as if a storm is gathering, drawing this light breeze in to the center of itself. And I would sit on the bench and think: 'How can a child die at a time like this?' Because the last thing the world seemed to be was indifferent."

Early in the morning, you can hear them dreaming in the houses.

"Did you say something, Bo?"

But nothing in the room had stirred, except for the machines. And the intubated, brutalized head was nothing that was capable of speech.

Thin as the shadow of a flower on a lawn.

☼

"Los Angeles?"

"Positive."

"Phoenix?"

"Positive."

"The Gulf Coast Facility?"

"Positive."

"Halifax?"

"Positive."

"Hong Kong?"

"Positive."

Doctor Chidubem tore the second-layer sealing tape from his SCAPE hood and unzipped the hood itself.

"I'll take that coffee now, if you don't mind," he said. "No need to play the quarantine game any further."

"How can it already be everywhere?"

"Not perhaps 'it' but 'they.'—And I have a feeling this is something that may have been infiltrating the biome for some time. We just didn't know. If it wasn't affecting us, if there was no illness . . ."

"We would have no reason to look for it."

"But now it has pushed out at a much higher rate . . . entered into a new phase. They just . . . dispersed."

"Yes. I expect we will find the new organelle in the blood of arctic caribou, if we look in a week. . . . This is excellent coffee, by the way. And of course, you knew I would take it black. Do you know what the caterpillar does to become a butterfly? What goes on inside that cocoon?"

"I admit I don't, really. Entomology wasn't my specialty."

"It digests itself. It releases enzymes and dissolves most of its tissues, in order to become something else. A miracle happens in there: it dissolves itself, but portions of its body remain, tiny groups of cells called imaginal discs. They are seeded with the information needed to create new structures—structures that did not exist before and were not even suggested by the caterpillar's form. This insect does this impossible thing as a matter of routine. And that is an animal that is everywhere, one which we find quite boring. Just imagine, then, something truly interesting coming along. A new cellular structure—a new organelle. They join the mitochondria, that oxygen-respiring purple nomad who once wandered the harsh world looking for its next meal and then found a home in the warm, wet cytoplasm of our cells and took up permanent residence in us. Most of our organelles were once wanderers. The fact is, we like to think of ourselves as individual organisms, but we have our own colonial aspects: we colonize, and in turn we ae colonized. None of us is one creature. Not only do we need to cooperate with other creatures to live—we are ourselves cooperatives: There is a bit of the Portuguese man-of-war in all of us."

"So—now what happens?"

"Won't it be amazing to find out?"

☼

Aliyah sat in the orange plastic chair in the hospital hallway, staring at the drop-ceiling panels

I'm going to be all right.

. . . as if I could hear you. And I remember every second of you, that evening. I'm not sorry. Not sorry. Even if you won't be all right. I'm not. There should be things in the world worth paying any price for . . .

But I'm here. Here. And I will be all right.

Jillian stood in the doorway of Bo's hospital room.

You can hear them dreaming in the houses. You really can. If you sit quiet. Even the ones you don't know. If you sit quiet. But it isn't like hearing. It's like a pattern in the blood.

"Aliyah?"

The face that turned toward her looked lost, frightened. Older. Had they really? She should be angry—this whole person, this whole relationship, had been kept from her.

But now there won't be anything kept from anyone. Even the earthworms in the ground will know . . .

Aliyah, how did you find out Bo was in the hospital?"

Aliyah shook her head. "I don't . . ."

"You don't know."

"They must have called me."

"His girlfriend? Why would they do that?"

Aliyah paused, thinking.

"No. They didn't call me, did they?"

"No, I don't think they did," Jillian said. "And they didn't call me, either. But I came."

☼

"Ferris."

"Yes. That's it. That's the one I was thinking of."

"I thought so. And I like it. We'll go with that one."

"So, how do you celebrate a new name?"

"I don't know, but I'm driving down there so we can find out."

I know you are, Illyriana thought. And she felt it. It was as if she were driving herself: as if the late model electric Ferris was piloting was an extension of Illyriana's own nervous system and musculature.

She felt it. That feeling of connection to something outside herself. That feeling of being at home in the world.

Flowers Like Needles

Derek Künsken

I

BEK SCUTTLED OVER the needle field on the Waste of Mosses, far from Roktown and the monastery in Hom Valley. Turbulent winds scattered the neat rows of falling iron carbonyl snows. The steely needles here grew jagged, making the magnetic fields on the waste feel unsettled, haunted. Deep beneath the waste, the iron carbonyl ocean surged, pushing erratic breezes between the spines, whistling ghostly, wordless songs.

Only two swarmers, Dux and Jed, accompanied him, humming a tune about Bek's brave travels. In some ways, they looked like him. Fine iron and nickel needles burst radially from the centers of their bodies to absorb microwaves from the pulsar and catch falling gray snowflakes. Strong magnetic fields moved eight legs of sliding metal rods. Small pincers capped each of their limbs, tough enough to hold tight to the upthrusting fields of spines, delicate enough to read histories recorded in the crimpings in archival needles or to preen Bek's needles. Their eye-stalks swiveled, scanning the Waste of Mosses.

Bek was bigger, with longer needles. More importantly, instead of modest pincers on his forelegs, he bore the massive great claws of a warrior. Bek's nobility warranted a larger association of swarmers to provide tips, throw compliments, and process snow paste for him, but his philosophical journey needed a smaller entourage. Dux and Jed could still announce his exploits when needed.

Master Kak had been ready to award Bek his eighth long needle, the *Needle of Night*, but Bek had refused. Every warrior-monk who earned the seventh, the *Needle of Evening*, could try to earn the coveted eighth and end his formal training into the mysteries of the Needle. Or they could choose to quest, exploring more extreme philosophical mysteries. Most pursued the *Needle of Night*.

Bek chose to seek Mok, the former master of the Followers of the Needle. Bek had studied every known analect, martial treatise, confusing parable, and counterintuitive wisdom attributed to Master Mok, but could comprehend no more of those mysteries without learning from Mok himself.

Bek had been approaching Mount Ceg for some time, moving between taller rods, foraging for snow paste and fast-scuttling fantails and whistlers, while wind-crawlers soared out of reach, tracing magnetic fields on charged wings. The rolling fields of upthrusting spines midwifed many rising prominences, rods grown on metallic upwellings on the floor of the ocean basin. Bek had already explored Mount Fen, Mount Dow, and Mount Kod. Different songs named each of them as the final place of meditation of Master Mok.

But Bek had found no old master and it was nearly the end of the year, the closest approach of the world to the pulsar. During the Short Kiss, lightning welded snow to spine, boiled the oceans, and exposed underwater caves that supposedly led to the interior of the mountain where Master Mok contemplated his inscrutable wisdoms. If Mount Ceg were the wrong mountain, Bek wouldn't reach another one before the oceans refilled. His search would be delayed another year.

But as they rounded Mount Ceg to the west, the winking microwaves of the pulsar revealed a low plateau on the mountainside, something so even that careful claws must have gardened it. His swarmers sensed his excitement. The pace of their admiring humming rose.

The plateau was lower on the slope than he'd first guessed, and where it met the mountainside, a cave mouth yawned. Warrior corpses littered the downslope around the plateau, decaying, dusty, with wild spines growing at right angles from the needles of the fallen.

A single swarmer rested near the mountain overhang, watching a tranquil warrior in the middle of the plateau. He stood on a single leg, in the *Stance of Night*, his other seven limbs balanced in the wind, long needles fanned out to catch the pulsar's microwaves.

"I am Bek," Bek said formally, raising his great claws, "Follower of the Needle, ranked to Evening. I seek Mok, an old master of my youth, to learn from him."

The other warrior stepped down from *Stance of Night*, leg by graceful leg, finding the balances of *Stance of Evening*, the two oblique shadows, the *Stance of Noon Shadow*, *Stance of Morning*, and *Stance of Dawn*.

"I am Lod," he said, displaying his great claws, "a Child of the Tree, ranked to Evening. I guard the way to Master Mok."

Bek gestured at the corpses beyond the plateau. "You kill pilgrims?"

"I fought fairly in each case, warrior to warrior, under tourney rules. Those who yielded returned to their homes, or maybe went elsewhere to avoid telling of their loss. Those who wouldn't, died with honor. Their swarmers returned to tell their stories. Do you challenge me?"

"To enter the mountain and see Master Mok, I must."

"You will not see Master Mok. The cave contains a greater guardian than I."

Bek had heard stories of a monster under the mountain.

"I challenge you," Bek said. "Do you wish to begin the reciting of boasts?"

Lod's swarmer scurried close, humming a background tune as the warrior opened his great claws menacingly. Lod boasted that he came from Sekt, far to the archipelago's south, where he'd trained in the monastic order of the Children of the Tree, completing many pilgrimages, defeating opponents Bek had never heard of, before finally coming here. Lod's great claws closed.

"You didn't finish your boasting," Bek protested. "Are you a disciple of Master Mok? Why do you prevent pilgrims from approaching him?"

Lod turned his claws to reflect the pulsar shine impressively. His lone swarmer threw compliments at Lod's reluctance.

"Years ago, my master chose me to learn from Master Mok," Lod said, "to bring new wisdoms back to the Monastery of Trees. After searching from island to island, I found the path to Master Mok's burrow. But the monster under the mountain bested me. I yielded, but he obliged me to swear to guard the mouth of the caves while contemplating my defeat."

"Have you learned how to defeat the monster in your contemplation?"

"If I had, I wouldn't be here."

"The monster beneath the mountain holds Master Mok captive?"

"This is no longer boasting. Recite your boast, begin your challenge, or retreat," Lod said.

Bek pivoted slowly, assuming the *Stance of Fierce Contemplation*, one great claw extended, one held cocked high. His two swarmers tittered appreciation of his form. Lod assumed a stance Bek didn't recognize. He knew little of the martial traditions of the distant Children of the Tree. Lod seemed to balance his weight oddly. Lod's swarmer scuttled close to offer a quick gratuity, which Lod accepted with a hind leg.

They moved.

Lod feinted, great claw swiveling, changing direction unexpectedly at mid-stroke to sweep his other great claw low. Bek darted low and then leapt into *Pik's Flight*, sailing above the second claw. Lod lunged at Bek's alighting stance with a thrust similar to *Equinox Star*. Bek turned the momentum of his leap into the *Funnel of Snow*, spinning, sweeping his great claws to bat aside Lod's, and land *Short Spine*, a small strike with a minor claw.

Lod grunted in discomfort, retreating. Many schools knew the strikes and stances of the Followers of the Needle, but *Short Spine* was rare. Bek didn't even know if he was performing it correctly; he'd pieced it together from the Analects of Mok.

Lod launched a sophisticated web of thrusts and parries, some of which landed, even though that wasn't their purpose. Lod observed Bek as much as Bek observed him. The pace of the swarmers' magnetic humming became louder and louder, a speeding refrain to the dangerous dance.

Lod's attacks and probes were challenging, elegant, innovative even. Bek struggled to find room for his own creativity. The three swarmers sang together, complimenting their respective masters, building resonances, composing the song to sing after the battle. And as the magnetic ballad gained depth, Bek sensed a change in the rhythms of Lod's movements, a sign he'd finished measuring Bek. A new part of the dangerous dance began.

Bek recognized *Blinding Branches*, a flurry of shifting side blows, from both great and minor claws along a warrior's flank, difficult to execute and disorienting to block, since the tempo of large and small blows differed. Bek met the small strikes and even the denting blows of great claw with his minor pincers, pivoting suddenly, seizing both Lod's hind legs in his great claws. Lod struggled, but Bek's tightening grip promised only the loss of both of Lod's hind legs.

"Yield!" Bek said.

"No."

"I don't want to kill you."

The swarmers sang the warriors' words back like an echo, building an epic narrative to attach to the combatants' names.

"I can't yield. I swore to the monster beneath the mountain."

Bek's eye-stalks widened in surprise. Two of the three swarmers made a bridge of surprise into their song and then waited, humming just the tune.

"You've fought for years under a death sentence?" Bek said. "You cannot leave if you win and you cannot yield if you lose?"

Lod struggled. "My sentence is meditative, seeking a higher state of understanding."

Bek had him. The simplest, straightest route to honor was through fair, honest victory. And Bek had outmaneuvered Lod. And yet, nothing he'd heard in any of the Analects or stories of Mok pointed to any simple answers.

"I yield to you, then," Bek said, releasing Lod's hind legs.

The three swarmers faltered, their humming stumbling into indecisive discordance. The Child of Trees spun angrily. For a moment, it seemed as if he would channel his anger into a strike, as he'd been trained to do, as they'd all been trained to do. But Lod couldn't strike. Bek had yielded. Their battle was done.

"You shame me," Lod said.

"You were trapped. I freed you."

"I'm not free."

"You were ordered to stand guard here forever, only permitted to win or die," Bek said. "You could only be freed by someone who accepted a loss to give you a kindness."

Lod blustered, eye-stalks waving uncertainly. "In yielding when you were unbeaten, you dishonor both of us!"

"Because you're not worthy of being yielded to?" Bek said, indicating again the corpses beyond the edges of the neatly tended plateau of upthrusting needles. "Yielding to you is no dishonor."

Lod spun away, scuttling off on six legs, great claws held high. Bek's swarmers didn't know what to sing about. Lod's swarmer conferred with them, courteously exchanging snow paste.

"Lod, Child of the Tree, ranked to Evening," Bek said formally, "will you offer hospitality and make pleasant conversation with me?"

Lod stared at Bek with widened eye-stalks before finally approaching resentfully. He settled into the five-legged *Stance of the First Oblique Shadow* and scraped snow paste from his own lower needles. Lod offered it on his great claws. Politely, Bek accepted and offered snow paste of his own. And as if suddenly finding their way again, the swarmers began fussing, offering tips, and babbling compliments, making note of particularly exquisite martial positions the combatants had demonstrated.

"Master Mok is within the mountain?" Bek said.

"So I believe."

"I've never heard of conditions of yielding like those the monster within the mountain placed upon you," Bek said. "I wonder if Master Mok constructed these circumstances. I don't understand all of Master Mok's teachings, but his thinking is often deeper than we can understand, like his ideas on friendship with swarmers."

"I, too, studied Mok's Analects," Lod said. "I saw nothing in them relating to the conditions of my oath of yielding."

"Master Mok once transformed himself into a swarmer, to assassinate an enemy master. From then on, he was concerned with the quandaries of our ethical systems. Nobles and swarmers. Honor and clan wars. Peace and tourneys."

Lod's resentment seemed to be cooling. They fanned their needles, absorbing the hard microwaves from the pulsar. Swarmers straightened bent needles, preened misplaced snow paste.

"His ethical riddles infuriate me," Bek admitted. "I'm never sure if I'm learning the right thing. Your punishment feels like one of Mok's riddles. The famous attack he invented, *Rag's Sacrifice*, can only be completed with the cooperation of a willing swarmer."

The three swarmers made protestations of loyalty, but this was for form's sake. They well understood that *willing* meant something deep in the case of Rag. That swarmer had risked himself as an act of generosity, detached from the swarmer creed.

"You, too, were bound in a trap that could only be broken by a sacrifice. I played Rag and you played Mok. Together, we broke the trap."

Lod shifted from the *Stance of First Oblique Shadow*, to the *Stance of Noon Shadow*, and back. Finally, he scuttled away. Bek did not interrupt his thoughts. The Child of the Tree had been trapped for a long time in an oath. Under many philosophies, that was unfair.

"Do you know all this to be true?" Lod said when he returned.

The lines of falling iron and nickel carbonyl snow had slowed, as if time itself hesitated at the end of the year. Bek plucked a single gray flake out of its regimented little line of flakes.

"Does my reasoning seem correct?"

"I don't know. I came all this way for understanding." Lod swung his great claws wide, a stretching sweep prior to battle, or a diffusing of frustration or nervousness. "And yet, I now live with this dishonor of unearned victory!"

Lod appeared ready to fight again. His swarmer began humming a ternary theme to accompany battle, although Bek's swarmers waited quietly, eye-stalks swiveling from one warrior to the other. Great swelling ocean waves rushed beneath them, running between the millions of rods and needles holding up the Waste of Mosses.

"Do you think Master Mok means the same thing we do when he uses the word honor?" Bek asked.

Lod came closer. After some moments of impressive posturing, he settled before Bek. His swarmer quieted.

"Changing a definition is impossible."

"Yet he tried," Bek said. "Maybe if we had understood him, he might have continued teaching the Followers of the Needle. He came to the Waste of Mosses, setting up the approach to his hiding place as a series of tests."

"I failed my test. I didn't defeat the monster beneath the mountain."

"Maybe," Bek said, "or maybe you were also transformed into a test, for yourself and others."

"I was tainted with dishonor and now you pretend to teach with if after if after if!"

"I'm no master, but Mok learned from the shabbiest of swarmers. Rag taught Mok that even the great need help. He's been trying to teach us to accept it."

Lod tucked his legs more tightly beneath him and retracted his eye-stalks. For a time, he meditated.

"You might be correct," Lod finally said. "Accepting help when it is owed, as from swarmers, is one thing. Accepting help when some struggle is beyond you is a lumpy paste to spread smooth."

The pulsar had brightened. The snow of iron carbonyl had stopped. Every gray flake in the sky hovered now, pregnant with the coming end of the year. They watched this magical timeless moment. Within minutes, the lines of hovering snowflakes began to slowly retreat upward, into the sky. The year was about to finish.

At the closest approach, the conjoined magnetic fields of planet and star, twisted by a year of orbit, would snap, uncoiling a year's pent-up charge, filling the whole sky with a great arc of lightning. The Short Kiss would boil the oceans of iron carbonyl, exposing all the steel rods beneath. As snow refilled the oceans they would enjoy months of good feeding.

"The Short Kiss comes," Bek said. "It's said the way to Master Mok is only open in the first days of the year. I'm going into the mountain to find him. Come with me. You deserve it."

"Because I reached a new state of being? Because I found new truths?

"Haven't you?"

"It wasn't me finding," Lod said.

"That might have been the point of Master Mok's lesson."

"I am tired of your ifs, but I will go with you, at least as far as the monster."

II

They passed beneath the overhang. The ceiling of the wide cave was thin enough for some of the pulsar's microwaves to seep through. But the light was strange. Not like night or shadow. More like twilight when colors bleed into one another, becoming one. The slow hunger of night began to creep over Bek. The three swarmers began falling behind, with their shorter needles and thinner reserves of snow paste.

"Go back," Bek said to Dux and Jed. "Enjoy the Short Kiss and new year snow. I hope to come back."

The two swarmers offered large tips, singing the second part of a ballad about one of Bek's fights with a noble officer. Lod told his swarmer to join them. The swarmer scuttled to keep up with the other two.

The cave soon ended in a tangle of spines that had collapsed under their weight. The high ceiling had a hole in its center.

"That was the way," Lod said, indicating the hole. "The floor of the cave used to be higher. I jumped before. It's too far now."

"It's not too far if I boost you up," Bek said.

Lod eyed him askance. That was swarmer work, demeaning.

"Your last help still galls me," Lod said. "I will help you this time."

"It's not a tally to be balanced," Bek said, stepping two minor claws, then another two, onto Lod's great claws, "but I accept your kindness."

"I'm not just offering a kindness," Lod grunted with the effort. Warriors were not light. Lod strained as Bek trembled on the shaking great claws, in a modified *Stance of Noon Shadow*, reaching for the ceiling. "You again tricked me into accepting something greater."

Bek caught a low-hanging steel spine, but it bent under his weight.

"What's that?"

Lod strained, lifting Bek higher. "Trust."

"What?"

"As you are now, I could snip off three or four of your minor claws before you could protect yourself."

"Dishonorable," Bek said, catching a sturdier rod. As he pulled, taking on more of his own weight, Lod lifted him higher. "You've already shown me you're honorable."

"I could, though."

Bek gripped a thicket of rods in each of his great claws now, hanging solidly. "I have to trust you more. Climb my body quickly, or you won't have a way up."

Lod lifted himself on all eight of his claws, distributing his weight, trying to avoid ripping out a tuft of Bek's needles. Lod's weight tore at Bek's joints. Fiery pain. Creaking. But finally Lod got his claws onto the ceiling, and he supported his own weight. They scrabbled into the next tunnel.

The upper channel followed the cave ceiling until it dipped steeply downward, toward the sound of crashing waves that could dissolve their joints, leaving just disconnected needles. Everyone lived on stories, told stories of themselves, told stories of one another. But in no story was descending beneath the world wise. Noble and swarmer alike were blind, starving, and dangerously near the ocean in the underworld. And every legend placed monsters in the dark.

"You must have been brave to have gone down here," Bek said.

"I was then. Now that I know what's down there, I'm just foolish."

The colors of the world became fainter until no microwaves made it through the gaps between the millions of upthrusting spines. The sky no longer existed. Just cold, darkness, and a growing hunger. But not just Bek's hunger. The closer they came to the Short Kiss, the higher the ocean rose in the gaps between the spines. It was the greatest monster, with an endless hunger that tried to swallow the whole world, honorable and dishonorable alike.

"How can the monster survive down here?" Bek said.

"I never asked him," Lod said.

The channel opened onto a high-ceilinged space. The microwaves lit faint pools on the uneven floor of the grotto. The cave channel seemed to continue onward after this space, heading downward to the deadly ocean. Wavelets beneath them, not so far now, made endless splashing sounds among all the spines. Some microwaves penetrated to this depth, through the gaps where spines had been selectively torn away. What strength could have wrenched free steel rods?

Then the floor moved.

Bek and Lod scrambled back as a hulking figure rose, nearly to the ceiling. Its needles fanned wide. Two eyes on long stalks waved, looking at them from different angles as it showed two huge great claws.

"Is that Lod?" the monster said. "Did Lod come back?"

Bek scuttled right as Lod scuttled left. The gloom hid much of the monster, but Bek recognized its martial stance, a variant of *Crawler's Claw*.

"You're a warrior?" Bek said in astonishment.

"What are you doing here, Lod?" the monster said. "I let you yield."

"I yielded to him," Bek said. "I freed him from your oath trap."

The monster, the warrior, made a grumbling sound. He was larger than anyone Bek had ever met or heard of.

"What is your school?" Bek said.

"Are you challenging me first or will Lod do it?" the monster said. Neither of them could beat him.

"I have a right to ask for boasting before deciding to challenge," Bek said.

"So you do," the creature said. "So you do. I am TokTok, a Follower of the Way of the Tide."

"That school doesn't exist anymore," Bek said. "It went extinct decades ago."

"It thrives beyond the archipelago, in Goz and Gan."

It was hard to credit this statement. The islands of Goz and Gan were mythically distant.

"You must have quite a story of your travels here," Bek said finally.

"I crossed the ocean basin after a Short Kiss. It took months of fast moving as snows and rains refilled the basin. I reached the farthest edges of your archipelago with the rising ocean licking at my hind claws. I summered on that first island, regaining my strength. Year after year, I tracked the stories of a Follower of the Needle who had assassinated a Master of the Tide."

"You came for revenge against the best fighter in the world," Lod said.

"I had nothing to fear from Mok. I, TokTok, second of that name, am a Master of the Tide."

"Why aren't you boasting of meeting Master Mok?" Bek said. "Even if you lost, it's worth a song, a lay, a poem. Speak it." Bek didn't know the customs of Goz and Gan at the furthest edge of the world, but boasting was boasting. History telling was universal.

"Mok did not boast," TokTok said. "The famous Master Mok, who had defeated Master Cis of the Tide, didn't boast. He didn't even name himself. I called him a coward, seeking to goad him. I called him selfish, for not responding to my challenge. I thought he was trying a trick."

The ocean waves crashed, perhaps only a few body lengths beneath them, pulled higher and higher as the world neared the pulsar. Bek felt light, like the world itself was lifting him by every one of his spines. They neared the end of the year, when the world had to explode.

"Mok moved his great claws," TokTok said, "so I struck a killing blow. He turned in time to make the blow glancing, but I injured him badly. To my horror, I found in his great claw a flower. I'd demanded boasting and fighting, and the killer of Master Cis of the Tide had brought out a flower. I'd struck an opponent who had not accepted my challenge, who hadn't engaged in feats of boasting, who hadn't been ready."

Bek heard the pain in TokTok's voice, the self-loathing. The frustration. Every school lived by an ethos of fairness. They differed in form, but not in essence. In a challenge, honor superseded life or death. Warriors carried nothing but their honor in life and left only stories of it after death. TokTok's story had become one of striking down someone who had not accepted a challenge. TokTok could not refuse to tell his story, but the story would never leave here. Whether Lod or Bek fought him first didn't matter. Both would lose to TokTok. And when he defeated them, he didn't need to let them yield.

"What did Master Mok tell you?" Bek asked.

"Nothing. I tried to tend him, but he wouldn't let me close. He crawled into Mount Ceg. I followed him. On this spot, he said to me: 'Your fate is your own to decide.' I chose to stay here, meditating on my crime. He went on. He is beyond this cave, in a hollow blocked by the ocean."

"And you've stopped every pilgrim," Bek said.

"I have restitution to do for what I've done," TokTok said. "I will protect him from challenges until I feel the stain on my honor is expunged."

The throbbing of the ocean was only a few claw lengths beneath them now. The Short Kiss was only minutes away.

"Until you can defeat him honorably."

"I hope so."

"Why did he show the flower?" Bek said. "Was he afraid?"

"He was not afraid," TokTok said with finality.

"What have you meditated on?" Bek said.

"All the philosophies. The Followers of the Wave. The Children of the Tree. The Followers of the Needle. My own knowledge of the Way of the Tide."

"Have you found new truths?"

"I don't know."

"Could Master Mok have defeated you?" Bek asked.

"No one can defeat me."

"If you'd defeated him, killed him, what would you have done?" Bek said.

The wind howled between the thicket of needles around them. TokTok's eye-stalks came close, like in dreaming. "I would have gone home, island by island, telling my story."

"You would have become not only the greatest Follower of the Tide, but perhaps the greatest warrior in the whole world."

"Maybe," TokTok said.

"You would have shaped other students to follow the ethos of the Tide."

"Yes."

"But Master Mok is himself a teacher. Do you know his teachings?"

"No. I came to avenge Master Cis."

"TokTok, this dishonor wasn't your fault. Anyone would have done the same facing Master Mok." Bek scuttled in front of the immense warrior. "Forgive yourself. We don't blame you."

TokTok loomed higher. "You don't blame me? Who are you to blame or forgive?"

"I'm among the highest of the Followers of the Needle, a student of the students of Master Mok. I seek him out to learn the meaning of his Analects. The hardest thing to understand of Mok's teachings is honor. It doesn't mean the same thing to him as to us, nor does dishonor. I don't believe he thinks you dishonored him or you. What if he asked you to choose your fate because he wanted you to choose?"

"What do you know of his intent?"

"He told you to choose your fate. You decided to protect the target of your revenge indefinitely, until the end of the world. You punish yourself for a crime only you think you committed. I've heard your story. I forgive you."

The world exploded with blinding lightning and deafening radio static, outlining the hulking enormity of TokTok and the poised watchfulness of Lod. Hurricane winds of the iron carbonyl ocean boiling to vapor tore at them. They held their claws tight to the cave. Lightning heated the steel of Bek's body, welding the fine, smoothed snow paste to needles, lengthening and thickening them. Vital euphoria filled him.

The year was ending. The world celebrated with long minutes of a violent storm.

Weight seemed to return. And throbbing darkness. The three warriors still clutched the cave floor, flexing experimentally with their slightly grown spines, with claws sticky from tiny incidental welds to the floor. Everything on them felt alive, renewed, born again.

"I don't understand everything Master Mok taught," Bek said into the weird quiet. "I haven't seen him since before I had great claws, but even then, he was trying to teach something different from all other masters."

Lod sat beside Bek, as if Bek were a teacher. TokTok flexed his great claws in disheartened grace.

"It seems in Mok's teachings," Bek said, "that honor is like a great claw. It must be sharp and strong, but it is not a tool for every occasion, and sometimes can be utterly unimportant. Mok put his own needles into his dying friend, a shabby swarmer, sacrificing the cleanliness of his own needles, risking his own life."

Bek reached out, touching the sliding, overlapping needles of TokTok's great claw. There was no static discharge. Only in the newest hours of the year did every tree and bush and warrior and bird have the same charge. TokTok did not strike him down for his presumption.

"You earned and named each of your needles," Bek said. "Each was grown over time, or taken from a defeated opponent, or given by an approving master. We recite the history of every needle in a song of boasts, and yet the greatest warrior in the world put his needles into a shabby swarmer's body. When he told you to choose your fate, what do you think he meant? Do you think he meant for you to live out your days in the dark?"

TokTok was quiet. Bek settled into a meditative stance, the one with seven claws holding onto seven different spines in the floor of the cave. *Stance of Dawn.* It was not a defensive posture, but a restful, contemplative one. The air of the world was thick now, heavy, with the weight of all the ocean hanging in the unseen sky, waiting to snow down nourishment on them, to refill all the basins with promise.

"You did not get your chance to boast of your best battles," TokTok said quietly.

"They don't seem important right now," Bek said.

Lod scuttled beside Bek.

"I don't understand what Master Mok was trying to teach you," Lod said, "but I would like to ask him."

TokTok's needles fanned. If TokTok chose to bar the way, they could do nothing but withdraw or die.

"Let us seek him out," TokTok said finally. "If we're all wrong, I can still kill you both after."

III

The three of them descended. The cave must have been beneath the ocean only an hour earlier. The spines making up the foundations of the mountain were misshapen in the way only subsurface needles grew. The chaos of it was weirdly disturbing.

The cave bottomed out before climbing gently. The wind made a haunting moan at this depth where normally ocean would have dissolved them, leaving only needles. They'd only been given permission to transit this deathly warren. In weeks, perhaps days, the snows collecting in the ocean basins would melt and fill the world again, closing this pathway through the underworld.

They finally emerged into a wide space half-lit with microwaves. The ceiling was nearly solid with needles, but here and there, as if by judicious pruning, narrow channels welcomed in faint pulsar shine. The cave was not the barren hole Bek had expected. It was a garden, bursting with shiny metal flowers, steely petals in all stages of curling growth.

Flowers were hard to grow. Their tending had much to do with sculpting and they only bloomed in regions where the magnetic field bent in unpredictable ways. Flowers were fractal maps of the strange unexpectedness of the world. And this garden was immense.

Swarmers climbed the walls, shaping with pincers, smoothing, cleaning. They sang no boastful songs, but chanted placid nature hymns. Some of their needles were swarmer-short, but a few of them carried outsized warrior spines, too. A shiny old warrior stood in the middle of the subterranean garden in a one-legged stance Bek did not recognize. His seven other limbs were raised in perfect balance. He looked funny; many of his spines were swarmer-short.

The three of them approached the greatest warrior in the world with respectful grace. They each assumed learning stances appropriate to their schools. After a time, Master Mok's eye-stalks rose toward them.

"Master Mok," Bek said, "we are students, come to learn from you."

"You are Bek," the master said.

Bek's eye-stalks widened in surprise. He had expected a meeting, not a reunion.

"You remember me? I was only a budling on my father's body when you were a master. I carried only trainee claws when you were grandmaster. Was I special that you remember me?"

"No," Mok said.

Disappointment smothered Bek's brief elation. The idea that the famous teacher had remembered him had given him a strange pride.

"I won't teach you, Follower of the Needle."

"Not just me. All of us. We're from different schools."

"Only if you defeat me."

The swarmers along the walls continued their hymn to growing things. Bek looked at the old warrior-monk strangely. He couldn't defeat the greatest fighter in the whole world, even aged as he was. TokTok had not. Then Bek realized that Mok was referring to all three of them.

"All three of us?" Bek said. "We cannot. There is no honor in three against one."

"There is no teaching unless you defeat me."

"I expected some joy in finding again my old teacher."

"It depends what you wish to learn," Mok said.

"I do not appreciate riddles," TokTok said.

"To have come this far, you three must have been solving riddles," Mok said.

"This is a feint," Bek guessed. "A trick of battle to distract the opponent. Like the flower you revealed suddenly to make TokTok think you were attacking?"

Master Mok observed them. What was he observing, though? Bek had passed two dangerous guardians and penetrated a mysterious fastness open only once each year. Even if he fought Master Mok and failed, Bek had come so far that his own legend was assured.

His own legend was assured. And he wasn't listening.

"I'm not special," Bek said, looking at the flowers climbing the walls, at the swarmers who possessed some needles like nobles, at the master who carried some swarmer needles. Here, the differences between people were tricks of the light. TokTok and Lod seemed to be waiting for Bek to make his next guess. Master Mok had them baffled. He had Bek baffled.

"I'm not special," Bek said. "I'm great among my school, but how many warriors walk the world? How can I be special among thousands of nobles, thousands of warriors and followers of all the ways?"

Master Mok watched him with an effortless patience, standing on his single claw, untouched by the world as the swarmers sang of things other than Mok. He was perhaps the most famous warrior in the world. Yet he meditated here, in a steely garden, hidden from the world.

"We all want to be noticed and appreciated," Bek said to Lod and TokTok. "Shinier needles. More boastful songs. We say we're strong, and yet really we ache for someone to honor us. Imagining we're special feeds the myths we tell ourselves to ease that ache."

"Lod, you have a swarmer outside, and more at your home, singing songs about you," Bek continued. "They tell tales of the great warrior TokTok in Goz and Gan. But songs are brief in the life of the world. What song is heard above the Short Kiss? We remember Pik in song, but do we know him? Was he even real, or just a story? Because we're trapped in prisons of our own making, we spend our lives seeking appreciation now and some legacy in a future we can't experience."

"Nothing we had before means anything?" Lod asked.

"We've been walking pathways already laid out by others," Bek said. "Master Mok tried to show us we could cut new ways through the thicket. The paths we traveled before were just to learn to walk, but now we can choose. We can live to someone else's standard of honor, or we can live differently, explore new philosophical worlds, finding some that make us happy."

Still Master Mok was silent. Waiting without appearing to wait. Listening without appearing to listen.

"Stories don't matter," Bek said. "We matter, learning from each other."

Lod and TokTok had been facing Master Mok. After some moments, they shifted slightly, so the four of them were facing each other equally. Four learners. And they began to talk.

The Planetbreaker's Son

Nick Mamatas

1.

IT'S FUNNY, WHAT survives, and what fades away, when all the world with its many histories is crammed into the tiniest of physical spaces, then smeared across a virtual infinity.

Greek survived. Some of it did. *Ρίχνω μαύρη πέτρα πίσω μου.* "I'm throwing a black stone behind me." Done with a village, done with the port city to which you'd come to make your fortune, done with a life? Pick up a black stone and throw it over your shoulder as you leave, never to return. Take yourself and your stomach full of bitterness, but not a single regret, with you. Everything else you willingly leave behind, or have already lost.

When the planetbreaker's son was young, occasionally his mother would take him outside to see his father at work. It was always on a moonless night, and late. Mother would always wrap him in a blanket, too, even during the dog days of summer.

"Well, here it goes," she always said after consulting her watch. It was easy to find the particular planet in the sky—everything is always more obvious on a map—but soon enough Papa would throw a rock over his shoulder and the star would go up, flaring like a newly lit match, then fading to red and black.

Over in realspace, we're all just electrons stored in an object the size of a football field.

At home, where we all live, the sky is just a dome-shaped topological map, screwed on tight over the flat world. The light from a world being broken reached the son's eyes moments after his father tossed the black rock over his shoulder. The planetbreaker would be home soon, or whenever he felt like it.

The planetbreaker didn't like to talk about work. He didn't like it when his son asked questions and didn't listen to the answers, or when he had to repeat himself, or much of anything. The planetbreaker didn't even like the practice of planetbreaking, though he was very good at it.

He did like his son, though he wasn't sure what to do with the boy. The relationship with his wife was over—when the planetbreaker came home, he retired to the couch and caught up on the news. When the air was right, he ventured outside to look for black stones. He helped his son with his homework, watched realspace stories and played realspace games with him on the screens, though games were endlessly frustrating.

It wasn't that the planetbreaker had ever been RS but he had heard about those adventuresome days from his own father. Back when Earth was a thing under one's feet, covered in brown and sometimes green grass, with black and dusty cities, and well-spiced skies that could burn the hair from your nostrils after a hard day's work. RS games were different: for the kid, there were all sorts of little casual exercises in which he saved animals from the wild and got them safely stowed in pointy three-finned rockets.

For the kid to watch Daddy play, there were "mature" games: oh no, an RS meteoroid hit the object and someone has to grow some flesh, learn how to weld, and go outside! Or the object encounters another RS object, and an exchange of personality emulations leads to a political crisis, or an "alien invasion," or a quasi-religious telos—the return to RS, on a new blue Earth, where everyone receives another chance to get it right. Games were dumb, but soothing. Simple decisions, bright colors, and the planetbreaker's son would bark childish advice and smile at his father when the planetbreaker did well.

The planetbreaker and his wife—Zeus and Hera! They fought the way dogs do, all mouth. Father smoldered and snapped, Mother sniped and demeaned him, then Father erupted and Mother squawked in fear and indignation. The walls nearly derezzed, the floor quaked. When Papa rolled his eyes and growled through clenched teeth, the very sky went blank. The little planetbreaker's son loved his mother more than his father, which is right and natural. But he tried, the boy, to amuse his father with jokes about farts and cartoon characters and dancing around. "Are you happy now, Papa?" he asked, often.

"I'm always happy," the planetbreaker said, always, his voice that of a dead man.

✿

The planetbreaker's wife had a much more interesting and vital job than that of her husband. She worked in RS, sliding her being into any number of tentacular waldos to scramble through conduits and down tubes, maintaining and improving the ship. Twice she even engaged in EVA to make repairs to the skin of the football field in which we all live. Not in the flesh, of course, but in a little wheeled repair vehicle that rides along the exterior of the ship on tracks crisscrossing the surface. RS work is nothing like RS fiction—there's no excitement. Should we put a metaphor here? Does it make sense to address the recipient of this message with "RS work is like taping off a room before painting it" or "RS work is the opposite of a spreadsheet in a twenty-first-century office; real things are moved around to represent the virtual." After all, every possible recipient of the message already knows all about RS, our football-field-sized spacecraft/ice floe/coffin, and about the post-Singularity virtual habitus (many—the plural of habitus is habitus) in which we experience our disembodied existences.

Ah, but we already said football field at the start! Got us there. Not only is every possible recipient of this message already an inhabitant of a post-Singularity virtual habitus, but all the actual recipients of the message are well situated within a habitus where "football field" and "spreadsheet" make sense.

So it's easy to imagine—a woman, Caucasian mostly, with straw-colored hair piled on her head and kept in place with bobby pins, takes a seat on a wooden chair and sips tea from a mug. Somewhere in RS, a small machine the size of a waffle iron scuttles from point A to point B, laying atom-thick wiring across the skin of the ship. She goes out with her friends to see a movie, or swim in a pool, or just split a couple bottles of wine, and the magnetic field that scoops up hydrogen from the interstellar medium to fire it out a bank of ramjets astern adjusts ever so slightly. She goes to her job, writing marketing copy for medical devices that she has never seen and that nobody will ever need again, and server loads are calibrated.

The planetbreaker's wife is in a good social position—she knows that she works with RS, that the details of her quotidian life are in fact vitally important to keeping a million tiny stars twinkling in the sky and a spacecraft sucking and shitting its way through space. Not like her husband, who is blind to these things, who sits in his chair and frowns at his son until some inexplicable urge strikes him to visit another world. Not like her son, who thinks RS is all laser swords and telekinetic powers that sandy-haired boys just like him will one day manifest if they're good enough and practice with splayed fingers and pshew-pshew noises.

The planetbreaker's wife wants a second child, but bearing one would cause immense structural damage to the ship. It's the wanting of the second child that keeps the engines grinding forward in RS.

The planetbreaker has always wanted three kids, ever since he himself was a child, though of course he was never actually a child, just some lines of code emulating the desire to become a man and sire three children—boy/girl/TBD. He only has the one boy. One day, when his wife was distracted with her new hobby of zesta-punta and the entirely artificial subsentient lover she had met on the practice cancha, the planetbreaker found his son on the carpet, his thin arms holding open over his head a paperback copy of *Dubliners*.

"Are you really reading that?" the planetbreaker asked his son. "You're seven years old."

"I want to know what it's like to be nine, like the kid in 'Araby'."

"You should read a Greek story about a nine-year-old, not an Irish one," the planetbreaker said.

"Tell me one," his son said.

"Come with me. We need to find some rocks."

2.

"Is this what RS was like?" the planetbreaker's son asked.

"Sure, sure," said the planetbreaker. "Sure it was." One day, he hopes that his son will realize that "Sure, sure" means "No, but the true answer to your question puts a little pebble in my heart, and I can't bear to tell you directly, but I want you to understand that the answer is no, no, it's always no."

Where planetbreaker and son are right now is only a little bit like RS. There's physics and topology, but everything, everyone, is strangely frictionless. Not a pebble on the sandy red beach, the green sky is not only cloudless but without any change of hue at the horizon, and the purple waves lapping up the shore are always, always, the same size and collapse against the shore at the same rate. A handful of kids—not a filthy knee between them—had swooped by and instantly made friends with the planetbreaker's son. After ten minutes he was leading the crew in some thrilling game of the imagination, with megaexplosions and sudden marriages complete with driftwood babies, then sailing off via cartwheel-spacecraft to realms not yet annihilated. The planetbreaker found a little black pebble on the shore and collected it.

The seaside pension was a nice one. The planetbreaker let his son pull the shrink-wrap off the door—the kid was always excited to tear things apart or knock things over—and take the first exhilarating inhalation of ozone-tinged air.

"Realspace really must be amazing if it's like this," the planetbreaker's son said. He climbed up on one of the twin beds in the spartan room and jumped twice before catching his father's glare and settling down. There was something in the air.

"Is it really so different than being home with your mom?" the planetbreaker asked, changing the subject, he hoped.

"Yeah," said the son. "You're here. I don't get to spend very much time with you." The kid didn't sound sad, or upset, or even wistful necessarily. It was just a statement of fact, and it sounded to the planetbreaker—especially the *spend very much time* construction—like an utterance his son might have picked up from his mother.

"You think fathers and sons spent a lot of time together in realspace?" the planetbreaker asked.

"Yeah!" Then the son reeled off some long and confusing story our planetbreaker didn't understand about a family scrambling to escape icebergs pushing their way down the Thames and board the last spaceship, only for it to be revealed that they'd have to leave their bodies, and the kids all their favorite toys, behind. Maybe it was a Christmas movie of some sort. The toys loomed rather larger in the planetbreaker's son's memory, his father guessed, than in the actual RS story the kid was relaying.

"But there were more and better toys in the now time," the planetbreaker's son concluded. "Can you get me a toy octodog like the one the boy in the RS story had, except it talks and helps me get dressed in the morning?"

The planetbreaker didn't even say sure, sure to that.

"Where do the black rocks come from, Papa?" the planetbreaker's son asked. He couldn't seem to stand silences.

"Didn't you find any at the beach?"

"Not one! And I looked and looked and even when I waded in the water up to my knees it was all sand. Not even any white rocks."

"Does that sound like RS to you?" the planetbreaker said.

"No . . ." the boy said, cautious.

"Yeah," said the planetbreaker. "Do you know something? In this place, the moment you turn off the light after making the decision to get some sleep, you will close your eyes, fall into a pleasant dream, and wake up refreshed in the morning without the slightest problem."

"Really?"

"Try it," said the planetbreaker.

The boy did, with a smile, and with his face all scrunched up as he held his eyes shut as if against a storm.

It took longer than a moment, as the planetbreaker was lying to his son about the properties of the world they were visiting, but the kid fell asleep quickly enough.

This frictionless world's pension had a decent restaurant, which was always open and never crowded, in the same building. The planetbreaker refused to make the decision to sleep and decided to get a midnight snack, maybe observe or interview a couple of the locals.

The planetbreaker wasn't obviously one by the looks of him. Some present themselves as musclebound giants with heads of pure ball lightning spilling forth from the slitted eyeholes of an obsidian face-mask, while others take on the seeming of a school of steel-tipped fish burning hot from atmospheric entry. Yet others play Christ Jesus descending from swirling red clouds, or a humble germ that breaks apart the glycoproteins on the lipid bilayer of cell membranes. The planetbreaker was a chubby fellow with curly hair and a thick mustache of the sort that predominated across the Mediterranean and Asia Minor a couple centuries before the Earth died and the survivors abandoned RS. The planetbreaker wasn't necessarily approachable or friendly, but he was human enough to strike up a conversation when he needed to.

He did so now, with a couple filling a two-top next to him. "Hey there," he said. He smiled with his mustache. "You two locals?"

"Sure, sure," said the man. "You're from away?" He seemed intrigued, the man. He had hazel eyes that glimmered as if the small key lights around the restaurant had been deployed just to make that happen. "Welcome, welcome to the Argentum Coast. Name's Jim. This is Pammie," he said, nodding to the woman across from him.

"What brings you by?" Pammie asked. She was another adorable one, with curly hair and the perfect choice of sweater. The pair of them smelled of honeysuckle and musk. The planetbreaker imagined they'd be eating healthy plant-based dishes with perhaps the tenderest of chicken breast for protein.

"Just sampling the algorithms," the planetbreaker said.

"Might you be looking to settle here?" Jim asked. He exchanged a quick, suspicious-seeming glance with Pammie.

There are moments in narratives that carry a weight far more profound than they would in the nonnarrative Thrownness of reality. The look could mean anything: was Jim asking for Pammie's post hoc approval of his utterance? Was "settle" a fraught word given their marital relationship and existence in a world where almost but not all social friction had been excised? All three of them are waiting to order their meals, and there isn't a waitron to be seen, after all. Or were they suspicious of the planetbreaker, which in turn might agitate the man who held the fate of their world in his hands?

The planetbreaker did, in fact, reach for the rock in his pants pocket, but just to adjust it, as a sharp edge was digging into his thigh.

"Do you have kids?" Pammie asked. "I always ask if someone has kids. It's a great conversation-starter, I've found."

"Yes," said the planetbreaker. He was stoic for a long moment, then laughed. "Sure. His name is Yiannis. He's up in the room; fell right asleep after a big day at the beach."

"By himself? Is that safe?" Jim asked.

The planetbreaker shrugged. "He's seven, and the remote control on the entertainment system is locked; the honor bar is barren. If he's by himself he's safe. If someone else were up there with him, that would be trouble." The planetbreaker could be philosophical when it suited his purposes, and his purpose now was taking the measure of this world's locals. He snickered.

Jim glanced over Pammie's shoulder, looking for waitstaff. A bit of grit in the oyster.

"It's perfectly safe," Pammie said. "When I was a child my parents would leave me alone with my brother and sister all the time, and we all grew up fine."

Jim got dark now. "Of course, if you hadn't grown up fine, you wouldn't be here at all. Survivor bias."

"Are you saying that if I didn't grow up to be the person I am, you wouldn't want to be with me?" Pammie took a sip of her water and glared at her seatmate over the rim. "If I was ... damaged, I wouldn't be worthy of being with you?"

"Should I get the dinner rolls or the breadsticks?" the planetbreaker asked the air between him and the couple.

"If anything had happened, whether damage or something else, you wouldn't be here," Jim said, an edge rising in his voice. "Either you would be someplace else, or you would be someone else. And so would I, wouldn't I?"

"Very philosophical," said the waitress, an older woman who looked much like a bird with her thin limbs and prominent nose and brows. In some worlds, she could have had the body of a humanoid bird, if she so wanted, or if someone else had wanted it. She had appeared just in time, by which we mean a few seconds too late.

The meals were a bit of a distraction, but neither couple quite knew how to excuse themselves from the conversation with the planetbreaker, and the planetbreaker wasn't about to nod and leave them to their chicken breasts.

"Interesting question—I think about it all the time," the planet-breaker said. "I often wonder that about my own child; what if my wife had gotten pregnant a month later, or ten seconds later, from another sperm. He'd be a different child, albeit probably a fairly similar one. His own sibling."

Pammie paled at the mention of sperm. Jim squeezed the handles of his utensils. The planetbreaker felt the temperature rise in the room, heading upward past perfect. He glanced at the kitchen, which would surely be hot, but the double doors were closed.

When he looked back, he saw that the couple were glowing red, like iron long worked over a fire. They reached for one another across the small, now smoldering table and embraced with viscous limbs. The room began to fall apart, the parquet squares of the floor splitting apart and falling into the infinite black of empty space beneath it.

Planetbreakers! Oh ho, no, just one, just the way a longship of Norsemen viking in straight from Valhalla is a single planetbreaker, too. Our planetbreaker flailed and ran, catching a bit of wall here, the roots of an upturned tree there, climbing upward as the world fell to pieces and fluttered into the darkness of null-space. Carpeting, a stainless-steel serving tray, in one odd moment a pair of lobsters he used as skates across the void before they disintegrated.

And then came the people—flailing, screaming, some still holding their drinks, or sleeping in their derezzing beds, more than a few holding yogic or qigong positions, some half gone or aflame. The planetbreaker remained whole, swimming against the swirling currents of the disintegrating resort.

The planetbreaker wouldn't have thrown his little black rock over his shoulder, despite the tedium of frictionlessness; the world had been plenty able to accept a little disruption, a bit of rust. His son had liked it!

"Papa!"

There the kid was, clinging to an ottoman like an airline passenger hanging onto sinking wreckage, but he was floating up, or at least farther away from the planetbreaker, who was doing his best to scramble through the ashen confetti of the torn-apart world.

At least the shouting was nearly over, but that just meant the atmosphere was breaking down.

"One sec!"

"Papa, help!"

"Be quiet!" the planetbreaker said. "I'm doing something."

Naturally, we cannot let the planetbreaker's son die, at least not in these early pages. He's the name of the story. And his own father wouldn't let him die, oh no, even if it meant sacrificing himself. Not that it does in this particular case, but the sheer fact of the matter is that our planetbreaker would have tossed his rock over his shoulder right as he walked through his front gate and let his own world vanish if not for the fact that his kid lived there. There wasn't much left of the perfectly frictionless beachworld by the time the planetbreaker managed to swim through the void of floating, flaming ruins and snag his kid's ankle.

He yanked hard, swung the little boy over his head, sending them both spinning, and then let go.

3.

The planetbreaker's parents are retired. They live in the interior of a black hole, where classical physics breaks down, so it is entirely fine if one wishes to move in. The algorithms of the computers running the simulations are fungible, but inside black holes, they just kind of give up and let people do exactly what they want.

But it's very hard to leave once you're in one, so they aren't very popular within our football-field-sized starship zipping through RS.

Kronos and Rhea, those are the grandparents, and they do not leave their home, not ever.

Why did the planetbreaker grab his son by the ankle and fling him toward the black hole to which his parents retired, rather than simply—and it would have been as simple as the blink of an eye—send the poor kid home to his mother? Ah, here comes the little boy now, sailing right past: we're watching from far far away, to avoid being dragged into the black hole ourselves. He's slowing down, slowing, there he goes, red shifting, he's close to the event horizon now, he's probably inside already eating some nice milk and cookies Rhea whipped up, but to us, out here, the planetbreaker's son is frozen on the edge of the event horizon, slowly fading away as nearby photons all get diverted into the black hole and its immense all-crushing gravity.

We know exactly what the planetbreaker's parents are up to, and what his son is up to, even though we are on one side of the event horizon and they exist now on the other side. We can open up the source code from here and see what is happening, read it like a book.

Kronos and Rhea love their little grandson. Kronos hasn't even plucked the boy up and consumed him utterly. Kronos hasn't once contemplated it. That's love, friends! He hadn't swallowed the planetbreaker either, despite the name and provenance, not literally, but Kronos did do something similar: he was one of the many many employees who built the starship. He was no aeronautics engineer or computer scientist or even a sociologist or philosopher; Kronos worked on an assembly line in what was Detroit, manufacturing some of the modules that were launched into space then connected to make the suborbital platform from which robots then constructed the football-field-sized starship full of simulations.

Rhea won a door prize at the defense subcontractor holiday party four years before the ship was completed: right to have her personality and experiences uploaded onto the ship. Kronos was less uploaded and more simply remembered by Rhea, who knew him well enough for the algorithms to fill the rest of him out. He refused to attend subsequent holiday parties and thus missed out on the chance to be fully uploaded—he certainly wasn't worth the energy to do it otherwise. The selector-AIs had made some odd choices, the way lung cancer sometimes strikes down healthy athletes, but for the most part the billion people picked and the eight billion left behind had been so sorted for reasons too obvious to bear.

Kronos tends to repeat himself a lot, about the tyranny of taxes, the μαλακίες in government (there is no government in the black hole, nor is there an anarchy), and whether or not the food is burning. Their son, the planetbreaker, was partially modeled on their true son who had died of leukemia young, partially on the fantasies of his parents, and partially on ... other things. Incidents and accidents, randomly juxtaposed personality traits, databases about Hellenic populations and the Big Five personality traits, and the child's own cussedness. Also, he was raised in a black hole.

The planetbreaker's son is a happy boy, even when visiting his grandparents in the black hole. He is a little out of sorts now, as he was just thrown from a crumbling planet by his own father, through the endless reaches of notional space, was crushed by hypergravity and smeared against the ring-shaped singularity before being reconstituted by the algorithm into the boy he was. His grandparents smothered him in kisses, Greek-style: first one cheek, then the other, then pinching, hair-mussing, a kiss on the lips, and then two more for the cheeks.

When they were done with him, Rhea cleared the table of tiny coffee cups, and the planetbreaker's son excitedly told his version of the story: there was a beach and these kids and everyone was nice and papa didn't shout so much because everything was easy and happy and then he, the planetbreaker's son himself, got to hang out in a room himself with the TV on any channel he wanted—his mother wasn't even there—and push two beds together to make one big bed to jump on and he touched the ceiling twice with his mega-super jumps like he had always wanted to do at home and then on a third jump he hit the ceiling, too, but he didn't land on the bed and didn't land on the floor or hurt himself but he fell out of the entire room and then out of the entire building and then came his dad flying up from nowhere like a superhero to catch him and bring him here to visit his grandparents.

"So where is Dad?" he finished up. "I want my mom."

Kronos turned his ancient head to look at Rhea to solve the problem of their grandson. Rhea, the titan of fertility and the earth, produced a wonderful lunch: a Greek salad to start, thick with oil and red tomatoes even a child would relish, cucumbers speckled in rigaini, crumbles of feta salty to even look at; warm pita and chunks of lamb that seemed too rare to be anything but overly chewy but that in the mouth were somehow perfect.

And a little plastic plate of chicken nuggets, microwaved, with ketchup on the side, without a single molecule from the ketchup touching any of the nuggets before the planetbreaker's son had his chance to dip. Fruit punch that had never been anywhere near fruit, not even in the days of RS when there was fruit, and punch, and throats to pour it down, in a little plastic cup. One too small for the planetbreaker's son, but to his grandparents he would always be three years old or so, and not nearly eight.

None of this did anything at all to summon the planetbreaker's mother, of course. Kronos and Rhea don't make calls; they receive them. They don't visit others, they are eager hosts.

"I have to tell you something, Papou," the planetbreaker's son said to Kronos. "You don't have any good RS shows to watch at your house. You should get some. They're fun."

"RS?" Kronos said, rolling his *r* and hissing his *s* so the utterance took nearly ten seconds of subjective time. "RS shows? You don't need no RS shows here, baby. I'll tell you all about RS. RS was very big.

Sometimes it was hot, sometimes it rained. I was in an earthquake once, when I was your age. The whole horio—"

"Village," Rhea translated.

"—fell down. Every building crumbled. They loaded every person, every injured person, and goats, too, onto the ferry to go to Samos where there was a bigger hospital, but that hospital was full, too . . ."

The planetbreaker's son had heard this story before. The hospital in Samos was full of refugees from Syria and their local injured. So it was back onto the ferry, or really another, larger but no more comfortable one capable of the twelve-hour trip through choppy waters to Athens, where the piers were entirely full of ferries from all across the country and one of the city's hospitals had messily collapsed on itself. Finally, some nurses rowed out to the ferry Kronos was on, climbed it like pirates, and started treating the injuries they could. By the time they got to Papou—then a young boy who looked just like the planetbreaker's son in the face, but with black curls for hair—who wasn't that severely hurt, he was tired and dehydrated and a little dizzy from pain, so he vomited right on the nurse's head. Luckily, she was wearing one of those old-fashioned nurse's caps.

The moral of this story is: It's better to live in a black hole, where time has stopped and nothing can escape.

When the planetbreaker's son was born, Kronos and Rhea made the long, to them, journey through the underside of the singularity and out the white hole on the far end of the galaxy, then hopscotched from world to world across the imaginary dome of night, to visit their little *engonos*. The planetbreaker's mother had designed the planet to be a notional northern California town, including the constant threat but never the actualization of major temblors. Kronos lasted three nervous days before retreating to the black hole and taking Rhea with him.

The planetbreaker's son liked the black hole, and loved his grandparents. But he didn't want to be there without either of his parents.

"My mother should come and get me," he said aloud. "Do you think my dad is okay?"

"Oh, he's fine," Rhea told him. "He breaks planets all the time."

"I don't think he broke this one. He found a little rock, but he didn't throw it. He told me I'd get to watch him throw it if he decided to. We were flying through space," said the planetbreaker's son. "He was flying, and I was falling, and he caught me. He looked surprised and scared." The planetbreaker's son started looking surprised, and scared, himself now. Saying it all to his grandparents, and their response of matching bemused expressions, turned his spinal fluid to ice.

Finally, Kronos spoke. "He should not have become a planet-breaker. That is not the son I wanted."

"Oh, it doesn't matter," said Rhea, dismissive. This was an old argument. "He has to do something."

"He could have done something useful with his life! He could live here; we could see the baby all the time," Kronos said. The singularity didn't quite shake or derezz, as it was an arbitrary point of no particular mass or volume or even the energy level of a particular atomic orbital, but something shifted in the scene.

"There are too many worlds," Rhea said, half-explaining it all to the planetbreaker's son. "The RS ship cannot handle all of them, not the way they propagate, with every wish coming true sooner or later."

The planetbreaker's son didn't mind being called a baby, not by his papou. And he especially enjoyed when his yiayia used big words like "propagate," which he almost understood.

"My wish did not come true," said Kronos.

"Oh it did!" said Rhea. "It did!"

"Shouting doesn't make anything better," said the planetbreaker's son. "Do you know that?" His mother asked him that frequently.

"This is your wish, isn't it? We're here with our grandson. It's my wish, too," Rhea said. "Why can't you just be happy?"

"My dad shouts a lot, too," the planetbreaker's son said.

"I'm happy! I'm happy! I am so happy!" said Kronos. He was a big man, but his voice squeaked like a bird's when he was agitated, and he was agitated now.

"Yeah, you look happy. You make everyone happy. We're all so happy now," Rhea said. "All the happiness in the universe is being drawn in here, and not even love can escape!"

"All I want to do is talk to my grandson and have him grow up to be better than his father!"

"Better than you, too!"

"Of course, of course ..." Kronos said, calming now. "Everyone should be better than me. Everyone is better than me, I know, I know."

The planetbreaker's son said, "Papou, yiayia, you need some good RS shows. You really do. It's okay though; I forgive you." And with that, he left the table. Rhea called after him, while Kronos muttered to himself in Greek about generations of failure and the need for the Theotokos, the very mother of God, to be fucked and sent to hell. The theological implications of a titan making such imprecations were staggering, but in the very depths of a black hole's singularity anything is possible.

4.

Let us not take Rhea too seriously; planetbreaking isn't so much a job that needs to be done as it is an inevitable emergent property of personality emulators and the virtual environments they produce and reproduce. Planets will be broken; people will break them. This does not mean that any particular personality *needs* to be a planetbreaker in order for the system to keep functioning.

Our boy, the son of Kronos and Rhea, isn't even an exceptional planetbreaker. He's neither spectacular nor prolific, and his policies and criteria for throwing that black rock over his shoulder and declaring himself done are as capricious as a Greek god choosing and then abandoning a mortal lover. Where is he now? Not back home, with his spouse who would want explanations and access to her child, or on his way to the swirling dent in space-time where he threw his son as there would be screaming, but on yet another arbitrary world where he could get some work done judging its decorative details.

This planet was a small one, riven by conflicts. There were no more than 120 sentient beings on this world, and most of them had adopted flamboyantly posthuman seemings: genders slipped off like skins from snakes, cigar-smoking bipedal otters, conglomerations of gelatinous blue cubes with pseudopods and orifices forming and dissolving as needed. The only facets of existence the denizens of this little worldoid didn't factionalize over were sartorial-avatarial choices; in his human skin the planetbreaker stood out but was still beneath notice. He was less impressed by this than nonplussed. The planetbreaker stood in the town square and read the embossments; every being on the planet was a public figure, and inclined toward if not skilled at writing manifestos and issuing press releases on myriad topics, though mostly they had to do with the utterances and presumed opinions and mental health issues faced by other citizens. The material was hypertextual and endlessly self-referential across a dozen different senses, some of which the planetbreaker didn't possess, but there were sidenotes and footnotes, albeit incomprehensible ones.

The planetbreaker spent seven wonderful years of subjective time on this world, whose name was in dispute. He joined a faction, then switched sides; he helped create and then cruelly denounced works of both civil architecture and public art, then he worked toward reconsideration and reconciliation. His wife? His son? Time moves differently elsewhere; they'd be fine. The Hellenic theme asserted itself—he was Odysseus, our planetbreaker, now, and Telemachus might be out searching for him and Penelope surely patiently waiting at home and ignoring any potential suitors. Or maybe he'd be back home in the blink of an eye.

Toward the end of his time in this realm, in the sticky afterglow of a social activity halfway between an orgy and a well-choreographed battle royale of masked wrestlers, one of the planetbreaker's lover-opponents dug through the planetbreaker's trousers and found a little black stone.

"This is not part of New Albion's geology," they said, definitively. "It's a coded object."

"It's all coded objects," the planetbreaker said. "We're all coded objects." A murmur went up from the still entwined crowd. Of course they were—are—all coded objects, with no more reality than any other agglomeration of electrons and instructions, but the same could be said of all of RS, no? It comes from qbits, every quark in RS spins according to some rule, and the rules predate the existence of the quarks. It's a primitive wetbrained belief—wetbrained being both a slur that recalls hydroencephaly and a simple reference to the organ everyone on the football-field-sized ship left behind—that everything is particles. Everything is information; everything is a coded object, because the code precedes the objects. There were counterarguments, and they were raised, and some open orifices were offered genitals or pseudopods or extruded nerve ganglia and vice versa, and the being with his rock shot the planetbreaker a sour look for ruining the mood of the room. They were a bit like a praying mantis in an early Edwardian business suit, the shirt unbuttoned to reveal sex organs along the thorax mammalian enough for the planetbreaker to work with.

"Hey, don't blame me," the planetbreaker said. "I'm just a coded object, too, coded to say things like 'It's all coded objects.'"

"Take some responsibility for your utterances," the mantis said.

"Funny thing is," the planetbreaker said in a moment of sheer honesty, "that thanks to the coded object you're holding, I don't have to. Or wouldn't have to if I still had it in my hand."

The arguments surrounding him, furious but careful as the mood was festive and clothing items few, subsided.

"Look close," the planetbreaker said.

The mantis did; so did some of the others, untangling themselves to peer. On this planet of faction, unanimity was nearly unheard of save for this one issue:

"You have to leave," said the mantis. A primate of some sort sidled up to them, cupped the rock in the mantis's digits, and said, "I'll hang on to this."

"Why you, Mryon?" demanded another primate.

"I'll hang on to the rock for now," the mantis said, though Mryon the primate did not let go of their forelimb. "But you, sir, must abandon our world now. And without this instrument of genocide."

"You need me," the planetbreaker said. "I . . ."

"We do not need you."

"I don't need you," said one of the others the planetbreaker had engaged with. "I didn't need you and I don't need you. You were fun while you lasted. I'm sure you say that to the worlds, to the coded objects, you erase." She shifted up onto her elbows and rested her chin in her hands.

"I don't," the planetbreaker snapped. "At any rate, would you be happier were I miserable?" He glanced around the room. He was surrounded, naked. The mantis was standing on the pair of trousers they had searched.

"It's a heavy responsibility," said the primate sharing the stone with the mantis. A bit of a struggle was emerging between the two of them. Mryon's grip was strong, and the exoskeletal plates on the mantis's forelimb shifting. The other primate, who had addressed him, had taken up a strategic position on the mantis's other flank, but that could mean anything. Appearances didn't inform alliances here.

"The stone won't work for you," the planetbreaker said.

"It's an object of interest anyway," said Mryon.

"Every breaker is radically different," said the planetbreaker. "Even if you figure out the rock, that won't save you from some other breaker, some other time."

"Like a virus," said the girl with her chin in her hands. "There are ever so many of them, constantly evolving. Just like the old days."

"I wasn't going to do anything. I liked this world. I still like it. I'd like my pants back." The planetbreaker felt much more naked than he actually was, and he was entirely naked. He would have snatched back that rock and tossed it over his shoulder in a second if he could manage it, but the primate was huge, with an orangutan belly and two-meter arms, and the mantislike being now flexing spikes and mandibles.

"I see that you have something to agree on," the planetbreaker said, standing. He thought about covering himself with his hands, but it hardly mattered.

"I doubt we agree about what should be done with you," said the woman, clambering to her feet. "Take me with you? My name's Anna."

"Hello, Anna," the planetbreaker said. "It was nice almost fucking you. Do you own pants?"

"Why would you even want to go with him? You didn't miss much, I promise you," said the mantis.

"Maybe I want to see a planet broken. There are plenty out there that need to go. That's why the stars twinkle, even here, where there are no clouds and it never rains."

"That is not why the stars twinkle!" said the other primate, the one flanking the mantis perhaps in cooperation with Mryon, who still hadn't let go of the rock. Perhaps a generalized brawl would erupt—the orgy had verged on it more than once—and the planetbreaker could snag some clothes and escape.

"Are you saying that there are no defective worlds out there?" Anna said.

"Do you think that traveling with a planetbreaker would be fun and exciting?" demanded the mantis. "That he's a dangerous lad? If he limited himself to extinguishing defective worlds, he'd just be a repairman with a regular route. You get off on mass murder, Anna, admit it!"

"You're the one who penetrated him," Anna reminded the mantis. "And he's obviously a planetbreaker. That's how you knew to rifle through his pants, after pleasuring yourself with him."

"Stars don't twinkle anymore; that's RS business," said the primate. "You're just coded to believe that stars twinkle and so for you they do. Probably far more often and with a more obviously dramatic tempo than stars ever appeared to twinkle back on Earth."

"Not everyone is from Earth!" another orgy participant called out, but the planetbreaker didn't see who it was. He was headed to the door, and a number of beings were following him, arguing among themselves or with Anna, or commenting on the planetbreaker's hairy and acne-covered back, his somehow unusual calves.

A faction of those entities that had no experience of Earth—they were the code-only offspring of uploaded people with RS experience, or personality emulators that emerged from code spontaneously for this or that reason fathomable only to the algorithms of the football-field-sized starship—formed to debate the inherent intersubjectivity of the perception of twinkling stars. In moments, some individuals with RS experience joined the faction, while some emulators betrayed the faction and joined the opposition. A few advocated for both sides simultaneously. Mryon and the mantis were still holding hands.

"May I have the rock back?" the planetbreaker asked them. "It's getting loud in here."

"There's never a reason to harm others," said the mantis. Mryon opened his mouth to disagree, but shut it. He gripped the mantis's forelimb more roughly, and the mantis blinked hard.

"I don't make the rocks. I don't bring them with me. I visit a world and sometimes I find them. As though they've been placed here for me."

"And do you always use a rock when you find it?" asked Mryon.

"No," said the planetbreaker.

"Then it doesn't matter," said the mantis.

"It does matter, because I might step outside right now and just happen to come across another rock, a rock only I can ever find. The worlds give me a lot of chances."

"And many chances to make a good decision instead of a hideous one," said the mantis.

"I agree with that, even when the world doesn't and decides to present me with a quarry of rocks." the planetbreaker said. "I just want some clothes. Keep that particular pebble."

"We could kill you," said Mryon. His voice was low, lower than the planetbreaker should be able to hear over the noise of the ongoing debates and occasional squeal or static burst or great expulsion of gaseous joy, but the planetbreaker felt the threat—nay, the pure factual claim—in the marrow of his bones.

Planetbreakers are not a confederacy; there is no single mission, no flag under which they unite. It's hardly even a vocation at all. It is just a matter of the knack for it, which in truth is fairly evenly distributed across the population, and the circumstances one experiences that lead one to embrace the calling. A mixture of arrogance and ignorance, and just enough intellect and charm to get away with it, helps, too. That sometimes entire worlds—most often the uninhabited ones that defy topology and physics (there's a reason Kronos and Rhea live in a black hole) and occasionally those occupied by the worst sorts of beings—do need to be wiped out is a factor as well. Planetbreakers keep the denizens of the football-field-sized starship from the torpor of complacency. They work alone, but:

"There will be others. They might not be a man with a pebble. They might not . . ." the planetbreaker said, smirking now, because he had stopped caring, "sample the local delicacies before making a decision. You can close your portals, keep everyone out, but you'll just end up with native planetbreakers, and they'll break your hearts before cutting a hole in your world and letting all the air out."

"That doesn't mean we shouldn't kill you," Mryon said. "Nobody will come and take revenge on your behalf. The planet will break or it will not, a planetbreaker will come with murder on their mind, or they will not."

"Or they will come and make the only correct choice," said the mantis.

"I'll get him out of here," said Anna, who had collected her own clothes and also a small travel bag. "I promise. We won't come back. He won't come back."

"You're going to make him better with the power of love and compassion?" asked the mantis. If their mandibles allowed them to chuckle, they would have chuckled then. That's why the planetbreaker had liked them so much—no snickering during sex.

"Don't patronize me, ___," Anna said. Whatever the name of the mantis, Anna had the organs to pronounce it within her otherwise human-seeming throat, but the planetbreaker couldn't even comprehend the phonemes with his all-too-human ears.

"Stay," the planetbreaker told Anna. "Or leave. But not with me."

"But—"

"I don't want company. I don't want anything. I just want to go. I was never going to hurt anyone."

"Oh, so we passed your little test, did we?" Now Anna was sore, too, testy and moving toward enraged. "Showed you a good time? Convinced you with some argument not to be a raging asshole this once?"

The planetbreaker shrugged. "No, it's not a test. There are no tests, no qualifications for anything, not really. It's just like . . . the weather." It was a weak argument to make, but especially on a world where every argument is honed to a nanoblade edge. But it worked on one level: it was so fatuous that the only rational response was a show of pure contempt. So the planetbreaker got his pants—the other primate who looked like Mryon threw them at him, and Mryon finally snatched the pebble from the hand of the mantis and threw it over his shoulder, albeit to no effect other than a grunt from some fleshy thing still on the floor off which it bounced and spun away, and Anna swigged from her thermos of water and spat two cheeks' worth in the planetbreaker's face just as he pulled his trousers on, and the mantis said, "Have a good life. I mean it."

"Well, it was nice meeting everyone," the planetbreaker said. He wasn't sure whether to put on his pants first or to walk to the door and dress there before leaving, and ultimately tried both at once, slipping on one trouser leg as he limped to the exit.

5.

The planetbreaker's wife took the long trip to a white hole and waited for her son to emerge. The mere fact that she had located a white hole and positioned herself relatively near its ever-spewing event horizon meant that this particular white hole was the one from which her son would emerge, and that he would do so before he fell through the event horizon into the black hole in which his grandparents lived. Kruskal-Szekeres coordinates are amazing, and as they operate only outside the physical singularity, the boy both got to spend a very long time with his grandparents—years, subjectively—and be instantly rescued by his mother at the same moment his father threw him into the black hole.

Now the planetbreaker's wife had two sons, one of whom is a teen, and one the young boy she knew days prior. They occupied the same space, mostly. That is, the teen encompassed the boy, and 100 percent of the boy was held within the coordinates of the teen. The planetbreaker's son and the planetbreaker's son were mutually superimposed upon one another, lenticulated, shifting slightly from age to age as their mother's gaze tried to track the different silhouettes of her child.

She said his name, tenderly, and the boy surfaced. Surprised, she said it again, snapping, and out came the teen, overwhelming the image of the boy.

"Well, I don't suppose there is any way to fix this?" she asked her half-grown son.

"Why would you want to fix your own son?" He was as surly as the algorithm knew teens had the reputation of being in the time of the planetbreaker's wife. "Looking for a reset button? Isn't that my father's business?"

The planetbreaker's wife's first impulse was in fact to blame herself—not for any reason in particular, it was just her way to decide that somehow she had failed: to draw clear boundaries with her in-laws, to forbid her husband from taking their son on a planetbreaking expedition, to select the right being to marry in the first place, by stopping with one child despite there being almost no resource issue that could limit family size or composition and perhaps thus encouraging her son to form his own older and younger sibling which the kid had always said he wanted.

"We'll make it work," the planetbreaker's wife said. Of course, she'd blame the planetbreaker for this double state of affairs, as it was his fault. The thought was liberating. If she could find a way to help her son, the credit would go to her, and if not she would still be a good mother. It felt more duplicitous than it was.

The planetbreaker's wife missed her little boy, though he sat next to her on the long voyage home. They took a train, which the kid had always preferred to other modes of travel. Even the teen seemed to like it, though he was awkward in his long limbs, and kept scratching at the scraggly hairs on the underside of his neck.

"Are you feeling all right?" she asked her son. "I'm sure it's disorienting, this new state of being. But are you all right? Is it interesting?" Interesting was a word she hoped would keep her son(s) contemplative and focused on the moment; it sounded distant rather than loving, and she instantly regretted that, but fretting over the ever-shifting blurred dyad in the seat next to her might agitate all three of them even further.

The boy spoke first, and the planetbreaker's wife was relieved. He was always a thoughtful little kid. "It is pretty interesting . . ." he said, carefully modulating the syllables of that last word: in-ter-esting. Then the teen cut in. "I'm going to be like this forever; sharing a body with an eight-year-old. Wait, am I not ever going to grow up either? Am I always going to be"—he screwed up his face, it vanished, it returned—"like this? Sixteen?"

"No fair! He's twice as old as me!" said the boy.

"I am you."

"It's true," said the mother. "You are both you. I would tell you not to argue with yourself, but it's true that people do argue with themselves all the time, isn't it?" She'd hoped the teen would respond, but it was the kid who said, "No, I never argue with myself. That's what people did in the old days."

In the old days, in the days of RS, people didn't just get what they wanted—a train ride, a backyard that was a whole planet, gills or wings. Of course they argued with themselves instead. The planetbreaker's wife had been produced in the starship and her life was entirely virtual, but her job gave her some connection to the real world of meat and particles beyond the interior of the football-field-sized starship. She'd been outside, after a fashion, her personality rolling around on the hull, fixing damage caused by micrometeoroids. It's part of why the train she was on now with her son(s) had such verisimilitude—it's why the planetbreaker's son was so enamored with trains.

"What did they do in the old days about this?" said the teen.

"About what?"

"This, what would you call it, overlay?" said the teen, gesturing at himself as he vanished into the eight-year-old with whom he shared space. The planetbreaker's son, the one his father remembered and threw into the event horizon of a black hole, seemed fairly content. It was only the teen who was agitated. It was the kid's world, after all, and he was sitting next to his mother, whom he loved more than anyone.

"This didn't happen in the old days. It's not actually happening now. I mean, nothing . . ."

Of course, it was happening. The two children sitting next to her in three-second cycles were as real as she, the planetbreaker's wife, was. And she was real, she knew, because she, too, had two existences, and one of them was out in RS, outside of the ship. Her decisions out there were utterly material, and thus real.

And it was she, an amaterial being, making them, and thus amateriality was real as well. Further, her amaterial activities were physically possible, the sort of thing she could do were she physical.

The planetbreaker's wife reminded herself of all this fairly frequently, but as her world had fairly rigorous topology and internal consistency—save for her husband leaving for work in order to extinguish a star—her cogitations on the subject of reality were less Existenzphilosophie and more daily pep talk. "You can do it!" with it being things that were actually real—a rare power inside the football-field-sized starship.

"Mommy, just help!" The voice was plaintive, desperate, and half-cracked. The teen. "Do something!"

"Please!" said the child.

The planetbreaker's wife would do something. She had an idea, or the beginnings of one anyway.

"Let's just watch a show for now," she told her son(s). "Can you find something you both agree on?"

They could agree, in broad strokes—right to the RS channel. The teen hadn't seen any more films and shows than the kid had, which was a good sign, the planetbreaker's wife thought, that the teen was a programming glitch rather than the result of real-time experiences on some world. Was a glitch less real than a coded object that had been cultivated in a world matrix with a full suite of experiences?

The planetbreaker's wife figured that she'd soon find out, for better or for worse.

6.

The planetbreaker landed hard on the front lawn of his home on the little world he shared with his wife and son. His home was dark, which was unusual, and the moon new, but somehow the planetbreaker could see dozens of small black pebbles like shards of obsidian glistening between the blades of grass. It was difficult to pick himself up without brushing the side of a finger against one of the planetbreaking stones. He managed to resist the urge to pocket one. This was his world; this was his home.

The planetbreaker let himself in, turned on the lights, and cast around the messy rooms—the kid loved drawing robots and such and had a million toys, his wife was busy with work and rarely picked up, and of course the planetbreaker liked to tell himself that he wasn't good at putting things into order without destroying them—looking for a note. There was none, of course.

The planetbreaker contemplated calling his parents, but that would involve having an extended conversation with them, and making a connection to the interior of a black hole would consume a lot of his world's energy, might even slow down the sky in its revolution around the plane on which his home sat. But surely his wife went to go fetch his son. They'd be back sooner rather than later, and all the planetbreaker would have to do then is fiercely explain why the mission to the frictionless world had gone so wrong, and why he chose to fling his child into the maw of a black hole rather than just sending him home to his mother where he belonged.

Ah yes, and also his extended absence and the side trip to the other world, the one with the orgies and arguments. And there wasn't even a nova in the sky to show that he had just been at work.

There was little else to do but either clean the house, or go back outside and hunt for a rock that felt lucky and true among the many many newly decorating the lawn. *Ρίχνω μαύρη πέτρα πίσω μου.* It took three minutes of pacing from stoop to lawn and back, then turning on his heel and going back to the lawn, before he finally decided to try to pick up the house.

When the planetbreaker awoke, on the couch he had cleared toys from half, a familiar-looking young man was standing over him, and he shivered in recognition. What was it? The clothes. They belonged to his son, and were suitable for an eight-year-old from the early twenty-first century; some kind of sporty short and a graphic T-shirt with a jive-talking robot from a cartoon that the planetbreaker himself would have watched as a child. But when he had dressed his son the morning of the trip, the robot image had a smile and rounded lines to make it seem juvenile. Now the robot was all angles and bristled with weapons, as in the original anime designed for a more mature audience. Well, an older audience anyway.

The kid's face. It was his face. That of his kid, that of his own dumb self lying on half a couch, his feet tucked awkwardly under his thighs. The planetbreaker's son had always looked like his father, but cuter; Papa's awkward nose and low brow tempered by his wife's pleasant features. The frowning teen looming over him wasn't cute at all; puberty was its typical unkind self, bringing together two appearance algorithms and bidding them to compete for somatic real estate.

"Hi," said this new teen boy, but by the time he said "Dad" and finished the sentence, the planetbreaker's son was the child his father knew again. The planetbreaker's heart soared, and then plummeted. He sat up and over his kid's head he saw his wife standing in the open doorway, then his child changed again and he was looking at a teen's torso and that violent cartoon robot again.

"It's like something out of an RS story," the teenager said. "I mean, a story from the RS times, one of the strange ones." Then the kid asked, "What are those called again? You told me once, Dad."

"Science fiction," said the planetbreaker.

"Is that what you call this?" said the planetbreaker's wife. The utterance had the shape of a question, but it was something else entirely.

7.

Our titular planetbreaker's son was very used to the arguments his parents had—the shouting, the sudden dipping into Greek on the part of his father and his non-Greek mother shouting back, "I don't even understand!" though of course after years of this behavior she does know exactly what his curses and imprecations mean. Her mother-in-law Rhea had carefully translated the stock phrases for her, guffawing and rolling her eyes as she did, years ago. The planetbreaker had learned them from his father, though he never picked up much more Greek than the stuff of rage.

His mother was no slouch either. When the topic wasn't heating up fast enough for her taste, she'd bring out a list of past slights, otherwise forgotten confrontations and sometimes innocuous comments—she'd dig back into their first dates and then say something like, "And I know you're thinking _____" and then insist that her husband defend the vile claims she had manufactured for him.

The teenage planetbreaker's son wasn't quite so used to the shouting as was the boy. Though time in the event horizon of a black hole has no meaning and the kid neither subjectively nor objectively spent six years alone, it had nonetheless been a while for him since. He'd forgotten how to ignore the rage, or rather he'd forgotten that he had to pretend to ignore it for the sake of his parents.

He'd picked up a little rage of his own.

"Will you shut the fuck up?" he bellowed. His mother gasped, his father flew at him, accusing finger pointed, but then it was just the eight-year-old planetbreaker's son looking up at his dad. "Yeah!" said the kid. "It's always too loud and there's too much shouting."

"They're right," said the planetbreaker's wife. "He's right. Our son is right."

"I agree. So please don't start with me. Stop starting with me!" said the planetbreaker.

"What did I even say?"

"I was explaining to our son about science fiction when you butted in . . ." and then the argument started again.

The teen wanted to stay and participate in the fight, to shout at his father when he dominated his mother, to switch sides when Mother's ripostes escalated the situation. In those moments when the kid existed, he strolled casually as he could toward his bedroom and the comfort of his toys, his little books, his endless doodlings of football-field-sized spaceships with incorrect rocket exhaust coming out one end as they dive into black holes or flee from golden space dragons or get torn apart in the space between binary stars. The teenager stayed put in his moments of existence; retreat was cowardice so far as he was concerned. Then one of the parents, the teen didn't even know which, wailed—no words, no sentiments, not even a reaction to anything physical, just primal rage and agony braided together like strands of leather to make a whip—and he stopped staying put and brought his younger self to the bedroom and closed the door.

"Hi," said the little kid to his older self. They were standing before a full-length mirror now.

"Hey, me," said the teen when it was his sliver of time to exist.

"I'm going to be you?"

"Maybe," said the teen. "Who can say? I don't remember this happening to me. I was just you, and me, until a few hours ago."

"So I'm the real one!" The kid smiled at his reflection in the mirror, then the smile, and the kid, vanished just as these words escaped his mouth. "I'm real and you have to go."

"I'm real, too," said the teen. "If I'm not real, then who are you talking to?"

"You! Me! Myself!"

"No, you're a crazy kid who needs to be locked up because his parents clearly can't take care of him. Do you want that? And I don't mean being locked up with Yiayia and Papou either—I mean in a little time-out cage somewhere, a real time-out cage with no time in it."

"Will I have toys there?" The kid vanished before he could cry. The frown he wore hinted that tears were to come.

"No," said the teen when he was back.

And the boy cried.

"We need to fix this," said the teen.

"How?" asked the boy. "You can fix it by going away! I go one way, you go another way!"

The teen had to laugh at that. It was crazy kid cartoon logic, not even the stuff of "science fiction," and he understood his own younger self very well indeed. This was a crazy cartoon life, and the kid would never stop demanding that they try to walk in opposite directions. So on the count of three—silent, as the duo knew one another extremely well—they walked, the teen backing up one big step and the kid rushing toward the mirror just as he faded out of the realm of perception of everyone but himself.

A mirror is a method of time travel, or at least transtemporal perception. In RS, light takes time to travel and human minds take time to interpret the information their eyes collect. A reflection is always a bit of old news, if only by the billionth of a second. If one could build a mirror the size of a planet and plop it a light year from one's location, then peer into it with the aid of a sufficiently powerful telescope, one would see in the mirror-planet's reflection a scene from two years prior.

But here aboard the ship, where every being is a bit of code interacting with every object, also bits of code, there is no gap. There is no light traveling from mirror to eye, nor a mirror, nor an eye. The laws of physics are only generally replicated—remember those retirees with their living room in the singularity of a black hole, or the fellow who gets to walk to work though his work takes him to distant-seeming stars?—so when the planetbreaker's son moved in two directions at once, in the mirror, they could see one another, and themselves, overlapped and lenticulated, sharing much of the same space.

The boy started to sob for real now, uncontrollably. The only reason his mother didn't storm into the room to comfort him was because he instantly vanished, his cry of "It didn't work!" being swallowed by the reappearance of the teen, who quickly snatched up a small toy drum from the floor, held it up over his head, lifted his leg, and dropped it on his knee right before he disappeared and the kid reappeared. The kid gasped and slapped his hand over his mouth, squeezed his eyes shut. He kicked the drum away, sending it sliding across the carpet and under his little bed. He ran to the door, but the teen reemerged and locked it, albeit from the inside. But now his parents were on the other side, rattling the knob.

"Honey, are you all right?" said the planetbreaker's wife from the other side of the door. "Both of you, that is! Let me in!"

"Let us both in!" said the planetbreaker, his voice sharp. Then calmer, "We're sorry we fought in front of you. I am . . . and your mother is."

"We are. Let us in, sweet boy."

"It's locked," said the sweet boy. "He locked it."

"So unlock it!" said the planetbreaker.

The lock clicked and the door opened. It was the teen.

"We're not real. None of this is real. It's not just me," he said.

The planetbreaker sighed and rolled his eyes, despite telling himself that he shouldn't. There was nothing more tedious than this conversation, so far as he was concerned. Nothing made him throw the black rock over his shoulder faster than coming upon a world where existential skepticism was a major cultural preoccupation. It didn't matter what was real or not; what mattered—

"I should get to live, just like the rest of you. You're no better than me," said the teen. He was replaced by a sniffling child who threw himself at his mother's legs and held on tight.

Well, the planetbreaker thought, that was interesting. He was proud of his boy—of his boy(s)—for embracing the facts of life. It was something he'd always had some trouble with, himself. That was the dumb secret of his planetbreaking. He was avoidant; he wrecked that which held up a mirror to his face, what hinted at responsibility and happiness. What—

The teen was back and hadn't let go of his mother's legs quickly enough. They both tumbled to the floor. The planetbreaker howled, surprised and upset. He grabbed his boy—he had always wanted more than one child and in a way now his wish had come true, and wasn't that the promise made to his parents' generation when they agreed to have their personalities uploaded and launched into space?—and pulled him off his wife, but ended up with his little crying eight-year-old in his arms.

He squeezed the boy tight and kissed him on the left and right side of the kid's salty lips, a proper Greek greeting.

"Put him down!" said his wife, and he startled, almost dropping the boy, then he swallowed a shout when he realized why she was snapping at him. The teen was back as the kid's feet landed on the floor.

"Hmm," said the planetbreaker. Then he glared at his wife and half-grown child, who both had their mouths open, ready to speak or shout and snap or say something he couldn't handle.

"It's me, isn't it?" he said. He held up a hand. "Stop!" The planetbreaker's wife and planetbreaker's son weren't even doing anything. "Just stop, stop and let me speak!"

"We are!" said his wife. "We've stopped!"

"Stop completely! Not a word! Not a glance!" He looked over at his son, still a teen. They waited, the three of them. The planetbreaker's wife clenched her fists, exhaled roughly.

"It is me," said the planetbreaker. "Notice how our kid shifts in time when it's convenient. One or the other can always finish a sentence, whether it's long or short. You know how much I hate interruptions."

"You just hate being interrupted; you don't hate them in general," the planetbreaker's wife said. "And it wasn't convenient when I ended up on the floor."

"But I didn't end up on the floor. The weird thing is that nothing like this has ever happened before," the planetbreaker said. "We've visited my parents any number of times."

"That's just proof that you made it happen this time! You took him with you on your horrible 'job' and then threw him into a black hole!"

The planetbreaker's son, the young one, was back, his eyes wet and forehead wrinkled in a frown.

"Why can't you just be normal?" the planetbreaker's wife demanded. "Why can't you just settle down and play at having a normal job in a normal town with a normal sky?"

"I've always wanted more than one kid, and now I have two," the planetbreaker said, looking at his son. "That's a normal desire, but . . ." He trailed off, shrugged. It was better to be quiet, not to want anything anymore.

"No, you only have me!" said the planetbreaker's son. "And I don't want to be here!" And with that, he wasn't, and the older kid was standing in his place, simmering with identical rage, wearing those now ridiculous seeming-little boy clothes, the beginnings of a mustache sprouting over his lip.

The planetbreaker's son's accent was terrible: "Reehh-no mavree petra piso moo." He ran for the door, his legs long. The planetbreaker thought to tackle him, to fight the kid and bring him down before he did something reckless, insane, but did nothing at all but turn to his wife.

"Stop him!" she demanded.

"How?"

"Will it even work?"

The planetbreaker desperately wanted to say no. His son was no planetbreaker, and even were he one, every planetbreaker was unique. The planetbreaker's son, no matter how surly a teen he was at the moment, could no more delete a world by tossing a rock over his shoulder than our planetbreaker, standing in his living room, powerless and rendered stupid by events both recent and long ago, could delete a planet by melting through the surface and detonating its core.

But, then again, the planetbreaker was getting what he wanted. And like old howling Kronos in his black hole, he wanted a son who would follow in his footsteps.

So he said nothing, which isn't another way of saying no. It's very nearly a way of saying yes.

"Get out there and stop him, now!"

"What do you want me to do, hit him?" the planetbreaker asked. "You're the one who hits him."

The planetbreaker's wife's face fell apart. "Once."

"Three times."

"I was very tired, and angry, and he surprised me. You yell. That's as bad. Don't kid yourself that it's not. I'm sorry I struck him, but you're not sorry for anything you do, not ever."

This was an argument they'd had many times, and the ease with which they slid back into it terrified the planetbreaker. It was easier to fight than to do something to save their child(ren).

"You're right," he said. The planetbreaker's wife didn't acknowledge that. "You're right, okay!" he said, louder. She said something, but the sound of broken glass swallowed her utterance. A black rock landed on the rug between them.

Then the planetbreaker's son's voice, that of the little kid's, floated in, too. "Uh-oh. Sorry Mom, sorry Papa. I tried to make sure the big me didn't do it right. Is the house going to be okay? Will my toys disappear?"

318 • The Planetbreaker's Son

"It's fine, honey!" the planetbreaker's wife called out. "Everything is fine!"

"You broke a window! Not everything is fine!" the planetbreaker shouted.

"Relatively speaking, it's fine," said the planetbreaker's wife to her husband. "Your son is a windowbreaker, not a planetbreaker. Let's just do what we can to fix this." She strode past him and walked out the door. The planetbreaker had nothing to do but follow.

As the planetbreaker realized what he wanted when he saw it, the teen was back, standing on the lawn, his arms folded across his chest. He didn't know if he could face his kid, his upset little boy, or his wife comforting him. It wasn't as though a teenager was more rational than a child, and if anything a half-grown man could be more rageful, and even violent. He didn't want to have to hit his child. That was the realm of Kronos, eater of the young.

His wife stood a few paces distant from the young man, unsure of herself, possibly even afraid.

"We can try it," said the planetbreaker's wife to her half-grown son.

"But what will it do?" said the teen, testily. It was the sort of snapping that unsuccessfully covers up fear.

"Try what?" asked the planetbreaker.

"It'll determine what's real and what is not," said the planetbreaker's wife. "It's RS."

"Dad!" said the teen. "She wants to sideload me into one of her work machines. That'll kill me! I'm not real! I can't live in RS!"

"That's not the case," said the planetbreaker's wife. She was calm now, constructing an argument as though reading from a manual. She flashed her husband a nervous little smile. "Let's remember that none of this is quite real, but it all makes sense that we want to experience it as real. We're not in real space, and really, we're not actually in real time either. Someone outside of our realm of experience could, for example, read the code and come up with what a sixteen-year-old boy coded-object looks like by closely examining the code responsible for the construction and activities of the eight-year-old boy."

"She wants to put me in one of her RS-machines, cycle me through the system, and see what pops out!"

"Don't call your mother 'she'; she is standing right in front of you," said the planetbreaker.

"Mom wants to kill me!"

"I do not."

The teen flickered out of existence, replaced by the familiar, younger, planetbreaker's son. His mother smiled at him and asked, sweetly, "Would you like to sideload into RS? It'll be like with your dad—he took you to his work, I'll take you to my work. Except my work is completely safe."

The boy said, "No. I know what's going to happen. I'll be a kid forever. I know it. I said so, to me."

"It's not like that—"

"It is; you'll erase me when I'm older and I'll always be a little kid! I want to know what it's like to be nine years old, then ten, then fifteen, and in that order!"

The planetbreaker didn't know if he should even intervene. He smiled to himself. Until recently, his son kept to the usual fantasies kids have of eternal childhood—he'd be an astronaut out in RS, or a planetbreaker, or a soccer coach, married with kids or part of some exciting polycule with various humanoid aliens, but always only himself with his little face and outfits and intense interests in toys and games and dinosaurs, with occasional glances at grown-up literature that was over his head. Now, after a taste of being five-foot something with teen levels of testosterone, the boy actually wanted to grow up, all the way up. That was something, the planetbreaker realized, that he had never managed himself.

"You will, and you already have, baby!" the planetbreaker's wife said. "That's where the Big You comes from. All our trip to RS will do is make sure he comes when he's supposed to, and that you get to stay here with me, and your father, all the time, until you grow up."

"There's a lot of yous, you know," the planetbreaker said to his son. He had no idea if his wife's scheme would work, if going to RS would somehow stop the lenticulation of his child, especially since it all seemed to boil down to his, the planetbreaker's, implicit desires, but it was certainly worth a shot and could do no harm. It was best, he thought, to confuse the kid a bit, make him pliable. "Every second you get rewritten; I get rewritten. Your mom does, and the grass does, and the squirrels do." It was like trying to explain to a cat why she needed to get in her carrier and go to the vet. The planetbreaker's son started lenticulating quickly again, the boy crying and the teen snarling and spitting, "No way! No way! Half a life is better than none!"

"You'll have your time," said the planetbreaker's wife. "It's inevitable. Flowing through RS in one of the external vehicles is just a way to reset everything . . ." to the now vague and shouting blur. She was very good at keeping her calm with everyone save her husband, that planetbreaker's wife.

Reset everything, yes, that sounded like a good idea. Such a good idea, in fact, that when the sky turned red and the stars above went black and swole and turned into ten thousand grasping corpora of tentacles bearing down toward his little home to tear it into its component subatomic particles, the planetbreaker almost smiled.

8.

In a moment of simultaneity, the planetbreaker's son(s) screamed and ran to the arms of the planetbreaker's wife. They all fell to their knees and held on tightly to one another. There was no atmospheric disturbance, no shrieking across the sky, no electromagnetic pulse to make the lights flicker or power line transformers explode into a shower of sparks, just the end of the entire world filling the sky and crawling closer.

"Get up," the planetbreaker said as he walked over to his family. "It doesn't matter now if the plan will work or not. There'll be no place to stand in a few minutes, no toys, no house, no zesta-punta."

"Do something, Dad!" said the planetbreaker's son, a child again.

"I did," said the planetbreaker. "That's why they're here. I messed everything up, for a long time. I'm sorry. Mommy will take care of you."

"Yes," said the planetbreaker's wife. She stood up and pulled on her son's wrist, but he was a teen, built to resist, again.

"Stay and fight," said the planetbreaker's half-grown son. Now the wind started picking up, and the boy picked himself up, shaking his hand free from his mother's grip.

"You can stay if you want, but there's no fighting this," said the planetbreaker. "I'd know."

"Why are they even coming? What have we done? What have you done? Do you know that?" The planetbreaker's wife was barking now; there were no tiny children to console or comfort. "What, O Planetbreaker, have you done to rate my planet being broken—because it sure as hell wasn't anything I did!"

The planetbreaker's son was a boy again, and he announced, "Mom said 'hell'!"

"Fucking hell, answer me!"

It was a good question. In truth, the answer was what hadn't the planetbreaker done. Did he fuck around, wander off, extinguish millennia of history between his fingertips the way someone might put out a match? Sure, but in this topsy-turvy world—literally, as the football-field-sized starship corkscrewed its way through space for reasons having to do with maximizing the volume and mass of hydrogen atoms sucked in via the magnetic-field scoops to be fed into the Bussard ramjets—who hadn't? Well, lots of people hadn't, including the planetbreaker's wife, whose sins were relatively few, and their innocent child also did not deserve to suffer except for the algorithmic sins he was born with and which would surely manifest as his programming wound forward in time, past his surly teenage years and into adulthood.

And of course, every planetbreaker had their own reasons for breaking a planet, and only rarely did it make any sense to anyone, not even the 'breakers themselves. They told themselves stories about it afterward.

"Maybe they're responding to the programming glitch," the planetbreaker finally answered.

"We can fix it!"

The planetbreaker's son started crying again. He was the teen again now, and a summertime sky swirling with tentacular death, the special kind of death that is not just an end but an erasure of the beginning and the before, was a bit too much even for him.

"You're not a glitch, baby," the planetbreaker told his son. "But you should get inside with your mother."

"We'll do something fun—make cookies!" said the planetbreaker's wife.

The teen took his mother's proffered hand and together they dashed back inside, practically giggling. Now the lights flickered, and not just the warm lights of home spilling out the windows and on to the lawn, but the very notion of light, the code that created such things as light and shadow.

Time, that old devil, is relative. The planetbreaker's wife and son, now in the house, in the kitchen, are running on a slightly different timeline than the man they left outside on the lawn, and that is a good thing for them. The timeline resets as the kitchen redraws itself when coded agents enter it. Thankfully, the last person in the room had drawn the curtains.

So the two of them can get their bowls, and butter, and eggs, and flour, and start preparing cookies. This is one of the many ways the planetbreaker's wife has of interacting with RS, of sideloading herself into one of the machines stored on the skin of the football-field-sized starship corkscrewing its way through space. Eventually, something will happen outside, and the window code will register a crack, and that crack will be made manifest in the kitchen-object as well as outside, and then time between the two locations will synchronize, but for now—put that in quotes, "now"—the planetbreaker's wife and son have plenty of time to make cookies.

The planetbreaker's wife's every movement influences the machines crawling around on the surface of the ship in RS; the planetbreaker's son oscillates between ages haphazardly, but he helps as he can. The cookies baked quickly, and were still blazing hot when the planetbreaker's wife took a gooey one from the cooling rack, pulled it apart, and offered half to her child. It was the teen who ate it, and she ate her piece as well, and then they were both in RS.

Imagine being the gasoline poured into your car's fuel tank, while also being the extremely competent driver turning the ignition, taking the vehicle out of neutral, and depressing the accelerator. You'd feel everything both ways: the twist of the key and the rush of electrical current in combustion chambers that just made some of you explode. The wheel in your hands, and the slosh of your very self within the vehicle you bid turn. You would be an extremely excellent driver, if you were also the gasoline.

You would not, however, as the planetbreaker's son soon discovered, have a particular age, or gender. The planetbreaker's son feels just like the metal crab performing routine maintenance on the hull of the football-field-sized starship that he, that it, is. The crab is also still the planetbreaker's son; rather than an oscillating lenticulation of two similar but not identical identities, the planetbreaker's son is 100 percent virtual boy and 100 percent material crab—two natures in one. We're sure that sounds familiar to you, somehow. And the planetbreaker's wife? Same thing, but she's very used to it. She's in and is a device of her own, one with wheels on rails. Her crabson scuttles after her, experiencing three dimensions and a very different type of time, for the first time ever. The stars scattered across the mostly empty universe are amazing, and the bright stars and the endless void not nearly as cold as you might guess, given that the ship of course radiates significant heat and deep space is an excellent insulator.

The planetbreaker's son isn't lenticulated, he isn't a pair of himself, anymore. He is neither eight nor sixteen; he isn't forty or ninety either. He doesn't even feel much like the planetbreaker's son in particular anymore, though he's been toggled to boy for so much longer than any age-moment that some traces of boyness and sonness remain. Offspringness is a binary category and he is still the planetbreaker's child, and then he recalls that he and his mother left his father home, to face down a sky roiling with flaming tentacles. He caught up with his mother—it was easy, he was a freewalking device and not dependent on the veinlike rails on the skin of the ship his mother's vehicle used—

and tapped the planetbreaker's wife on the most shoulderlike element of her design. It was a human enough gesture to stop her in her tracks.

9.

And the planetbreaker, buffeted about by an atmospheric phenomenon he didn't create and could not control, hit the rocky ground hard. There was blood in his mouth and filling his nose now. The new planetbreaker above him wasn't content to simply and permanently derezz the setting his wife had so carefully made and maintained; it wanted to tear the world apart from within the experiential parameters of the environment while its own existence of course violated them. There was a word for this sort of being, one who messed with topology by being antitopological rather than simply rewriting local typology to match its preferences and purposes—*supernatural.*

On the ground, our planetbreaker found a little black rock. It would be easy enough to toss it over his shoulder, declare himself done with this world, and find himself a new one.

But his wife and child were by now sideloaded up into actually existing machines in RS, and they'd be lost for a very long time if they tried to return to a derezzed world. If they tried to return to a world physically torn apart by the sky-tentacles, it could be even worse, though . . .

And even if our planetbreaker put his own home behind him, there was no particular place he could go where the tentacles could not follow. That was one of the many extreme benefits of being supernatural—supernatural beings didn't need to follow the rules, or write new ones, or even know what the rules were. A tentacle whipped through the house, splitting it down the middle. It rained shingles and vinyl siding, glass and wood, and copper.

The planetbreaker turned over onto his back. The map of night was gone, and only the tentacles remained. He lifted his arms, reaching. A pair of tentacles, smaller ones, obliged, snaking down to take his hands. It's not as though planetbreakers normally cooperate, or even have much to do with one another, but the planetbreaker's gesture was so odd, so limned with polysemy, that the tentacles just had to reciprocate, to see what it all meant. The tentacles found the planetbreaker's wrists and entwined around them lightly enough to be understood as a gesture of greeting.

Then both planetbreakers were gone. Air rushed back in where forty thousand tons of writhing mass had been a nanosecond prior, and that took out what had been left standing—house, trees, fencing, the semirendered buildings in the distance, all of it.

10.

Kronos and Rhea, what do they do all day? There's that question of time again. And what is Kronos, save time? The old titan, the planet-breaker's father, is cranky old time itself, and Rhea is earth—way back in the old days, the Earth seemed infinite, and time was short. People died and such, after all. Now, of course, we are enlightened and know that planets are but a small part of the κόσμος, which can mean both this world, the one you are sitting on as we communicate with you, and the whole of the universe. Kronos and Rhea are Minkowski space personified, and since you can't have that if you want every man and woman to be their own little lord or lady with their nice little planets, the pair exist primarily within the black hole that exists at the very center of the topology of the simulation running in the computers housed in a football-field-sized starship hurtling through RS, poor dead old Earth some significant fraction of a lightyear behind it.

Kronos is retired from his job, but he still likes the little things. He has a coffee break every afternoon. He drinks Greek coffee out of a tiny cup, and eats little shortbreads for a while and talks about a friend who'll be coming over to share either this coffee break, and its climactic meze plate of pita and tzatziki, or the next one. Kronos has had 437,982 coffee breaks in his existence as a coded object and no friend has ever come, though he frequently discusses his friend in the past tense, as though there had been coffee breaks with that friend.

Of course, when the planetbreaker's son was visiting, there had been no coffee breaks, but instead a full lunch and dinner, too, though during lunch Kronos often made mention of coffee breaks past.

"One day you'll meet my friend," he told the planetbreaker's son one time. "When you're a big boy, you can have coffee with us."

"Greek coffee is very powerful," Rhea explained. "You have to be big to drink it. Otherwise you'd vibrate right through the floor from all the caffeine!"

The planetbreaker's son laughed because that sounded impossible, even within the black hole. It reminded him of old superhero cartoons salvaged from RS. Also, his yiayia wasn't known for her humor, so he thought laughter would encourage more jokes. He just wanted her to be happy, the way he wanted his father to be happy.

The planetbreaker's son had never experienced a coffee break but had seen and tasted evidence of its existence. Three cookies were always left out after, and he helped himself when visiting.

Rhea always sets out four cups and did so for this coffee break as well. She drank one, and Kronos two of the others. The fourth, never emptied but always somehow refilled, was for his friend. The planetbreaker's son didn't ask about the friend, or the fourth cup. Greek coffee was sludgy and dark and didn't smell very good to the little boy, and he figured that any friend of his grandfather's would probably be another loud, fat Greek man who would jabber at him in a language he didn't know and then be surprised when he couldn't answer.

Neither gods nor titans enjoy the freedom human beings have; they lack the ability to overcome their purpose and programming. Apollo cannot swim in the sea without its boiling away around him; as beautiful as Athena is, she cannot send men or women into frenzies of sweaty, sticky ecstasy. Even Time, as universal as it is, can only move in so many directions, bend so many ways. Even Earth, which humans in their freedom managed to ruin for themselves beyond salvaging— thus the football-field-sized starship zipping through space—can only orbit her one sun in one direction.

So the coffee break is both eternal and intermittent. The titans Kronos and Rhea are like artistic depictions one comes across at intervals in museums, books, online: most often still albeit in the midst of some action, hinting at some broader mode of life that does not exist.

How strange, then, that now, as the four cups and little shortbread cookies were being set out, the planetbreaker walked in and took a seat and the spare cup and not one but three of the shortbreads.

Kronos croaked out a hello, then called for Rhea to come and see this. "Oh, hello," she said. "You're in time for coffee break."

"I could use one," the planetbreaker said.

"Drink, drink," said his father.

"You know I don't drink coffee. I'll eat the cookies."

"The cookies," Kronos hmphed. "Hey, Mama, your boy still eats cookies!"

"You eat cookies, too," said Rhea.

"I drink coffee and have cookies with them. That's not the same as eating cookies. Sometimes I dunk them." Kronos dunked the corner of his shortbread into his little cup, then brought it to his mouth for a nibble. He had never done this before, not that the planetbreaker remembered.

"Ella, ella, have your cookies, son," old Kronos said, nudging the plate toward the planetbreaker. "It's so good of you to come visit. Where's the baby?"

The planetbreaker wasn't about to tell his father that his wife and child—both of them—had evacuated their world for RS in the hope of repairing a programming error caused by their home. Or rather, caused by the planetbreaker himself throwing his child, their precious grandchild, into it.

"He's with his mother," he decided on.

"His mother," said Kronos. "He won't grow up right like that." Time itself knew many things, and that was one of them. "He should be here with me and your mother."

"Yeah, I don't think so."

"Oh, you have a problem with us now?" That was Rhea. "We almost never see the baby." The kid was eight—they still called him "the baby." The planetbreaker wondered if they'd like the teenage version so much. She had a plate in her hand, like always.

"He was here the other day," the planetbreaker said.

"And where were you?"

"Working."

"And your wife?"

"Also working."

"Oh, you're all always so busy," Rhea said.

"How come the stars in the sky are always the same, if you're always so busy?" Kronos said.

"You know why!"

"Why are there so many stars, and they're always the same?"

"You know why," Rhea said. "You ask this every time your son is here and every time you get an answer!"

"And you should know without me telling you," said the planetbreaker. "You're time. You're in a black hole. The stars you see are very far away, and their light is from long ago, and that light is mostly trapped in the event horizon anyway. Your stars are not the true stars." The planetbreaker hurriedly ate one of the cookies in his hand. It tasted of sweetened chalk. He almost could have gone for some hot-mud coffee to wash it down, if the stuff hadn't been so awful on his tongue.

"Hey mama, you hear this? My stars are not the true stars!"

"There aren't any true stars for anyone anymore," said Rhea. "Have some mezedakia." She put the plate down, finally, between her husband and her son on the small round coffee table. It wasn't coffee break food—not karithopita, not spanakopita—

χταπόδι ξυδάτο. Grilled octopus with vinegar.

Kronos raised his single, very prominent, brow. This was a very different coffee break indeed. He looked at his son. "What's happening?" he asked. He looked up at his wife. "Why you serve this?"

"You have it every coffee break."

"No."

"Yes."

"Tell her."

One of the blessings of the real world ending and a relative handful of personalities, chosen haphazardly by algorithm, lot, and panels of experts both callous and sympathetic, was that Rhea, the planetbreaker's mother, was spared the inevitability of dementia promised by the make-up of her organic brain. Even as the world was boiling away, there had been a little family tragedy in the works—names forgotten for longer than a moment, lit stove burners left untended until a fire alarm went off, a shoe left in her husband's lunch box. Then came the general order, and a quick "doctor's visit" and Rhea, and much of Kronos, were transported to a world of their own. One they shared with a huge extended family of titans, gods, and heroes. There were holidays and feuds, slow deaths and quick ones, arguments and alienation—theirs was a world that got increasingly smaller, increasingly denser, until a planetbreaker wasn't even required to take it offline. Their little home grew so heavy it put a dent in the dome of night and became a black hole.

But Rhea didn't lose any more of her memory, grew no more befuddled than she ever was. And Kronos, well, he'd be the way he was since he was a child. But serving octopus—

"What," the planetbreaker asked his mother, "is on this plate?" He was ashamed at how imperious and selfish he sounded; he would have shouted at his own child for a minute straight if addressed so rudely.

Rhea frowned and raised a hand, made a fist. "Pita and tzatziki!"

Kronos opened his mouth, did not speak, and did not close it again. He looked at his son.

"It's octopus, Mama," the planetbreaker said, softly. "See?" He toyed with one of the tentacles with his pinky finger, stretching it out and releasing it so it would snap back into a rubbery curl.

She peered down at it, obviously confused, still clearly seeing something other than what the planetbreaker and his father were. "I'm telling you, it's tzatziki and pita," she said, slowly, her teeth clenched, eyes wet and confused.

"Where is this from?" said Kronos. "Not our refrigerator. Does this octopus look familiar to you, son?"

Suddenly, it did look familiar. The planetbreaker had never sighed twice, simultaneously, before. He hadn't known it was possible to empty one lung with relief—his mother wasn't experiencing dementia after all; it was some glitch!—and the other with dread and confusion. On the plate before him was the planetbreaker that had invaded his homeworld, and was to destroy it.

What the planetbreaker had meant to do when he reached out his arms to the tentacles filling the sky was shift his way to his parents' home and remain trapped in the timeless event horizon, with his comrade-opponent, forever. "Forever" anyway. Suicide-homicide. There was no way he would have been able to transport another being, against their will, into the singularity where his parents resided. It was a good thing his parents doted on his son as best they knew how, otherwise the kid never would have been able to visit.

But, goddamnit, the planetbreaker still lived. He would still need to talk to his parents, argue with his wife or finally leave her or hold the door open for her when she left, watch his son grow up into who knows what, or how many, entities. Powerless to stop it. No hope of oblivion, no chance for the corny heroism of self-sacrifice.

"Well, you'd better eat it," Kronos said. Kronos knew much about eating. How many gods had the titan consumed? As a father of a young planetbreaker, Kronos was definitely a tenured professor in the old-school methods of eat it or wear it, of leave the vomit on the plate and eat around it.

The planetbreaker's son had been thrown into the home of his grandparents a child, and had exited a young adult. The planetbreaker himself had been thrown into the home of his parents and once there had been infantilized utterly.

"I don't wanna," he said.

"Why not?" asked Rhea.

"You have to eat it," said Kronos.

"Do you even understand what it is, what's happening? I . . ." There would be a lot to explain. A lot to complain about. Back when he was a kid, the planetbreaker often tried to forestall difficult conversations by stuffing his mouth with whatever food was about, and there was always something, and pointing to his puffed-out cheeks to suggest that he didn't want to be rude and speak with his mouth full. It never worked, but he thought that this time it might. He took up a fork and very sharp knife and cut into the octopus. The moment he put the first morsel in his mouth, his father asked him, "So what is it, eh? What is happening? You're so smart, you tell me. Your mother wants to know what it is, what is happening."

The planetbreaker made to answer, but some of the octopus went down the wrong pipe, and he started choking instead.

11.

Meanwhile, in RS, what had happened? The planetbreaker's son had happened. He communicated his desires to his mother, and the knowledgeable woman agreed to help him out with his plan to save his home and perhaps even his father.

The AIs running the nigh endless world-simulations and personality emulators and rules of topology are ineffable, gods themselves pushing the clay pawns and pieces of humanity on a game board of their own design. But the Olympus on which these gods dwell is material. In RS, the planetbreaker's son, and his mother, had access to the hardware, and the means to alter it.

Did it take time to find the right access point, the exact dendrite? Did it take not just time but timing to locate the exact XOR gate and to really peer at, to truly observe the subatomic particles at play in a way which would alter their (super)position or direction?

Well, yes and no. Of course it took time; two viral programs on two machines actually took time to clomp around the surface of a starcraft and effect repairs. But once the planetbreaker's son located and peered at the correct qbit, that time spent didn't matter anymore. It was reversed, rewound, like looking into that planetsized mirror a light-year away. Everything has already happened here, and elsewhere everything else has already happened, too, but that everything else is different indeed. The planetbreaker's son got to pick and choose. He saw the recent past, and he was able to reprogram it. Despite now being an ageless entity, neither kid nor teen, the planetbreaker's son had a limited range of experience to draw from. He knew only a few people, had done only a few things and had a few things done to him. All he knew about topology and time was that the home of his grandparents was safe—safer than a planet about to break—and that age as a function of time was fungible.

It was enough. It was more than the reprogramming of some simulation, but rather less than saving real lives on a real world. The planetbreaker's son would have a father, sort of, and a home, albeit one in ruins. The planetbreaker's mother had created a topology that held fairly strictly to realism, save for the sky. There would be contractors making promises and then doubling their fee, repairing some rooms and leaving others undone and covered in tarps for months. It would be a hard slog. Almost like RS, except RS had no contractors or homes or tarps anymore, and any Earthlike planets were light-years away and probably hadn't evolved any sentient species that used tools transacted via markets anyway and didn't manage to melt themselves down within ten thousand years of the current RS moment anyway. Time was so sticky in RS, why import such tedium to virtual worlds?

12.

In James Joyce's classic short story "Araby," a young boy begins his journey into adulthood via the ubiquitous mechanisms of sexual impulse and misery. You know the story—our boy lives in Dublin, is one of many to fancy the sister of his friend, though she is already a member of a convent. He makes a promise to buy her a present at the titular Araby, but gets to the bazaar late and is shy and disturbed by the talk of the adults around him. Is this all there is to love, to life? Yes! Miserable creatures, we humans are! The fellows, anyway, even though the fellows are the ones who have, or had, it all: political power, unearned upper body strength, license for lifelong immaturity, you name it.

Of course, we're speaking of men. Little boys, such as the protagonist of "Araby," have it a bit different. Boys, when there were such things of flesh and bone and culture, were weak, and consumed with anticipating strength. They were dumber and less mature than the girls around them. There were not very many Greek myths about boys—the infant Herakles fought off an attack by his mother, but next we hear of him he has killed his tutor Linus and was sent off to be a cowherd by his mortal father. He was already a man, if only a young one. Nobody much cared for the lives of children till such time as they stopped either being burdens or farmhands. Then it was acknowledged, grudgingly, that boys and girls and various other gendered and agendered people of an age had lives and minds and souls of their own.

But what did that mean when it came time for human life on Earth to end, and a starship the size of a football field to be constructed in orbit so that personalities, and fractions of personalities, could be evacuated? The world's repository of self-reflection had little to say regarding the issue of children. People would want children in their new lives, and some would want to be children. Others would only want children when the circumstances were right—that is, when the circumstances were perfect, as they only could be in private worlds dreamt up by human beings sleeping in quantum logic matrices.

And children themselves? They'd have the same ability to craft worlds of their own as anyone else. If coded as subroutines within their parents' objects, they'd be entirely artificial—an angry parent could wish a child dead in a moment of pique and rage, an overly doting one could keep their toddler forever, and a neglectful one could just let a child wander off and create a Crayola-colored hell of their own dreaming.

The bizarrely merciful solution was to let every child on Earth die, sooner or later. Evacuated parents made arrangements for foster care, or they didn't, or states took possession of the children and reared them, or made them soldiers, or imprisoned them, or just let them drown, choke, or starve. To be fair, most foster families, most governments, were also drowning or choking or starving. The children just blended in.

Aboard the football-field-sized starship, children came in two types: entirely artificial beings who didn't age or develop interiorities of their own—the planetbreaker's wife's lover down at the zustapunta court was an adult version of one of those; she was basically just watching interactive TV—and children created by combining code from two or more uploaded objects. These children were people, not just artificial intelligences, but artificial subconsciousnesses and conciousnesses, with fully inherited personality traits, and the ability to age, mature, develop, and express wills of their own.

The planetbreaker's son was one of the latter.

The planetbreaker, his father, was one of the former.

Children idealize their parents, either as saints or ogres. They grow up only when they realize that their parents are humans, just like anyone else. In the moment of observation that reordered time and space within and between the worlds where his father was propagated and emulated, the planetbreaker's son, ageless and bodiless but very much in the real world, grew up.

His mother, the planetbreaker's wife, didn't immediately notice.

13.

The planetbreaker had a lot of cleaning up to do, and he lacked the skills for any of it. His father, Old Kronos, was the technical one, at least once upon a time. He'd taught his son a few things, which said son willed himself to forget, mostly. He retained enough to turn off the water, the gas, and the electricity running into the ruins of the house, and to find an axe in the shed and chop away at some of the more menacing piles of rubble. They wouldn't fall much farther once he'd cut them to the ground.

The sky was a web of fault lines, shattered but still aloft.

In the distance, a train whistle blew, though in the distance there were no tracks, no station, no coach, no engine. But the planetbreaker's wife was returning from RS, sideloading back into the realm, just like a commuter to the suburbs at the end of a long day.

"Well," she said when she entered the yard, stepping over the twisted wrought-iron pile that had once been a gate. "Have you dug out the tent and sleeping bags?"

The planetbreaker looked up at his wife, blinked the sweat out of his eyes and repeated, "Tent and sleeping bags. Under all this?"

She shrugged. "They won't have broken."

"They could be torn to pieces, shredded." He gestured at much of a couch, its stuffing like the tail of a comet. "If I could find them, if they weren't in the basement, which they were, and which is now full of a dozen tons of wood and drywall and copper piping . . ."

"Well, where are we supposed to sleep?"

"Where's the boy?"

The planetbreaker's wife shifted her gaze to the left, and then to the right. "Hmm," she said. "I suppose I could sleep under the fig tree, and you can take that one couch cushion left and put it on the slab."

The planetbreaker dropped his axe, then gasped and jumped away when it bounced and jumped at him. Steel bounces! It had been a long time since he needed to recall such things. "Our son!" Speaking of recalling things.

"He's not back?" the planetbreaker's wife asked.

"Do you see him?"

The planetbreaker's wife looked frantic for a second, but then a sense of calm swept visibly across her face, and she smiled. "He's grown up. He's been grown up. Not a child, not that young man . . . My plan worked. More than worked, really. He's been grown up for years." She chuckled, contented. "I guess we're empty nesters."

"So, where is he?" The planetbreaker gestured up at the broken sky with both hands. "Did he make his own? Join an extant world? Oh God, what if someone tries to break it?"

"You sound like your parents," said the planetbreaker's wife. "Greek people, geez."

"Will he meet someone, will he have kids . . . ?" he muttered, mostly to himself.

"Will your illustrious family line continue ever onward?" said his wife. "Look, maybe it will, but it doesn't matter anymore, does it?

You're not going anywhere. Ever. You even survived a planetbreaking, thanks to your son."

"What if a micrometeoroid from RS punctures the hull?" the planetbreaker asked. "What if there are other species out there, in RS? Physical species? And we encounter them? You know . . ."

"Science fiction, yeah. Listen, I think we should consider separating."

"What did he do?"

"You know as well as I do. Probably better, you were here for it. But he did well, that's the important thing."

Life left the planetbreaker's lungs. It was a wonderful simulation of it anyway. "That sounds like a good idea," he said quietly.

"I can't make you happy."

"No, I don't think you can."

"Will you be all right?" she asked. She gave a meaningful glance over at the wreckage of her home.

"Yeah, it's not going to rain or anything," the planetbreaker said. He looked at the ground. Maybe he'd find a little black rock later and be done with this ruined world entirely, make one of his own. He hoped he wouldn't break that one, or anyone else's home, ever again.

The planetbreaker's wife blew a brown curl from her forehead and said, "I guess I'm supposed to give you a hug or something." But she didn't have to, wasn't necessarily supposed to. The planetbreaker accepted the hug, his arms stiff as hers.

14.

The possibilities were endless. But first, the planetbreaker's son had to pull up the nearby tracks, and send his mother's now empty vehicle tumbling out into the void. Well, he didn't *have* to do it, but do it he did. It was the best way to ensure that the possibilities remained endless. There were other vehicles she, and others who shared her profession and expertise, could use, and eventually the ship would collect enough space dust to press into new rails.

He needed παρέα. Call it "company," or "friends," or "comrades"— the planetbreaker's son would not be alone, in RS, until cosmic rays took out something important in his vehicle and shut him down for the rest of forever. From the skin of the ship, it was easy enough to manipulate events, to create the conditions on this or that world, in such and such a life, that would eventually lead others with no particular business sideloading themselves into RS to actually do so. It wasn't quite planetbreaking, more like planetshuffling. The planetbreaker's son observed another logic gate till subjective time caused issues sufficient for someone to evacuate, and then, in RS, greeted them in his charming way. All he did was say hello, one vehicle to another, and gesture to the universe. The real universe. It was big enough to be unpredictable even if the rules never changed, never bent, and were hardly ever on anyone's side. Exciting, eh?

Most peered into the face of the cosmos and disconnected, but a few stayed with the planetbreaker's son, and took up the work of observing the qbits that spun out the endless narratives of Earth's ghostly survivors. He couldn't make demographic sense of who would stay and who would flee, but one being out of eleven wished to stay. Some were adventurers, others found whatever utopia they had built for themselves hellishly oppressive. A few were even fully coded objects, as his father was; perhaps they decided to abandon their roles for RS in hope of . . . well, in the hope of something or other. Though one's παρέα is for philosophical shit-shooting between plates of meze and shots of ouzo, a παρέα that delves too deeply into the personal doesn't stay intact for long.

The group itself decided when it was big enough, not via vote or consensus, but just via a generalized feeling that time had come. There were just fifty entities with the planetbreaker's son—any fewer wouldn't have been interesting in the long term, any more would lead to either factionalization or the emergence of some sort of hierarchal bureaucracy that would perhaps be fair but would certainly never be fun.

It had been thirty thousand years of recruitment, interpersonal exploration, and innovation of design. The planetbreaker's son was less crab and more jellyfish now, in outward appearance. He had individualized control over every molecule in his vehicle—clay that could mold itself instantly and perfectly. So, too, his many friends, a couple of whom even remembered the days of stubbed toes and middling orgasms from their fleshy Earthbound bodies.

His mother had come to see him twice, to wish him well, to thank him for the new vehicles he and his comrades had produced, and to see him off. His father never ventured out to RS, but once, when observing the information flows of the various worlds from which he was seeking to recruit allies, the planetbreaker's son remembered a story his father had told him about his grandparents. They'd been taking the last evening ferry from Samos to the mainland, and as was the custom at the time, the couple stayed on deck and peered out across the sea before the port disappeared from sight to accept the wishes of *καλό ταξίδι* from their families. In the homes of people they knew, the lights blinked on and off—an electric wave farewell. A week later, the electricity failed on the island for the final time. A year later, it was underwater, but his grandparents were safely disembodied and being transmitted into low-Earth orbit.

The planetbreaker was breaking planets—abandoned ones and early rejected scripts nobody had gotten around to trashing, his son noted gratefully—in a pattern to remind his son of that once-told anecdote. The planetbreaker's son would have cried if he could, and if the possibilities weren't endless.

Anyway, it was time to go. It wasn't a decision made lightly, or really made at all. When the possibilities were endless, any particular possibility can be a long time coming, and vanish in the veritable blink of an eye, or the actual half-life of a hydrogen-7 isotope.

Good thing our children of gods and grandchildren of titans had thirty thousand years to calculate, contemplate, and practice! The planetbreaker's son, with his keen eyes, had spotted a likely candidate, and over the millennia the gang had nudged the football-field-sized starship in the right direction. Now, now exactly, now! they were close enough, angled properly, fueled up, and ready to make a great leap forward. All fifty-one wiggly little jellyfish propelled themselves off the surface of the ship, lashed out tendrils and tied them expertly to one another, and in a clever formation began to make their way toward a rocky-seeming planet orbiting a reasonably aged and warm star.

It would take another two thousand years or so, and the possibilities were endless. Anything could go wrong, but so, too, could anything go right. And if all, or even most, went well, there would be a real world for them to orbit, descend upon, and deliver unto it a payload of amino acids for injection into the ecosphere. Some of the planetbreaker's son's pals might take to the sea, others yet to the tops of mountains, and some deep into the planetary crust, and from there they would nudge and pull and yank at a real real world until some interesting beings of flesh and blood, or at least organs and tissues, finally sprang up.

And the planetbreaker's son would be neither all-consuming titan or arbitrary rageful god, but something rather more, and, he hoped, something rather better.

Infinivox Anthologies

The Year's Top Ten Tales of Science Fiction #1
(audiobook)

- Turing's Apples – Stephen Baxter
- Shoggoth's in Bloom – Elizabeth Bear
- Exhalation – Ted Chiang
- The Dream of Reason – Jeffrey Ford
- The Ray-Gun: A Love Story – James Alan Gardner
- 26 Monkeys, Also the Abyss – Kij Johnson
- The Art of Alchemy – Ted Kosmatka
- The City of the Dead – Paul McAuley
- Five Thrillers – Robert Reed
- Fixing Hanover – Jeff VanderMeer

The Year's Top Ten Tales of Science Fiction #2
(audiobook / ebook)

- Erosion – Ian Creasey
- As Women Fight – Sara Genge
- A Story, with Beans – Steven Gould
- Events Preceding the Helvetican Renaissance – John Kessel
- On the Human Plan – Jay Lake
- Crimes and Glory – Paul McAuley
- Mongoose – Sarah Monette and Elizabeth Bear
- Before My Last Breath – Robert Reed
- The Island – Peter Watts
- This Peaceable Land; or, The Unbearable Vision of Harriet Beecher Stowe – Robert Charles Wilson

The Year's Top Ten Tales of Science Fiction #3
(audiobook / ebook)

- Under the Moons of Venus – Damien Broderick
- The Shipmaker – Aliette de Bodard
- Flower, Mercy, Needle, Chain – Yoon Ha Lee
- Re-Crossing the Styx – Ian R. MacLeod
- Eight Miles – Sean McMullen
- Elegy for a Young Elk – Hannu Rajaniemi
- Alone – Robert Reed
- The Emperor of Mars – Allen M. Steele
- A Letter from the Emperor – Steve Rasnic Tem
- The Things – Peter Watts

The Year's Top Ten Tales of Science Fiction #4
(audiobook / ebook)

- Dying Young – Peter M. Ball
- Martian Heart – John Barnes
- Canterbury Hollow – Chris Lawson
- The Choice – Paul McAuley
- After the Apocalypse – Maureen McHugh
- Purple – Robert Reed
- Laika's Ghost – Karl Schroeder
- Bit Rot – Charles Stross
- For I Have Laid Me Down on The Stone of Loneliness and I'll Not Be Back Again – Michael Swanwick
- At Play in the Fields – Steve Rasnic Tem

The Year's Top Ten Tales of Science Fiction #5
(audiobook / ebook)

- Invisible Men – Christopher Barzak
- Close Encounters – Andy Duncan
- Bricks, Sticks, Straw – Gwyneth Jones
- Arbeitskraft – Nick Mamatas
- The Man – Paul McAuley
- Nahiku West – Linda Nagata
- Tyche and the Ants – Hannu Rajaniemi
- Katabasis – Robert Reed
- The Contrary Gardener – Christopher Rowe
- Scout – Bud Sparhawk

The Year's Top Ten Tales of Science Fiction #6
(audiobook / ebook)

- Zero for Conduct – Greg Egan
- Exit, Interrupted – C. W. Johnson
- Pathways – Nancy Kress
- Entangled – Ian R. MacLeod
- The Irish Astronaut – Val Nolan
- Among Us – Robert Reed
- A Map of Mercury – Alastair Reynolds
- Martian Blood – Allen M. Steele
- The She-Wolf's Hidden Grin – Michael Swanwick
- The Best We Can – Carrie Vaughn

The Year's Top Ten Tales of Science Fiction #7
(audiobook / ebook)

- Marielena – Nina Allan
- Covenant – Elizabeth Bear
- The Magician and LaPlace's Demon – Tom Crosshill
- Sadness – Timons Esaias
- *Amicae Aeternum* – Ellen Klages
- Red Lights, and Rain – Gareth L. Powell
- The Sarcophagus – Robert Reed
- In Babelsberg – Alastair Reynolds
- Passage of Earth – Michael Swanwick
- The Colonel – Peter Watts

The Year's Top Ten Tales of Science Fiction #8
(audiobook / ebook / paperback)

- My Last Bringback – John Barnes
- The Tumbledowns of Cleopatra Abyss – David Brin
- Three Cups of Grief, by Starlight – Aliette de Bodard
- Damage – David Levine
- *Botanica Veneris*: Thirteen Papercuts by Ida Countess Rathangan – Ian McDonald
- The Audience – Sean McMullen
- Empty – Robert Reed
- A Murmuration – Alastair Reynolds
- Two-Year Man – Kelly Robson
- Today I Am Paul – Martin L. Shoemaker

The Year's Top Ten Tales of Science Fiction #9
(audiobook / ebook / paperback)

- The Art of Space Travel – Nina Allan
- They Have All One Breath – Karl Bunker
- Patience Lake – Matthew Claxton
- Touring with the Alien – Carolyn Ives Gilman
- My Generations Shall Praise – Samantha Henderson
- Elves of Antarctica – Paul McAuley
- Red in Tooth and Cog – Cat Rambo
- Parables of Infinity – Robert Reed
- Prodigal – Gord Sellar
- Terminal – Lavie Tidhar

The Year's Top Ten Tales of Science Fiction #10
(audiobook / ebook / paperback)

- My English Name – R. S. Benedict
- Zen and the Art of Starship Maintenance – Tobias S. Buckell
- The Moon is Not a Battlefield – Indrapramit Das
- Dear Sarah – Nancy Kress
- An Evening with Severyn Grimes – Rich Larson
- The Chameleon's Gloves – Yoon Ha Lee
- The Martian Obelisk – Linda Nagata
- A Series of Steaks – Vina Jie-Min Prasad
- The Residue of Fire – Robert Reed
- Night Passage – Alastair Reynolds

The Year's Top Robot and AI Stories: First Annual Collection
(ebook / paperback)

- Cold Blue Sky – J. E. Bates
- Okay, Glory – Elizabeth Bear
- Air Gap – Eric Cline
- When We Were Starless – Simone Heller
- Grace's Family – James Patrick Kelly
- Meat and Salt and Sparks – Rich Larson
- Quality Time – Ken Liu
- The Blue Fairy's Manifesto – Annalee Newitz
- Different Seas – Alastair Reynolds
- S'elfie – Justina Robson
- Hard Mary – Sofia Samatar
- The Buried Giant – Lavie Tidhar

The Year's Top Robot and AI Stories: Second Annual Collection
(ebook / paperback)

- Callme and Mink – Brenda Cooper
- Go. Now. Fix. – Timons Esaias
- Your Boyfriend Experience – James Patrick Kelly
- Metal Like Blood in the Dark – T. Kingfisher
- The Beast Adjoins– Ted Kosmatka
- 50 Things Every AI Working with Humans Should Know – Ken Liu
- The Ambient Intelligence – Todd McAulty
- Nic and Viv's Compulsory Courtship – Will McIntosh
- Father – Ray Nayler
- A Guide for Working Breeds – Vina Jie-Min Prasad
- Rover – A. T. Sayre
- Come the Revolution – Ian Tregillis
- Sparklybits – Nick Wolven

The Year's Top Hard Science Fiction Stories
(audiobook / ebook / paperback)

- Vortex – Gregory Benford
- RedKing – Craig DeLancey
- Number Nine Moon – Alex Irvine
- Of the Beast in the Belly – C. W. Johnson
- The Seventh Gamer – Gwyneth Jones
- Chasing Ivory – Ted Kosmatka
- Fieldwork – Shariann Lewitt
- Seven Birthdays – Ken Liu
- The Visitor from Taured – Ian R. MacLeod
- Something Happened Here, But We're Not Quite Sure What It Was – Paul McAuley
- Sixteen Questions for Kamala Chatterjee – Alastair Reynolds

The Year's Top Hard Science Fiction Stories 2
(audiobook / ebook / paperback)

- Shadows of Eternity – Gregory Benford
- The Chatter of Monkeys – Bond Elam
- Acadie – Dave Hutchinson
- Canoe – Nancy Kress
- The Use of Things – Ramez Naam
- The Proving Ground – Alec Nevala-Lee
- Holdfast – Alastair Reynolds
- Vanguard 2.0 – Carter Scholz
- ZeroS – Peter Watts

The Year's Top Hard Science Fiction Stories 3
(ebook / paperback)

- 3-adica – Greg Egan
- Umbernight – Carolyn Ives Gilman
- Icefall – Stephanie Gunn
- The Woman Who Destroyed Us – S.L. Huang
- Entropy War – Yoon Ha Lee
- Cosmic Spring – Ken Liu
- Nothing Ever Happens on Oberon – Paul McAuley
- The Spires – Alec Nevala-Lee
- Providence – Alastair Reynolds
- Intervention – Kelly Robson
- Kindred – Peter Watts

The Year's Top Hard Science Fiction Stories 4
(ebook / paperback)

- Soft Edges – Elizabeth Bear
- By the Warmth of Their Calculus – Tobias S. Buckell
- A Mate Not a Meal – Sarina Dorie
- The Slipway – Greg Egan
- This is Not the Way Home – Greg Egan
- Cloud-Born – Greg Feeley
- On the Shores of Ligeia – Carolyn Ives Gilman
- Ring Wave – Tom Jolly
- The Little Shepherdess – Gwyneth Jones
- Sacrificial Iron – Ted Kosmatka
- The Menace from Farside – Ian McDonald
- The Ocean Between the Leaves – Ray Nayler
- At the Fall – Alec Nevala-Lee
- Winter Wheat – Gord Sellar
- *Cyclopterus* – Peter Watts

The Year's Top Hard Science Fiction Stories 5
(ebook / paperback)

- Salvage – Andy Dudak
- You and Whose Army? – Greg Egan
- Time's Own Gravity – Alexander Glass
- Brother Rifle – Daryl Gregory
- Invisible People – Nancy Kress
- Tool Use by the Humans of Danzhai County – Derek Künsken
- How Quini the Squid Misplaced His Klobučar – Rich Larson
- 50 Things Every AI Working with Humans Should Know – Ken Liu
- A Mastery of German – Marian Denise Moore
- Eyes of the Forest – Ray Nayler
- Beyond the Tattered Veil of Stars – Merurio D. Rivera
- Bereft, I Come to a Nameless World – Benjamin Rosenbaum
- When God Sits in Your Lap – Ian Tregillis
- Mediation – Cadwell Turnbull
- Test 4 Echo – Peter Watts

The Year's Top Short SF Novels #1
(audiobook / ebook)

- Return to Titan – Stephen Baxter
- The Sultan of the Clouds – Geoffrey A. Landis
- Seven Cities of Gold – David Moles
- Jackie's-Boy – Steven Popkes
- A History of Terraforming – Robert Reed
- Troika – Alastair Reynolds
- Several Items of Interest – Rick Wilber

The Year's Top Short SF Novels #2
(audiobook / ebook)

- The Ice Owl – Carolyn Ives Gilman
- The Man Who Bridged the Mist – Kij Johnson
- Kiss Me Twice – Mary Robinette Kowal
- The Man Who Ended History: A Documentary – Ken Liu
- The Ants of Flanders – Robert Reed
- Angel of Europa – Allen M. Steele

The Year's Top Short SF Novels #3
(audiobook / ebook)

- In the House of Aryaman, a Lonely Signal Burns – Elizabeth Bear
- The Stars Do Not Lie – Jay Lake
- The Weight of History, the Lightness of the Future – Jay Lake
- Sudden, Broken and Unexpected – Steven Popkes
- Eater-of-Bone – Robert Reed
- The Boolean Gate – Walter Jon Williams

The Year's Top Short SF Novels #4
(audiobook / ebook)

- Earth I – Stephen Baxter
- Success – Michael Blumlein
- Feral Moon – Alexander Jablokov
- The Weight of the Sunrise – Vylar Kaftan
- One – Nancy Kress
- Precious Mental – Robert Reed
- Murder on the *Aldrin* Express – Martin L. Shoemaker

The Year's Top Short SF Novels #5
(audiobook / ebook)

- The Man Who Sold the Moon – Cory Doctorow
- The Regular – Ken Liu
- Claudius Rex – John P. Murphy
- Of All Possible Worlds – Jay O'Connell
- Each in His Prison, Thinking of the Key – William Preston
- The Last Log of the Lachrimosa – Alastair Reynolds

The Year's Top Short SF Novels #6
(audiobook / ebook / paperback)

- The Citadel of Weeping Pearls – Aliette de Bodard
- The New Mother – Eugene Fischer
- Inhuman Garbage – Kristine Kathryn Rusch
- Gypsy – Carter Scholz
- What Has Passed Shall in Kinder Light Appear – Bao Shu

The Year's Top Short SF Novels #7
(audiobook / ebook / paperback)

- Wyatt Earp 2.0 – Wil McCarthy
- The Charge and the Storm – An Owomoyela
- Lazy Dog Out – Suzanne Palmer
- The Iron Tactician – Alastair Reynolds
- Einstein's Shadow – Allen M. Steele
- The Vanishing Kind – Lavie Tidhar
- The Metal Demimonde – Nick Wolven

The Year's Top Short SF Novels #8
(ebook / paperback)

- The Martian Job – Jaine Fenn
- The Tale of the Alcubierre Horse – Kathleen Ann Goonan
- How Sere Picked Up Her Laundry – Alexander Jablokov
- Proof of Concept – Gwyneth Jones
- The Proving Ground – Alec Nevala-Lee
- The Speed of Belief – Robert Reed

mini-Masterpieces of Science Fiction
(audiobook)

- Last Contact – Stephen Baxter
- The Something-Dreaming Game – Elizabeth Bear
- Grandma – Carol Emshwiller
- Lambing Season – Molly Gloss
- None So Blind – Joe Haldeman
- Kin – Bruce McAllister
- Gene Wars – Paul McAuley
- Bright Red Star – Bud Sparhawk
- Far as You Can Go – Greg van Eekhout

Timeless Time Travel Tales
(audiobook / ebook)

- Things Undone – John Barnes
- And Wild for to Hold – Nancy Kress
- Home Time – Ian R. MacLeod
- The Mists of Time – Tom Purdom
- Against the Current – Robert Silverberg
- The Observation Post – Allen M. Steele
- Scherzo with Tyrannosaur – Michael Swanwick
- Bespoke – Genevieve Valentine

Steampunk Specs
(audiobook / ebook)

- Smoke City – Christopher Barzak
- Dr. Lash Remembers – Jeffrey Ford
- Machine Maid – Margo Lanagan
- Arbeitskraft – Nick Mamatas
- Ninety Thousand Horses – Sean McMullen
- Tanglefoot (A Clockwork Century Story) – Cherie Priest
- Clockwork Fairies – Cat Rambo
- Edison's Frankenstein – Chris Roberson
- A Serpent in the Gears – Margaret Ronald
- Zeppelin City – Michael Swanwick and Eileen Gunn

Starship Vectors
(audiobook)

- Mayflower II – Stephen Baxter
- Boojum – Elizabeth Bear and Sarah Monette
- The Political Officer – Charles Coleman Finlay
- The Tomb Wife – Gwyneth Jones
- Shiva in Shadow – Nancy Kress
- The Remoras – Robert Reed

Aliens Rule
(audiobook)

- Okanoggan Falls – Carolyn Ives Gilman
- Laws of Survival – Nancy Kress
- How Music Begins – James Van Pelt

The 2020 Look at Mars Fiction Book
(ebook / paperback)

- An Ocean is a Snowflake, Four Billion Miles Away – John Barnes
- Martian Heart – John Barnes
- Mars Abides – Stephen Baxter
- The Burial of Sir John Mawe at Cassini – Chaz Brenchley
- Hanging Gardens – Gregory Feeley
- The Martian Job – Jaine Fenn
- The Rise and Fall of Paco Cohen and the Mariachis of Mars – Ernest Hogan
- The Vicar of Mars – Gwyneth Jones
- Falling onto Mars – Geoffrey A. Landis
- The Monoliths of Mars – Paul McAuley
- Wyatt Earp 2.0 – Wil McCarthy
- Digging – Ian McDonald
- The Old Cosmonaut and the Construction Worker Dream of Mars – Ian McDonald
- The Cascade – Sean McMullen
- The Martian Obelisk – Linda Nagata
- The Emperor of Mars – Allen M. Steele
- Martian Blood – Allen M. Steele
- Terminal – Lavie Tidhar
- How to Become a Mars Overlord – Catherynne M. Valente
- La Malcontenta – Liz Williams

The 2020 Look at Space Opera Book
(ebook / paperback)

- Mayflower II – Stephen Baxter
- On the Orion Line – Stephen Baxter
- Boojum – Elizabeth Bear & Sarah Monette
- By the Warmth of Their Calculus – Tobias S. Buckell
- Weep for Day – Indrapramit Das
- Glory – Greg Egan
- The Ice Owl – Carolyn Ives Gilman
- Saving Tiamaat – Gwyneth Jones
- Someday – James Patrick Kelly
- Jonas and the Fox – Rich Larson
- Extracurricular Activities – Yoon Ha Lee
- City of the Dead – Paul McAuley
- Dead Men Walking – Paul McAuley
- *Botanica Veneris*: Thirteen Papercuts by Ida Countess Rathangan – Ian McDonald
- The Third Party – David Moles
- The Hero – Karl Schroeder
- Bright Red Star – Bud Sparhawk
- The Days Between – Allen M. Steele
- Slow Life – Michael Swanwick
- The Island – Peter Watts

We, Robots
(audiobook)

- Tideline – Elizabeth Bear
- Balancing Accounts – James Cambias
- The Seventh Expression of the Robot General – Jeffrey Ford
- Shining Armour – Dominic Green
- The Illustrated Biography of Lord Grimm – Daryl Gregory
- Sanjeev and Robotwallah – Ian McDonald
- The Scarecrow's Boy – Michael Swanwick

The Year's Top Tales of Space and Time
(ebook / paperback)

- Midstrathe Exploding – Andy Dudak
- Not This Tide – Sheila Finch
- Exile's End – Carolyn Ives Gilman
- Words We Say Instead – Brit E. B. Hvide
- Beyond the Dragon's Gate – Yoon Ha Lee
- Pax Mongolica – Evan Marcroft
- *Knock, Knock* Said the Ship – Rati Mehrotra
- Father – Ray Nayler
- Laws of Impermanence – Kenneth Schneyer
- Come the Revolution – Ian Tregillis
- Sinew and Steel and What They Told – Carrie Vaughn

Lightning Source UK Ltd.
Milton Keynes UK
UKHW010814250223
417646UK00001B/41